Withdrawn

POPULARMMOS

Popular MMOs (aka Pat) is one of the most popular YouTubers in the world. Pat and Jen (aka Gaming With Jen) created their *Minecraft*–inspired channel, PopularMMOS, in 2012. Since then, they have entertained millions of fans around the world with their gaming videos and original characters.

Pat and Jen live in Florida with their cat, Cloud. *PopularMMOS Presents: Zombies' Day Off* is their third book.

For Aunt Kim—D.J.

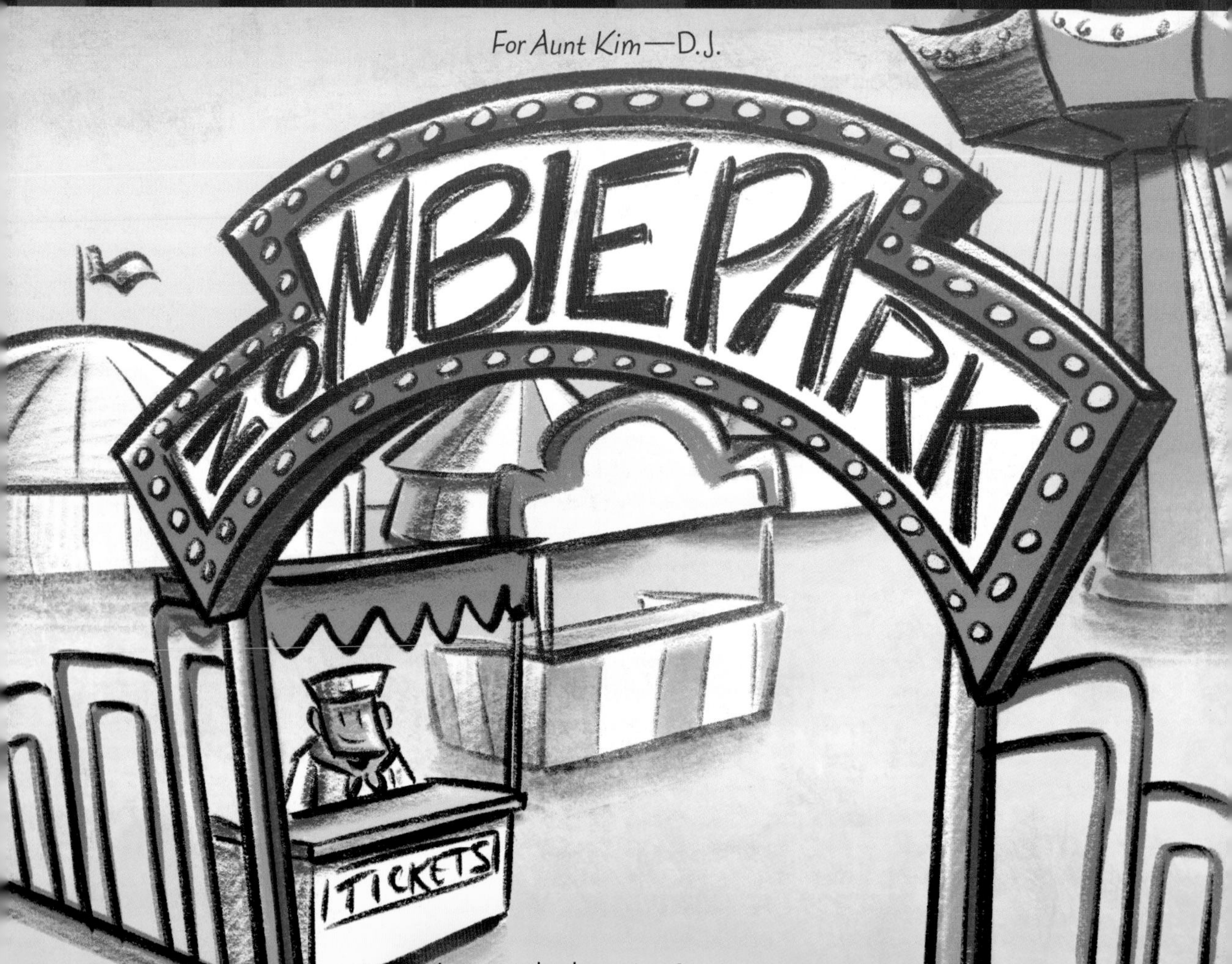
ZOMBIE PARK
TICKETS

A special thanks to Joe Caramagna
for all his creative help!

 For information address HarperCollins Children's Books, a division of HarperCollins Publishers,
195 Broadway, New York, NY 10007.
www.harpercollinschildrens.com

Library of Congress Control Number: 2020941016
ISBN 978-0-06-300651-5 (trade bdg.) — ISBN 978-0-06-304210-0 (special edition)
ISBN 978-0-06-304777-8 (special edition) — ISBN 978-0-06-307162-9 (special edition)

The artist used an iPad Pro and the app Procreate to create the digital illustrations for this book.
Typography by Erica De Chavez 20 21 22 23 24 TC 10 9 8 7 6 5 4 3 2 1 ❖ First Edition

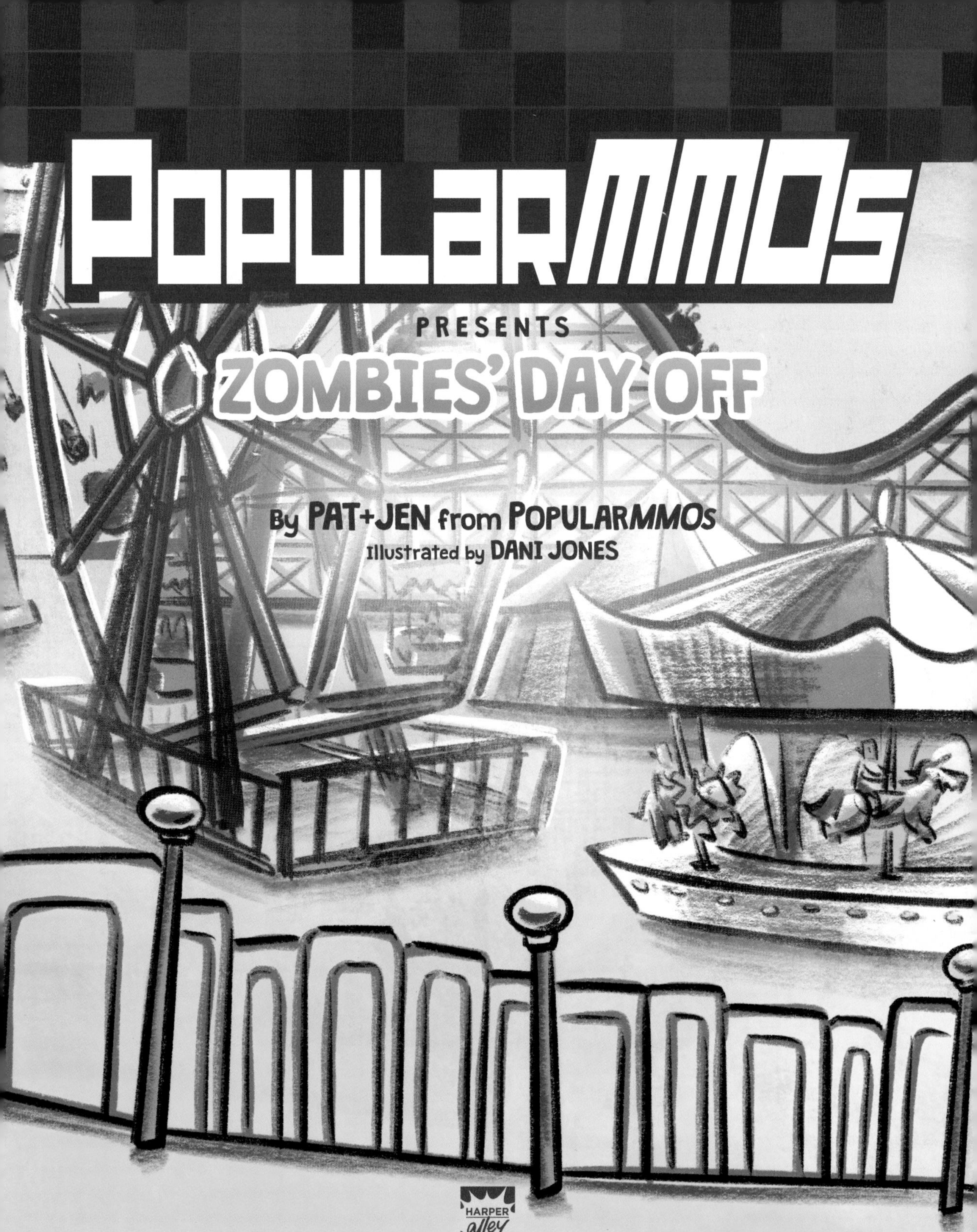

PopularMMOs

PRESENTS

ZOMBIES' DAY OFF

By PAT+JEN from POPULARMMOs

Illustrated by DANI JONES

HARPER alley

An Imprint of HarperCollinsPublishers

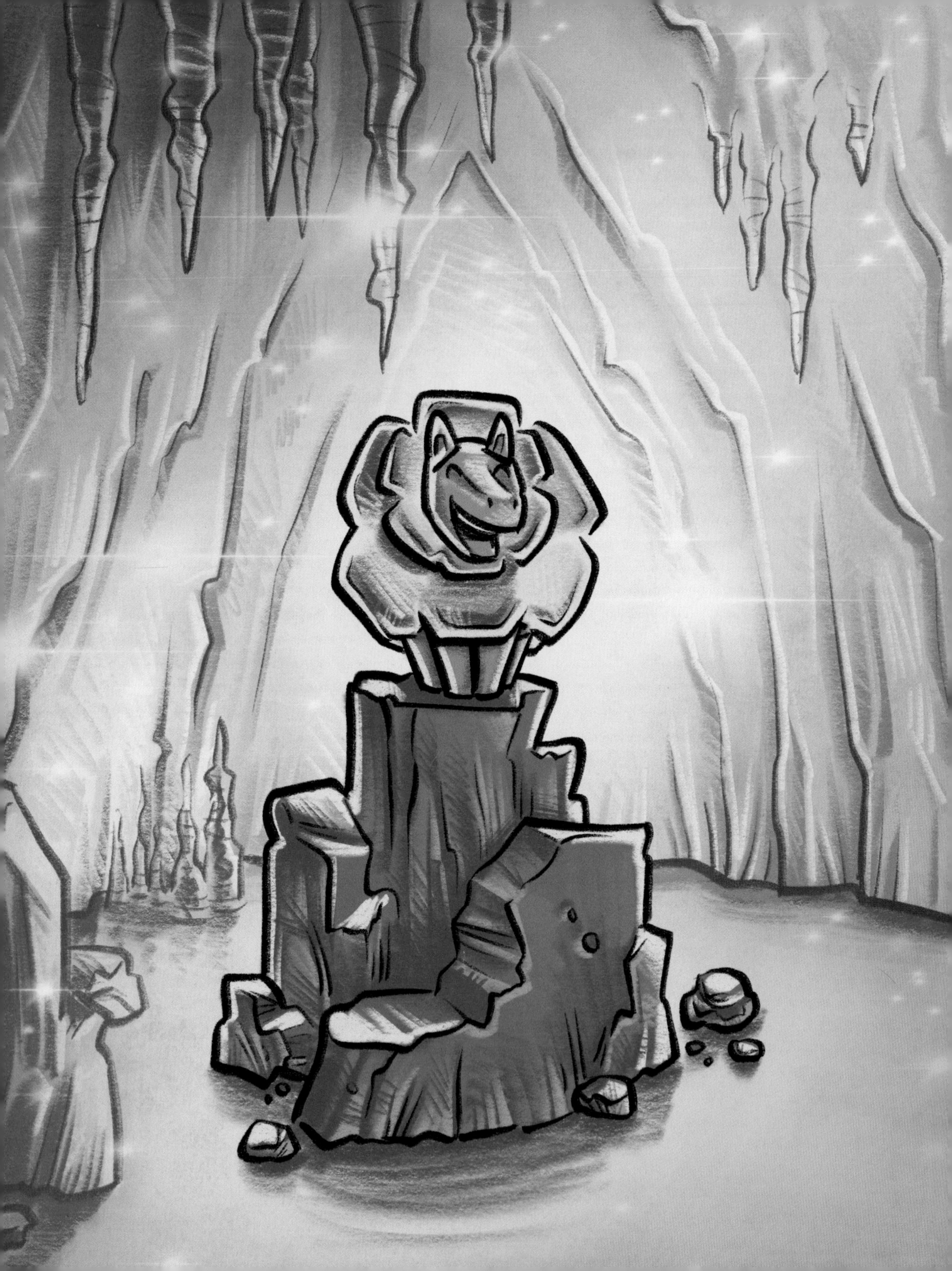

Welcome back, guys!

We can't believe it's our third book! We've already fallen into bottomless holes, battled vicious zombies, and blown up mountains, but we're back now for what might be our greatest adventure yet—to find out the truth about Jen's family. Of course, to do that, we'll have to visit a zombie amusement park, battle Herobrine, and use more TNT than we've ever done before. It's a story unlike any we've ever told, and we're so thrilled that you've decided to come along for the adventure. (And we do love adventure!)

Anyway, we hope you enjoy the book. We made sure it was filled with all your favorite characters from our videos—plus a few new stars that you might not have seen before. What we love most about the world of PopularMMOs is that on YouTube and in our books, Jen and I get to go anywhere, do anything, be anyone—all we have to do is let ourselves imagine it for it to happen. We hope this book encourages you to do the same, to tell your own stories, dream up your own worlds. It's fun, and it's actually pretty easy—and it doesn't have to be perfect. It just has to be yours. Actually, honestly, that's the best part—it's all yours.

And with that, we welcome you to *Zombies' Day Off.* Enjoy!

—Pat & Jen

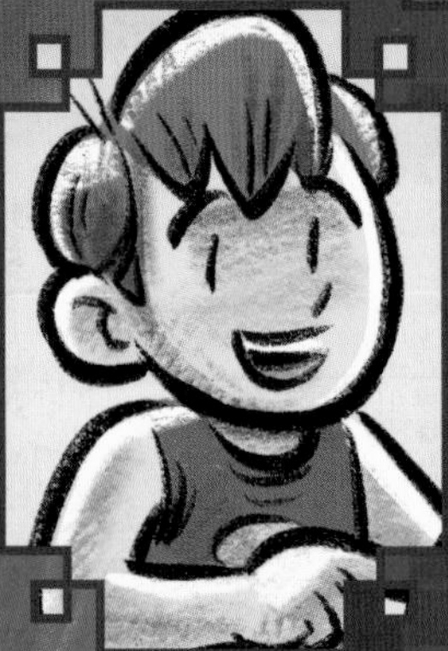

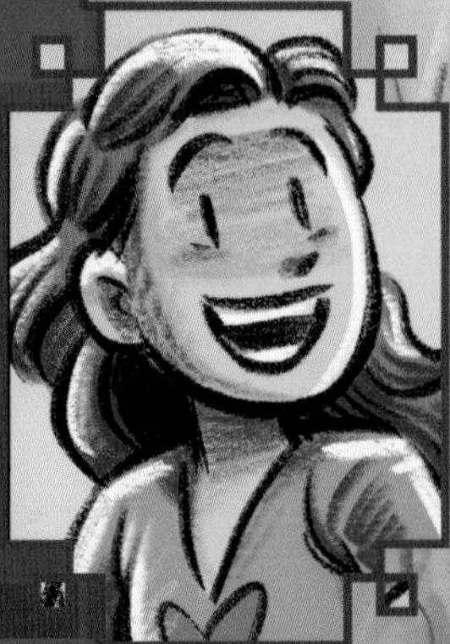

PAT & JEN

Pat is an awesome dude who's always looking for an epic adventure with his partner, the Super Girly Gamer Jen. Pat loves to have fun with his friends and take control of every situation with his cool weapons and can-do attitude. Jen is the sweetest person in the world and loves to laugh, but don't let her cheeriness fool you—she's also fierce. In fact, she could be an even greater adventurer than Pat . . . if she weren't so clumsy. Together, along with their cat, Cloud, they have a bond that can never be broken.

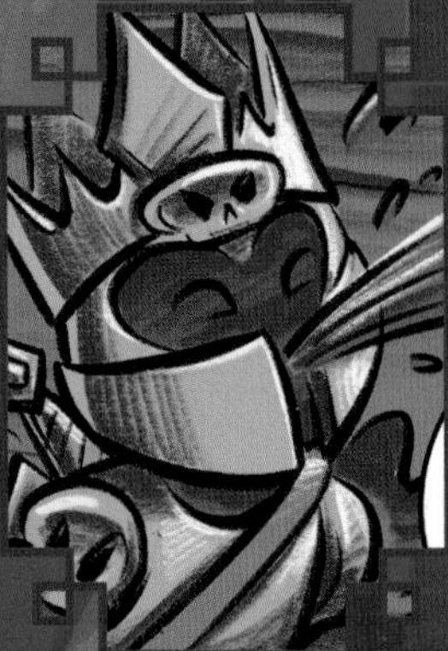

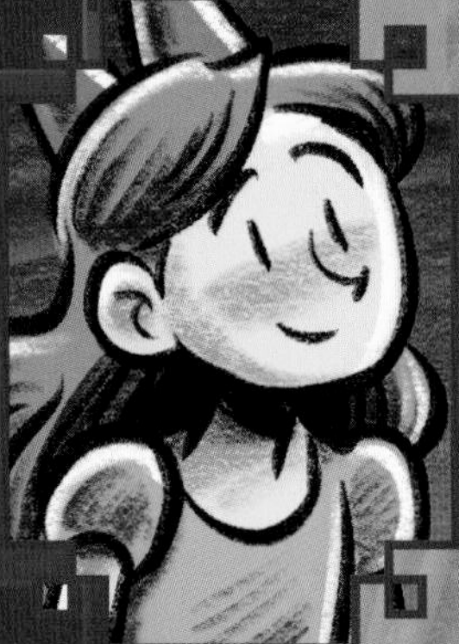

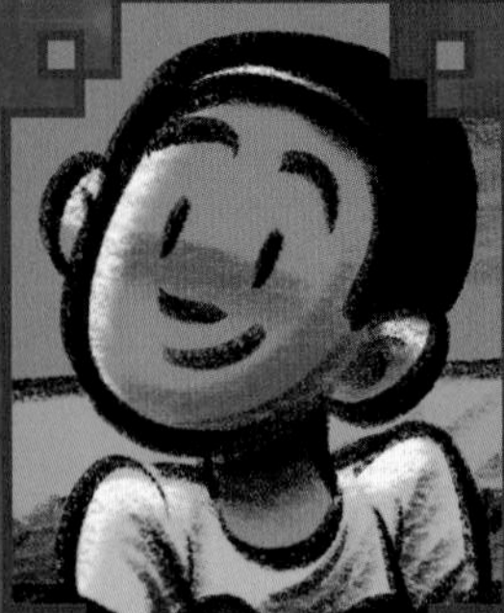

CARTER

Carter is Jen's best friend and biggest fan, but he doesn't seem to like Pat very much at all. Carter is also not very smart and sometimes carries a pickle that he thinks is a green sword!

CAPTAIN COOKIE

No one is quite sure if Captain Cookie is a real sea captain or if he just dresses the part. He doesn't seem to be very good at anything, but that doesn't stop him from bragging about how great he is! He's rude to everyone he meets but always in a funny way.

EVIL JEN

Evil Jen's favorite thing is chaos. She lives for wreaking havoc on the world. What makes her truly evil, however, is that she would take someone as sweet as Jen and become an evil version of her. She even looks *exactly* like her (just don't tell Jen we said that!).

HEROBRINE

Herobrine longs to be the king of all realms. He's as evil as evil gets, and he'll stop at nothing to get what he wants. But Herobrine also has a secret that will change everything for Pat and Jen.

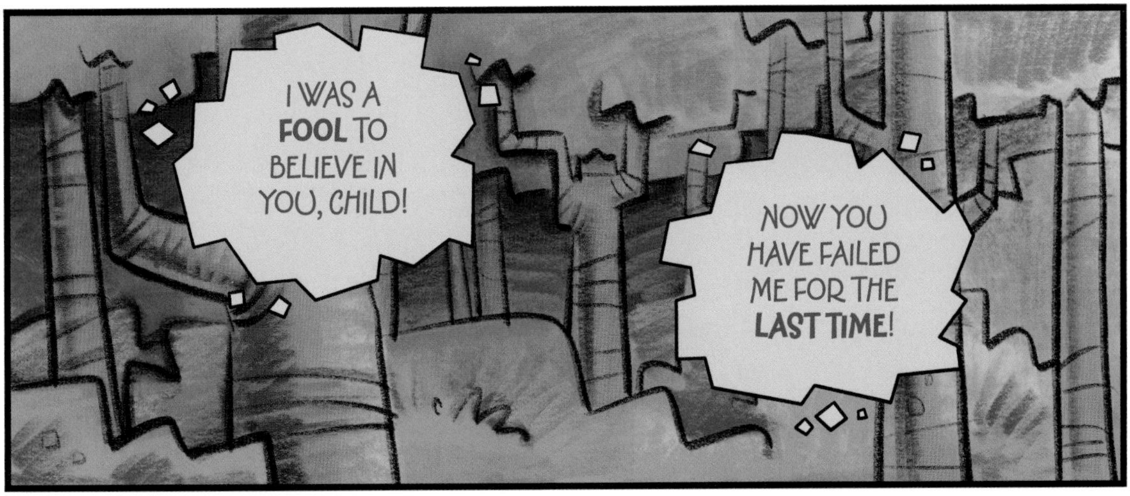
I WAS A FOOL TO BELIEVE IN YOU, CHILD!
NOW YOU HAVE FAILED ME FOR THE LAST TIME!

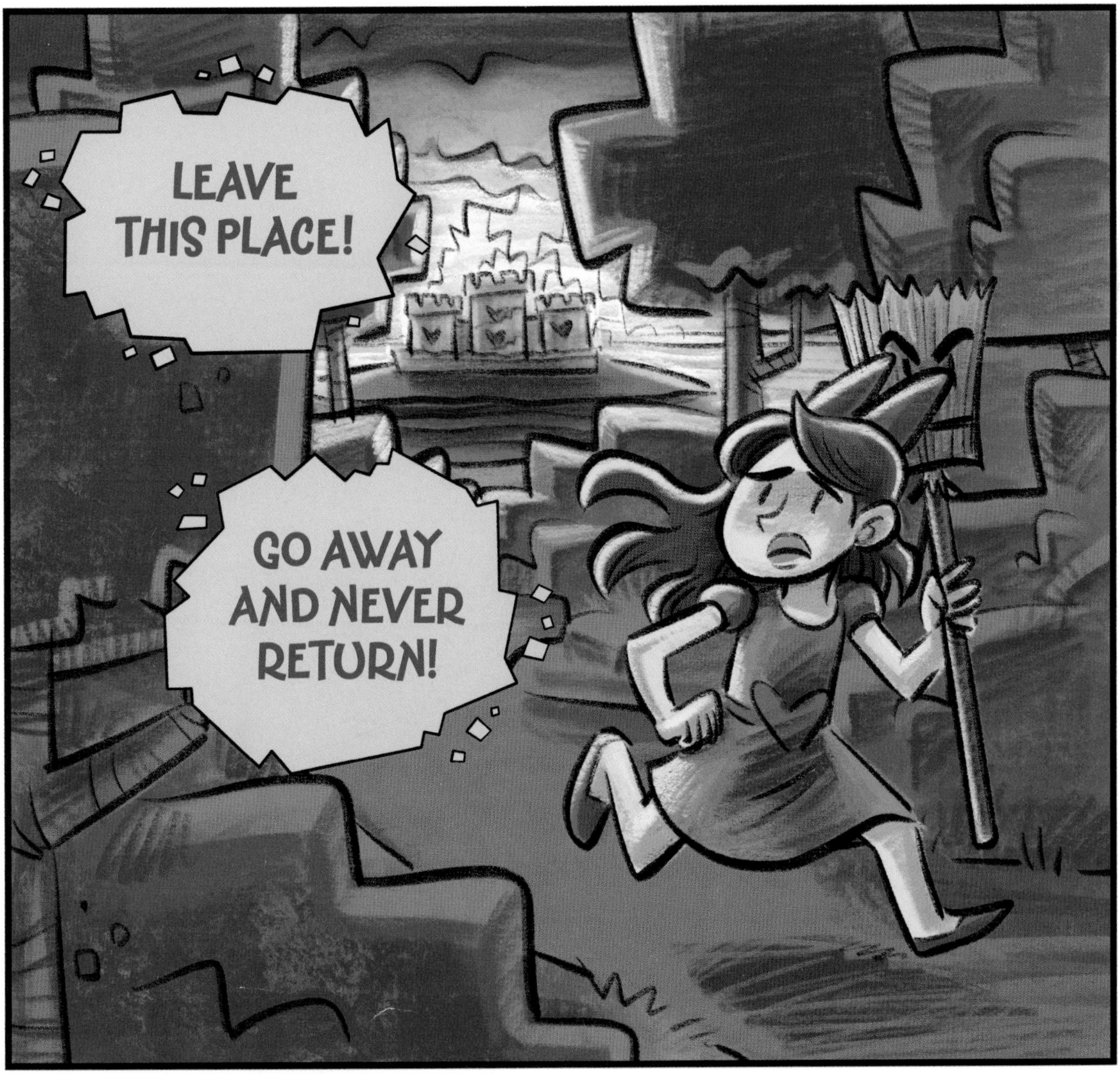
LEAVE THIS PLACE!
GO AWAY AND NEVER RETURN!

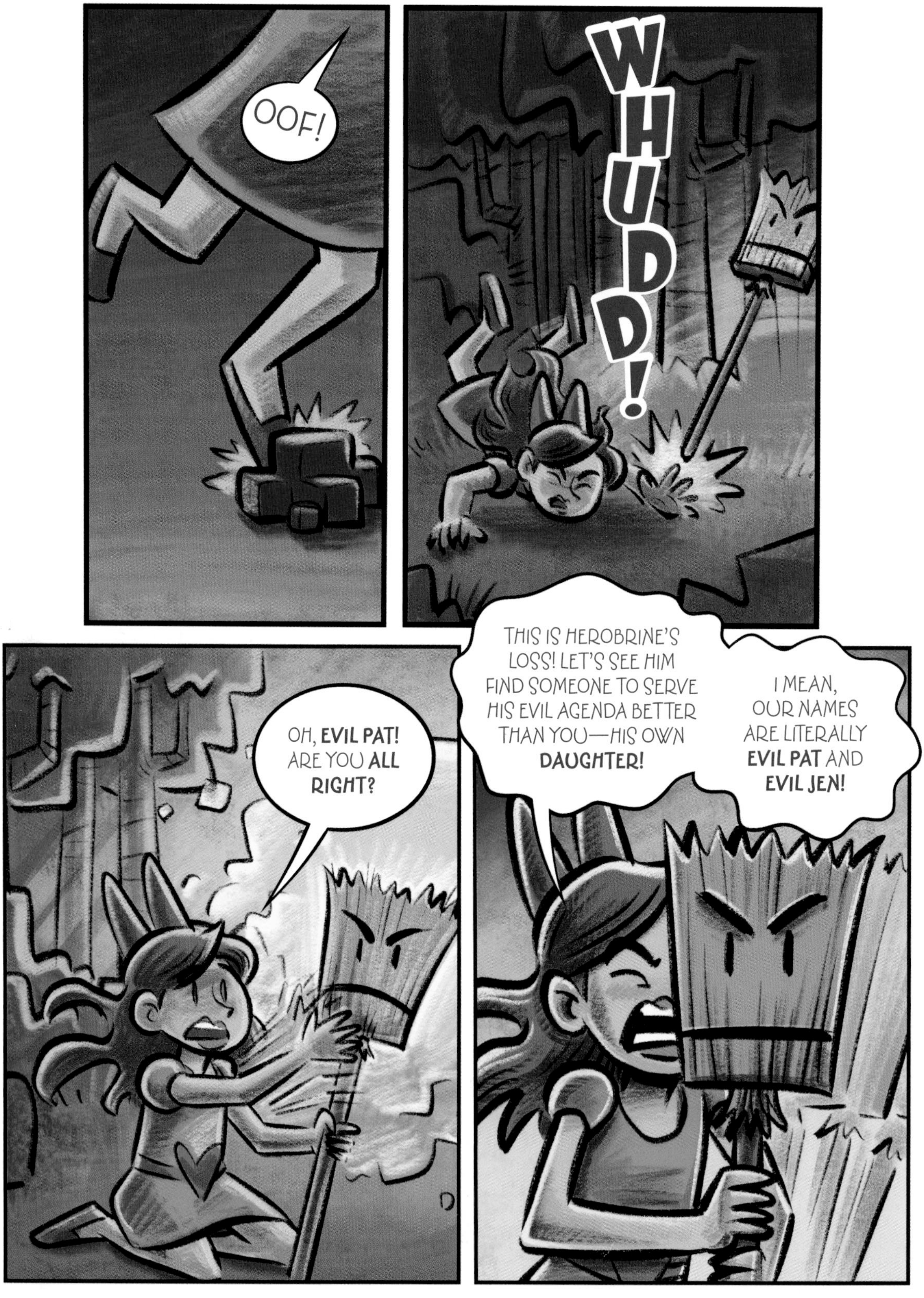
OOF!
WHUDD!
OH, EVIL PAT! ARE YOU ALL RIGHT?
THIS IS HEROBRINE'S LOSS! LET'S SEE HIM FIND SOMEONE TO SERVE HIS EVIL AGENDA BETTER THAN YOU—HIS OWN DAUGHTER!
I MEAN, OUR NAMES ARE LITERALLY EVIL PAT AND EVIL JEN!

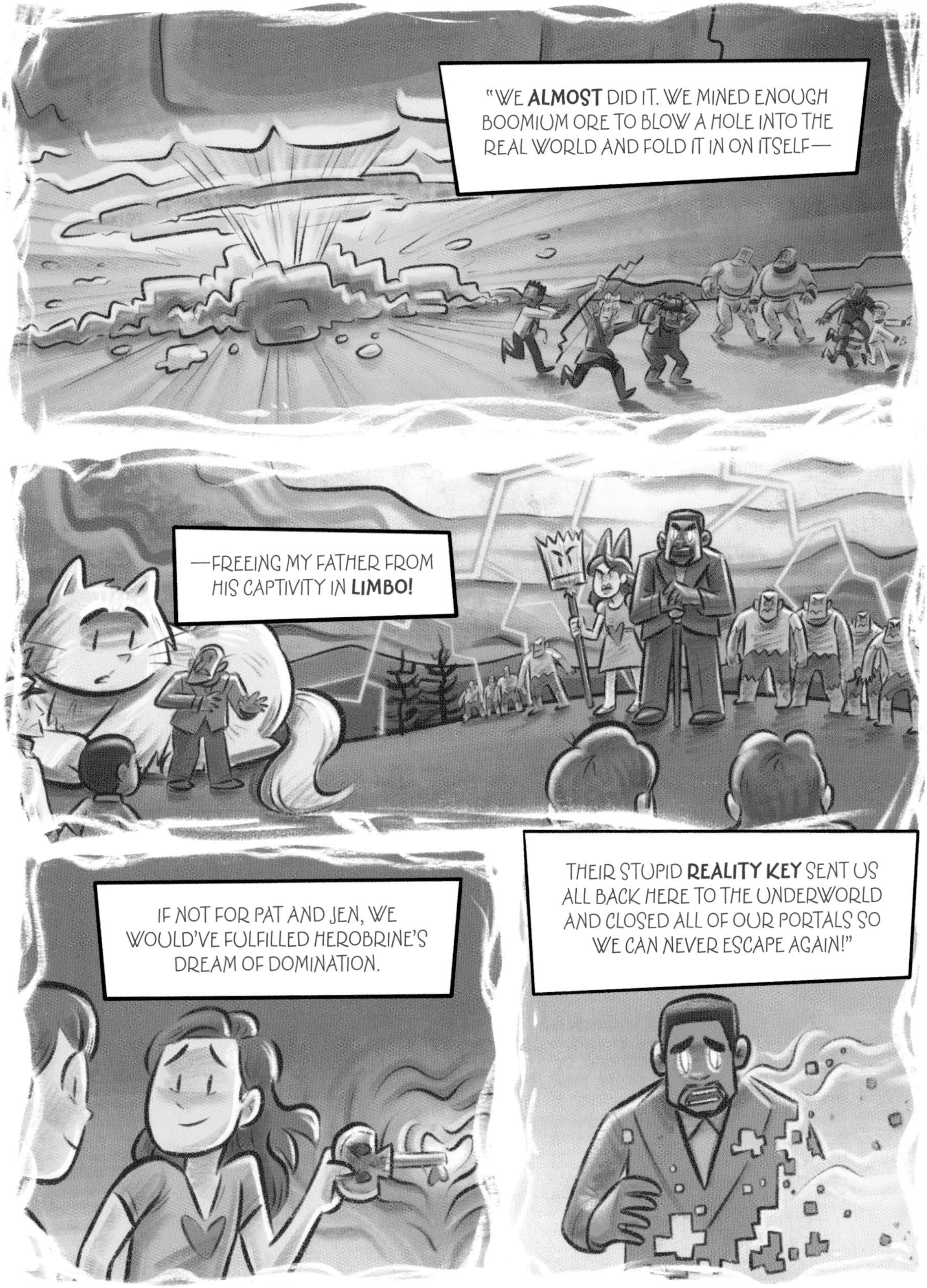
"WE **ALMOST** DID IT. WE MINED ENOUGH BOOMIUM ORE TO BLOW A HOLE INTO THE REAL WORLD AND FOLD IT IN ON ITSELF—
—FREEING MY FATHER FROM HIS CAPTIVITY IN **LIMBO!**
IF NOT FOR PAT AND JEN, WE WOULD'VE FULFILLED HEROBRINE'S DREAM OF DOMINATION.
THEIR STUPID **REALITY KEY** SENT US ALL BACK HERE TO THE UNDERWORLD AND CLOSED ALL OF OUR PORTALS SO WE CAN NEVER ESCAPE AGAIN!"

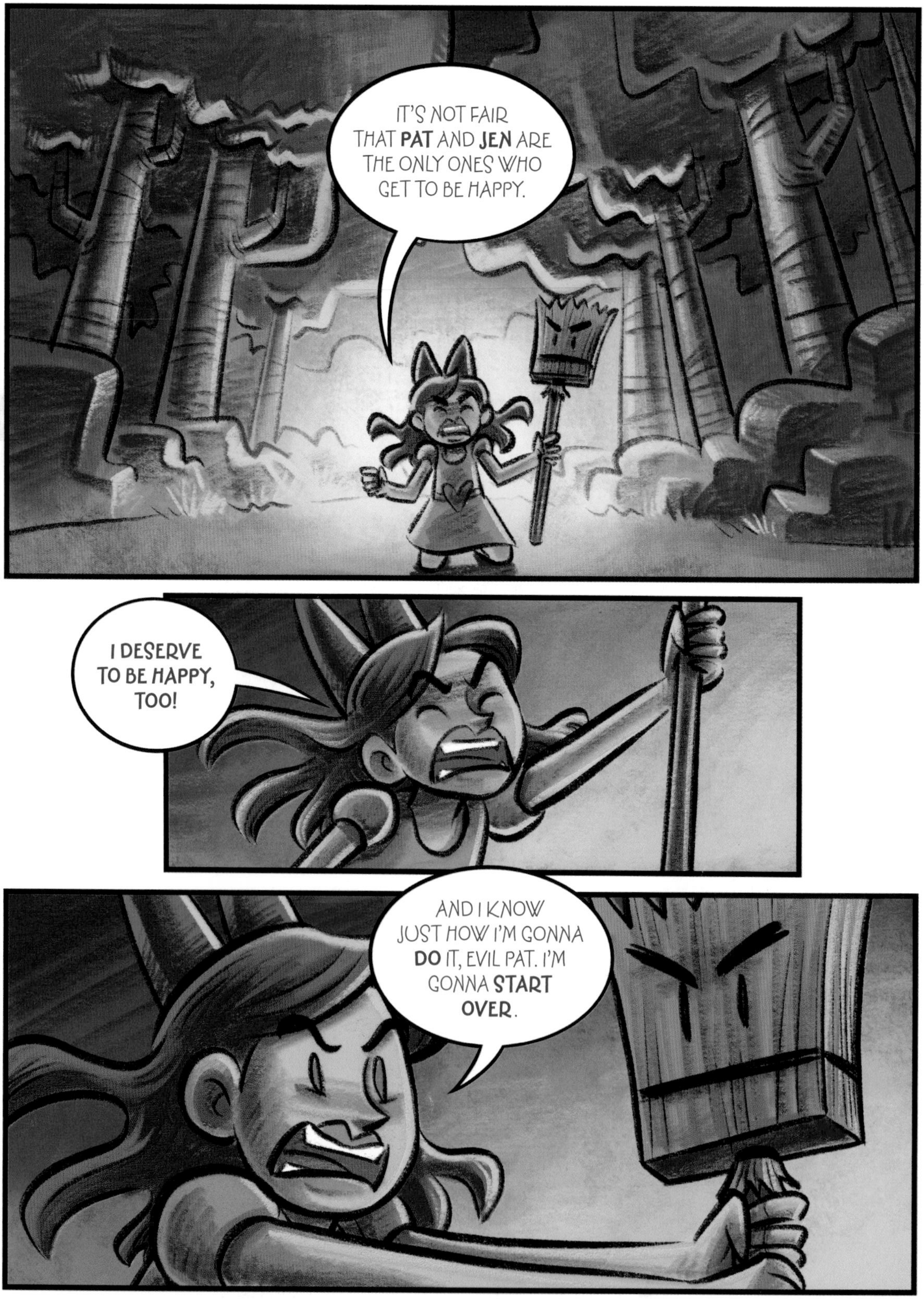
IT'S NOT FAIR THAT **PAT** AND **JEN** ARE THE ONLY ONES WHO GET TO BE HAPPY.
I DESERVE TO BE *HAPPY*, TOO!
AND I KNOW JUST HOW I'M GONNA **DO** IT, EVIL PAT. I'M GONNA **START OVER**.

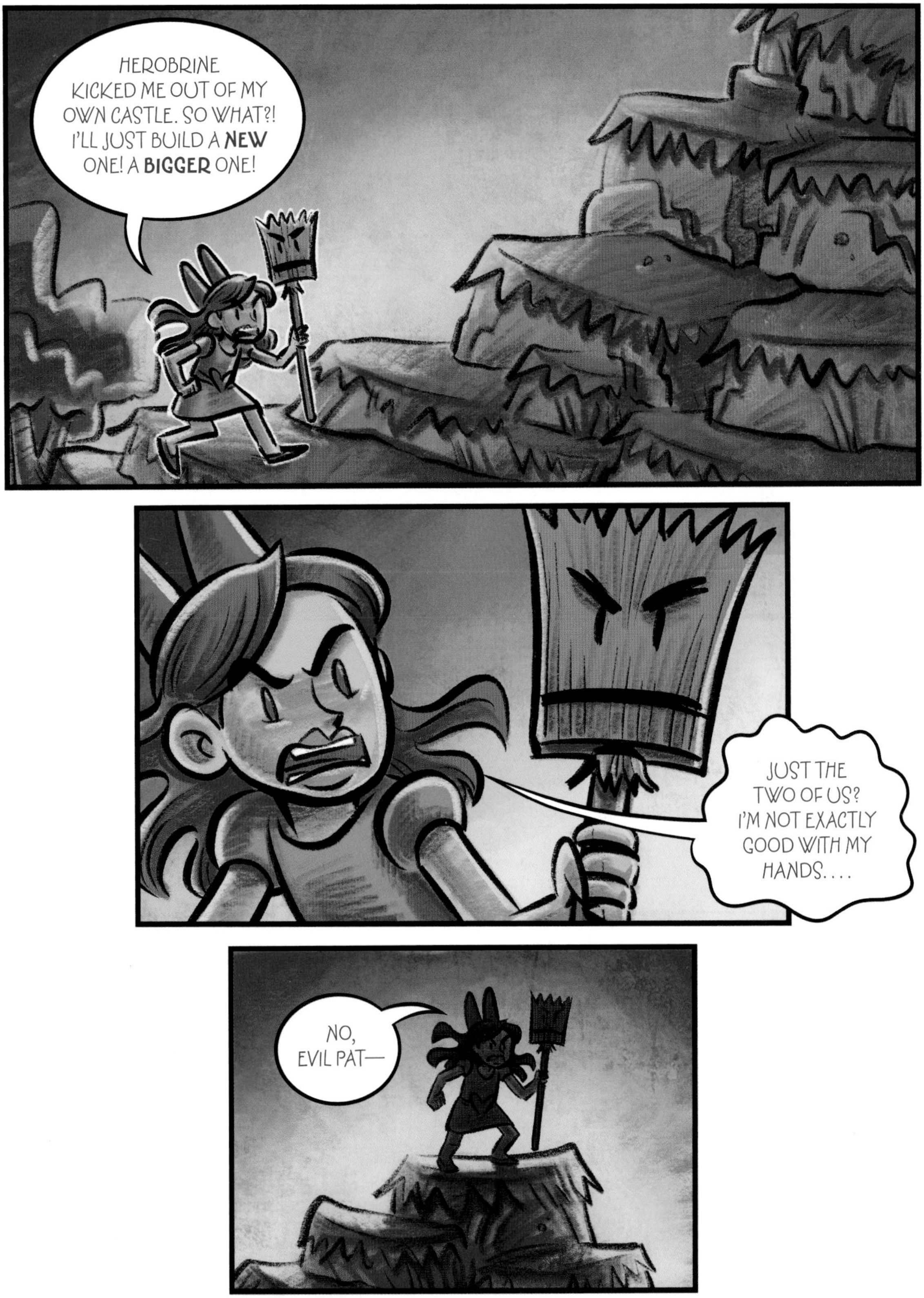
HEROBRINE KICKED ME OUT OF MY OWN CASTLE. SO WHAT?! I'LL JUST BUILD A **NEW** ONE! A **BIGGER** ONE!
JUST THE TWO OF US? I'M NOT EXACTLY GOOD WITH MY HANDS. . . .
NO, EVIL PAT—

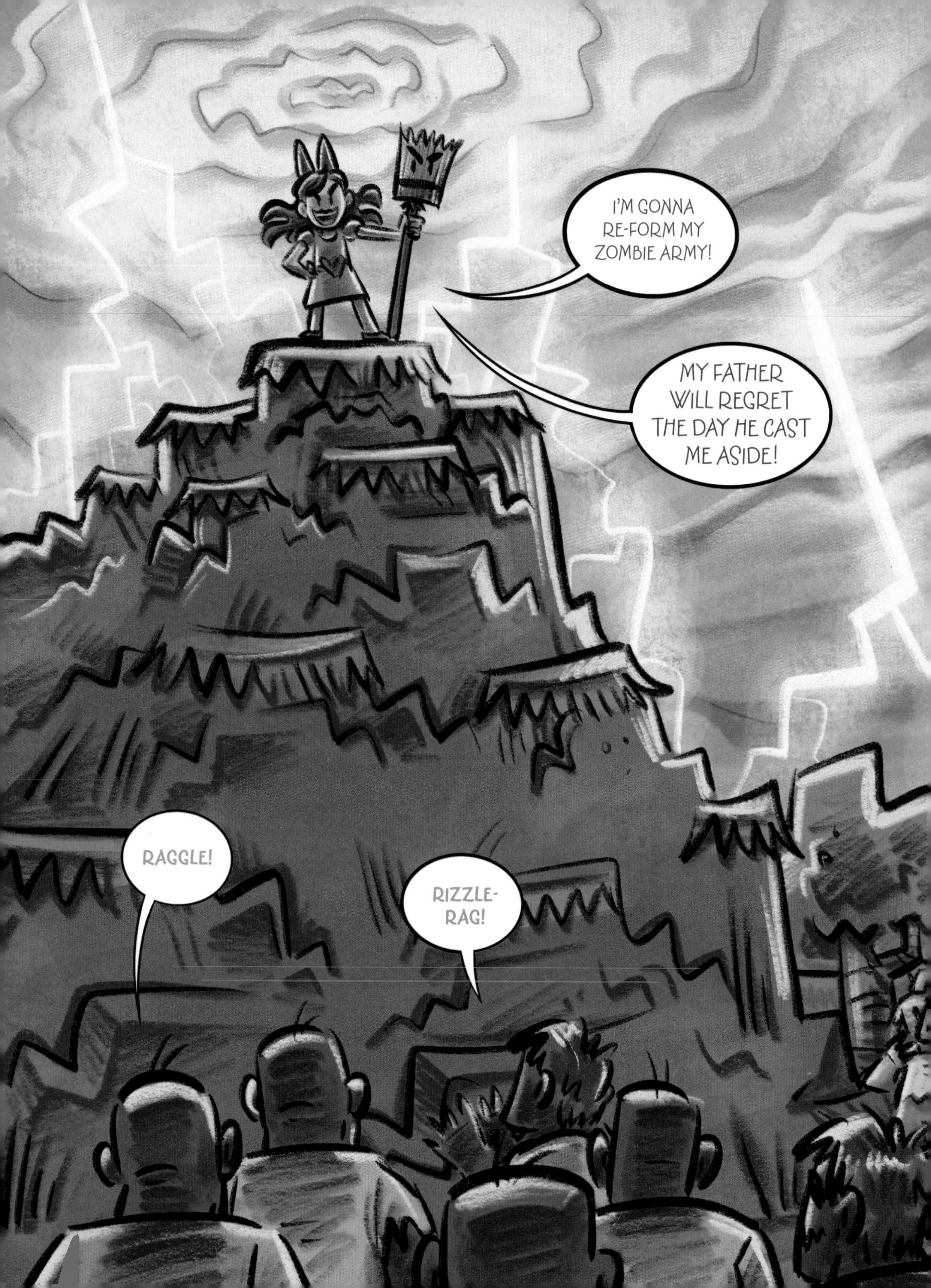
I'M GONNA RE-FORM MY ZOMBIE ARMY!
MY FATHER WILL REGRET THE DAY HE CAST ME ASIDE!
RAGGLE!
RIZZLE-RAG!

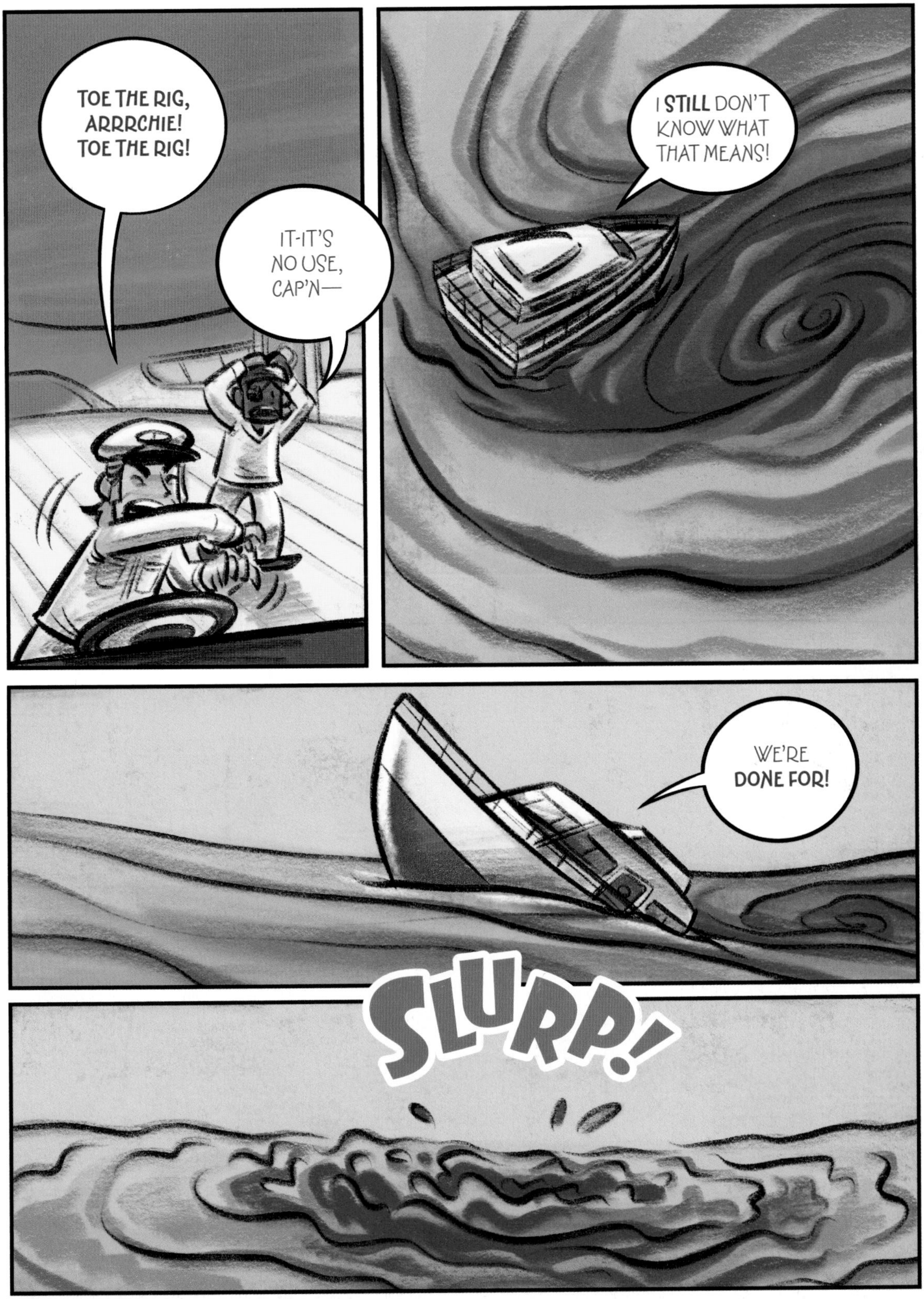
TOE THE RIG, ARRRCHIE! TOE THE RIG!
IT-IT'S NO USE, CAP'N—
I STILL DON'T KNOW WHAT THAT MEANS!
WE'RE DONE FOR!
SLURP!

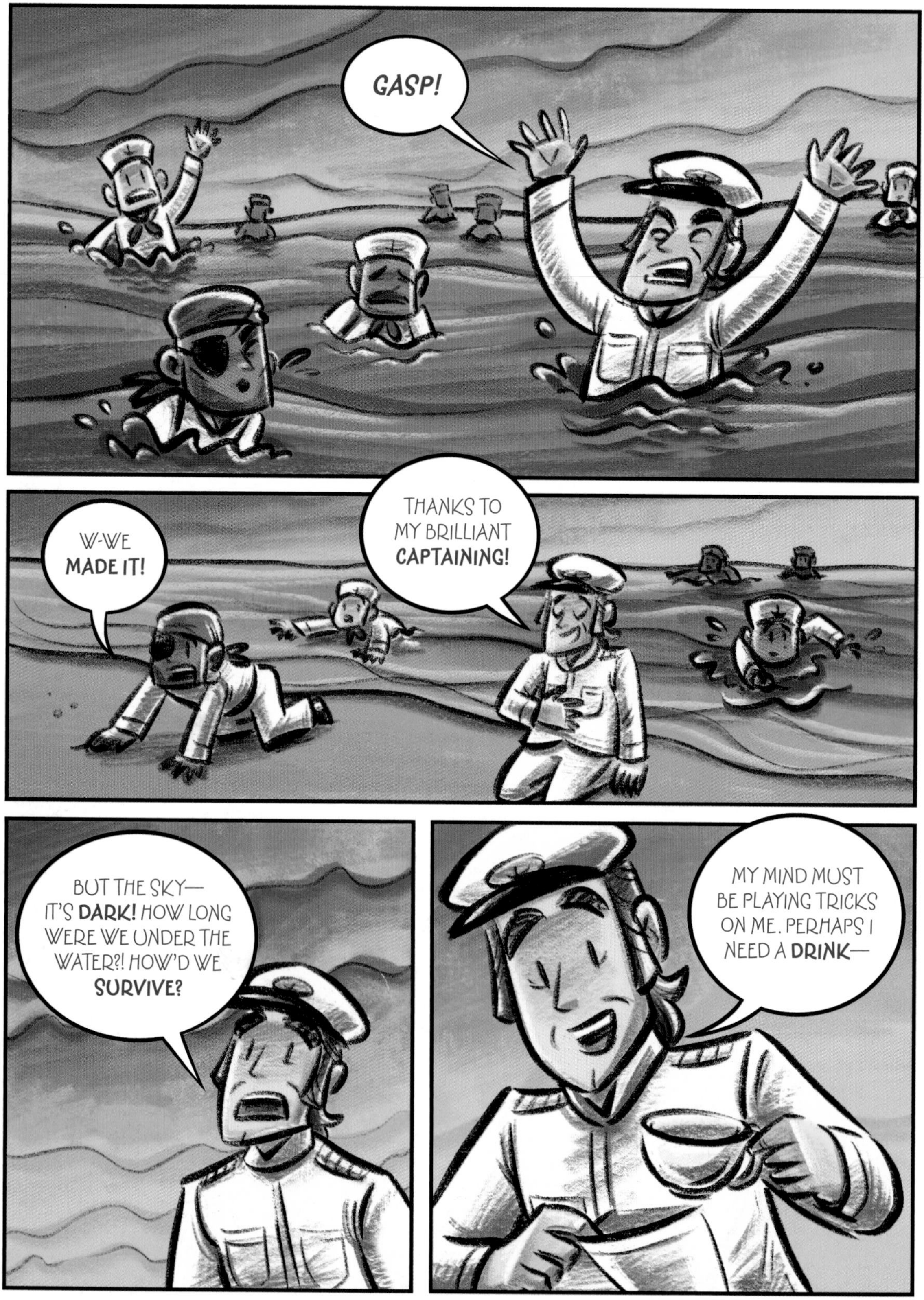
GASP!
W-WE MADE IT!
THANKS TO MY BRILLIANT CAPTAINING!
BUT THE SKY— IT'S DARK! HOW LONG WERE WE UNDER THE WATER?! HOW'D WE SURVIVE?
MY MIND MUST BE PLAYING TRICKS ON ME. PERHAPS I NEED A DRINK—

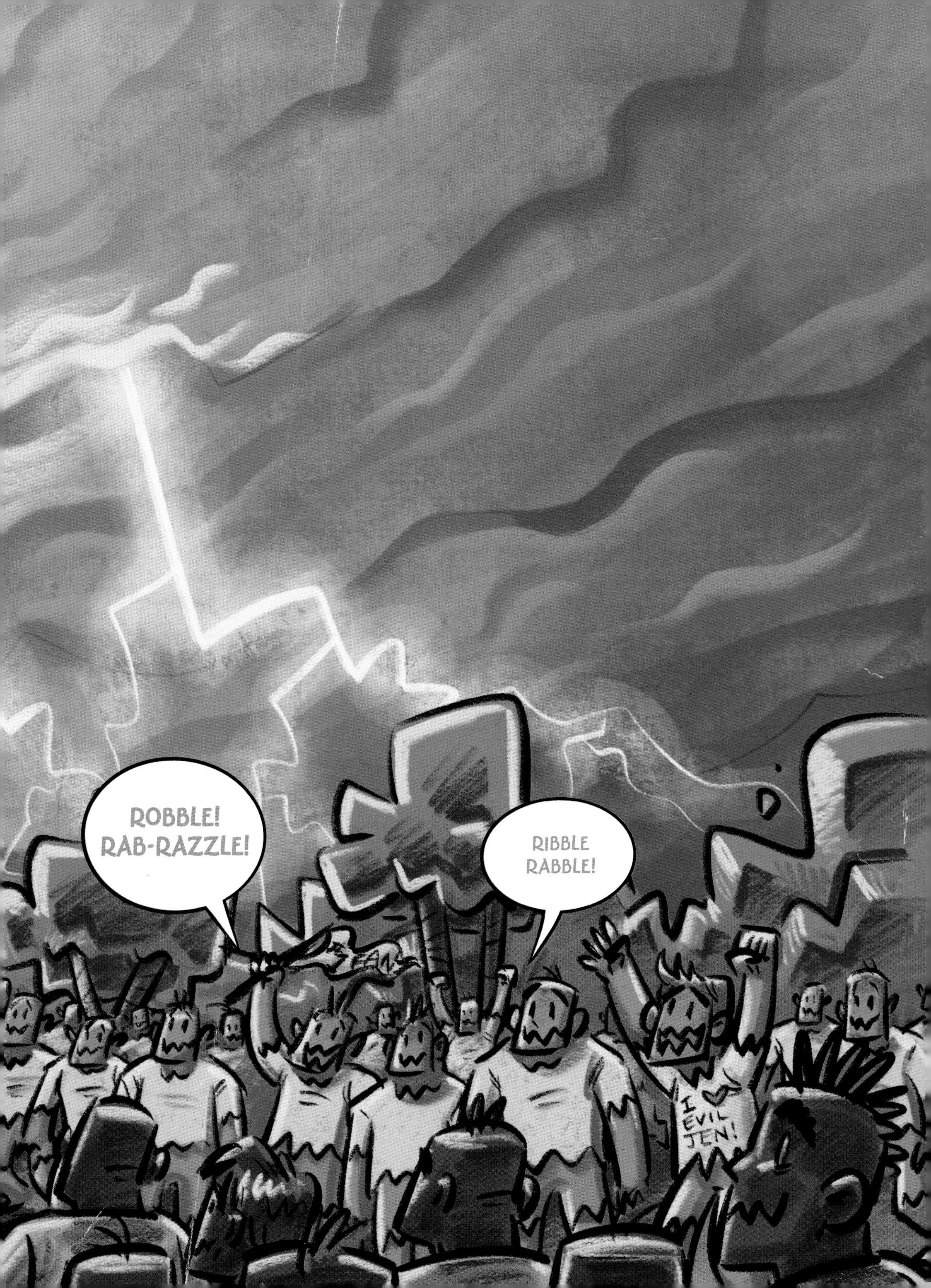
ROBBLE! RAB-RAZZLE!
RIBBLE RABBLE!
I ♥ EVIL JEN!

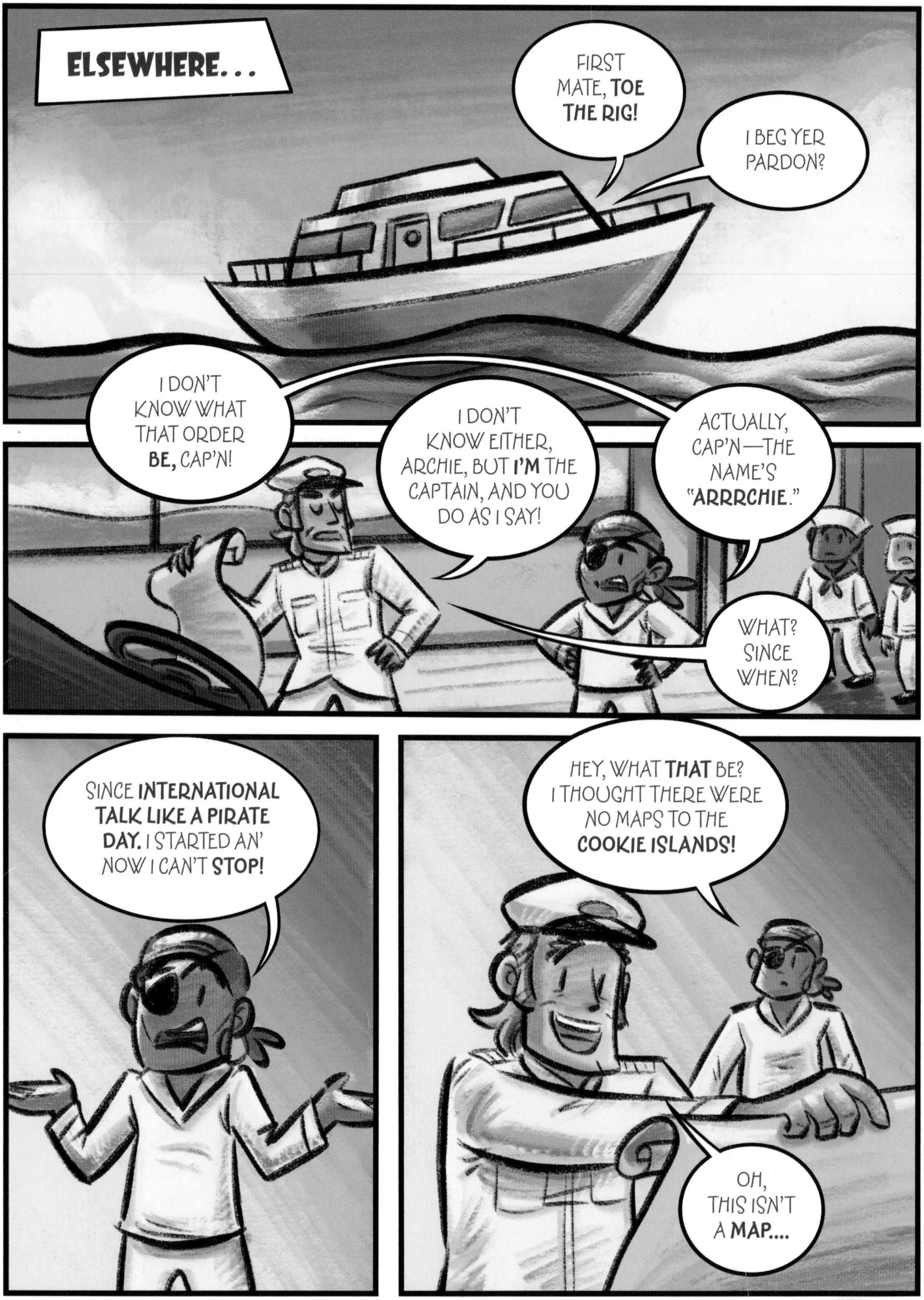
ELSEWHERE...
FIRST MATE, TOE THE RIG!
I BEG YER PARDON?
I DON'T KNOW WHAT THAT ORDER BE, CAP'N!
I DON'T KNOW EITHER, ARCHIE, BUT I'M THE CAPTAIN, AND YOU DO AS I SAY!
ACTUALLY, CAP'N—THE NAME'S "ARRRCHIE."
WHAT? SINCE WHEN?
SINCE INTERNATIONAL TALK LIKE A PIRATE DAY. I STARTED AN' NOW I CAN'T STOP!
HEY, WHAT THAT BE? I THOUGHT THERE WERE NO MAPS TO THE COOKIE ISLANDS!
OH, THIS ISN'T A MAP....

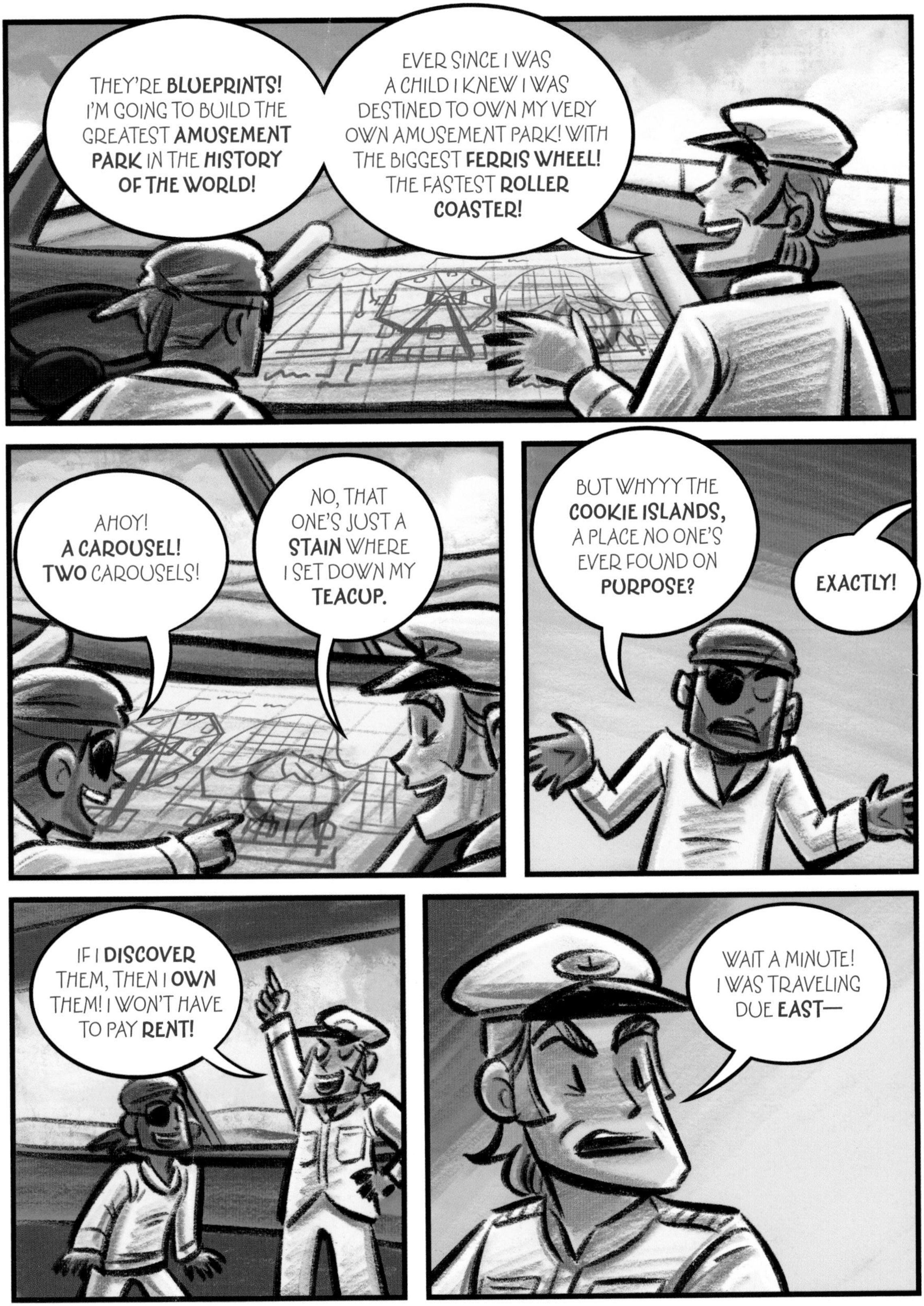
THEY'RE **BLUEPRINTS!** I'M GOING TO BUILD THE GREATEST **AMUSEMENT PARK** IN THE **HISTORY OF THE WORLD!**
EVER SINCE I WAS A CHILD I KNEW I WAS DESTINED TO OWN MY VERY OWN AMUSEMENT PARK! WITH THE BIGGEST **FERRIS WHEEL!** THE FASTEST **ROLLER COASTER!**
AHOY! **A CAROUSEL! TWO** CAROUSELS!
NO, THAT ONE'S JUST A **STAIN** WHERE I SET DOWN MY **TEACUP.**
BUT WHYYY THE **COOKIE ISLANDS,** A PLACE NO ONE'S EVER FOUND ON **PURPOSE?**
EXACTLY!
IF I **DISCOVER** THEM, THEN I **OWN** THEM! I WON'T HAVE TO PAY **RENT!**
WAIT A MINUTE! I WAS TRAVELING DUE **EAST—**

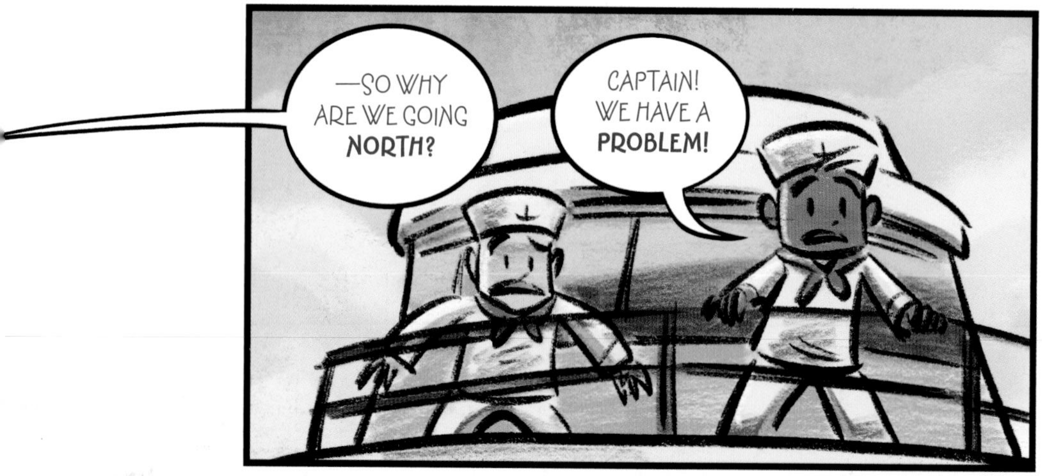
—SO WHY ARE WE GOING NORTH?
CAPTAIN! WE HAVE A PROBLEM!

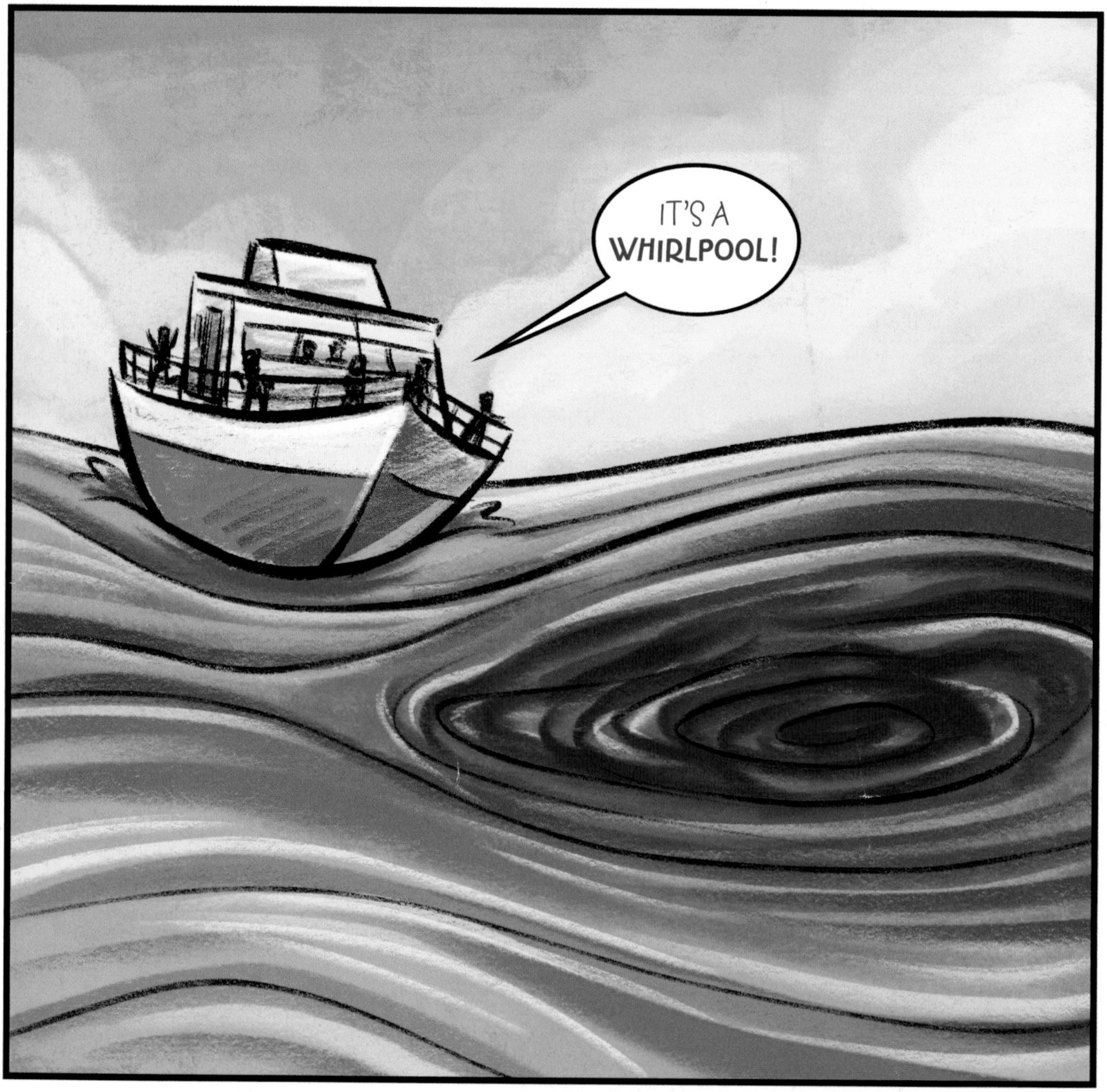
IT'S A WHIRLPOOL!

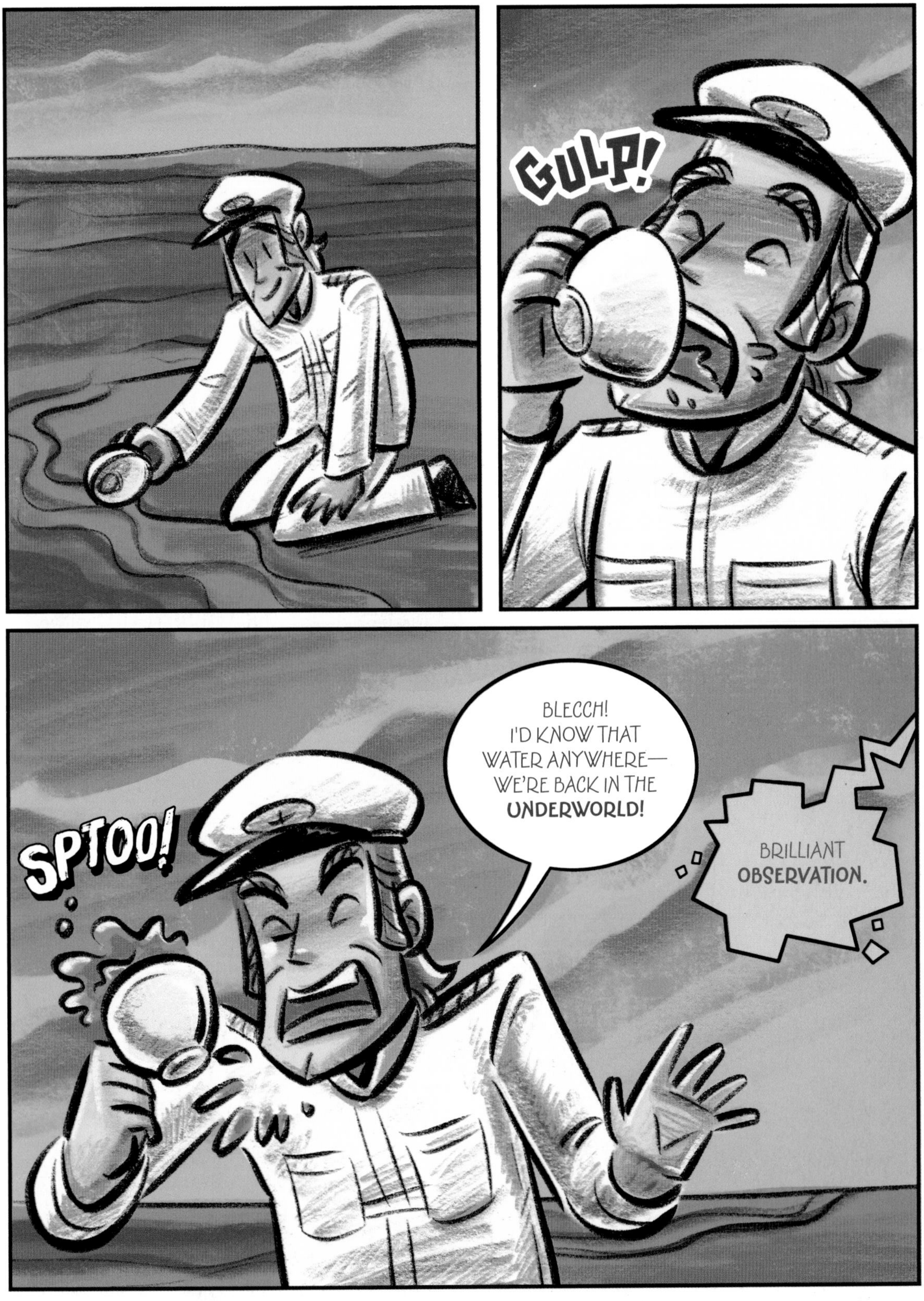
GULP!
SPTOO!
BLECCH! I'D KNOW THAT WATER ANYWHERE— WE'RE BACK IN THE UNDERWORLD!
BRILLIANT OBSERVATION.

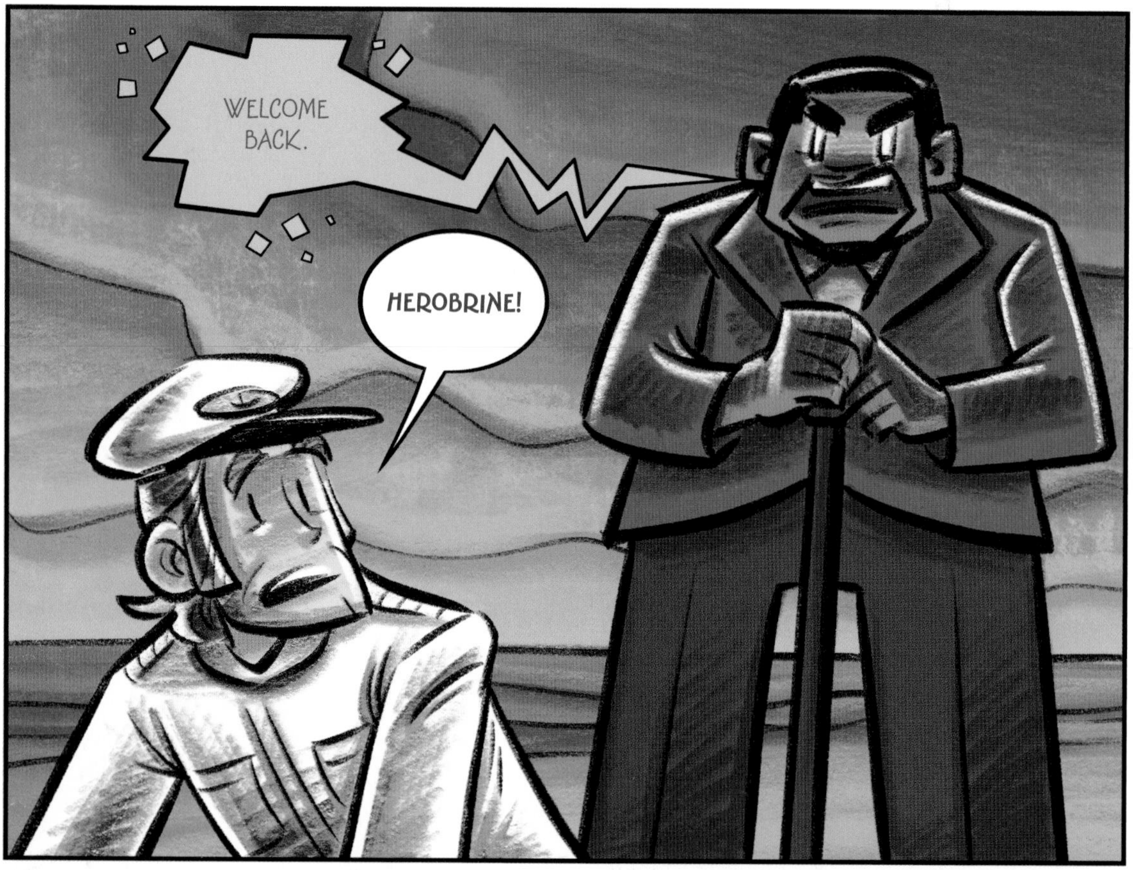
WELCOME BACK.
HEROBRINE!
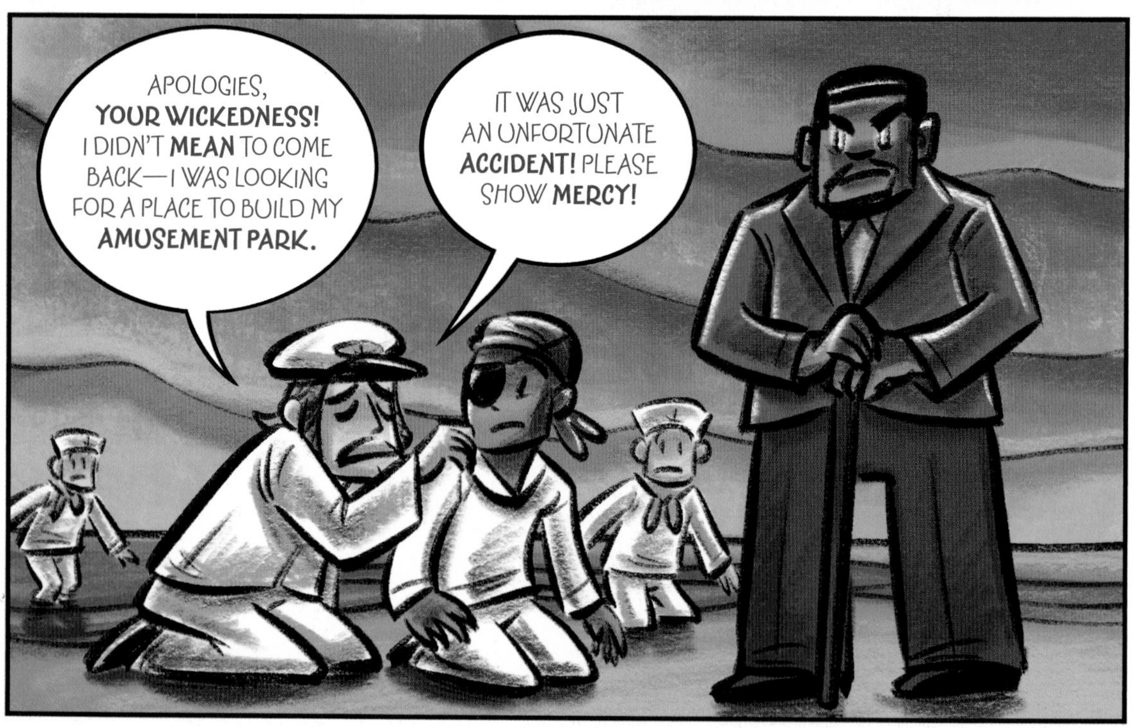
APOLOGIES, YOUR WICKEDNESS! I DIDN'T MEAN TO COME BACK—I WAS LOOKING FOR A PLACE TO BUILD MY AMUSEMENT PARK.
IT WAS JUST AN UNFORTUNATE ACCIDENT! PLEASE SHOW MERCY!

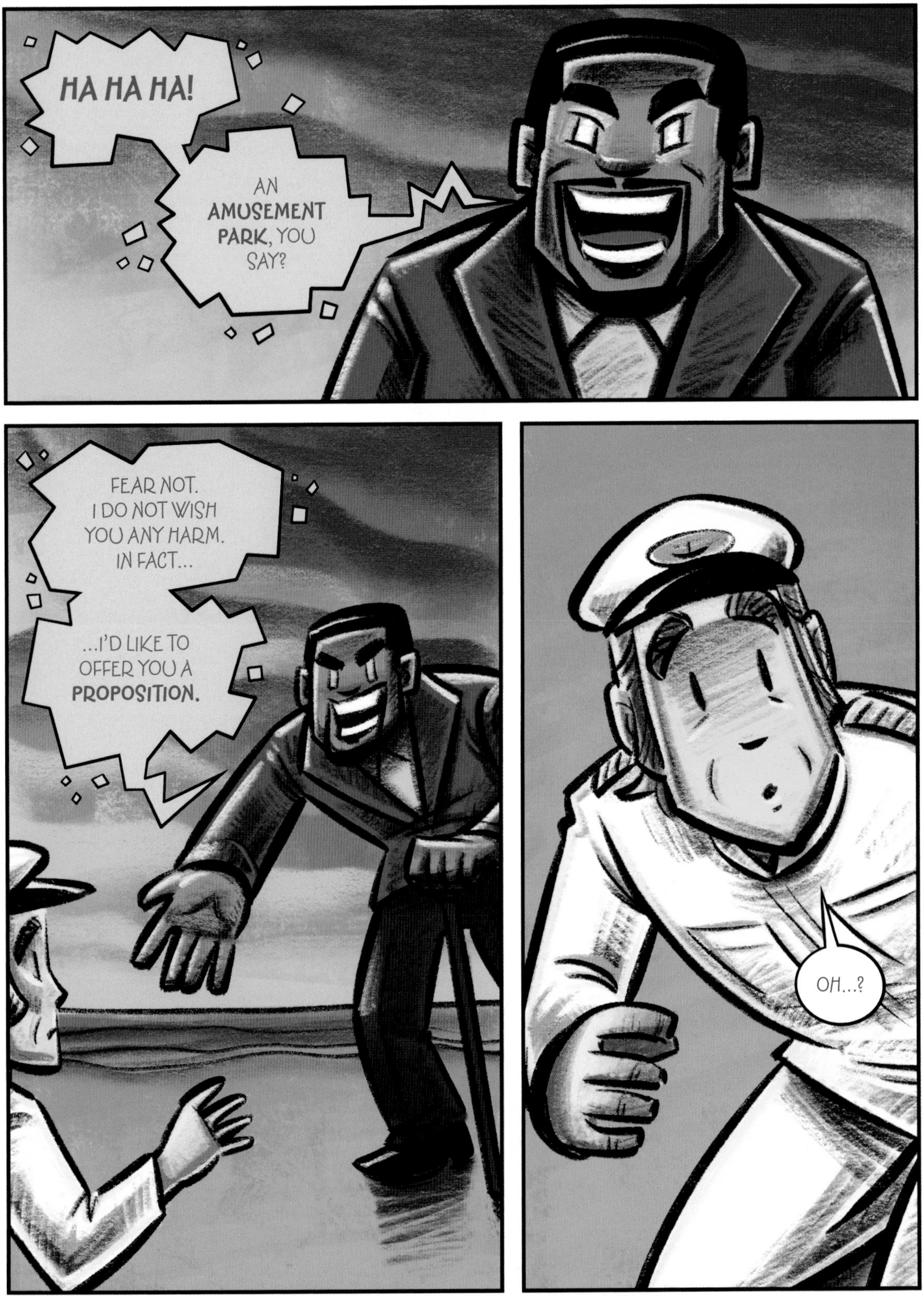
HA HA HA!
AN AMUSEMENT PARK, YOU SAY?
FEAR NOT. I DO NOT WISH YOU ANY HARM. IN FACT...
...I'D LIKE TO OFFER YOU A PROPOSITION.
OH...?

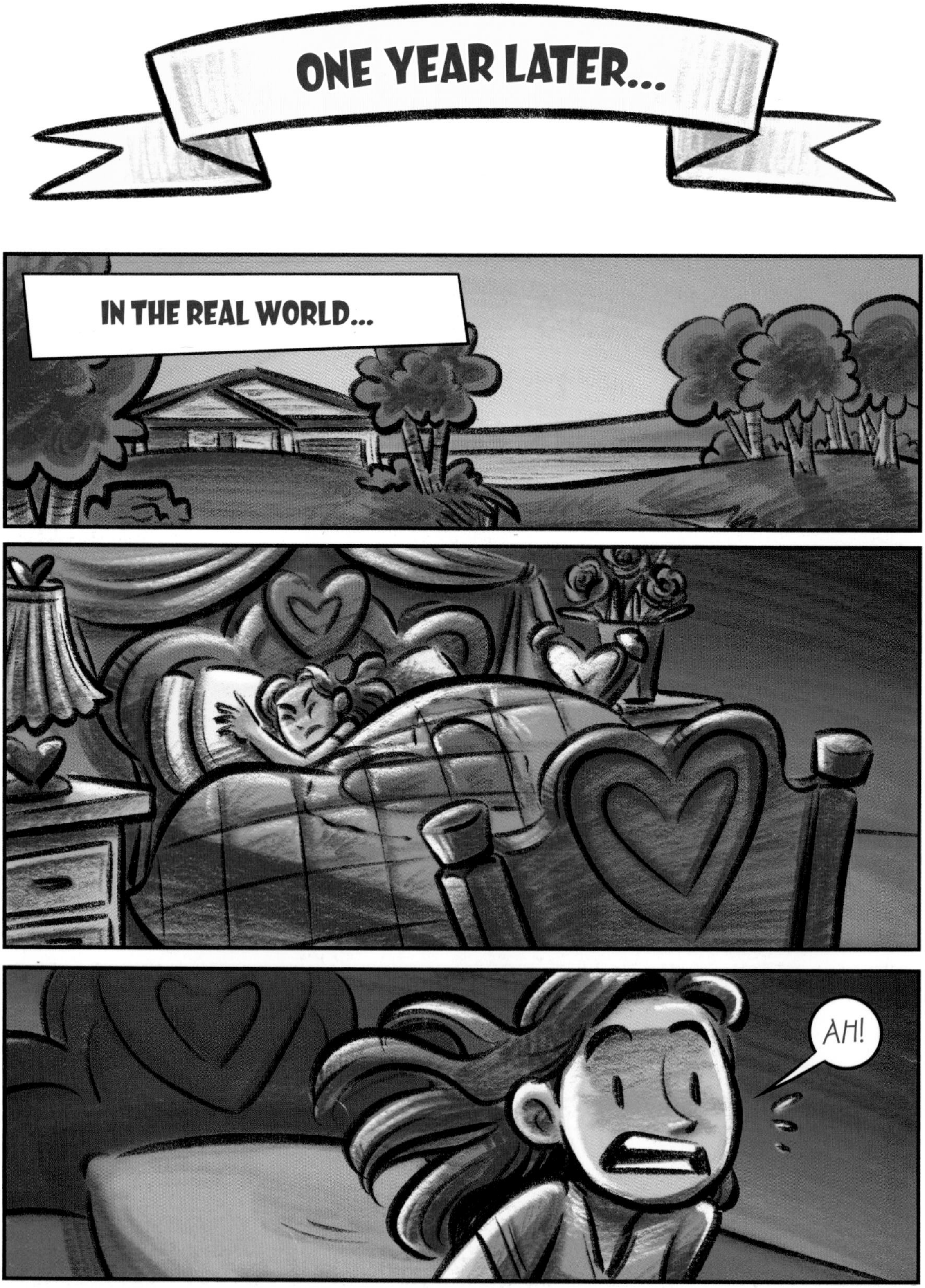
ONE YEAR LATER...
IN THE REAL WORLD...
AH!

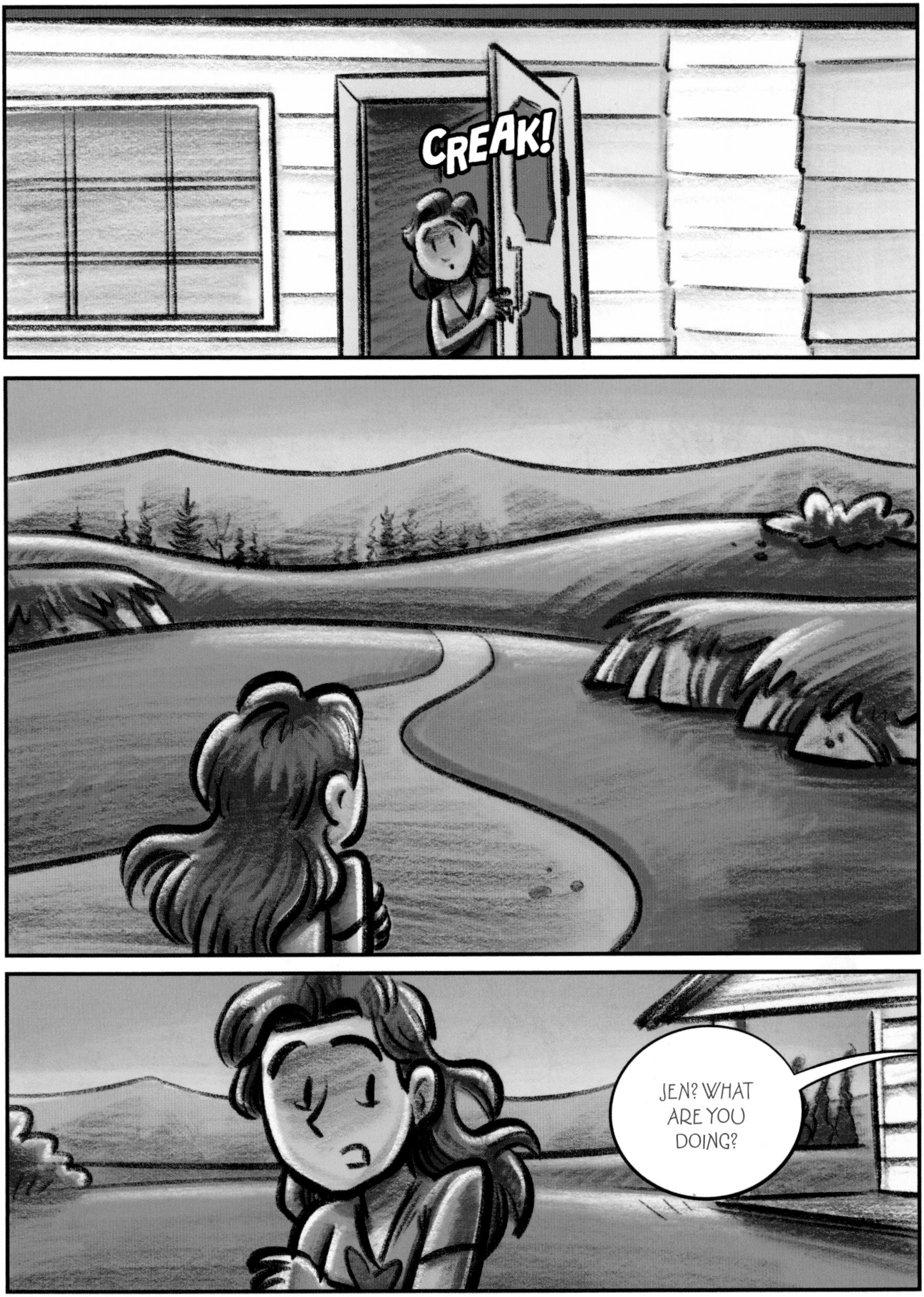
CREAK!
JEN? WHAT ARE YOU DOING?

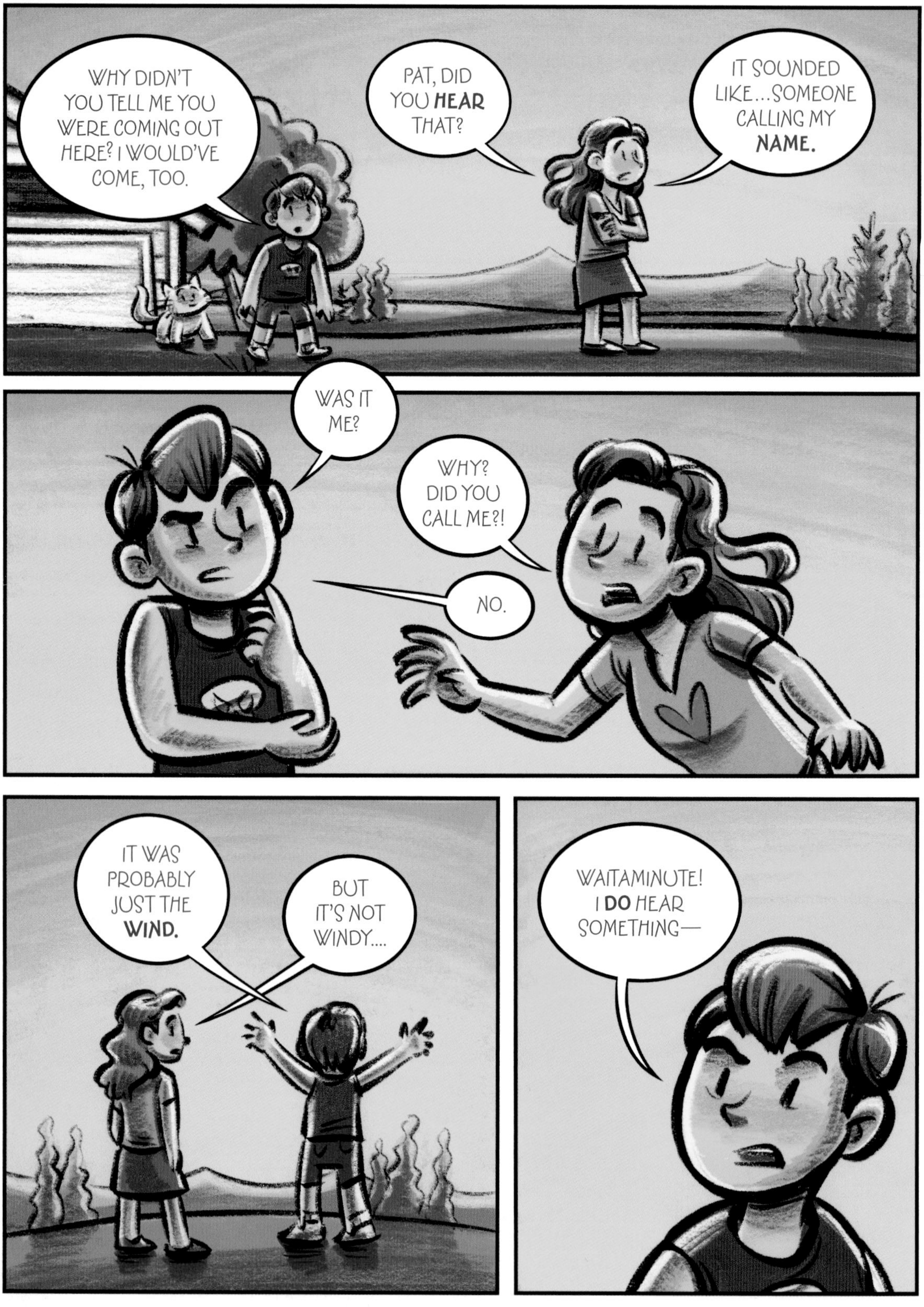
WHY DIDN'T YOU TELL ME YOU WERE COMING OUT HERE? I WOULD'VE COME, TOO.
PAT, DID YOU **HEAR** THAT?
IT SOUNDED LIKE...SOMEONE CALLING MY **NAME.**
WAS IT ME?
WHY? DID YOU CALL ME?!
NO.
IT WAS PROBABLY JUST THE **WIND.**
BUT IT'S NOT WINDY....
WAITAMINUTE! I **DO** HEAR SOMETHING—

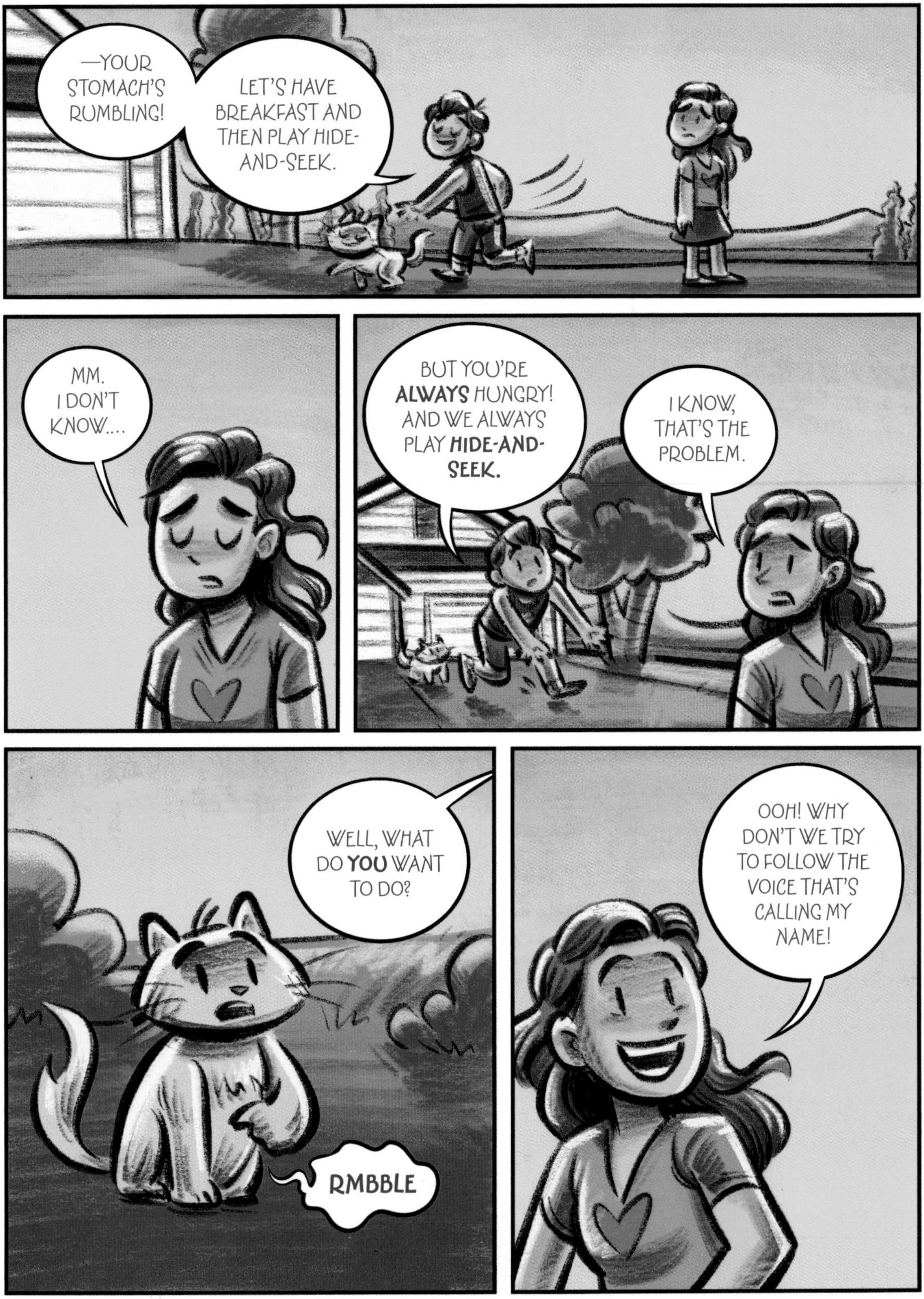
—YOUR STOMACH'S RUMBLING!
LET'S HAVE BREAKFAST AND THEN PLAY HIDE-AND-SEEK.
MM. I DON'T KNOW....
BUT YOU'RE **ALWAYS** HUNGRY! AND WE ALWAYS PLAY **HIDE-AND-SEEK.**
I KNOW, THAT'S THE PROBLEM.
WELL, WHAT DO **YOU** WANT TO DO?
RMBBLE
OOH! WHY DON'T WE TRY TO FOLLOW THE VOICE THAT'S CALLING MY NAME!

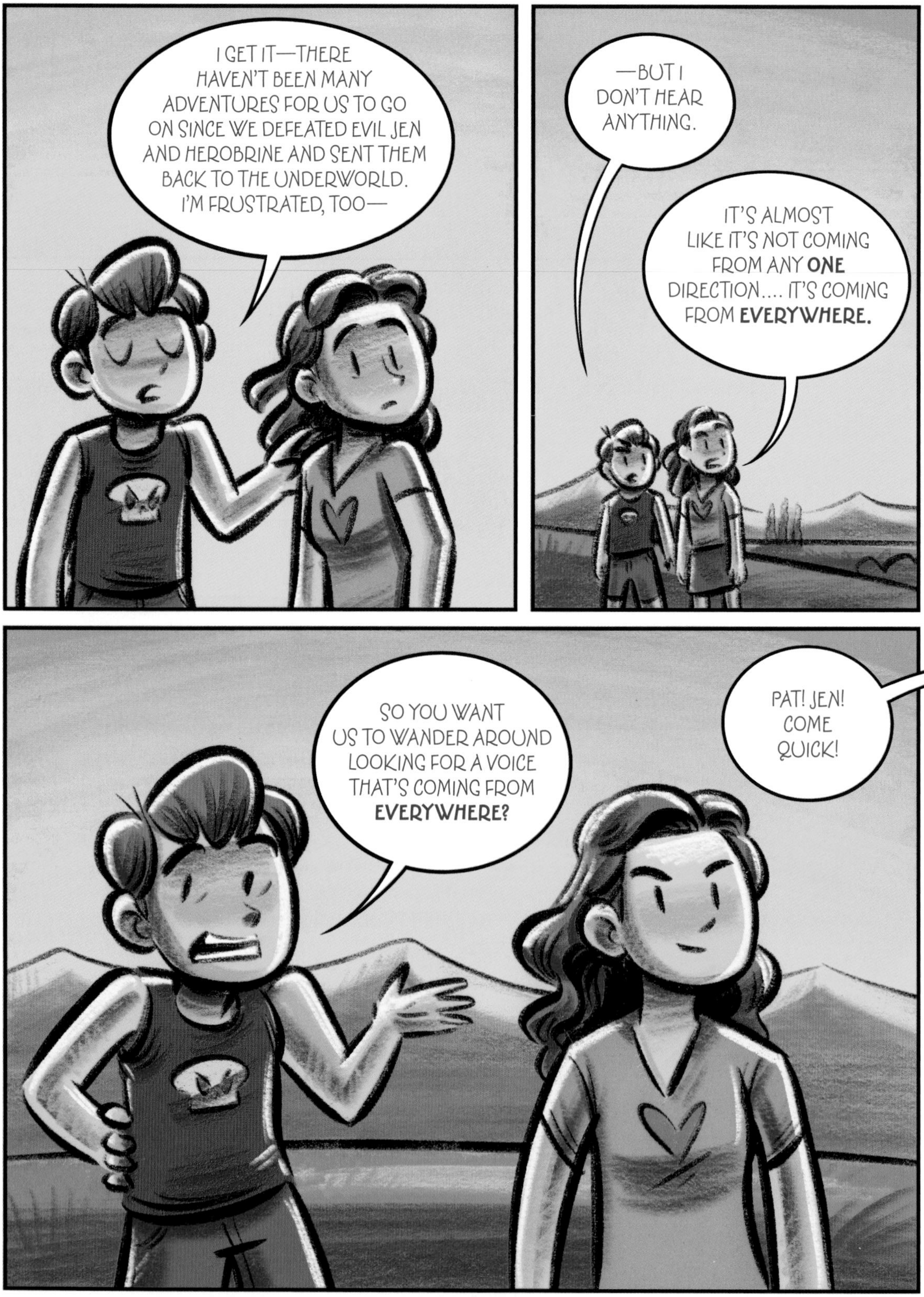
I GET IT—THERE HAVEN'T BEEN MANY ADVENTURES FOR US TO GO ON SINCE WE DEFEATED EVIL JEN AND HEROBRINE AND SENT THEM BACK TO THE UNDERWORLD. I'M FRUSTRATED, TOO—
—BUT I DON'T HEAR ANYTHING.
IT'S ALMOST LIKE IT'S NOT COMING FROM ANY **ONE** DIRECTION.... IT'S COMING FROM **EVERYWHERE.**
SO YOU WANT US TO WANDER AROUND LOOKING FOR A VOICE THAT'S COMING FROM **EVERYWHERE?**
PAT! JEN! COME QUICK!

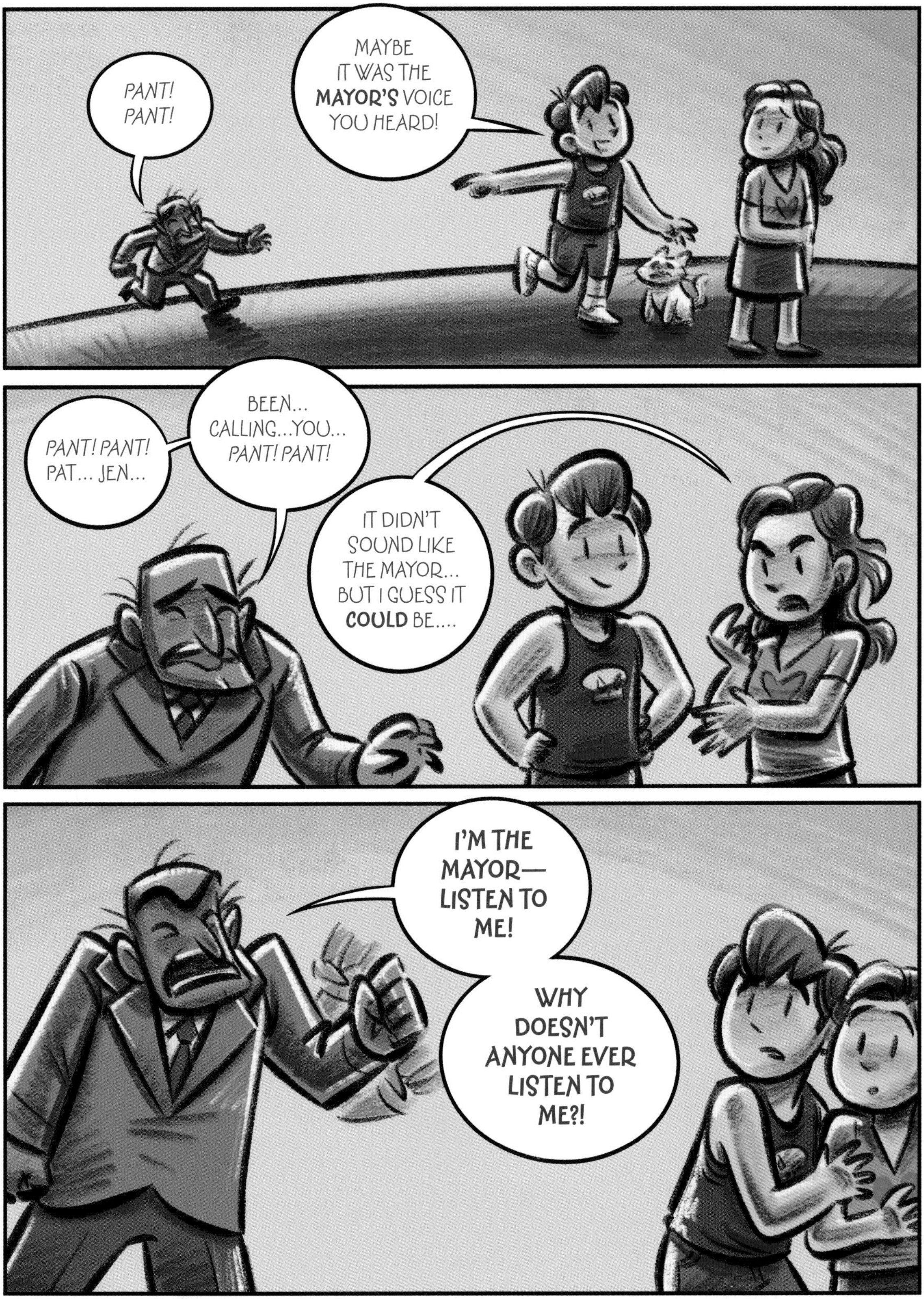
PANT! PANT!
MAYBE IT WAS THE MAYOR'S VOICE YOU HEARD!
PANT! PANT! PAT... JEN...
BEEN... CALLING...YOU... PANT! PANT!
IT DIDN'T SOUND LIKE THE MAYOR... BUT I GUESS IT COULD BE....
I'M THE MAYOR— LISTEN TO ME!
WHY DOESN'T ANYONE EVER LISTEN TO ME?!

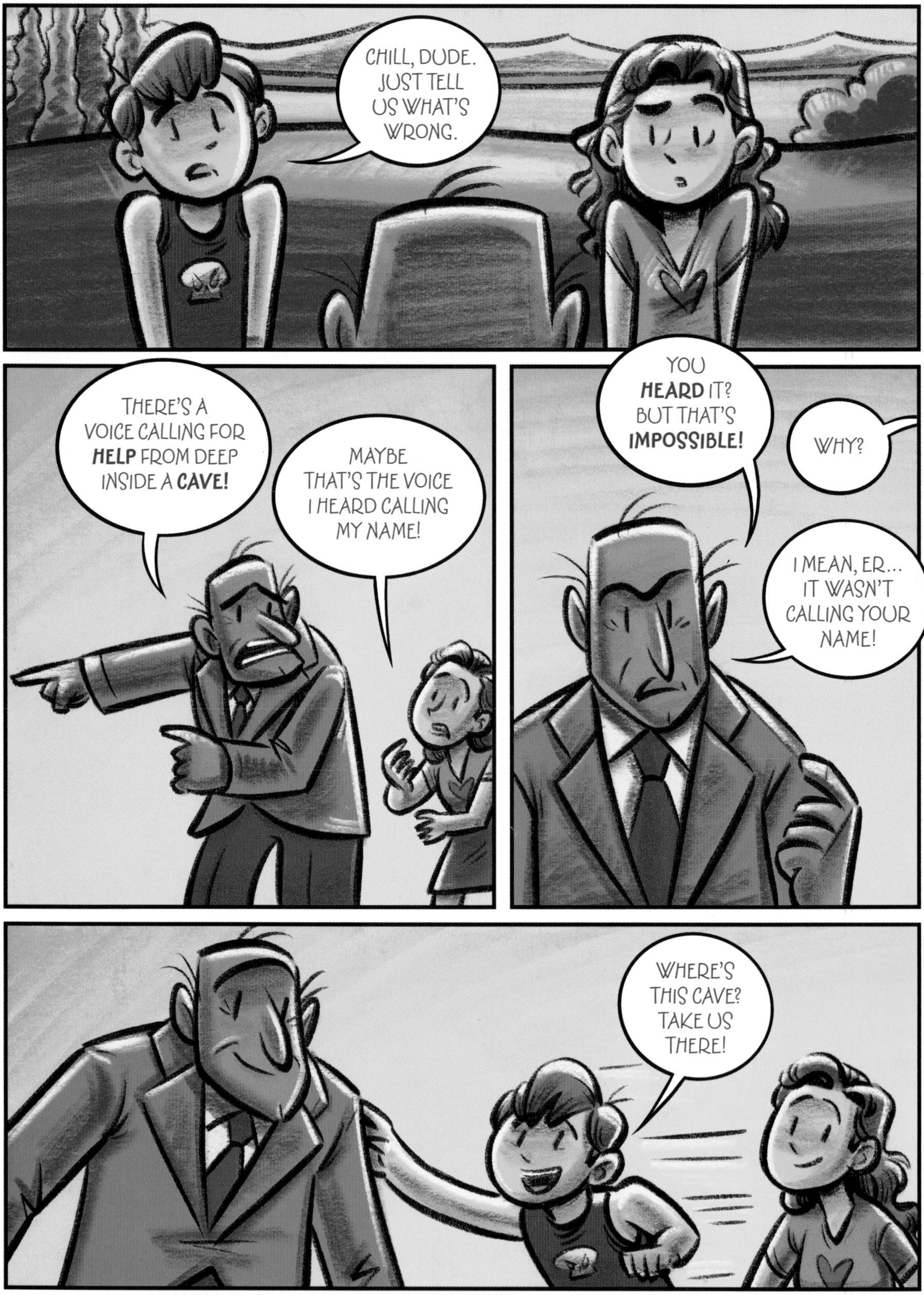
CHILL, DUDE. JUST TELL US WHAT'S WRONG.
THERE'S A VOICE CALLING FOR **HELP** FROM DEEP INSIDE A **CAVE!**
MAYBE THAT'S THE VOICE I HEARD CALLING MY NAME!
YOU **HEARD** IT? BUT THAT'S **IMPOSSIBLE!**
WHY?
I MEAN, ER... IT WASN'T CALLING YOUR NAME!
WHERE'S THIS CAVE? TAKE US THERE!

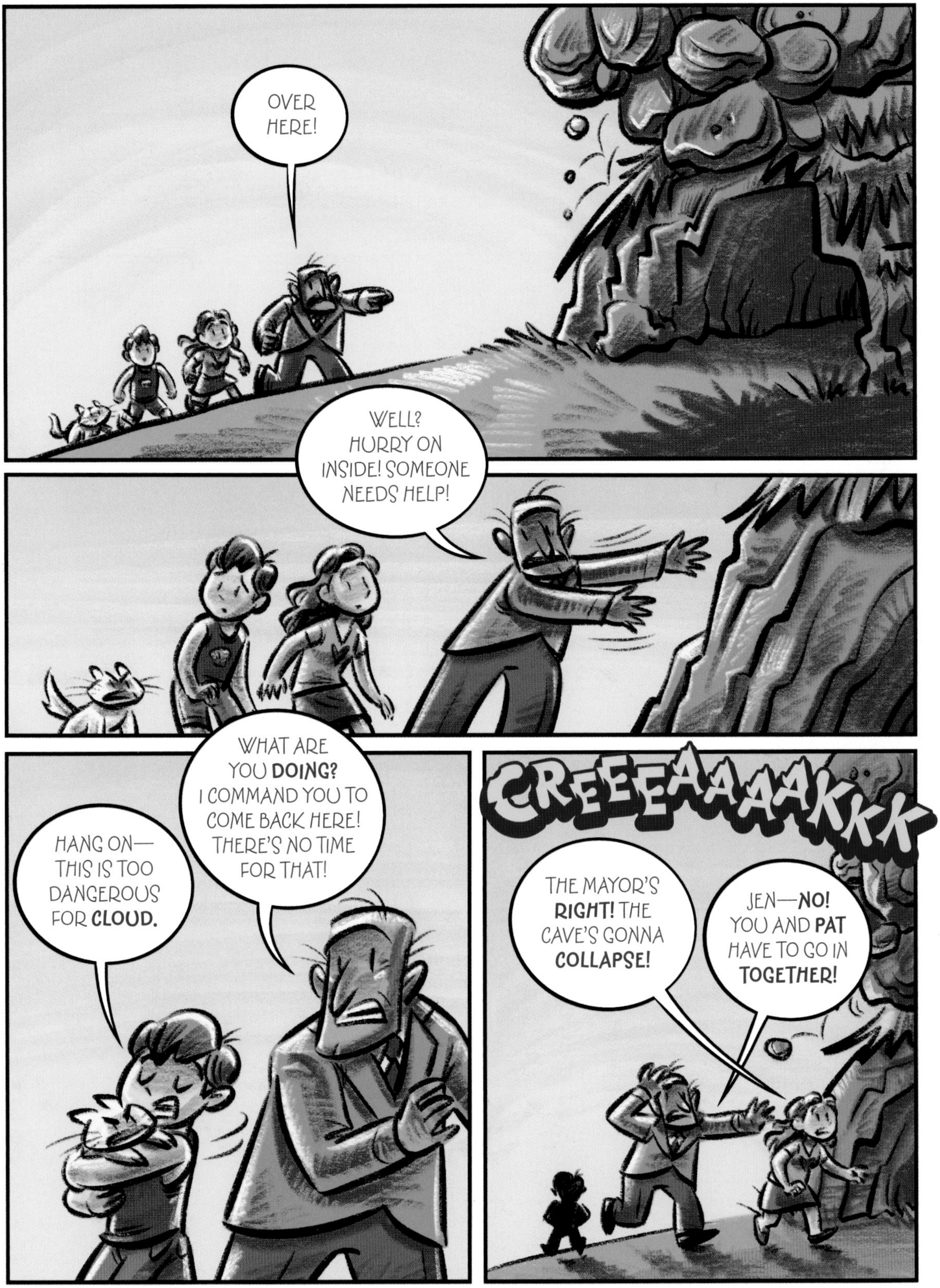
OVER HERE!
WELL? HURRY ON INSIDE! SOMEONE NEEDS HELP!
HANG ON— THIS IS TOO DANGEROUS FOR **CLOUD.**
WHAT ARE YOU **DOING?** I COMMAND YOU TO COME BACK HERE! THERE'S NO TIME FOR THAT!
CREEEAAAAKKK
THE MAYOR'S **RIGHT!** THE CAVE'S GONNA **COLLAPSE!**
JEN—**NO!** YOU AND **PAT** HAVE TO GO IN **TOGETHER!**

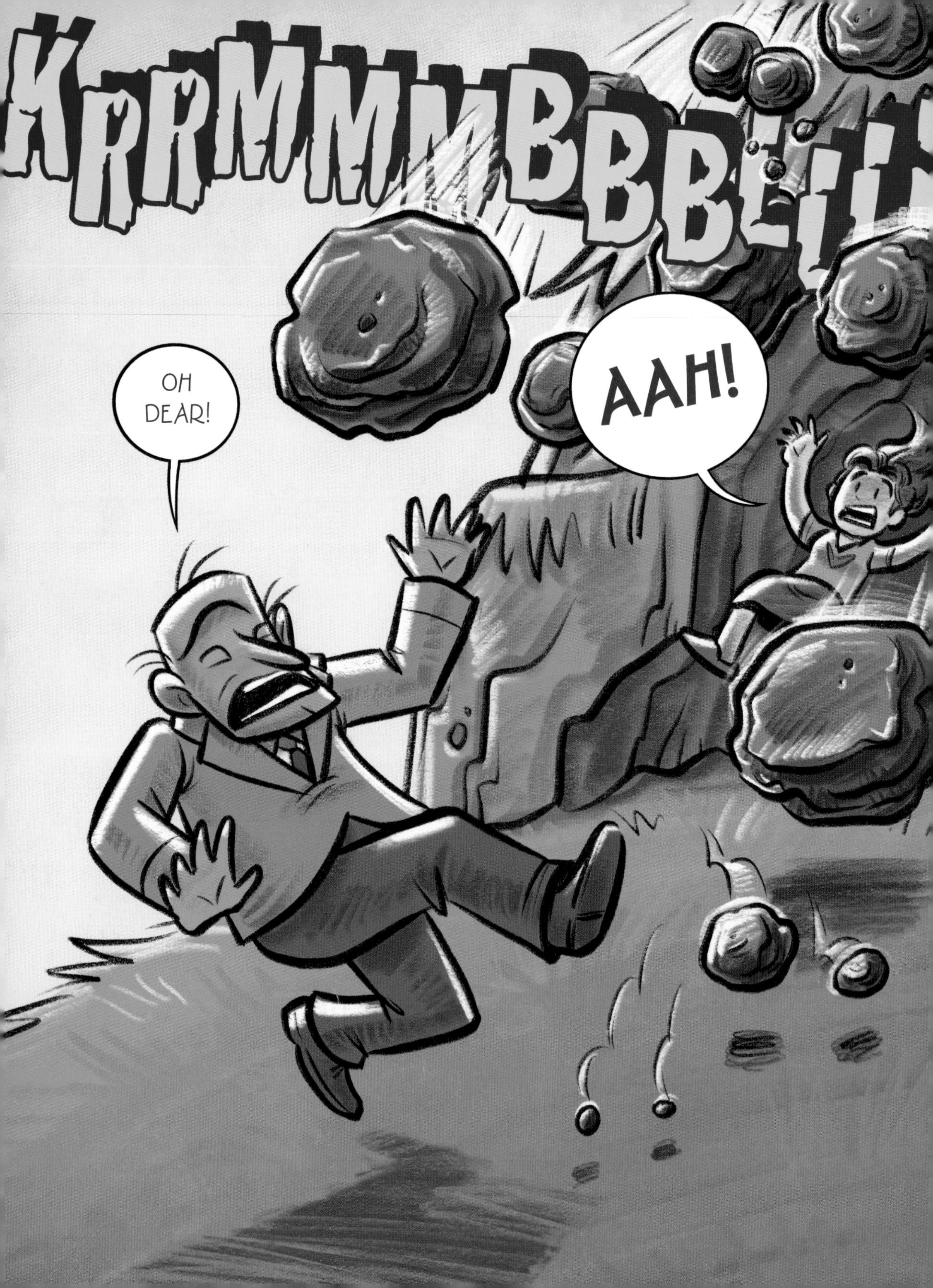
KRRMMMMBBBLE!!
OH DEAR!
AAH!

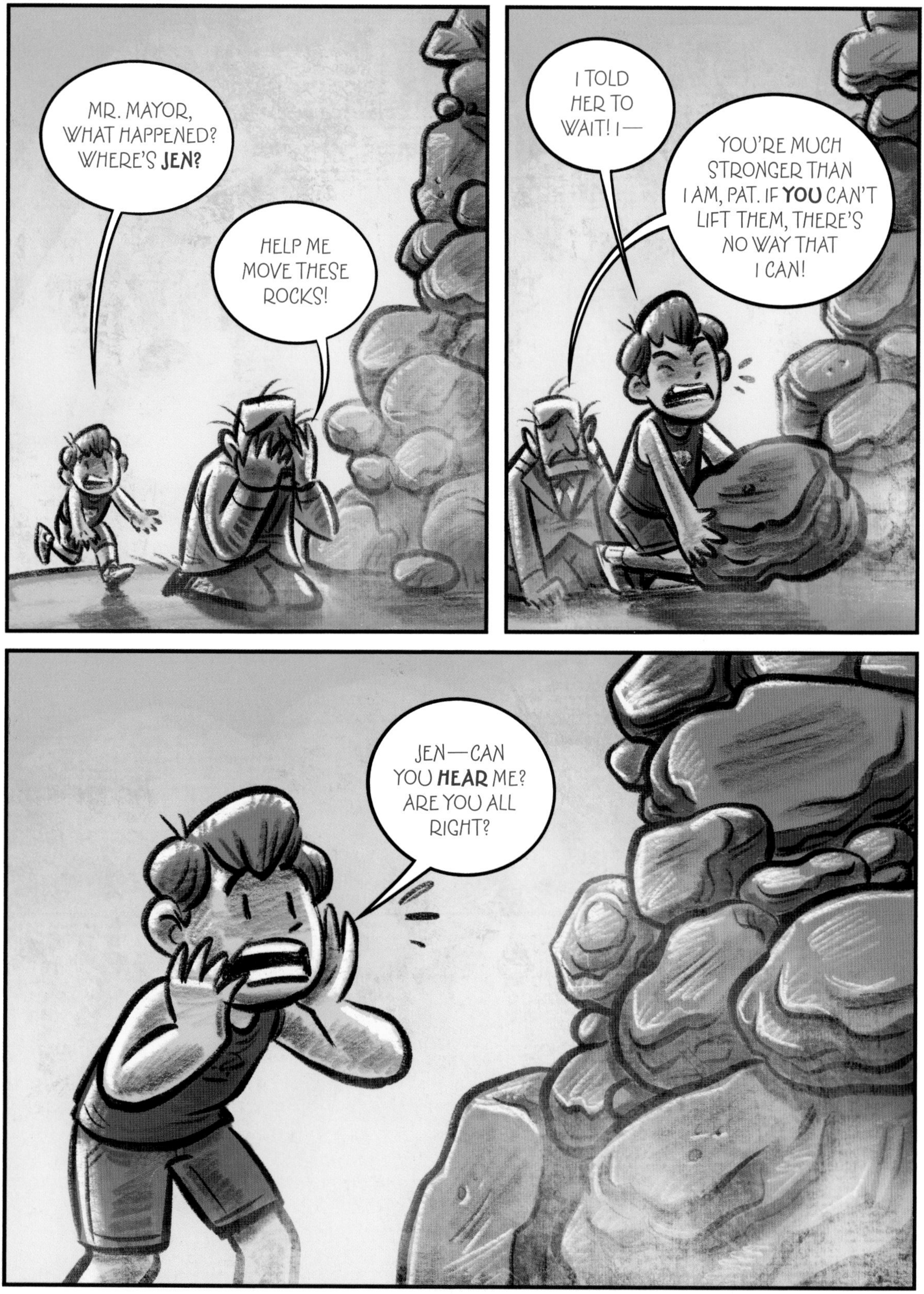
MR. MAYOR, WHAT HAPPENED? WHERE'S **JEN?**
HELP ME MOVE THESE ROCKS!
I TOLD HER TO WAIT! I—
YOU'RE MUCH STRONGER THAN I AM, PAT. IF **YOU** CAN'T LIFT THEM, THERE'S NO WAY THAT I CAN!
JEN—CAN YOU **HEAR** ME? ARE YOU ALL RIGHT?

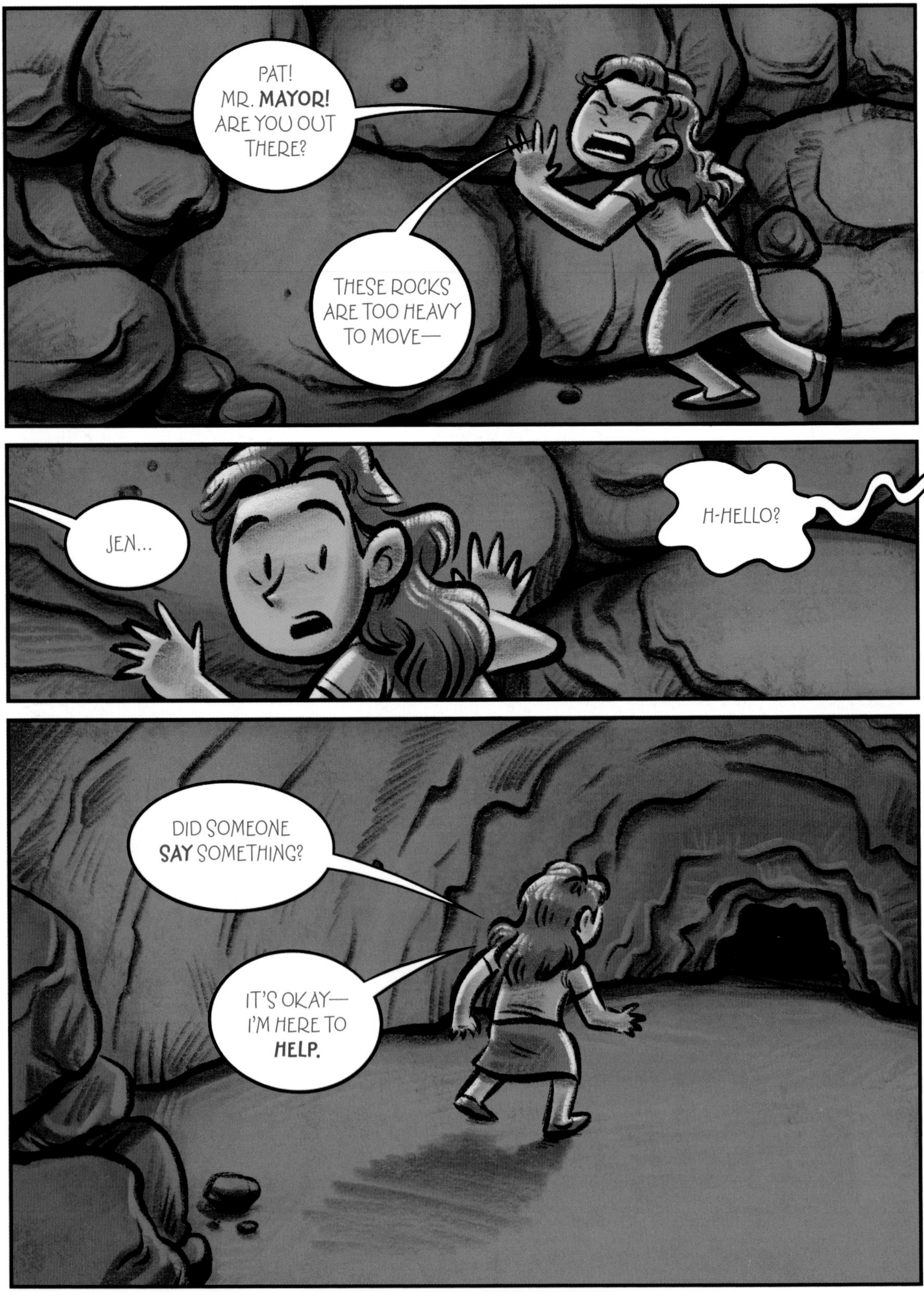
PAT! MR. MAYOR! ARE YOU OUT THERE?
THESE ROCKS ARE TOO HEAVY TO MOVE—
JEN...
H-HELLO?
DID SOMEONE SAY SOMETHING?
IT'S OKAY— I'M HERE TO HELP.

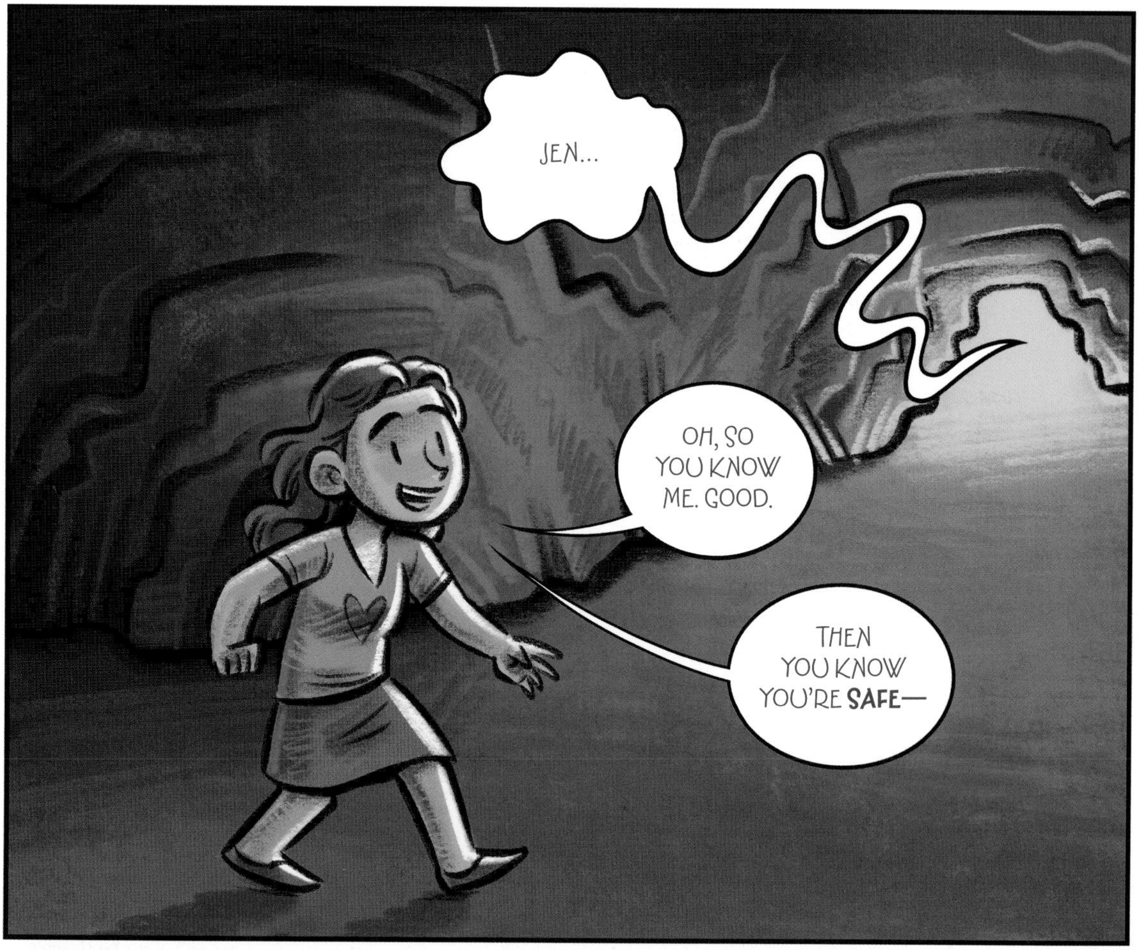
JEN...
OH, SO YOU KNOW ME. GOOD.
THEN YOU KNOW YOU'RE **SAFE**—

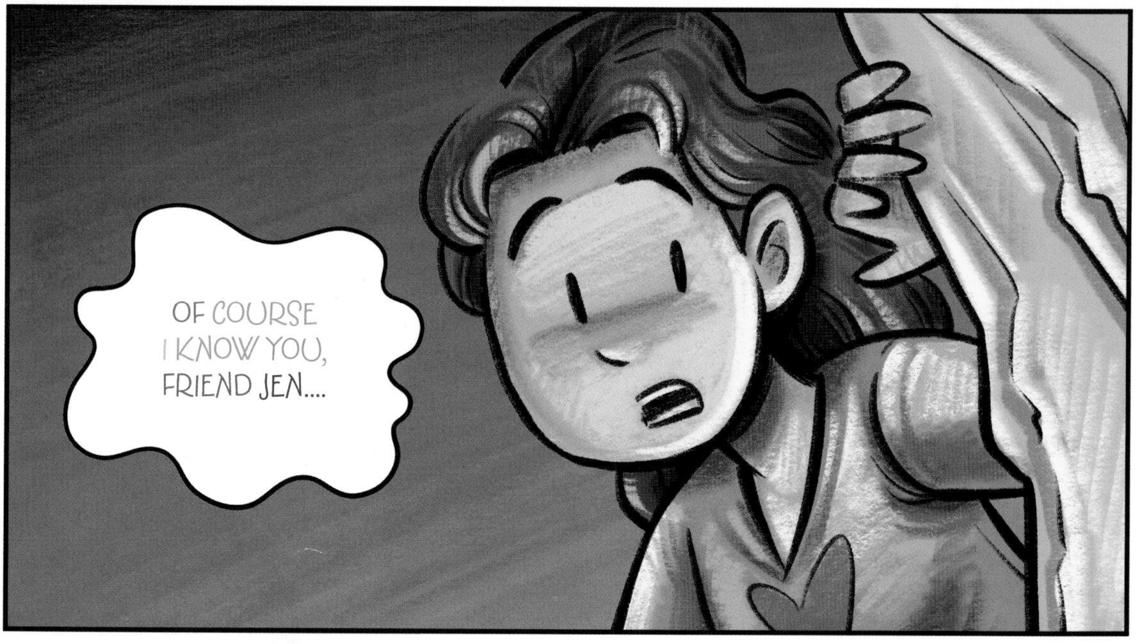
OF COURSE I KNOW YOU, FRIEND JEN....

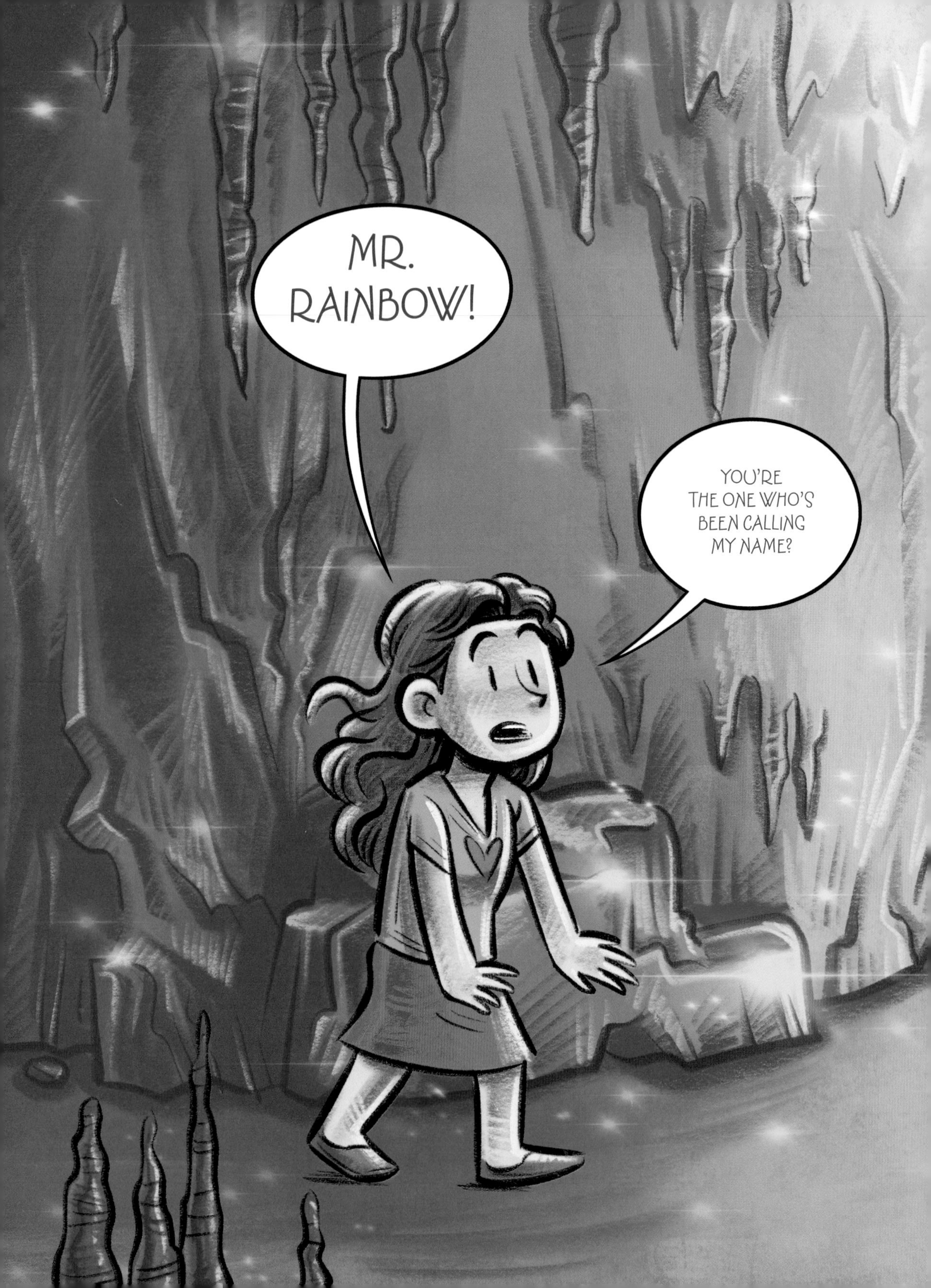
MR. RAINBOW!
YOU'RE THE ONE WHO'S BEEN CALLING MY NAME?

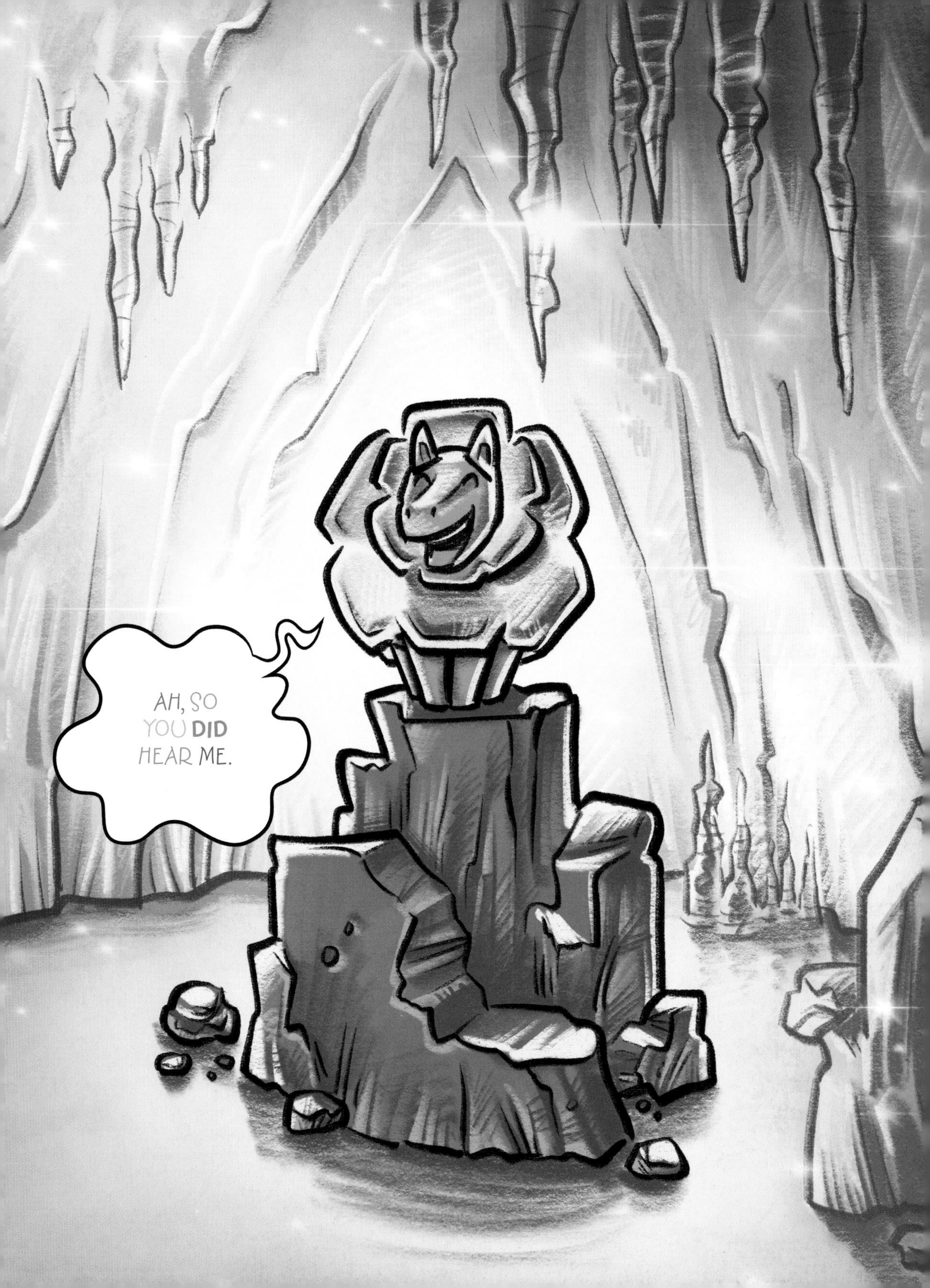
AH, SO YOU DID HEAR ME.

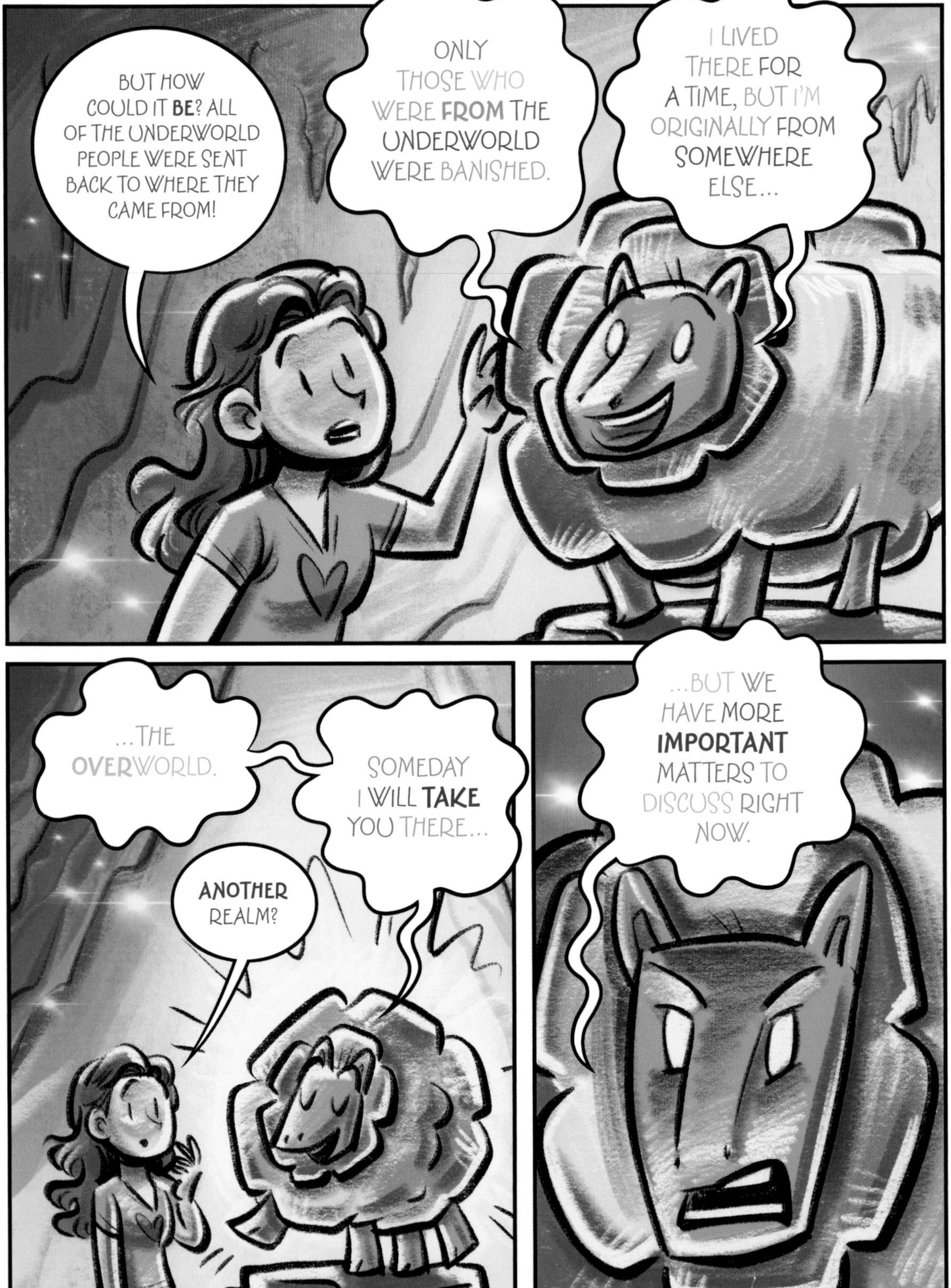
BUT HOW COULD IT BE? ALL OF THE UNDERWORLD PEOPLE WERE SENT BACK TO WHERE THEY CAME FROM!
ONLY THOSE WHO WERE FROM THE UNDERWORLD WERE BANISHED.
I LIVED THERE FOR A TIME, BUT I'M ORIGINALLY FROM SOMEWHERE ELSE...
...THE OVERWORLD.
SOMEDAY I WILL TAKE YOU THERE...
ANOTHER REALM?
...BUT WE HAVE MORE IMPORTANT MATTERS TO DISCUSS RIGHT NOW.

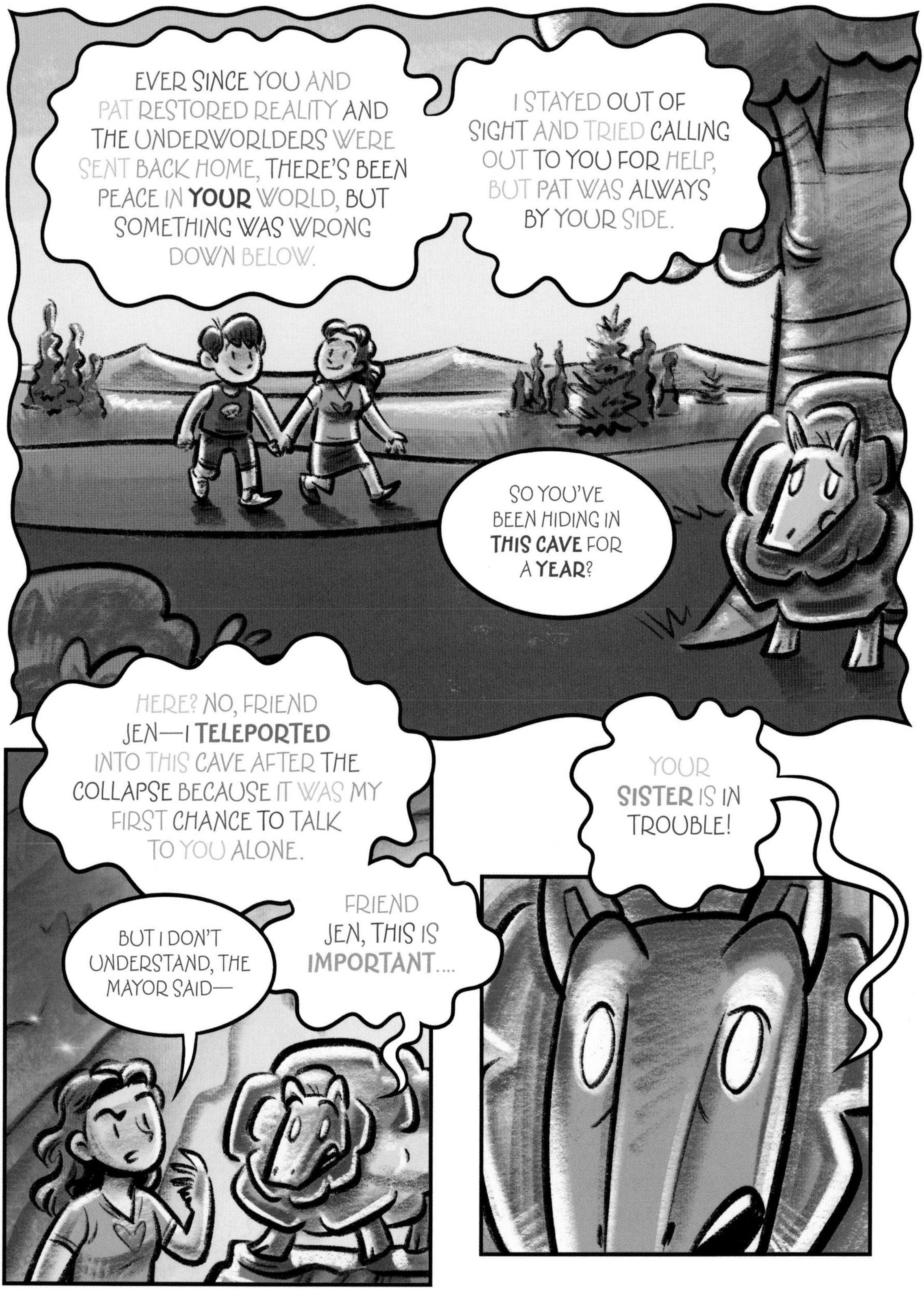
EVER SINCE YOU AND PAT RESTORED REALITY AND THE UNDERWORLDERS WERE SENT BACK HOME, THERE'S BEEN PEACE IN **YOUR** WORLD, BUT SOMETHING WAS WRONG DOWN BELOW.
I STAYED OUT OF SIGHT AND TRIED CALLING OUT TO YOU FOR HELP, BUT PAT WAS ALWAYS BY YOUR SIDE.
SO YOU'VE BEEN HIDING IN **THIS CAVE** FOR A **YEAR**?
HERE? NO, FRIEND JEN—I **TELEPORTED** INTO THIS CAVE AFTER THE COLLAPSE BECAUSE IT WAS MY FIRST CHANCE TO TALK TO YOU ALONE.
BUT I DON'T UNDERSTAND, THE MAYOR SAID—
FRIEND JEN, THIS IS **IMPORTANT**....
YOUR **SISTER** IS IN TROUBLE!

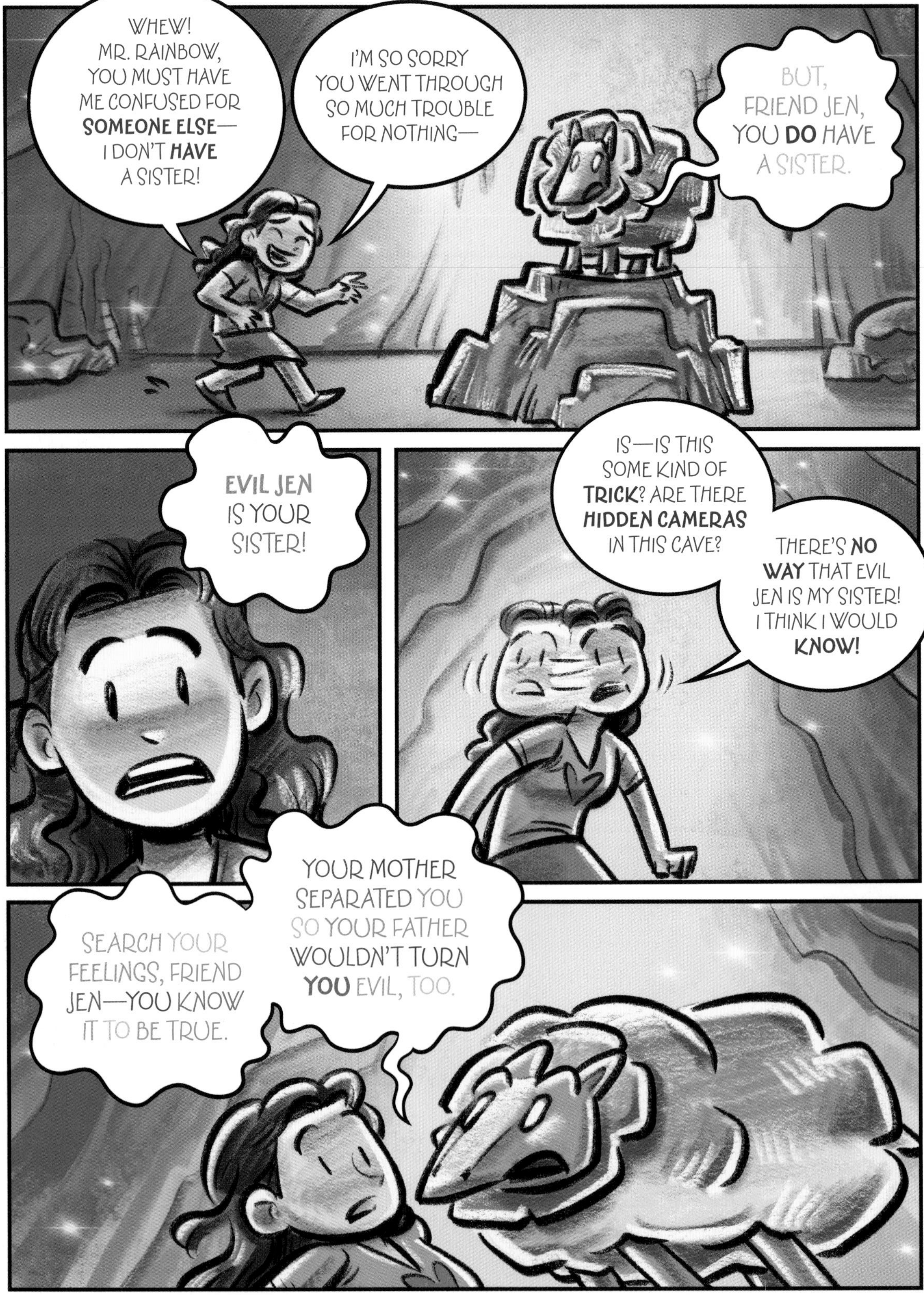
WHEW! MR. RAINBOW, YOU MUST HAVE ME CONFUSED FOR **SOMEONE ELSE**— I DON'T **HAVE** A SISTER!
I'M SO SORRY YOU WENT THROUGH SO MUCH TROUBLE FOR NOTHING—
BUT, FRIEND JEN, YOU **DO** HAVE A SISTER.
EVIL JEN IS YOUR SISTER!
IS—IS THIS SOME KIND OF **TRICK**? ARE THERE **HIDDEN CAMERAS** IN THIS CAVE?
THERE'S **NO WAY** THAT EVIL JEN IS MY SISTER! I THINK I WOULD **KNOW!**
SEARCH YOUR FEELINGS, FRIEND JEN—YOU KNOW IT TO BE TRUE.
YOUR MOTHER SEPARATED YOU SO YOUR FATHER WOULDN'T TURN **YOU** EVIL, TOO.

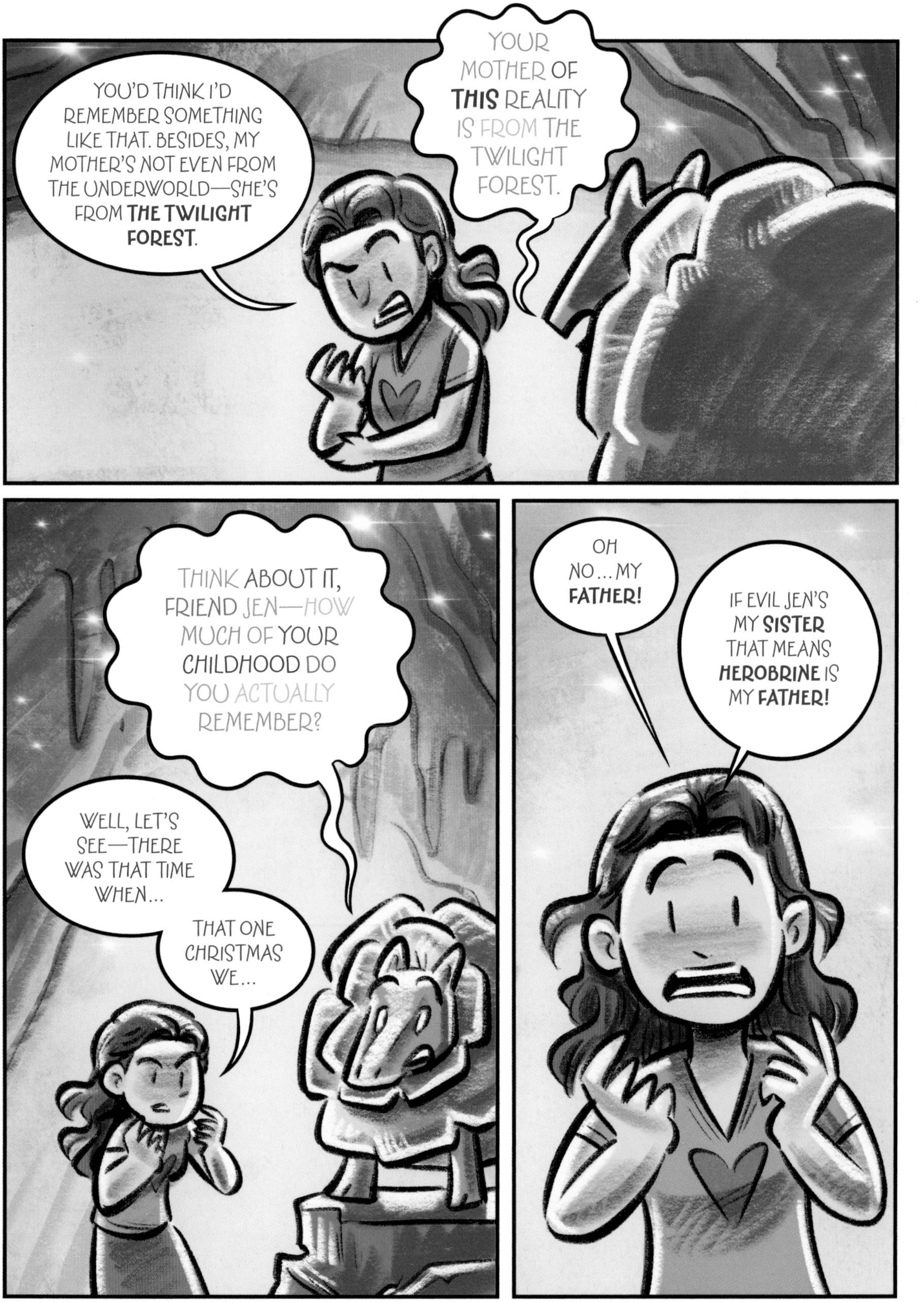
YOU'D THINK I'D REMEMBER SOMETHING LIKE THAT. BESIDES, MY MOTHER'S NOT EVEN FROM THE UNDERWORLD—SHE'S FROM THE TWILIGHT FOREST.
YOUR MOTHER OF THIS REALITY IS FROM THE TWILIGHT FOREST.
THINK ABOUT IT, FRIEND JEN—HOW MUCH OF YOUR CHILDHOOD DO YOU ACTUALLY REMEMBER?
WELL, LET'S SEE—THERE WAS THAT TIME WHEN...
THAT ONE CHRISTMAS WE...
OH NO... MY FATHER!
IF EVIL JEN'S MY SISTER THAT MEANS HEROBRINE IS MY FATHER!

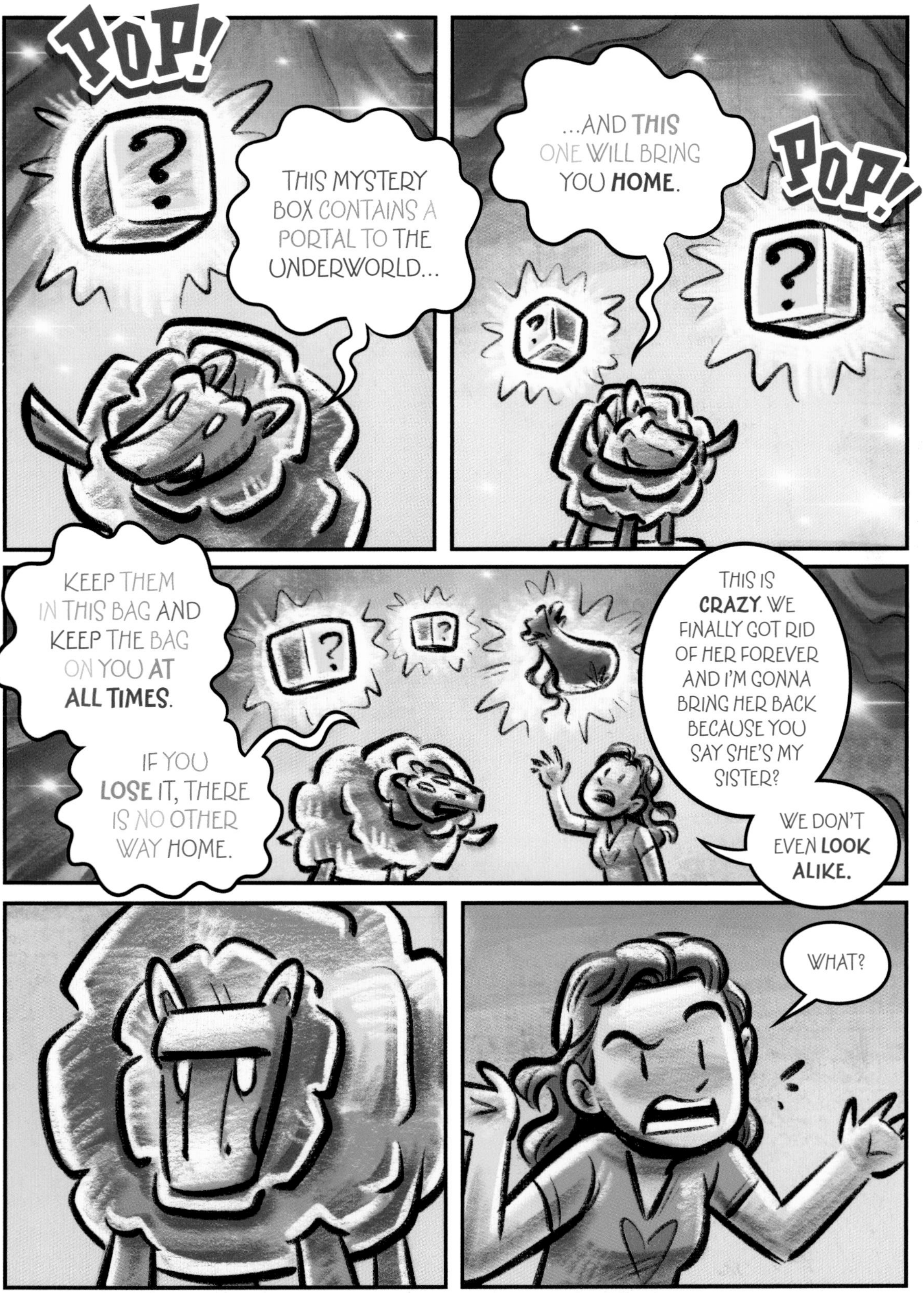
POP!
THIS MYSTERY BOX CONTAINS A PORTAL TO THE UNDERWORLD...
...AND THIS ONE WILL BRING YOU HOME.
POP!
KEEP THEM IN THIS BAG AND KEEP THE BAG ON YOU AT ALL TIMES.
IF YOU LOSE IT, THERE IS NO OTHER WAY HOME.
THIS IS CRAZY. WE FINALLY GOT RID OF HER FOREVER AND I'M GONNA BRING HER BACK BECAUSE YOU SAY SHE'S MY SISTER?
WE DON'T EVEN LOOK ALIKE.
WHAT?

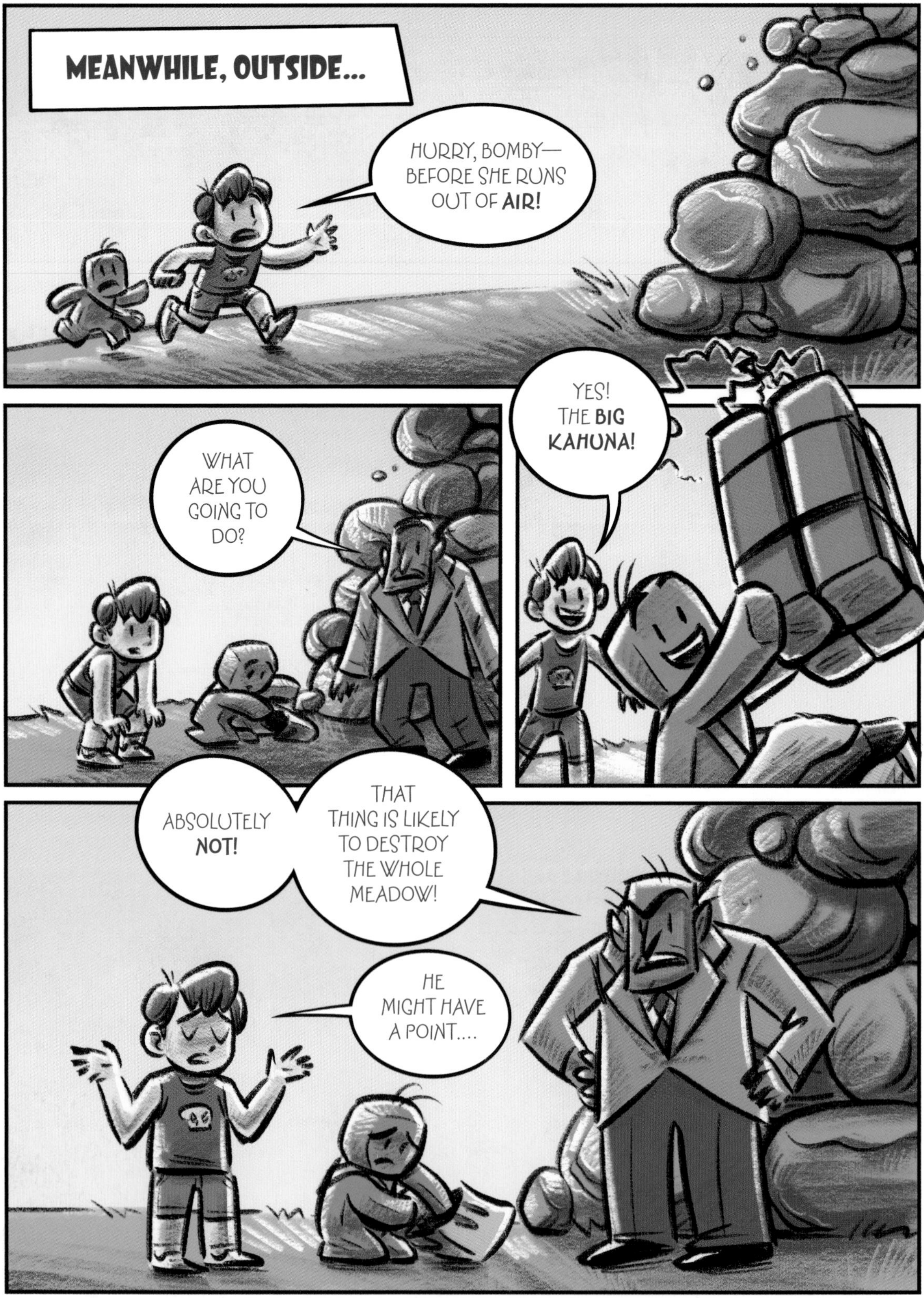
MEANWHILE, OUTSIDE...
HURRY, BOMBY— BEFORE SHE RUNS OUT OF AIR!
WHAT ARE YOU GOING TO DO?
YES! THE BIG KAHUNA!
ABSOLUTELY NOT!
THAT THING IS LIKELY TO DESTROY THE WHOLE MEADOW!
HE MIGHT HAVE A POINT....

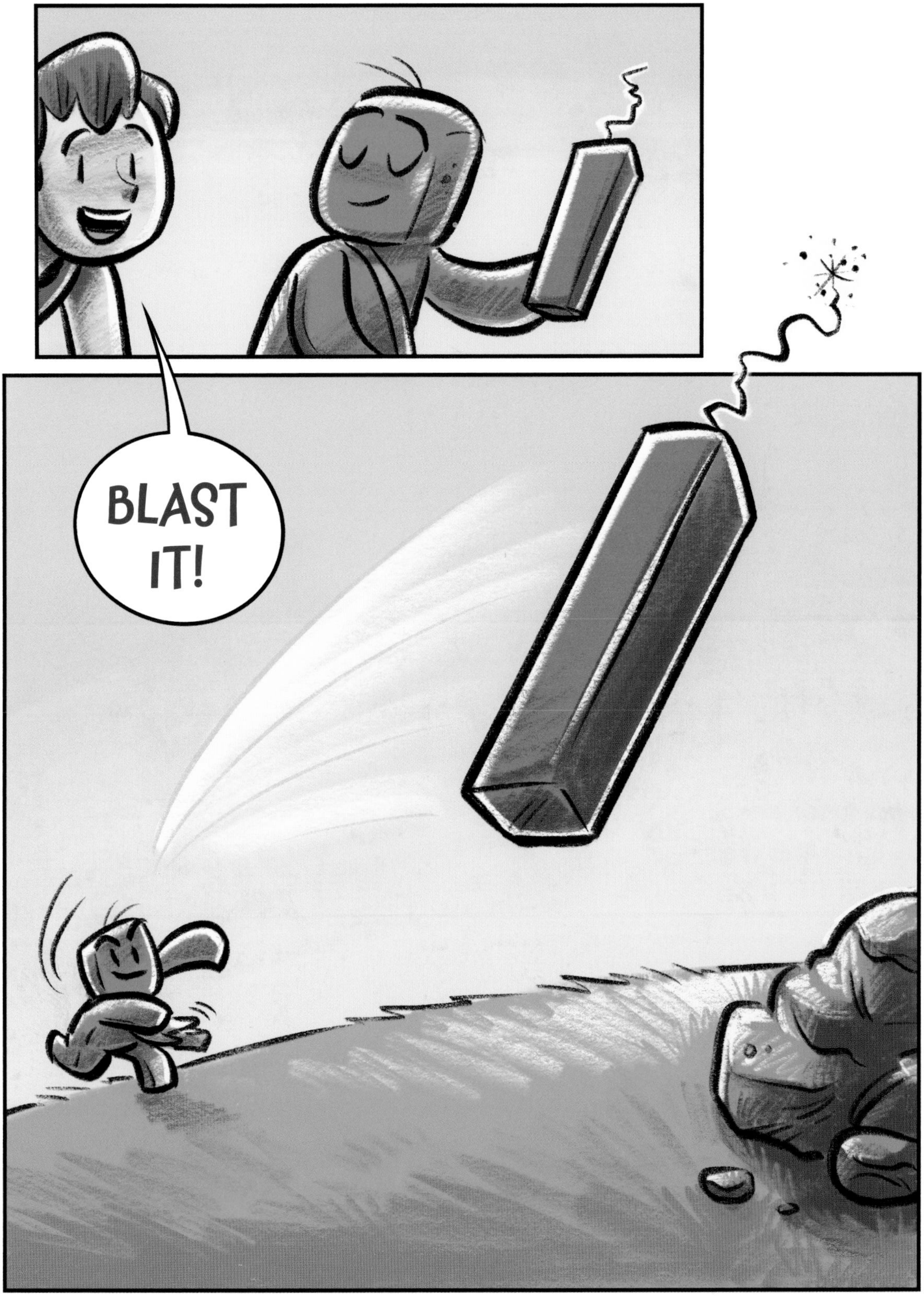
BLAST IT!

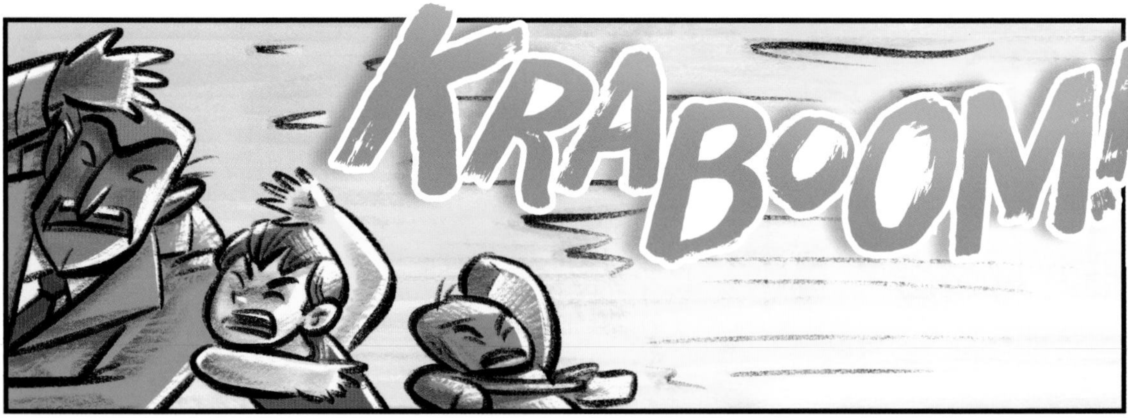
KRABOOM!

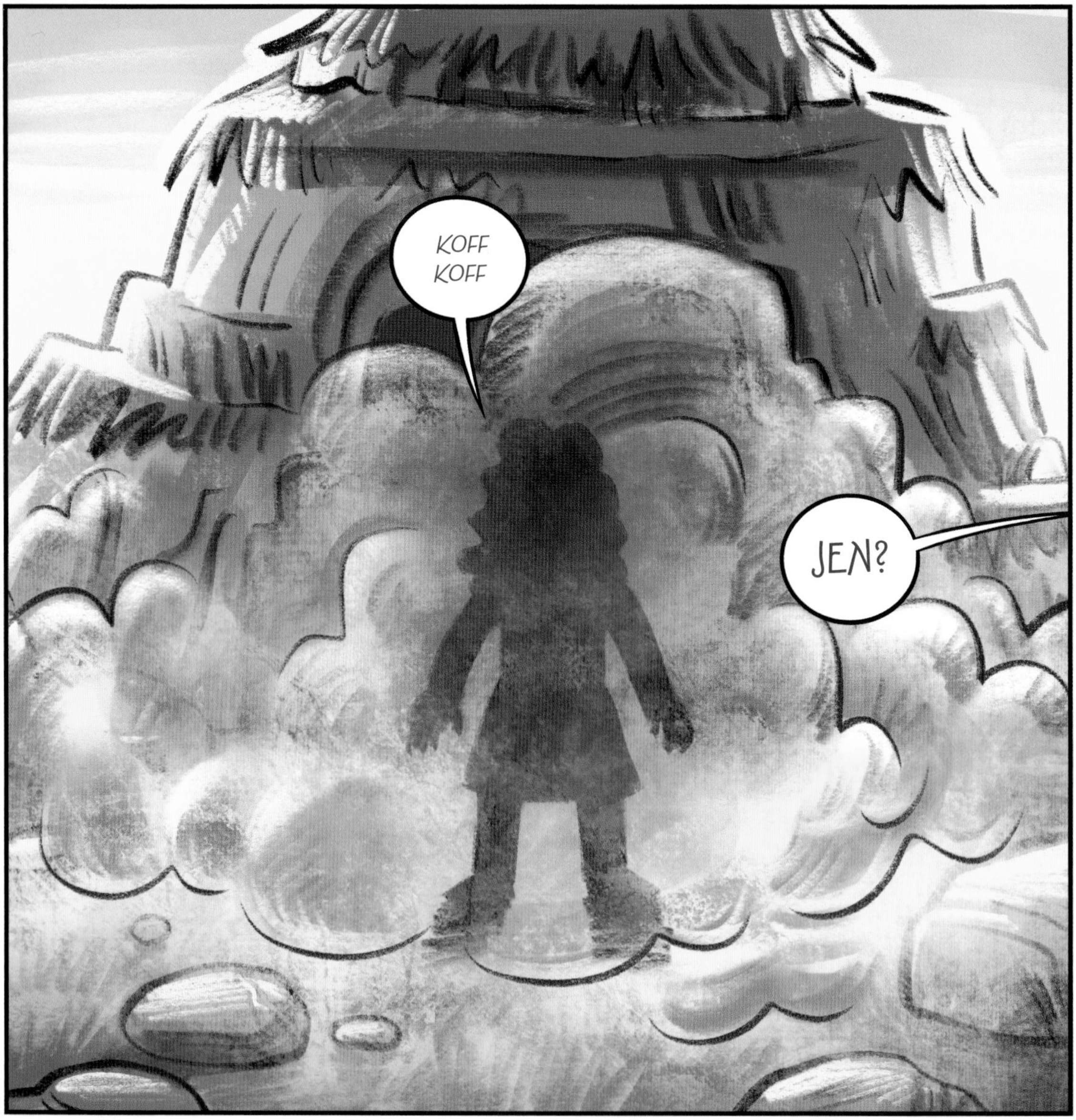
KOFF
KOFF
JEN?

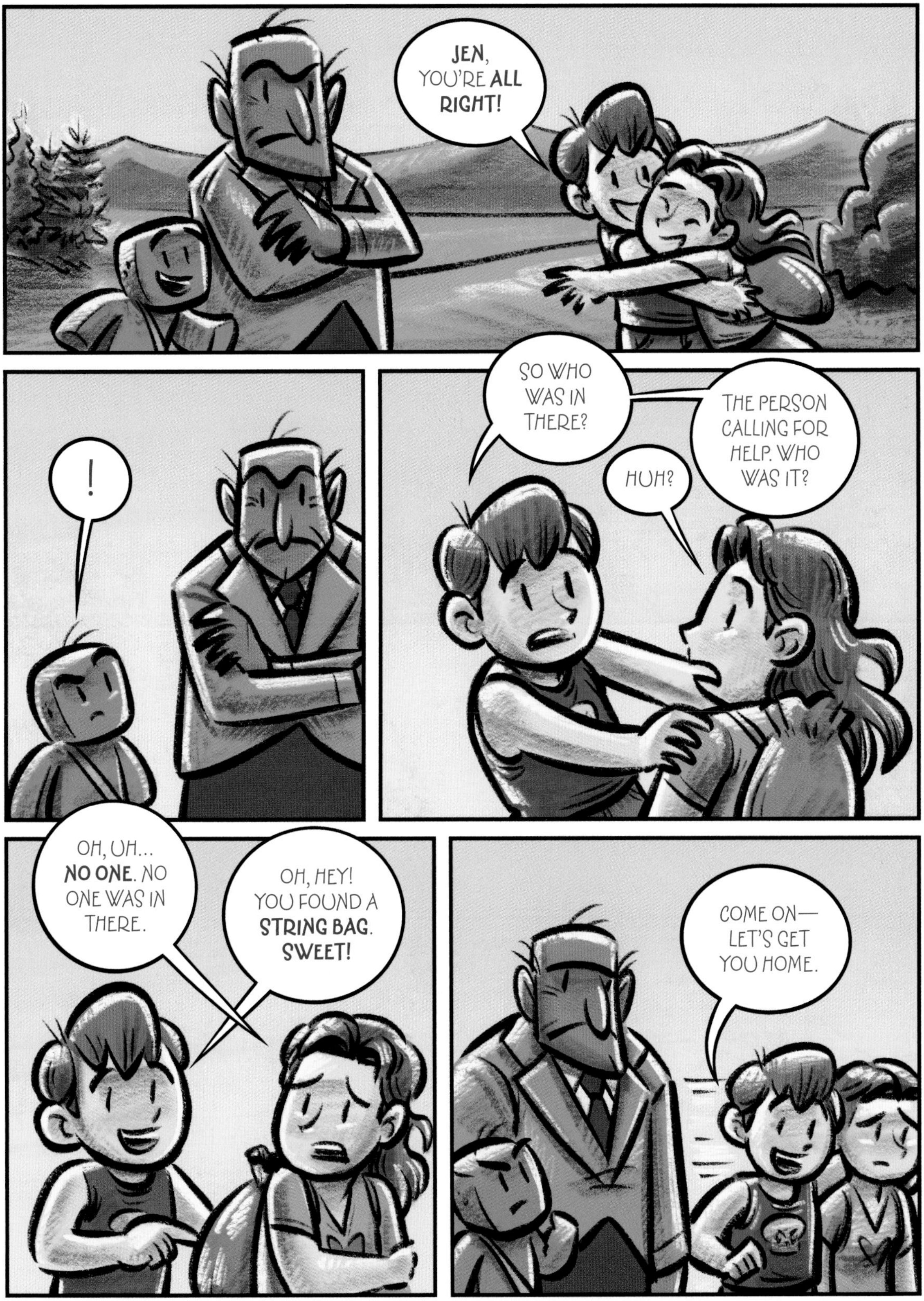
JEN, YOU'RE **ALL RIGHT!**
!
SO WHO WAS IN THERE?
HUH?
THE PERSON CALLING FOR HELP. WHO WAS IT?
OH, UH... **NO ONE**. NO ONE WAS IN THERE.
OH, HEY! YOU FOUND A **STRING BAG**. **SWEET!**
COME ON— LET'S GET YOU HOME.

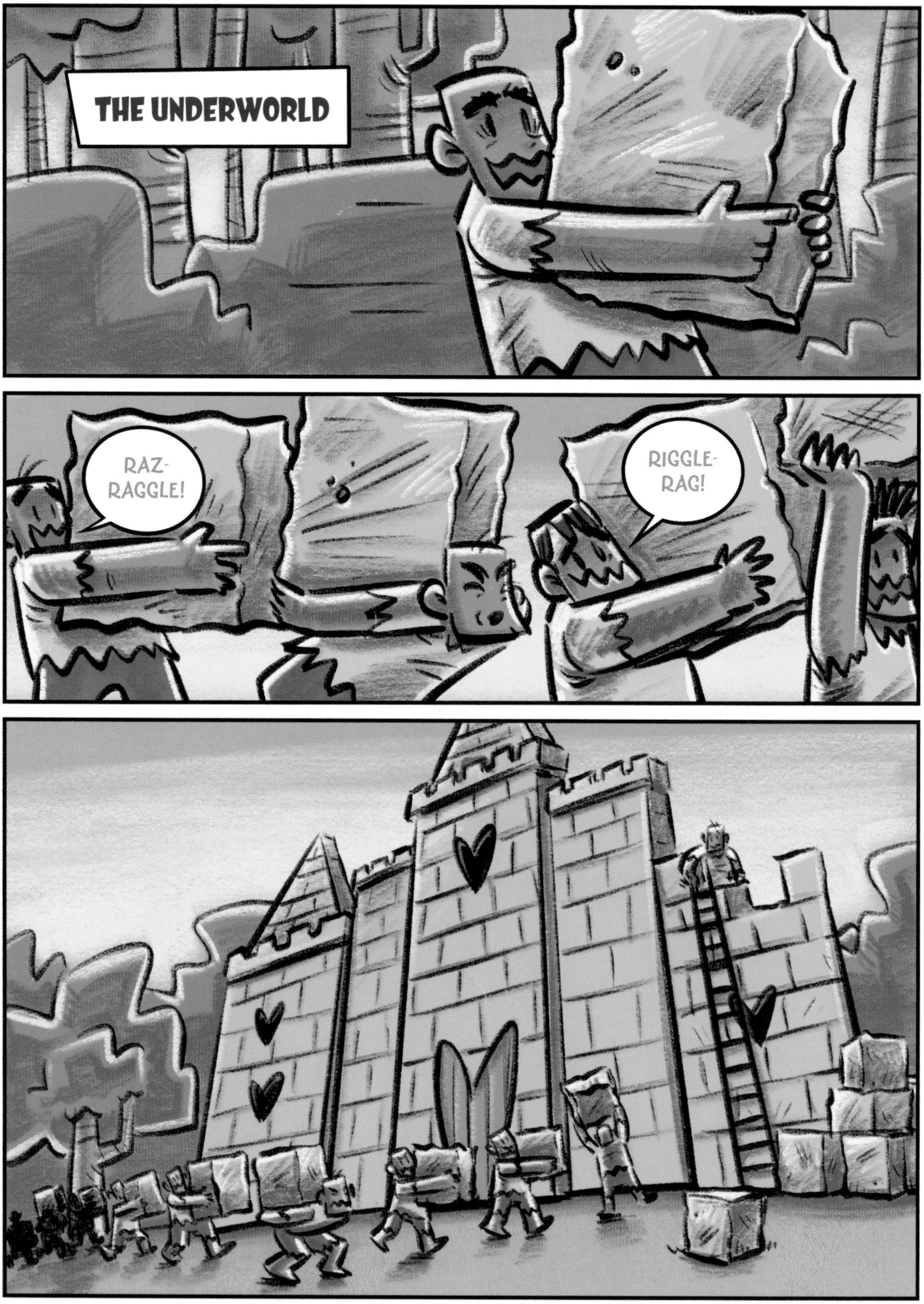
THE UNDERWORLD
RAZ-RAGGLE!
RIGGLE-RAG!

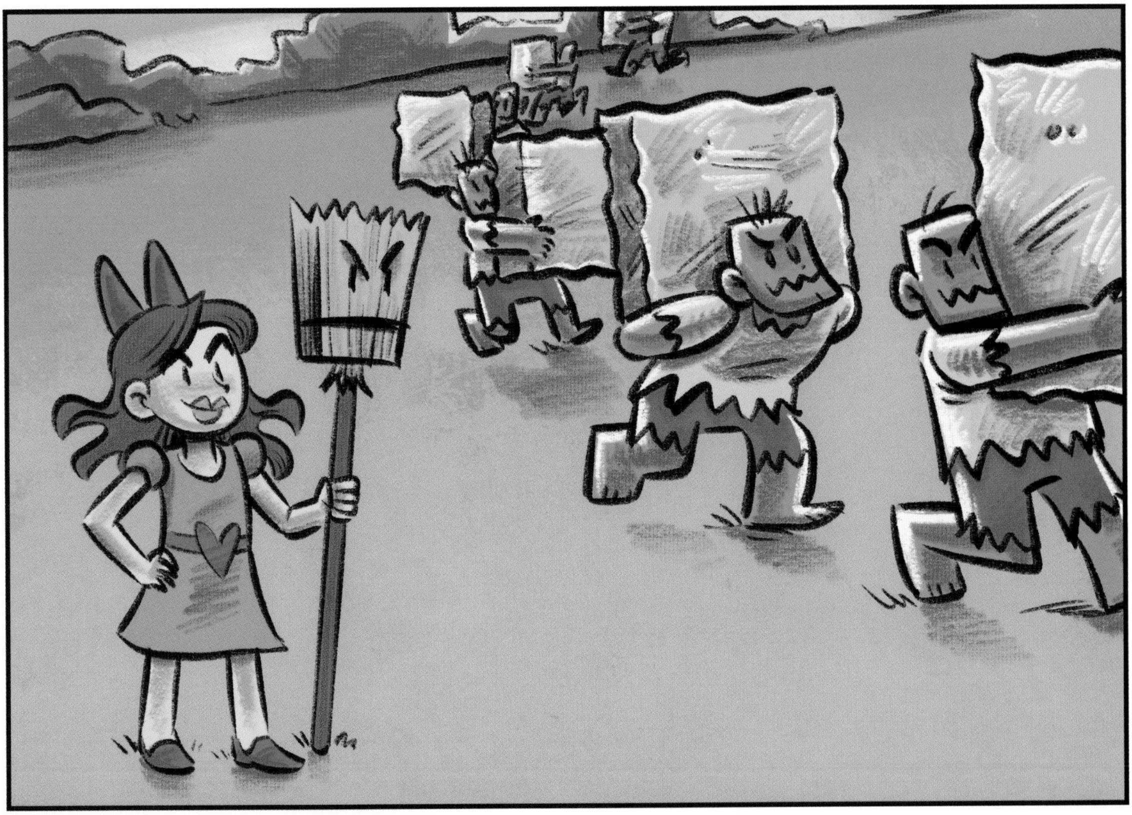

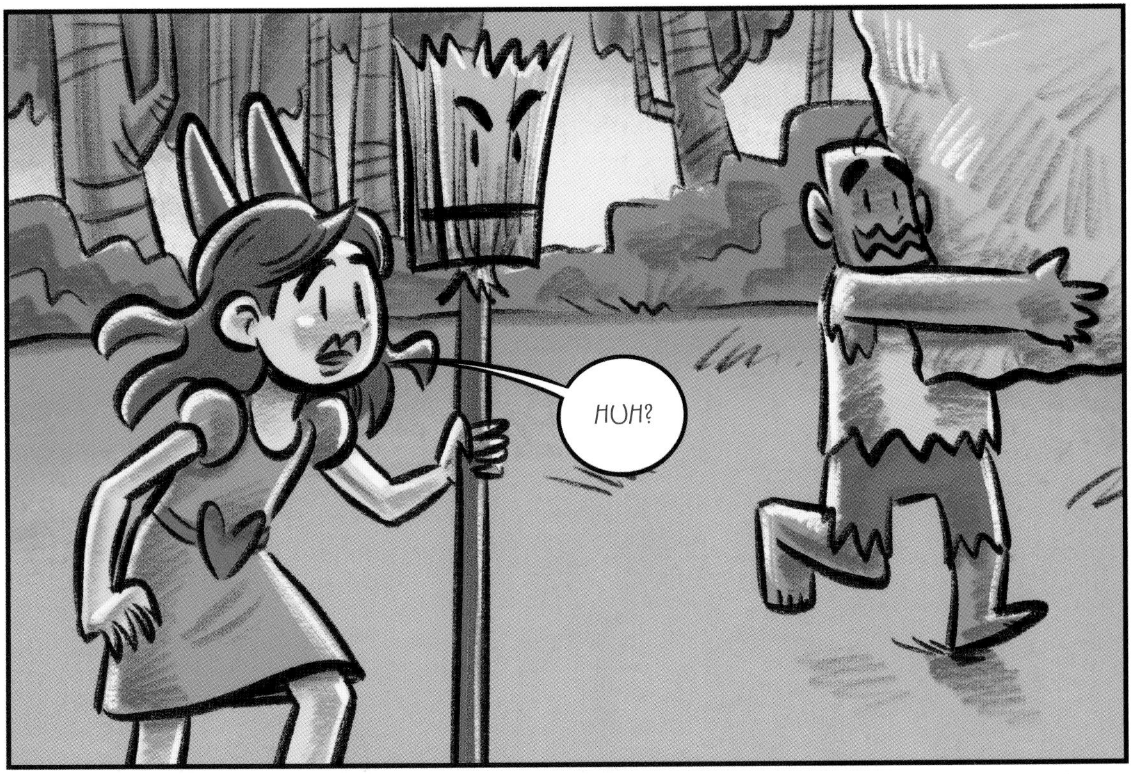
HUH?

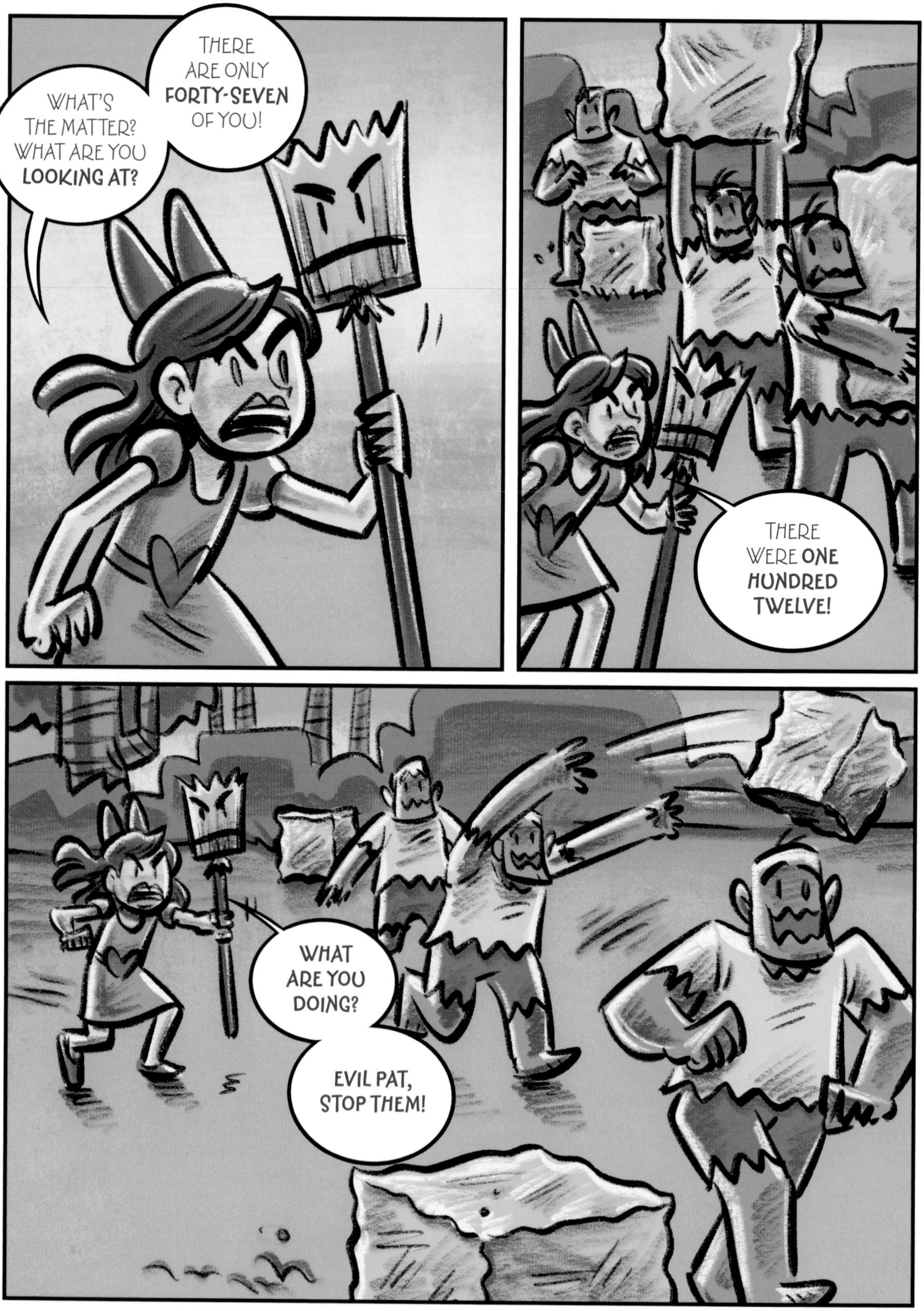
WHAT'S THE MATTER? WHAT ARE YOU LOOKING AT?
THERE ARE ONLY FORTY-SEVEN OF YOU!
THERE WERE ONE HUNDRED TWELVE!
WHAT ARE YOU DOING?
EVIL PAT, STOP THEM!

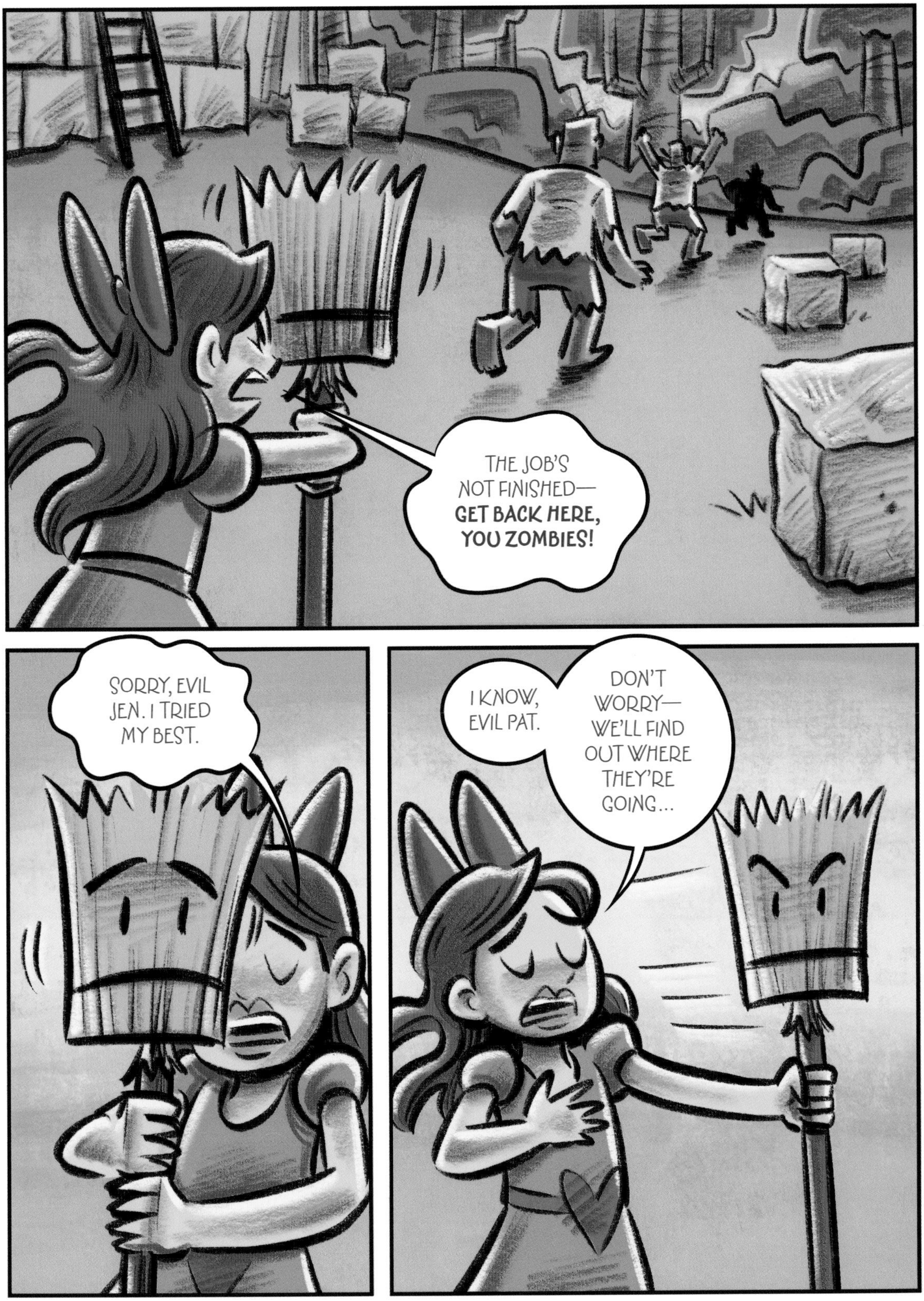
THE JOB'S NOT FINISHED— **GET BACK HERE, YOU ZOMBIES!**
SORRY, EVIL JEN. I TRIED MY BEST.
I KNOW, EVIL PAT.
DON'T WORRY— WE'LL FIND OUT WHERE THEY'RE GOING...

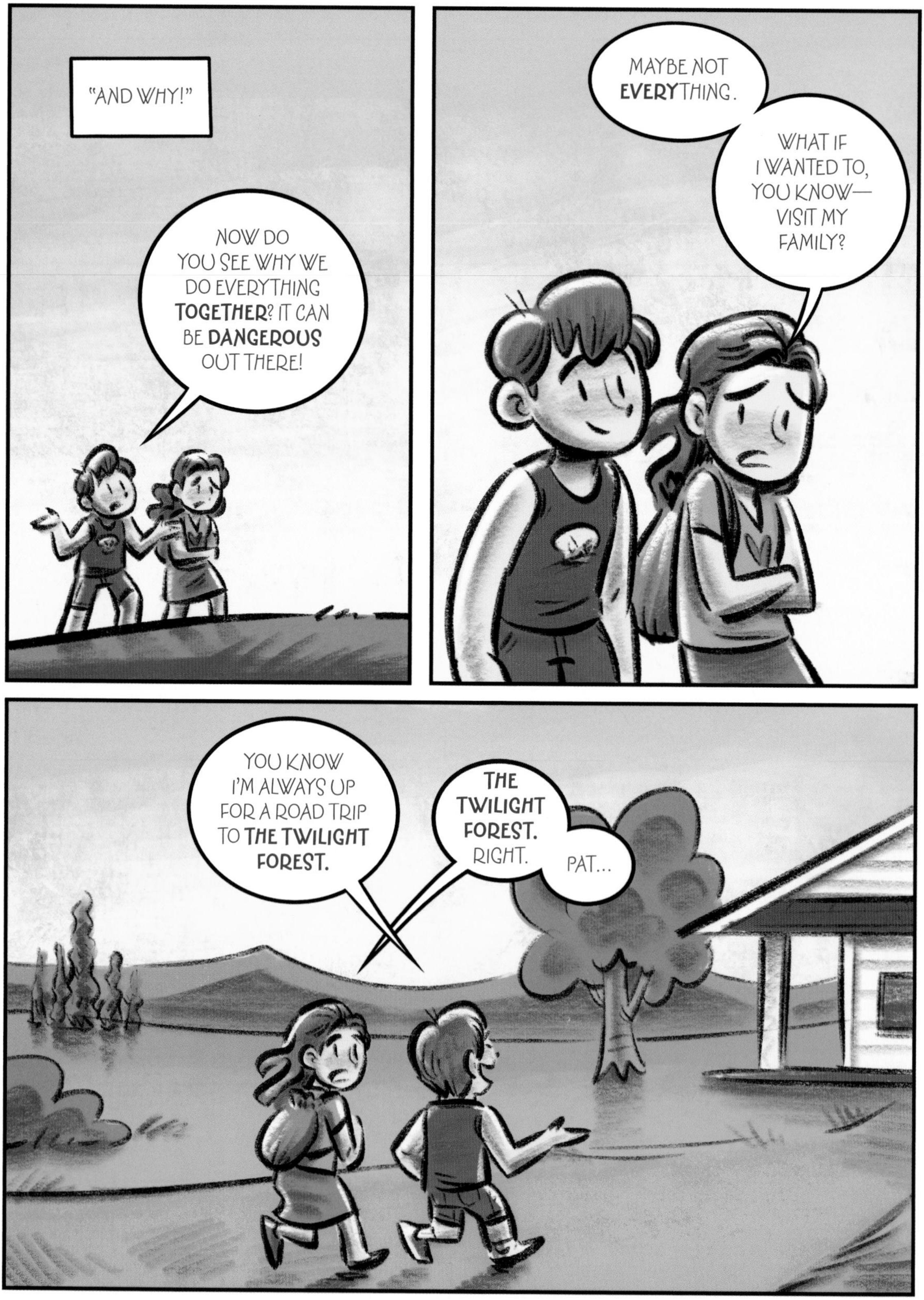
"AND WHY!"
NOW DO YOU SEE WHY WE DO EVERYTHING **TOGETHER**? IT CAN BE **DANGEROUS** OUT THERE!
MAYBE NOT **EVERY**THING.
WHAT IF I WANTED TO, YOU KNOW— VISIT MY FAMILY?
YOU KNOW I'M ALWAYS UP FOR A ROAD TRIP TO **THE TWILIGHT FOREST.**
THE TWILIGHT FOREST. RIGHT.
PAT...

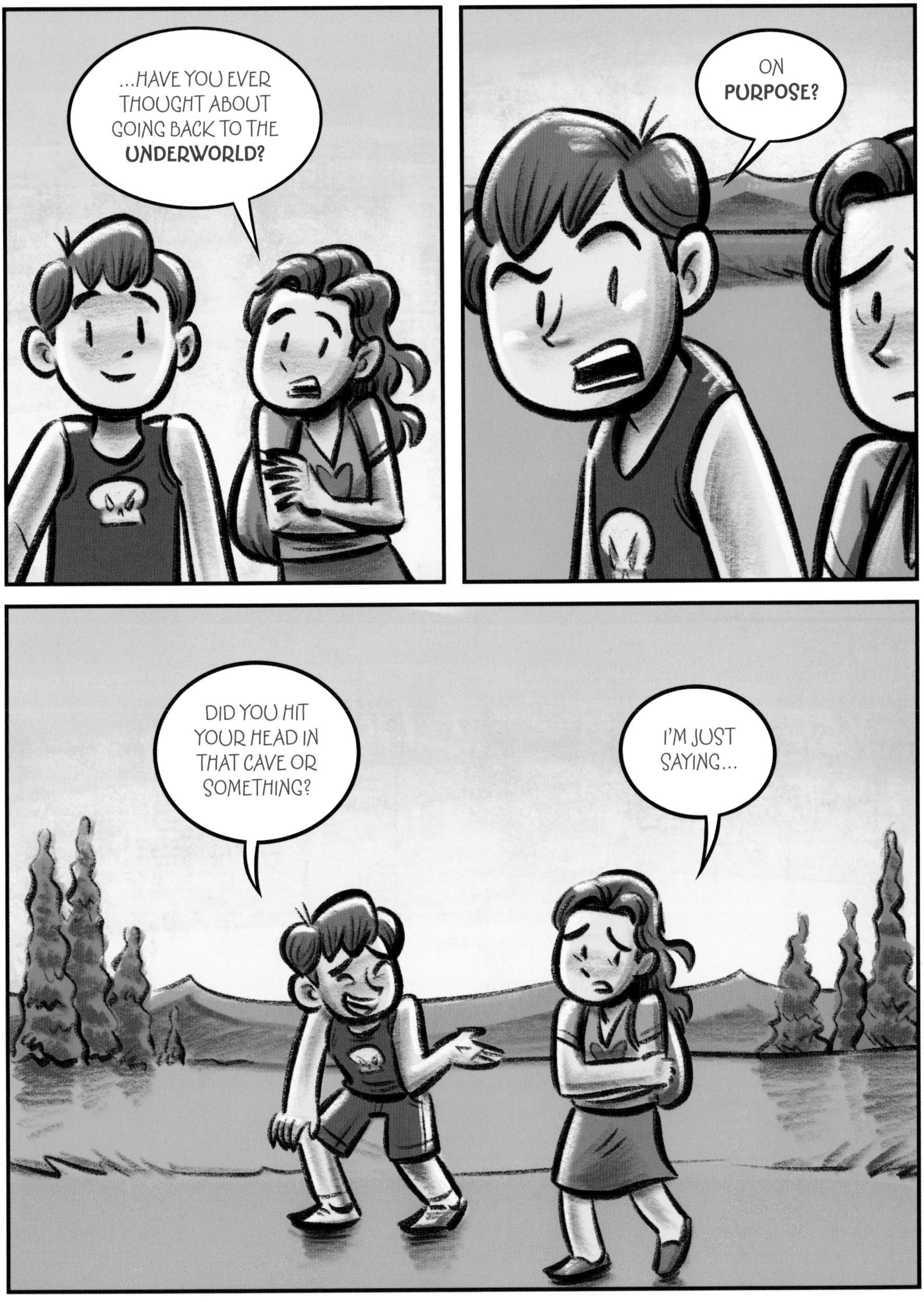
...HAVE YOU EVER THOUGHT ABOUT GOING BACK TO THE **UNDERWORLD?**
ON **PURPOSE?**
DID YOU HIT YOUR HEAD IN THAT CAVE OR SOMETHING?
I'M JUST SAYING...

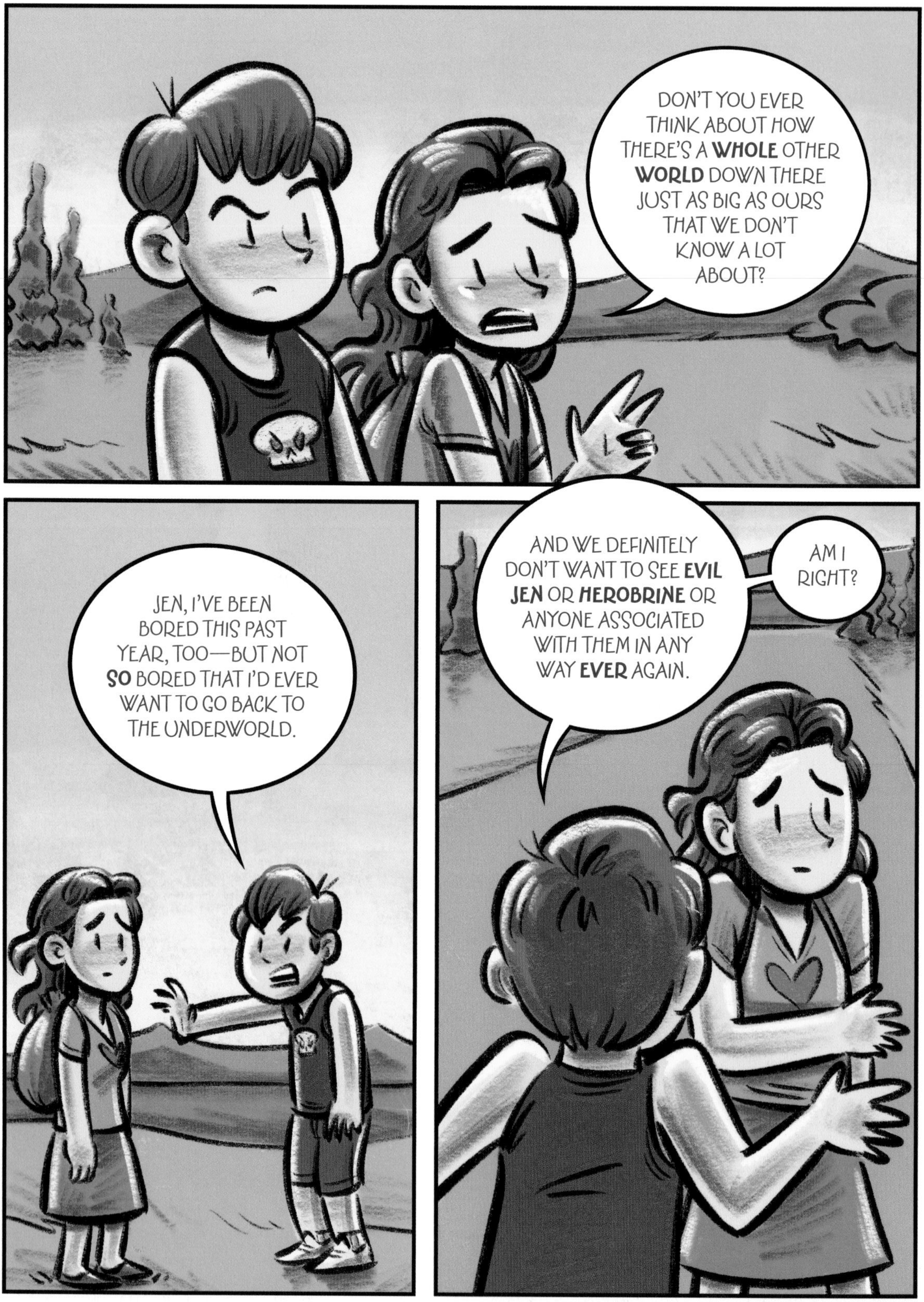
DON'T YOU EVER THINK ABOUT HOW THERE'S A **WHOLE** OTHER **WORLD** DOWN THERE JUST AS BIG AS OURS THAT WE DON'T KNOW A LOT ABOUT?
JEN, I'VE BEEN BORED THIS PAST YEAR, TOO—BUT NOT **SO** BORED THAT I'D EVER WANT TO GO BACK TO THE UNDERWORLD.
AND WE DEFINITELY DON'T WANT TO SEE **EVIL JEN** OR **HEROBRINE** OR ANYONE ASSOCIATED WITH THEM IN ANY WAY **EVER** AGAIN.
AM I RIGHT?

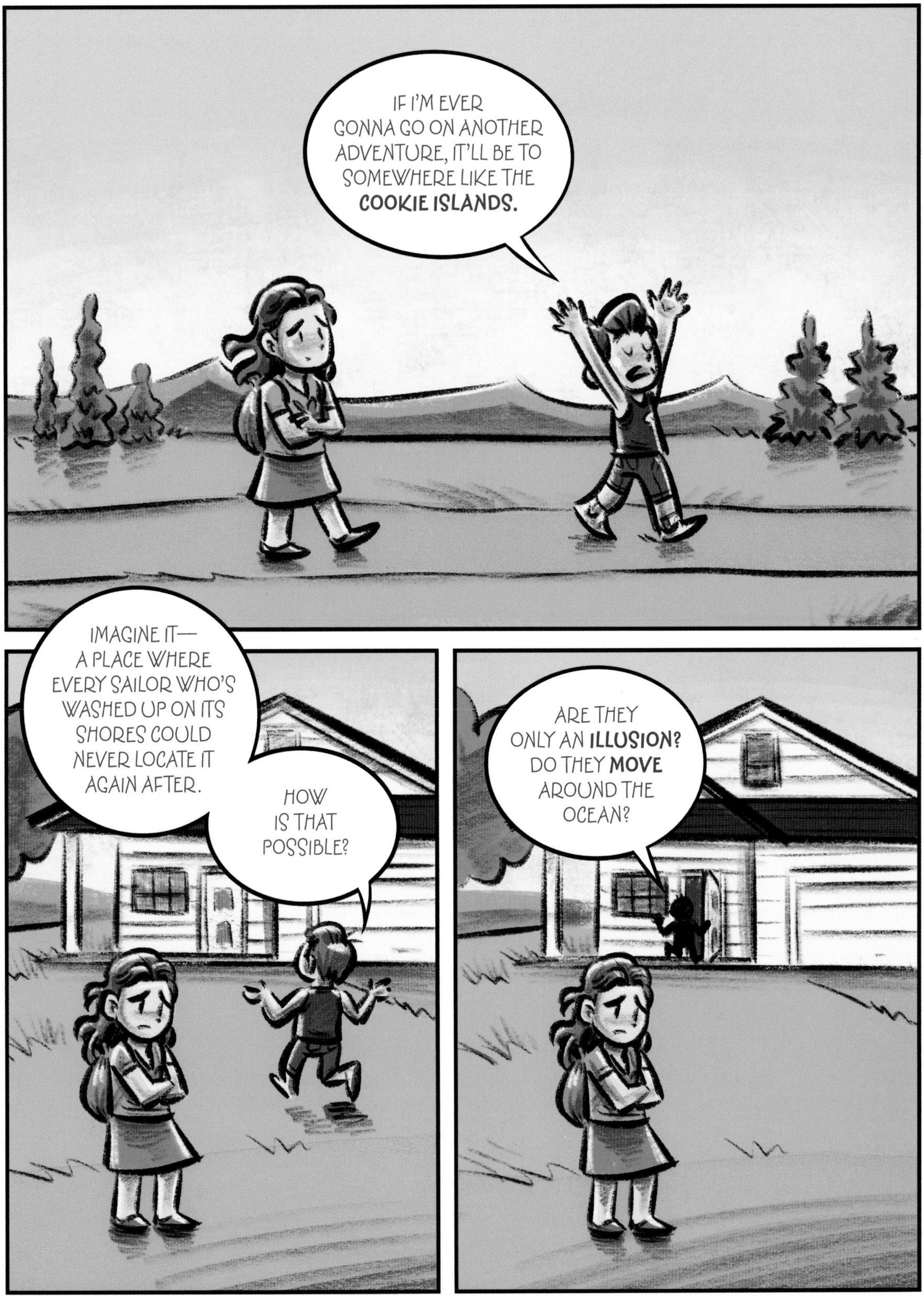
IF I'M EVER GONNA GO ON ANOTHER ADVENTURE, IT'LL BE TO SOMEWHERE LIKE THE **COOKIE ISLANDS.**
IMAGINE IT— A PLACE WHERE EVERY SAILOR WHO'S WASHED UP ON ITS SHORES COULD NEVER LOCATE IT AGAIN AFTER.
HOW IS THAT POSSIBLE?
ARE THEY ONLY AN **ILLUSION?** DO THEY **MOVE** AROUND THE OCEAN?

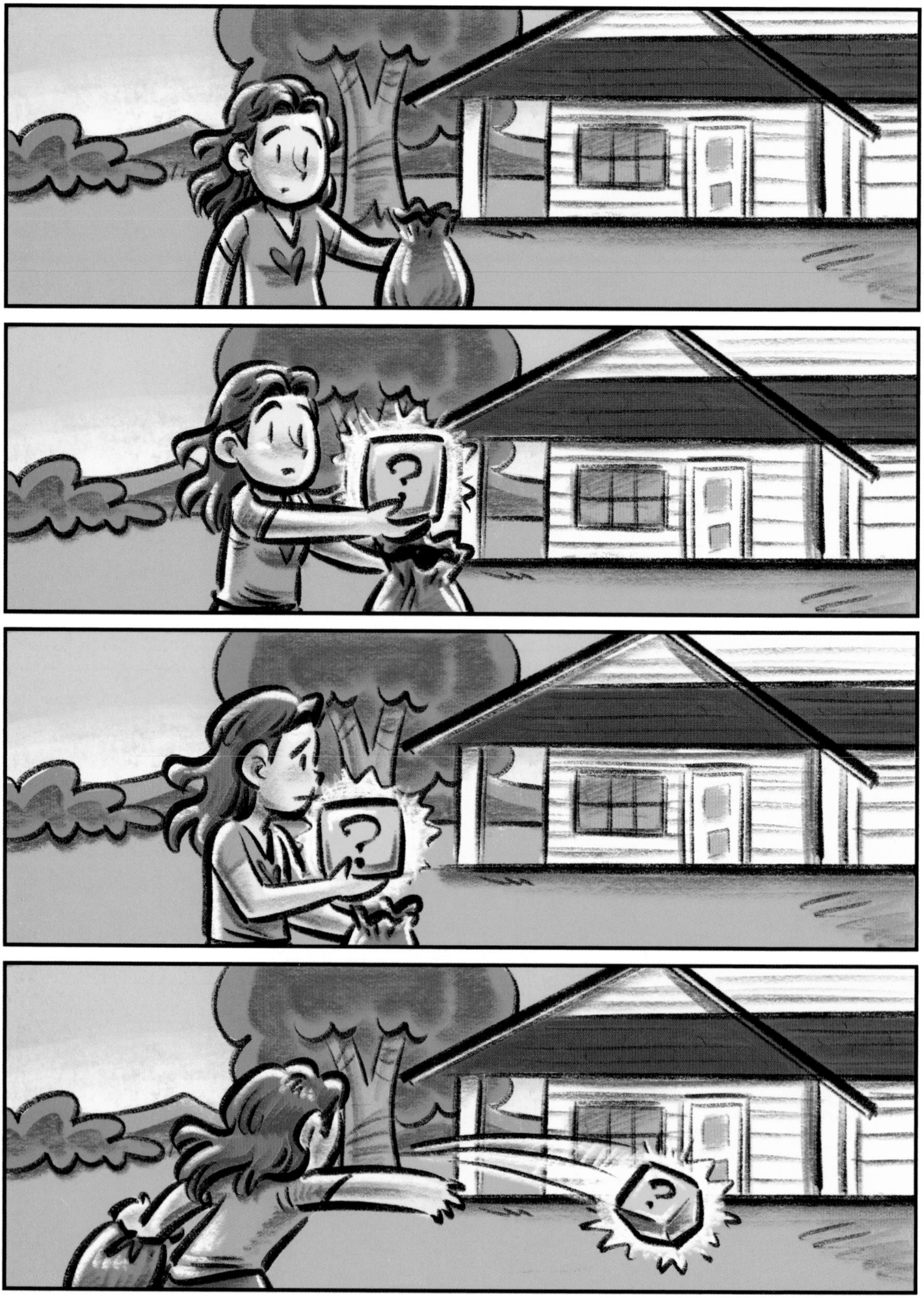

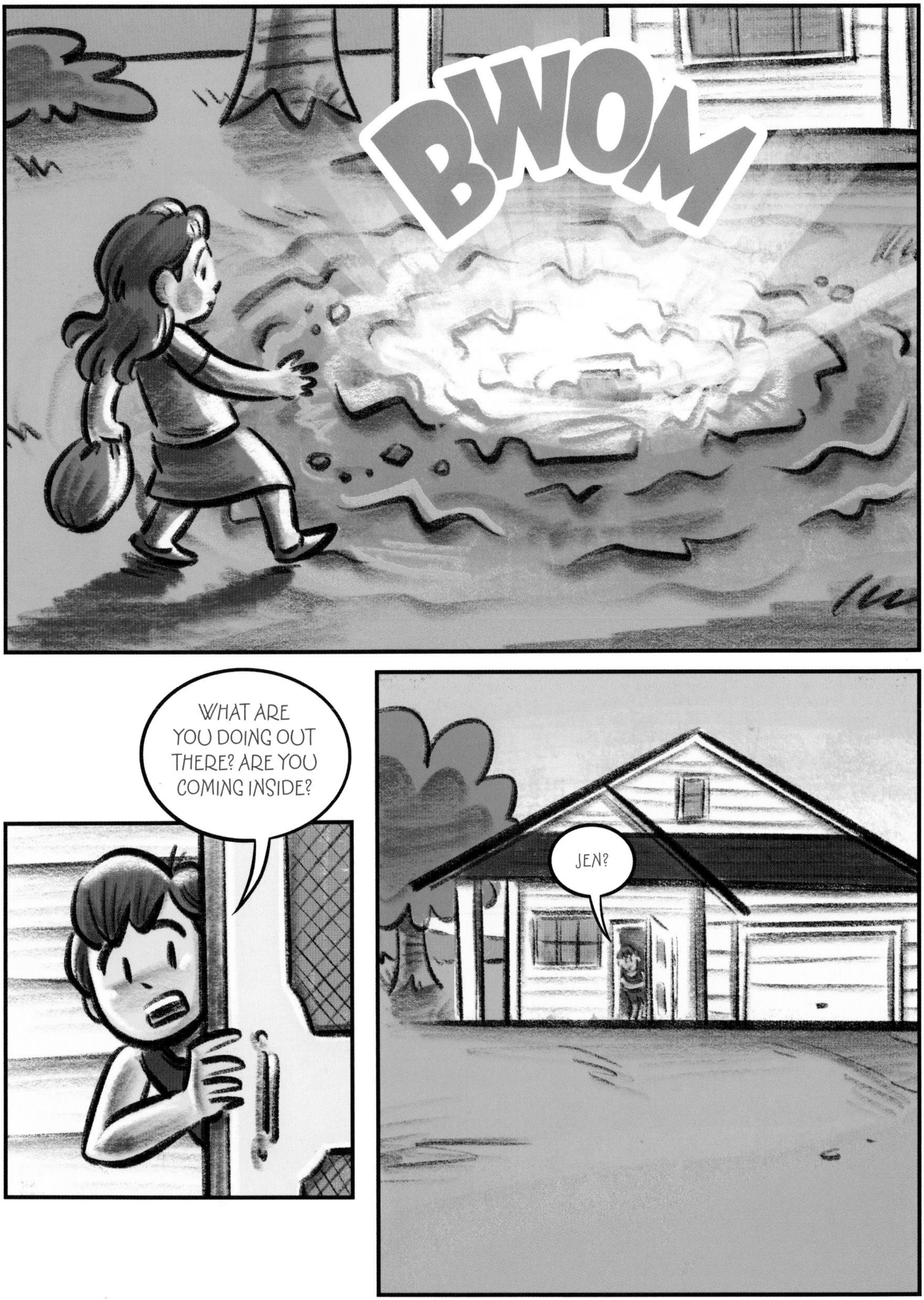
BWOM
WHAT ARE YOU DOING OUT THERE? ARE YOU COMING INSIDE?
JEN?

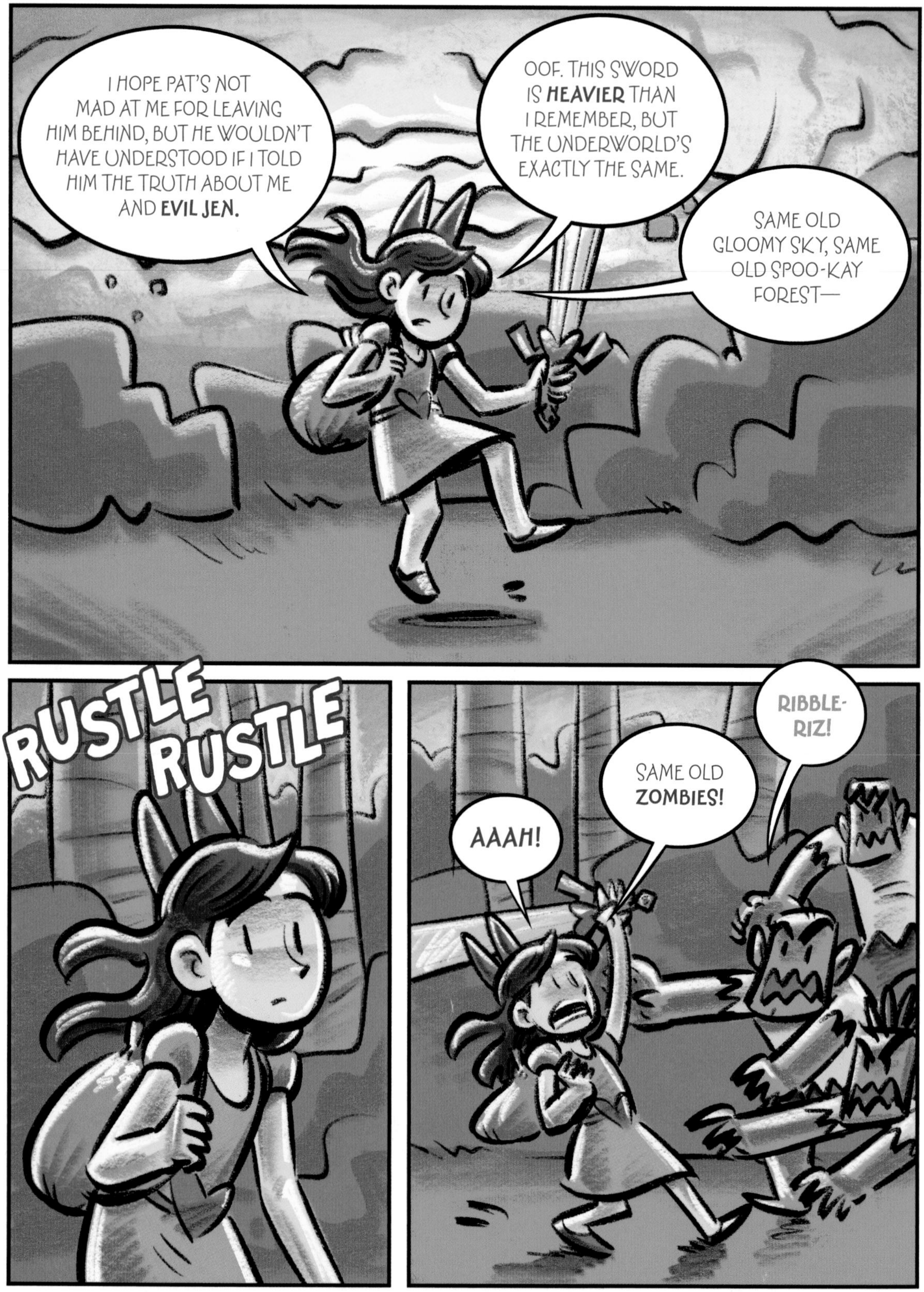
I HOPE PAT'S NOT MAD AT ME FOR LEAVING HIM BEHIND, BUT HE WOULDN'T HAVE UNDERSTOOD IF I TOLD HIM THE TRUTH ABOUT ME AND **EVIL JEN.**
OOF. THIS SWORD IS **HEAVIER** THAN I REMEMBER, BUT THE UNDERWORLD'S EXACTLY THE SAME.
SAME OLD GLOOMY SKY, SAME OLD SPOO-KAY FOREST—
RUSTLE RUSTLE
AAAH!
SAME OLD **ZOMBIES!**
RIBBLE-RIZ!

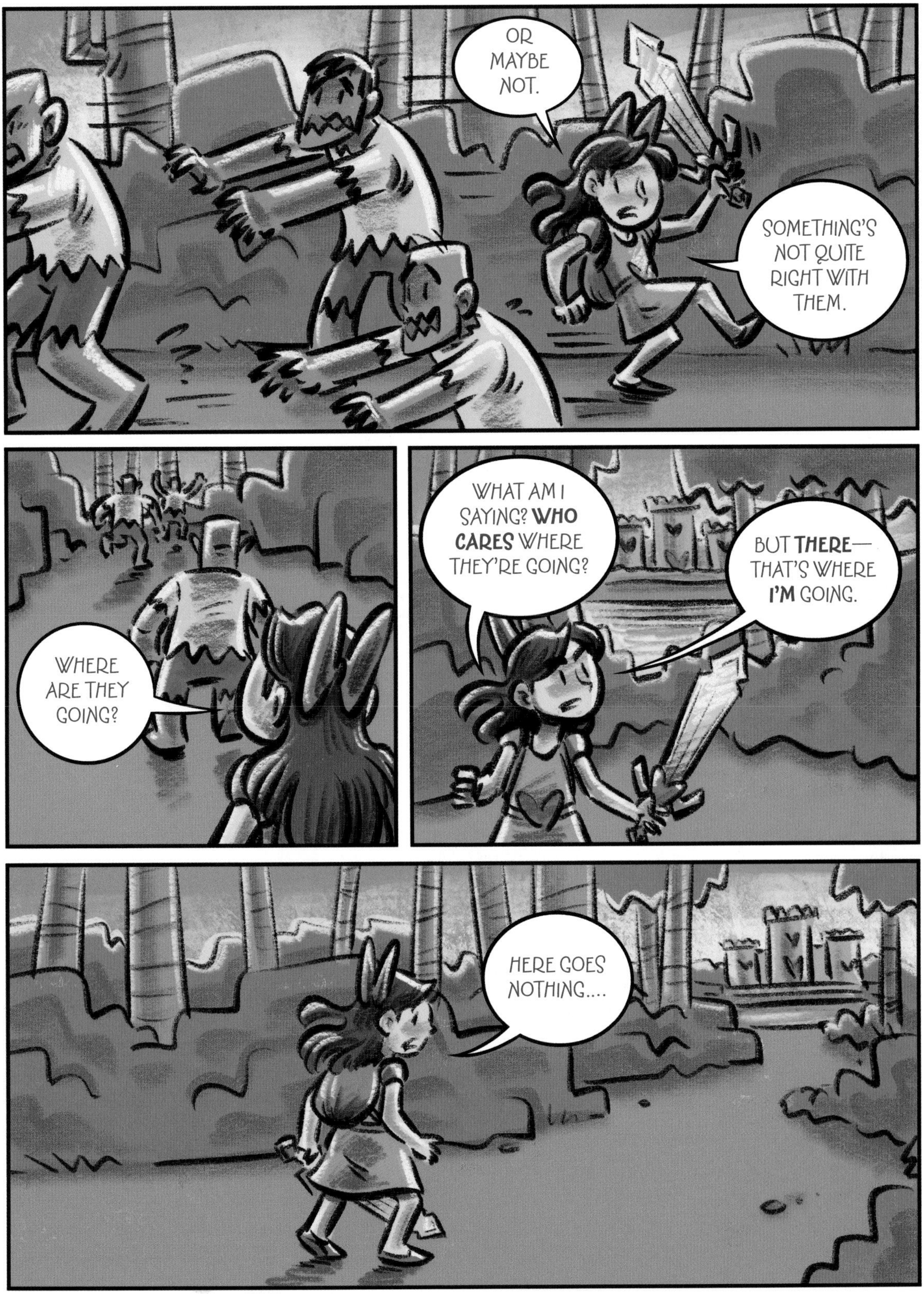
OR MAYBE NOT.
SOMETHING'S NOT QUITE RIGHT WITH THEM.
WHERE ARE THEY GOING?
WHAT AM I SAYING? **WHO CARES** WHERE THEY'RE GOING?
BUT **THERE**—THAT'S WHERE **I'M** GOING.
HERE GOES NOTHING....

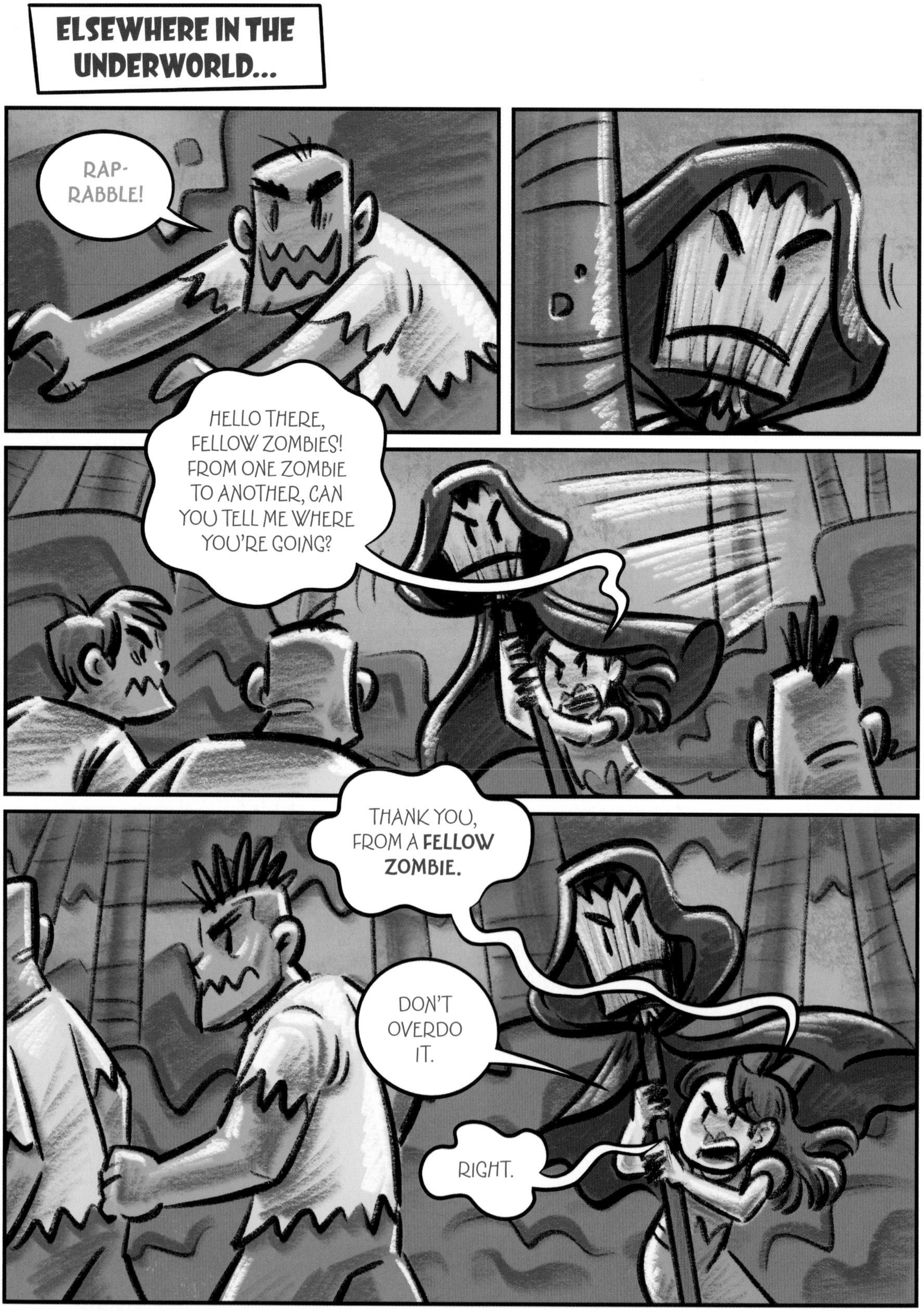
ELSEWHERE IN THE UNDERWORLD...
RAP-RABBLE!
HELLO THERE, FELLOW ZOMBIES! FROM ONE ZOMBIE TO ANOTHER, CAN YOU TELL ME WHERE YOU'RE GOING?
THANK YOU, FROM A **FELLOW ZOMBIE.**
DON'T OVERDO IT.
RIGHT.

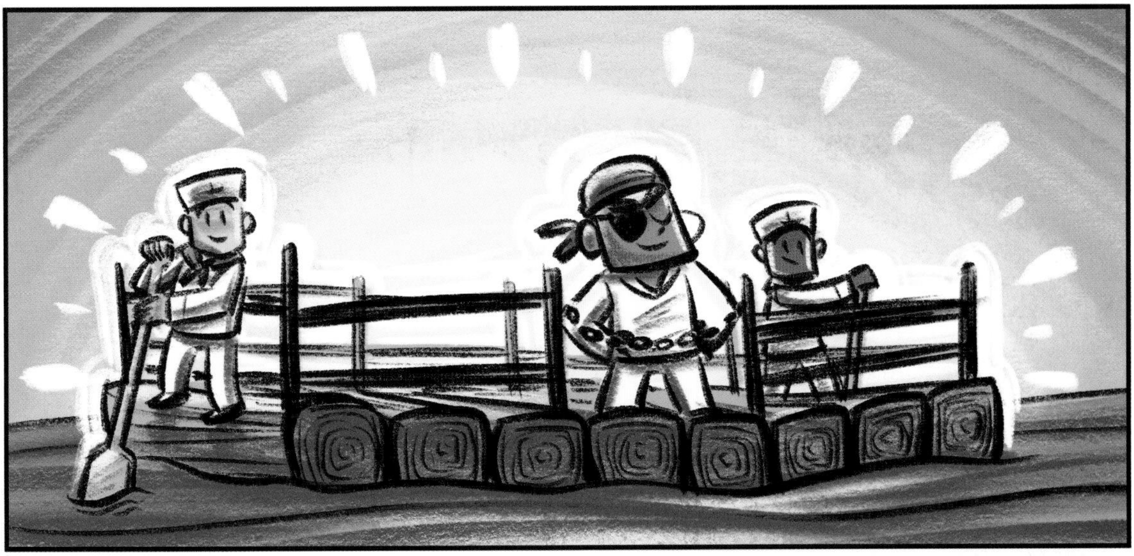

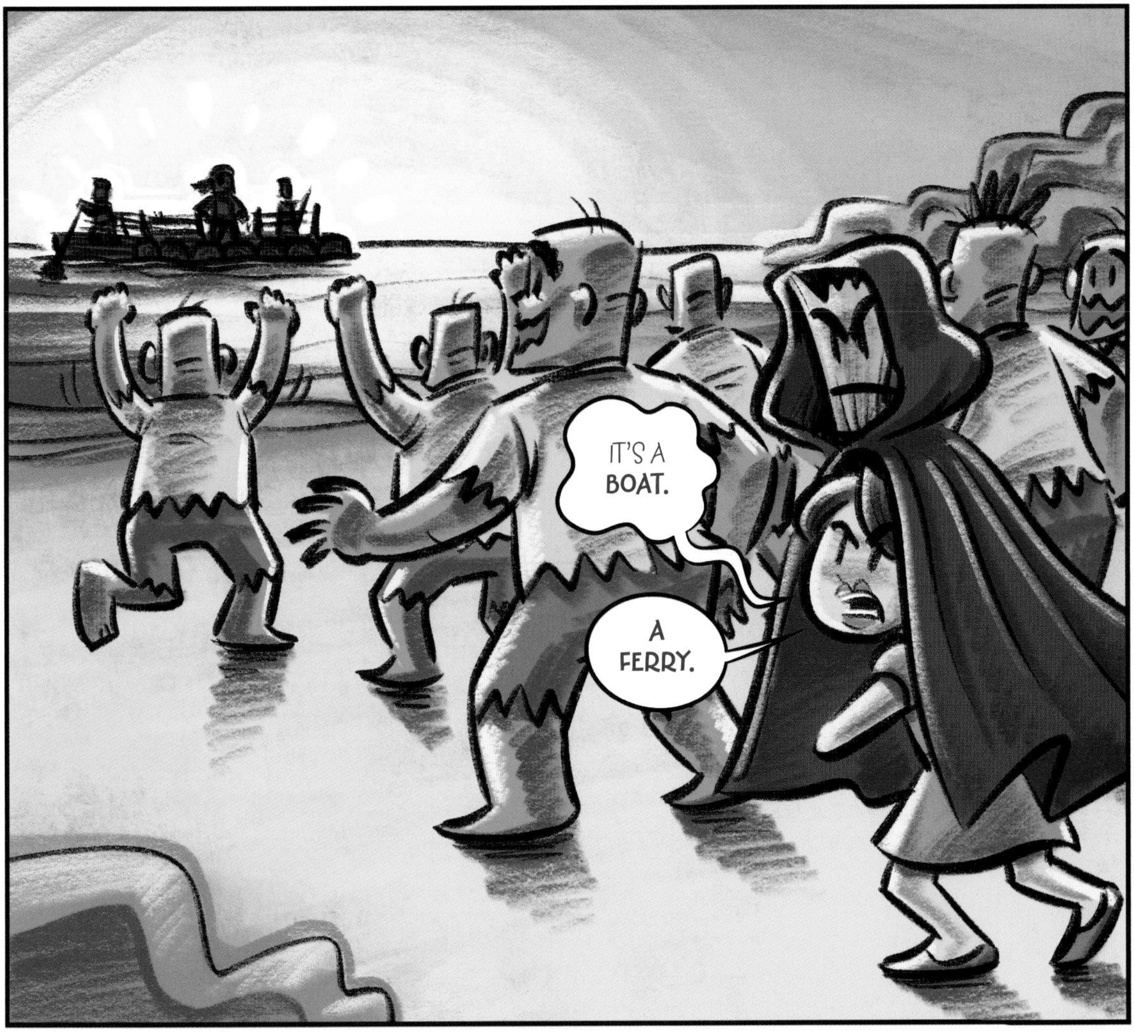
IT'S A BOAT.
A FERRY.

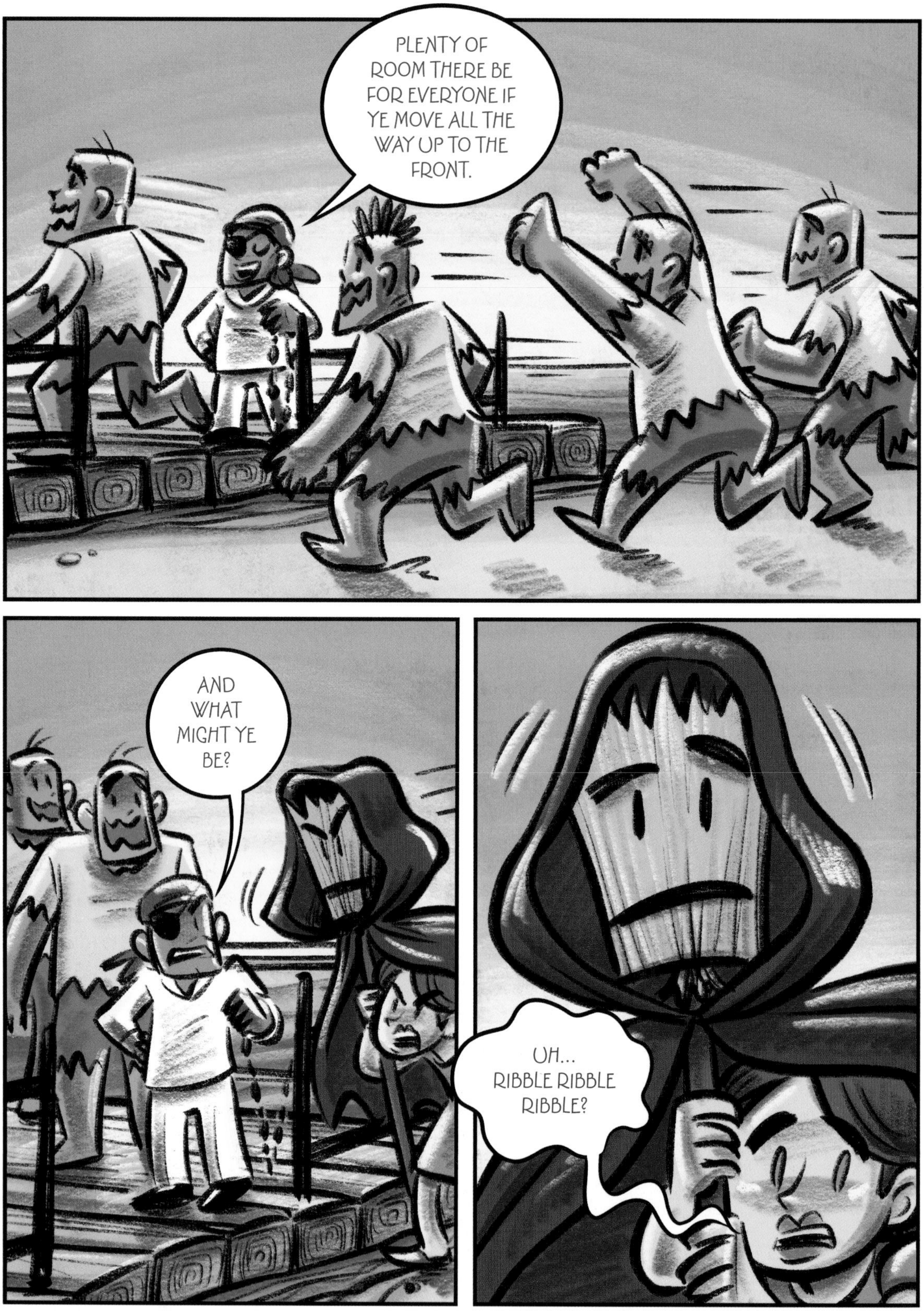
PLENTY OF ROOM THERE BE FOR EVERYONE IF YE MOVE ALL THE WAY UP TO THE FRONT.
AND WHAT MIGHT YE BE?
UH... RIBBLE RIBBLE RIBBLE?

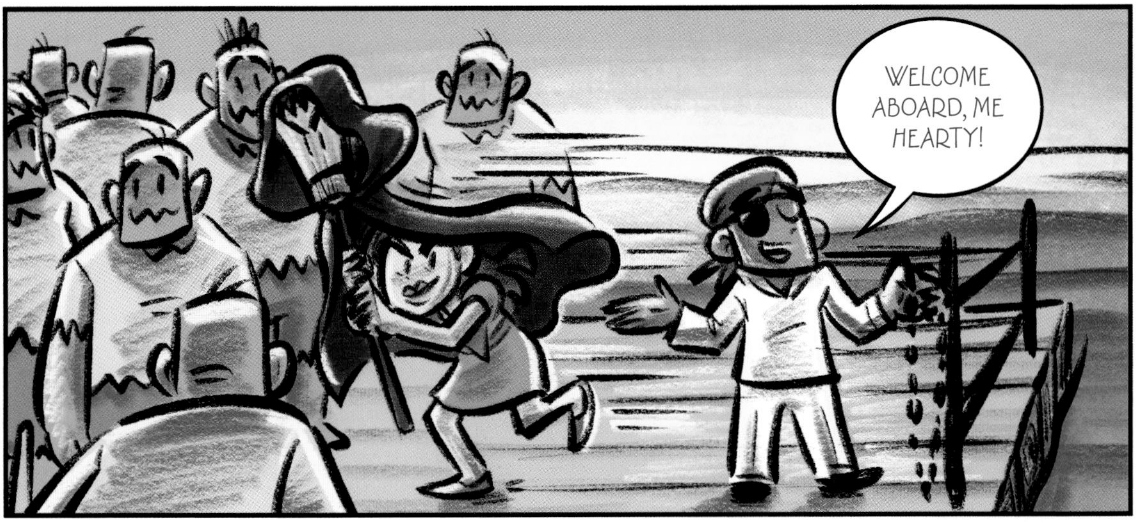
WELCOME ABOARD, ME HEARTY!

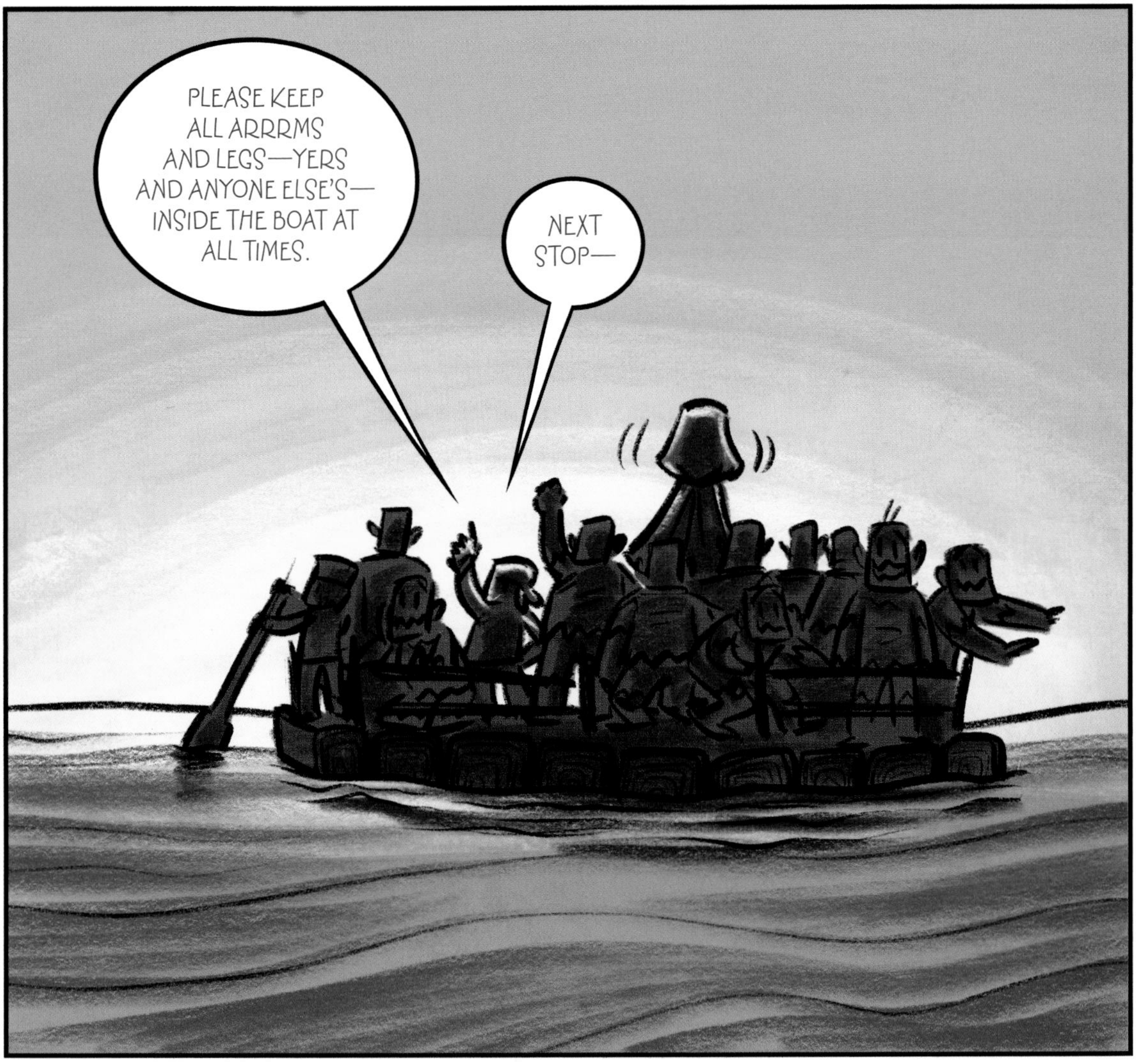
PLEASE KEEP ALL ARRRMS AND LEGS—YERS AND ANYONE ELSE'S—INSIDE THE BOAT AT ALL TIMES.
NEXT STOP—

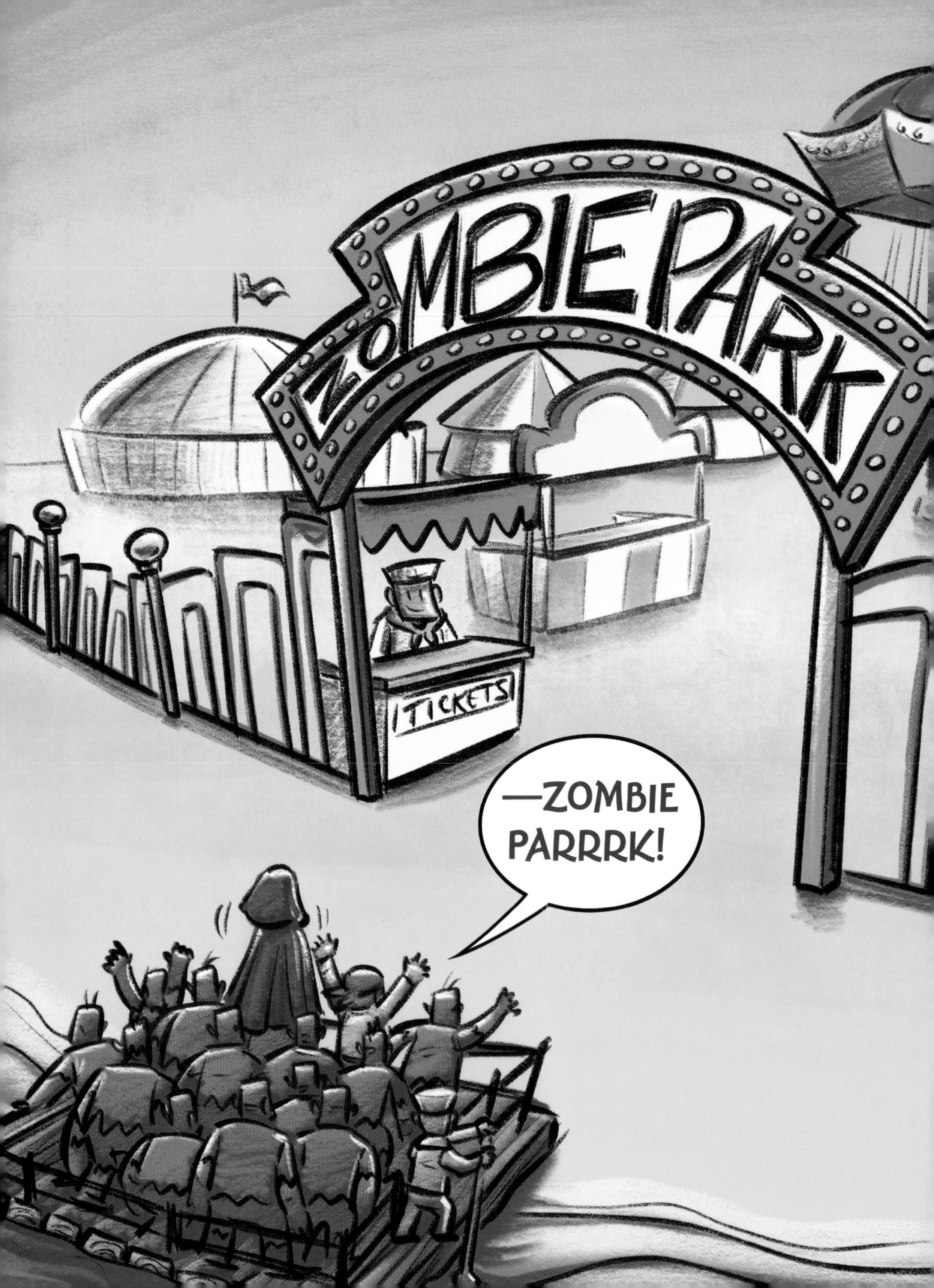
ZOMBIE PARK
TICKETS
—ZOMBIE PARRRK!

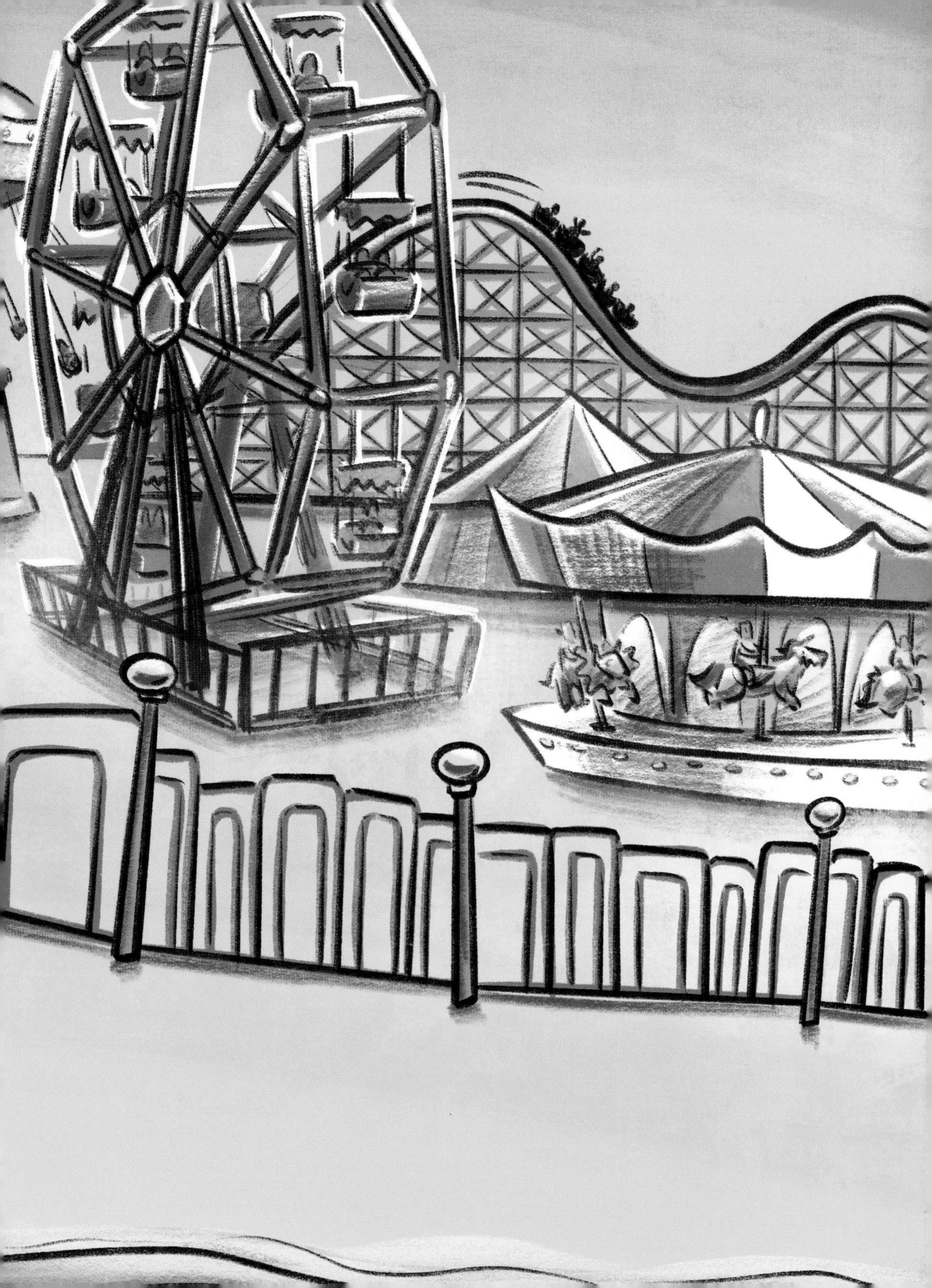

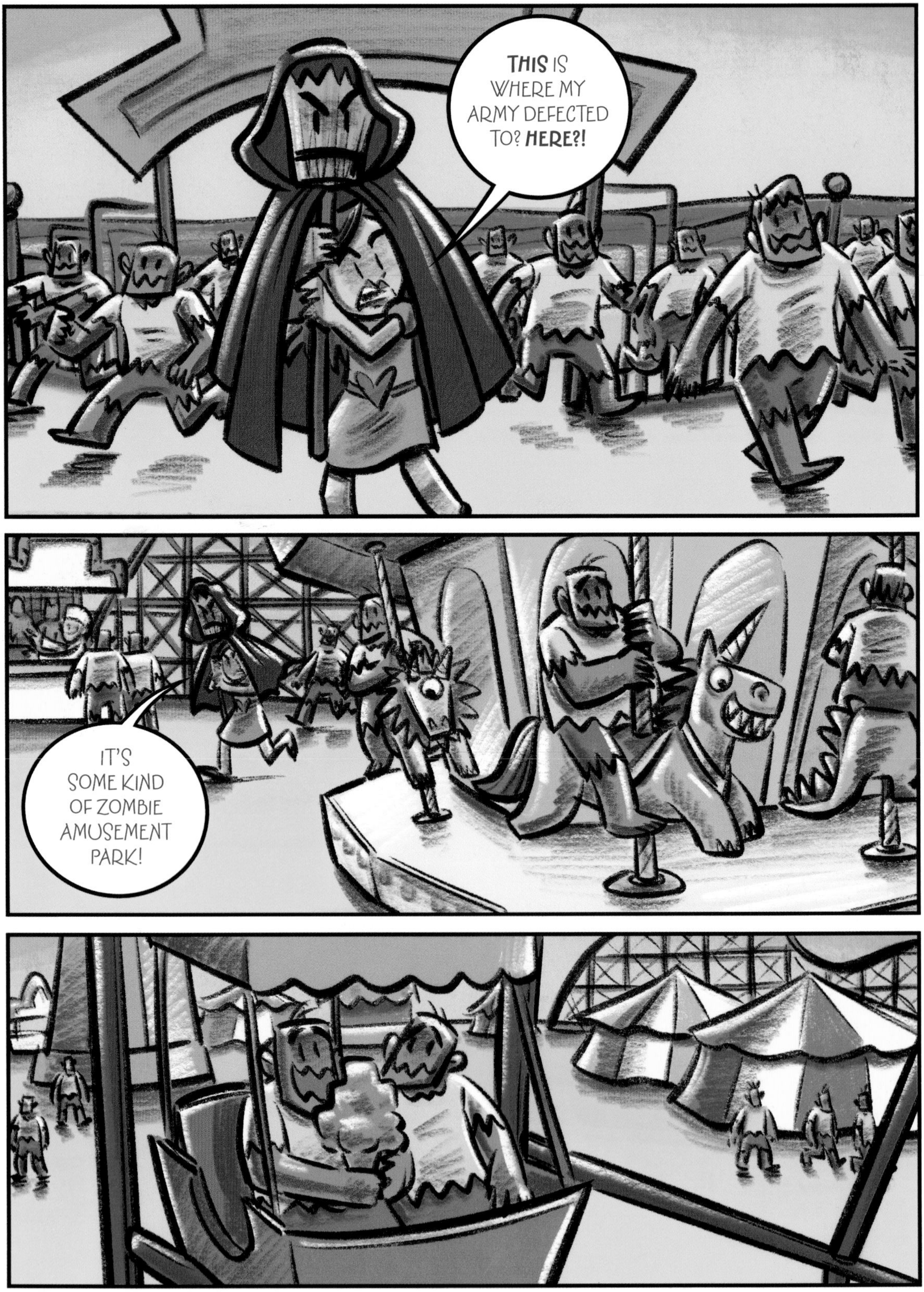
THIS IS WHERE MY ARMY DEFECTED TO? HERE?!
IT'S SOME KIND OF ZOMBIE AMUSEMENT PARK!

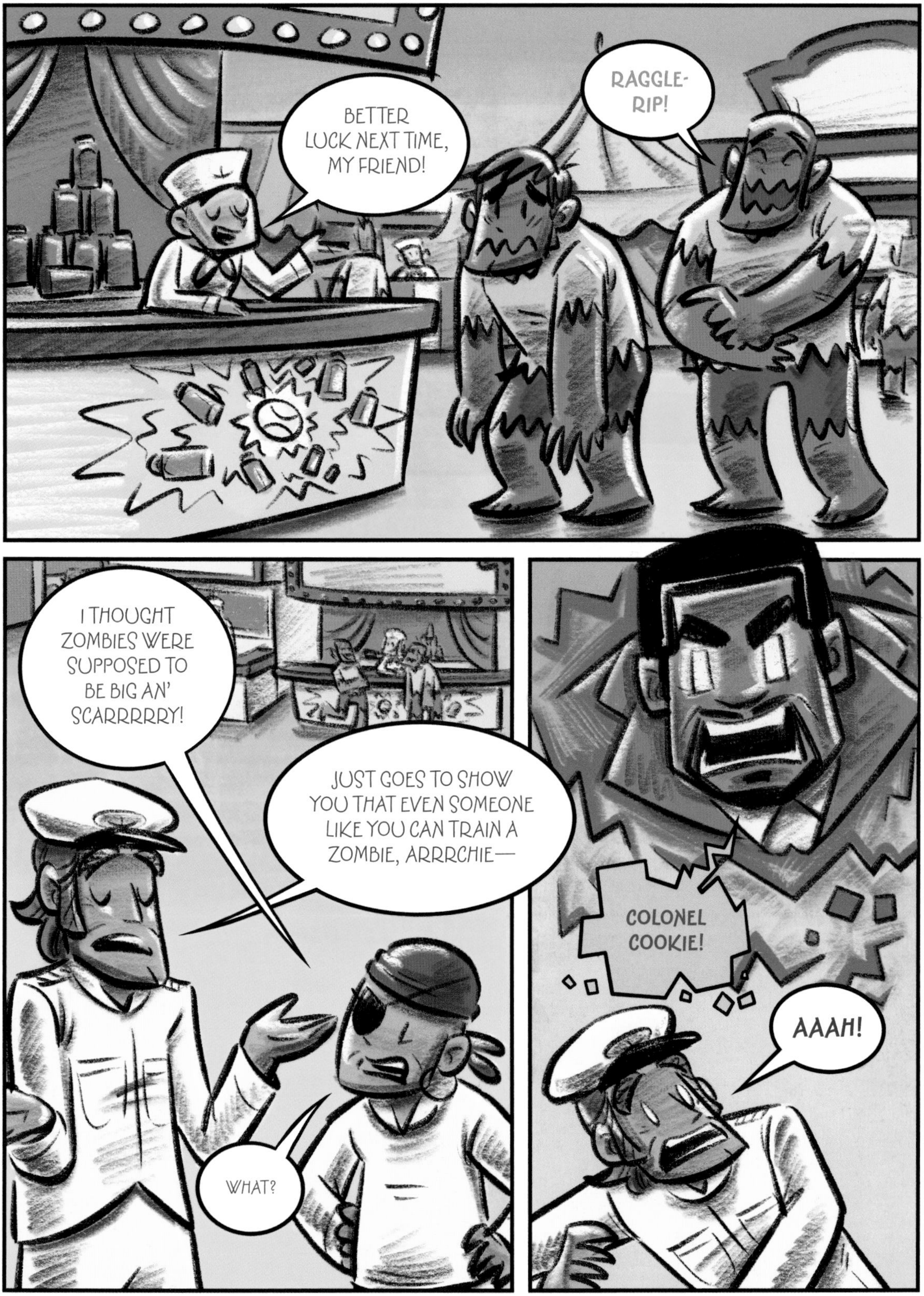
BETTER LUCK NEXT TIME, MY FRIEND!
RAGGLE-RIP!
I THOUGHT ZOMBIES WERE SUPPOSED TO BE BIG AN' SCARRRRRY!
JUST GOES TO SHOW YOU THAT EVEN SOMEONE LIKE YOU CAN TRAIN A ZOMBIE, ARRRCHIE—
WHAT?
COLONEL COOKIE!
AAAH!

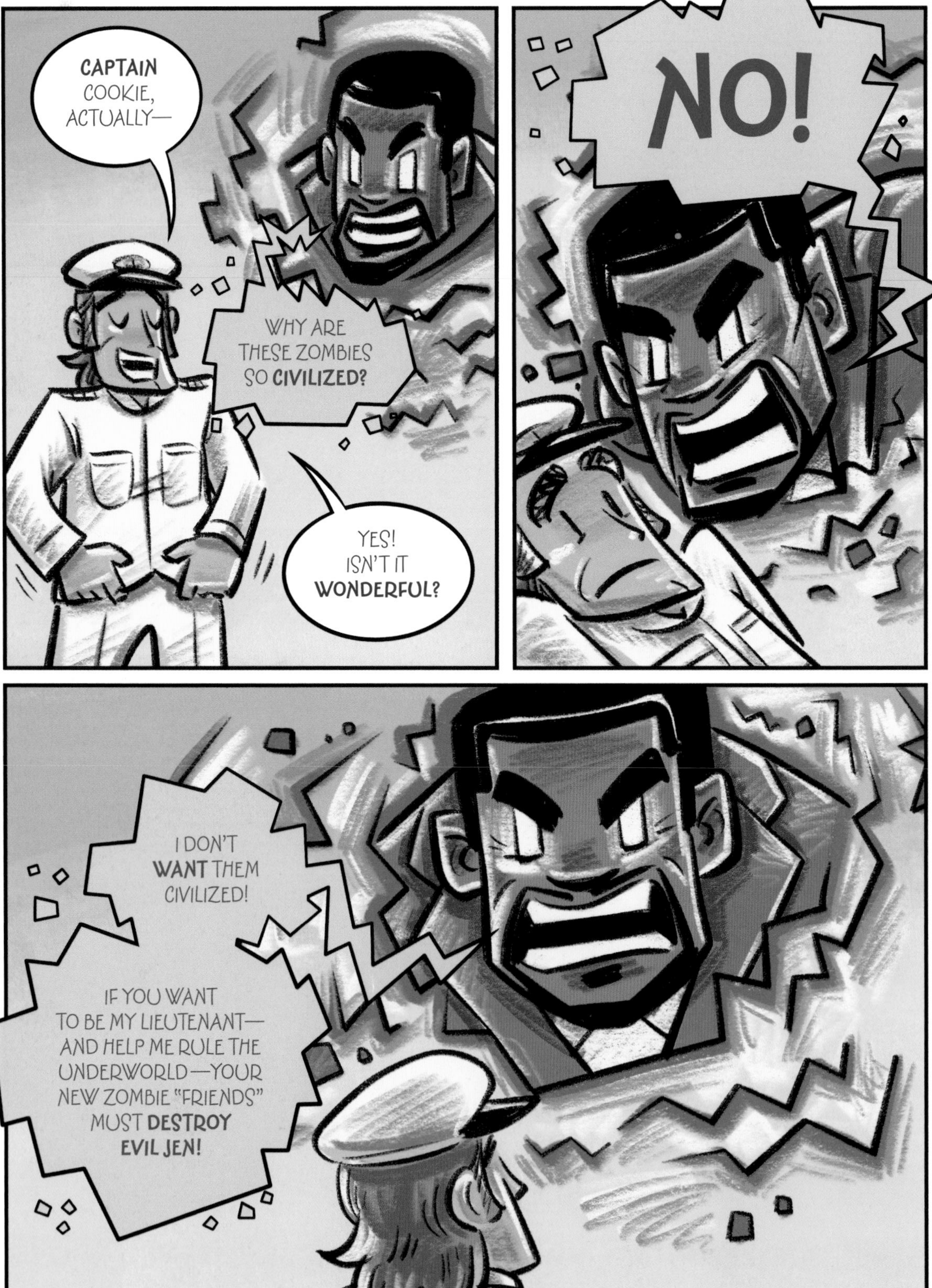
CAPTAIN COOKIE, ACTUALLY—
WHY ARE THESE ZOMBIES SO CIVILIZED?
YES! ISN'T IT WONDERFUL?
NO!
I DON'T WANT THEM CIVILIZED!
IF YOU WANT TO BE MY LIEUTENANT—AND HELP ME RULE THE UNDERWORLD—YOUR NEW ZOMBIE "FRIENDS" MUST DESTROY EVIL JEN!

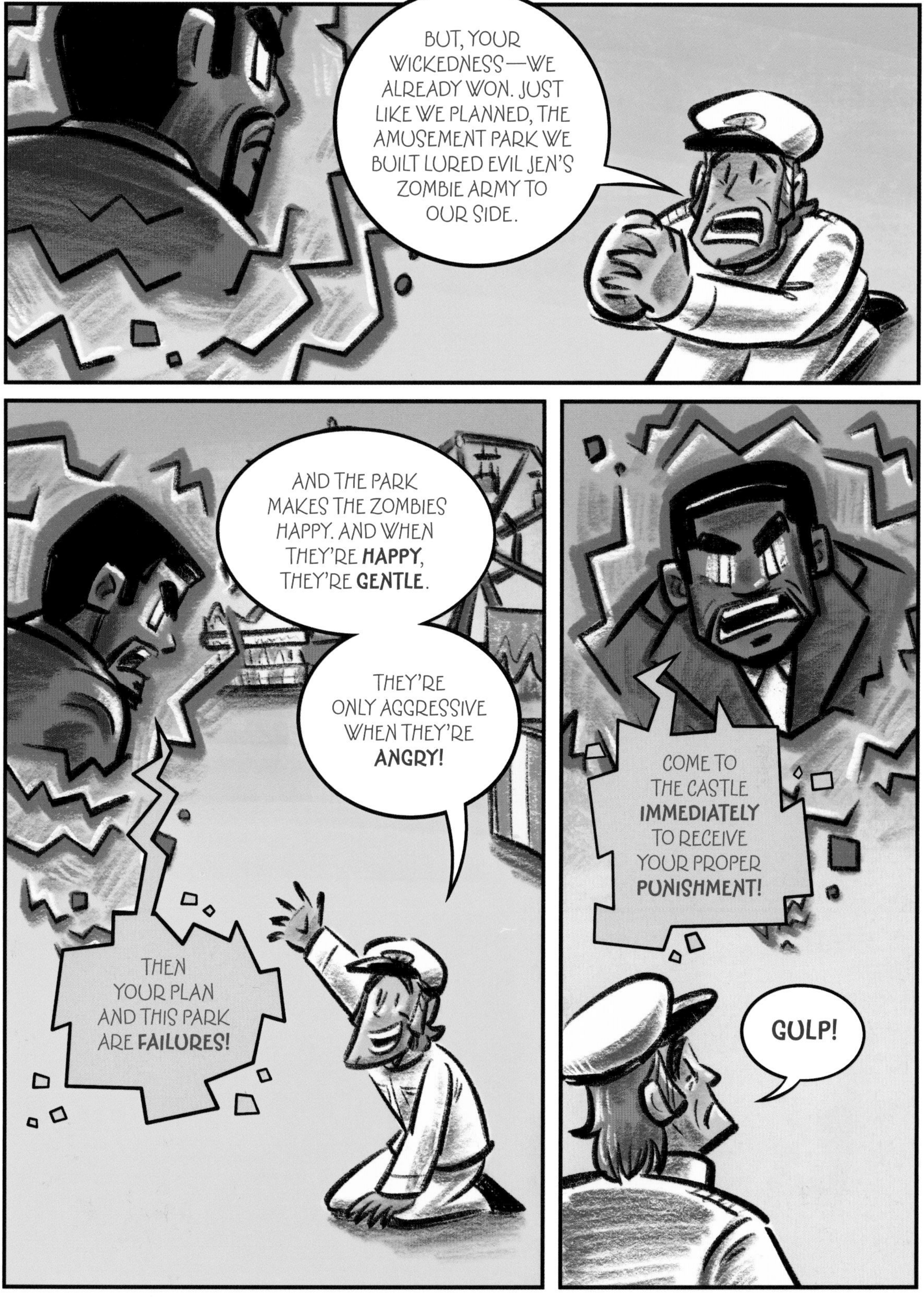
BUT, YOUR WICKEDNESS—WE ALREADY WON. JUST LIKE WE PLANNED, THE AMUSEMENT PARK WE BUILT LURED EVIL JEN'S ZOMBIE ARMY TO OUR SIDE.
AND THE PARK MAKES THE ZOMBIES HAPPY. AND WHEN THEY'RE **HAPPY**, THEY'RE **GENTLE**.
THEY'RE ONLY AGGRESSIVE WHEN THEY'RE **ANGRY!**
THEN YOUR PLAN AND THIS PARK ARE **FAILURES!**
COME TO THE CASTLE **IMMEDIATELY** TO RECEIVE YOUR PROPER **PUNISHMENT!**
GULP!

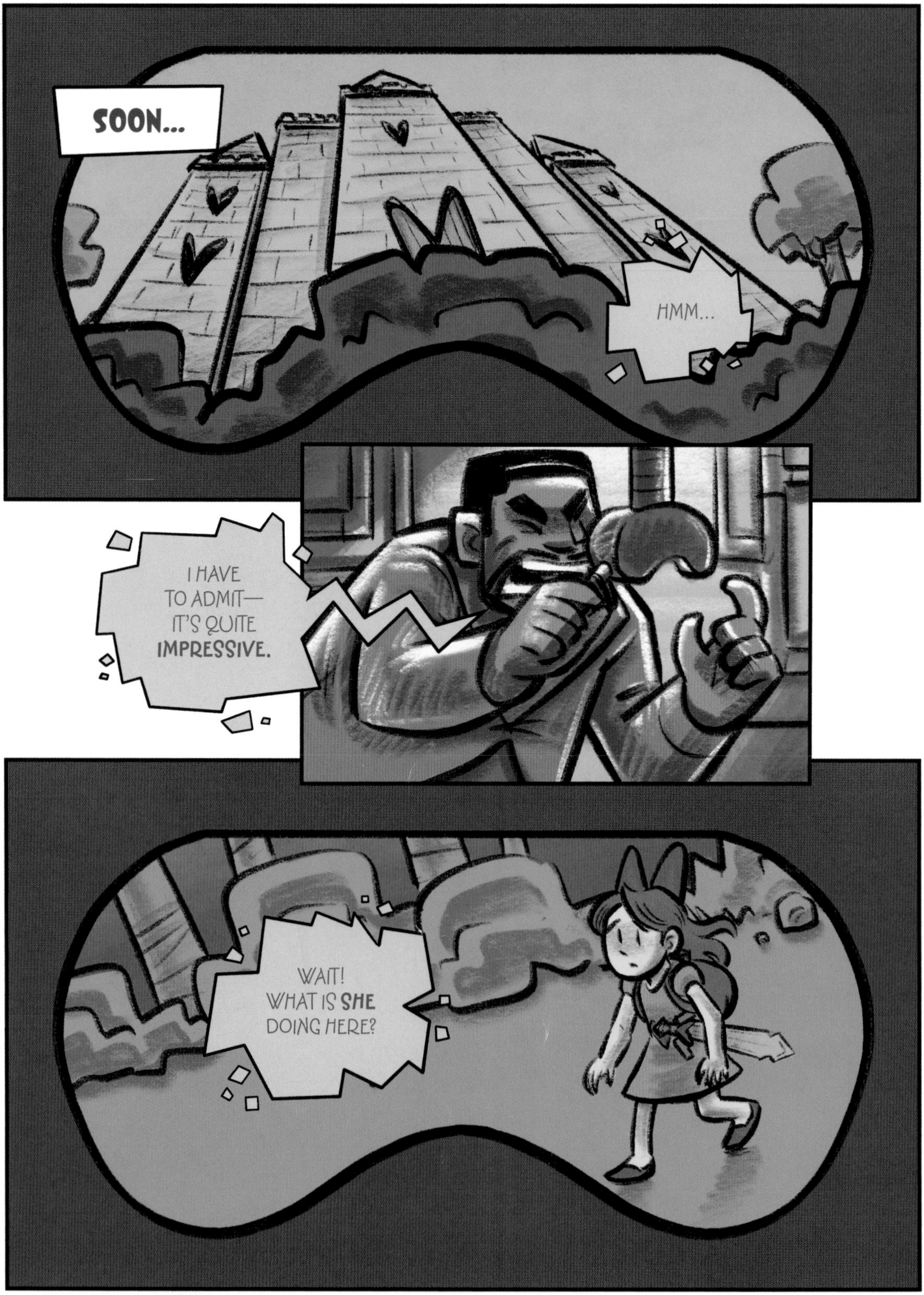
SOON...
HMM...
I HAVE TO ADMIT— IT'S QUITE IMPRESSIVE.
WAIT! WHAT IS SHE DOING HERE?

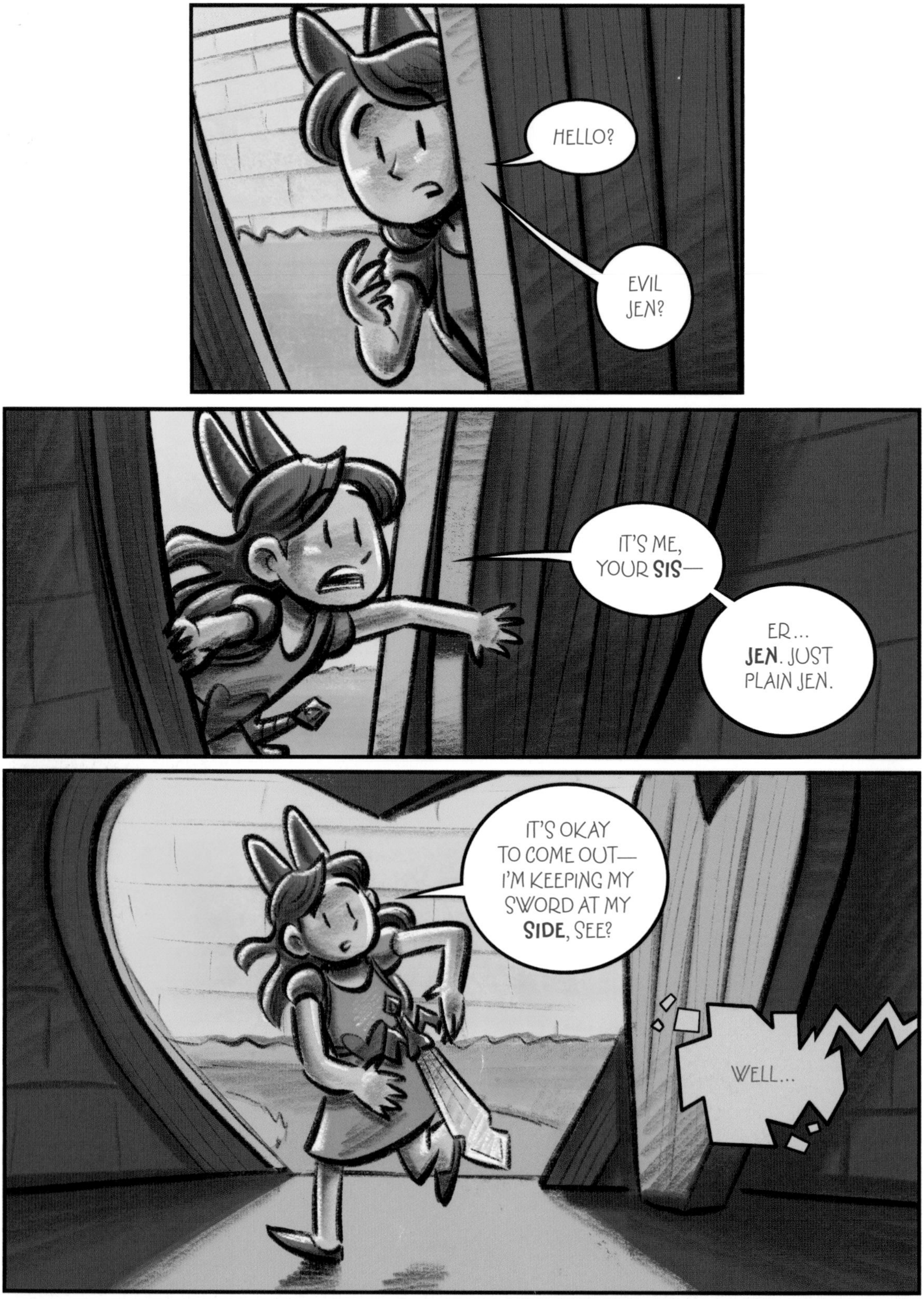
HELLO?
EVIL JEN?
IT'S ME, YOUR SIS—
ER... JEN. JUST PLAIN JEN.
IT'S OKAY TO COME OUT— I'M KEEPING MY SWORD AT MY SIDE, SEE?
WELL...

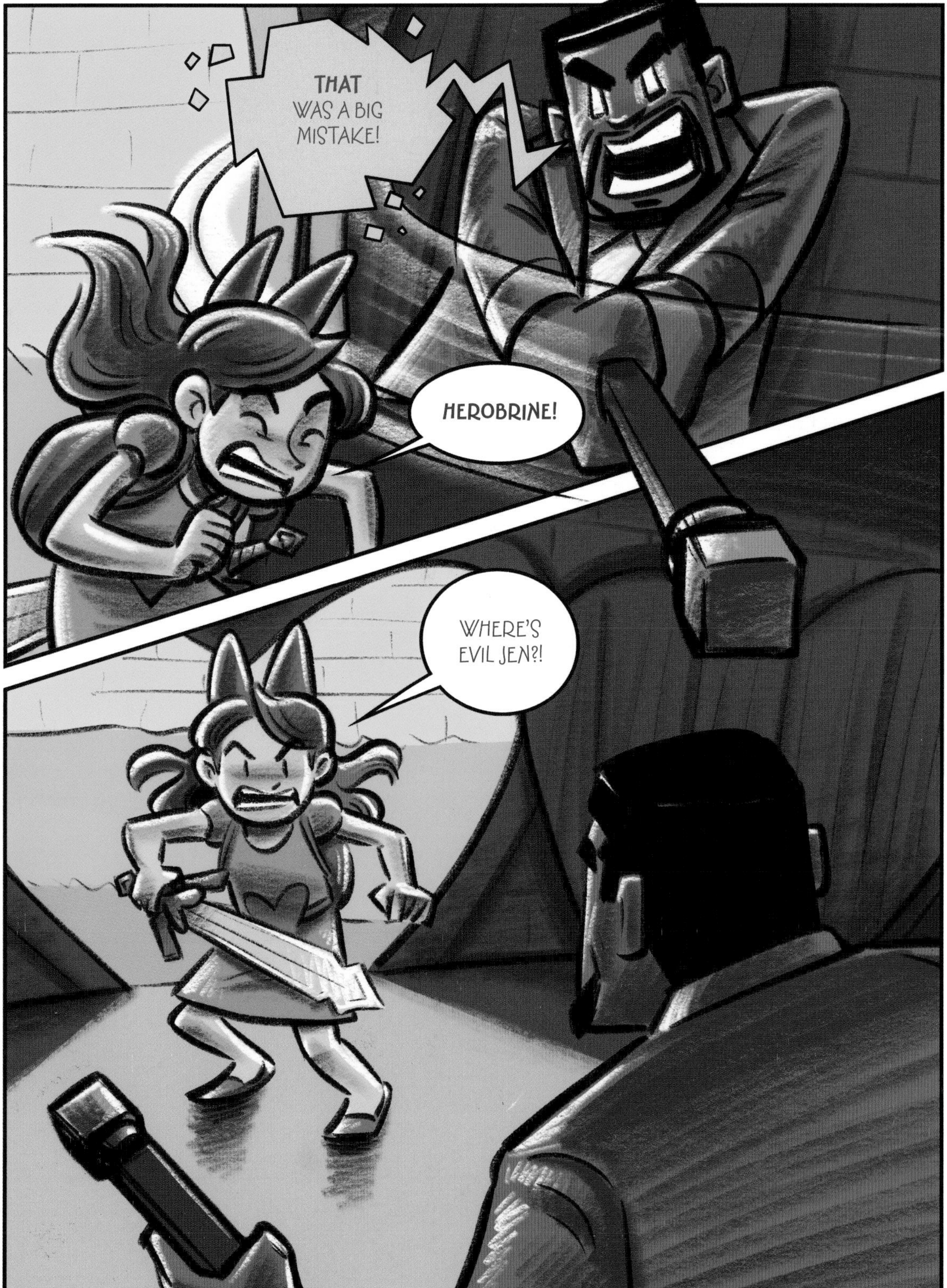
THAT WAS A BIG MISTAKE!
HEROBRINE!
WHERE'S EVIL JEN?!

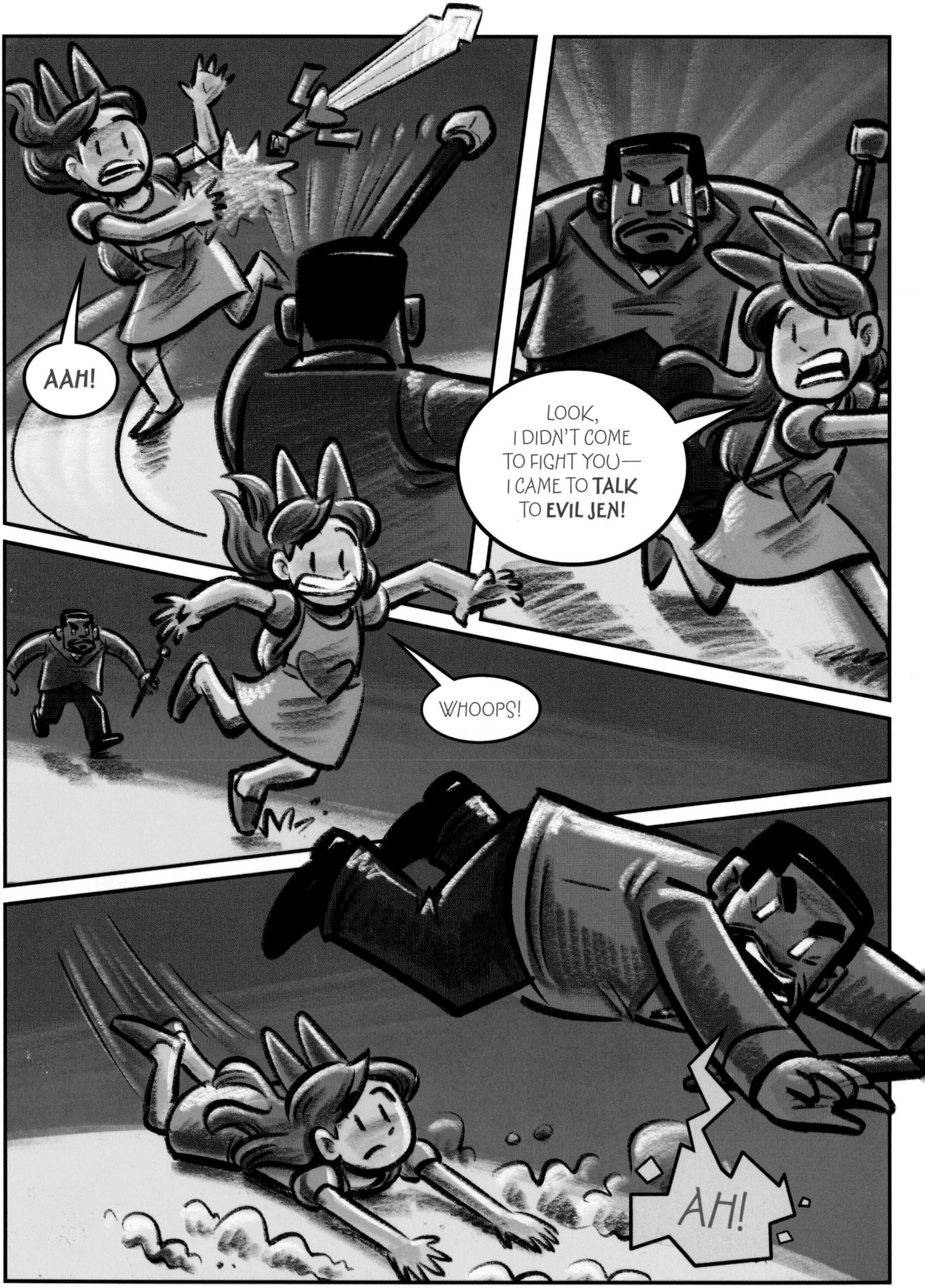
AAH!
LOOK, I DIDN'T COME TO FIGHT YOU— I CAME TO TALK TO EVIL JEN!
WHOOPS!
AH!

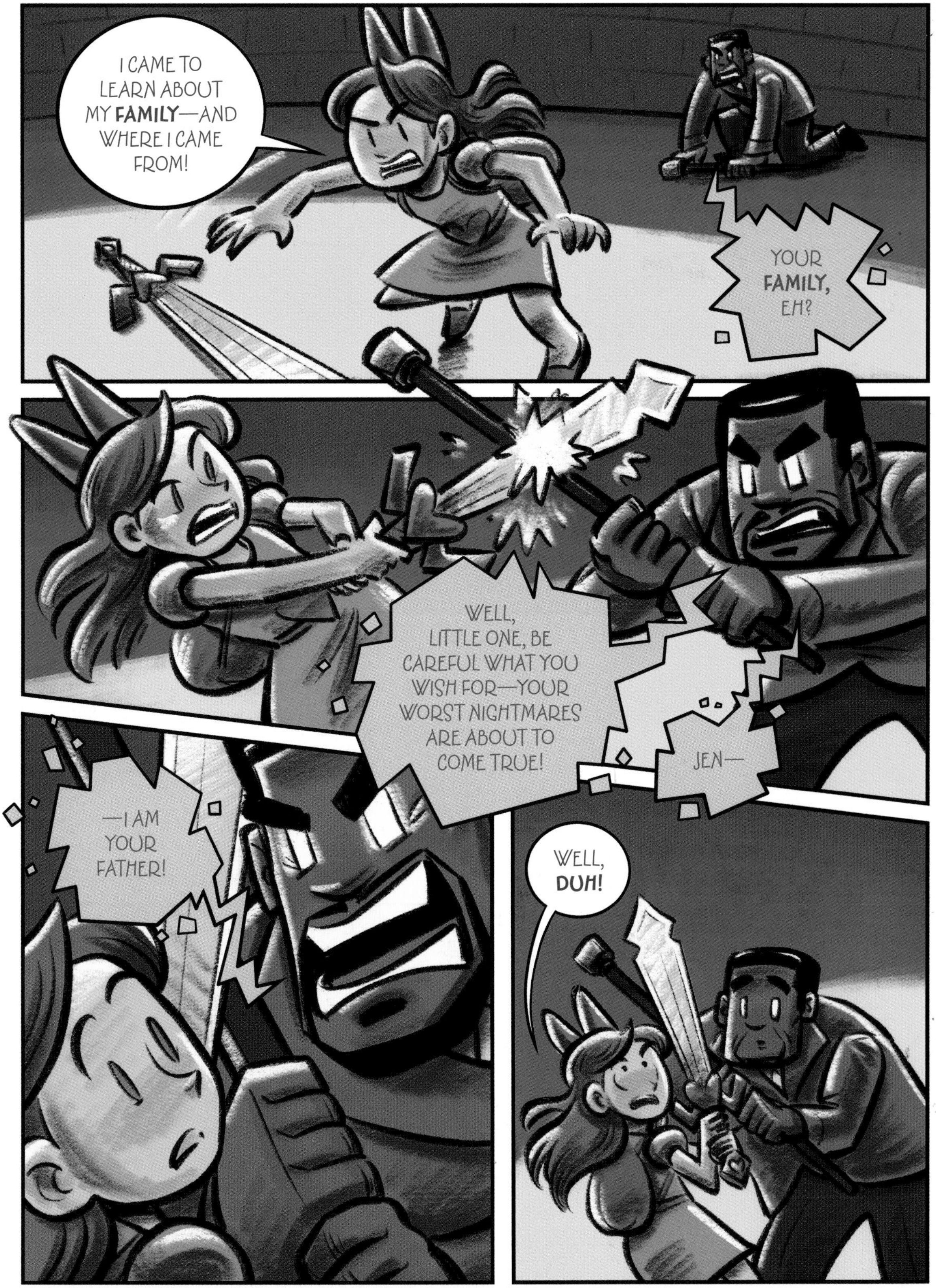
I CAME TO LEARN ABOUT MY **FAMILY**—AND WHERE I CAME FROM!
YOUR **FAMILY,** EH?
WELL, LITTLE ONE, BE CAREFUL WHAT YOU WISH FOR—YOUR WORST NIGHTMARES ARE ABOUT TO COME TRUE!
JEN—
—I AM YOUR FATHER!
WELL, **DUH!**

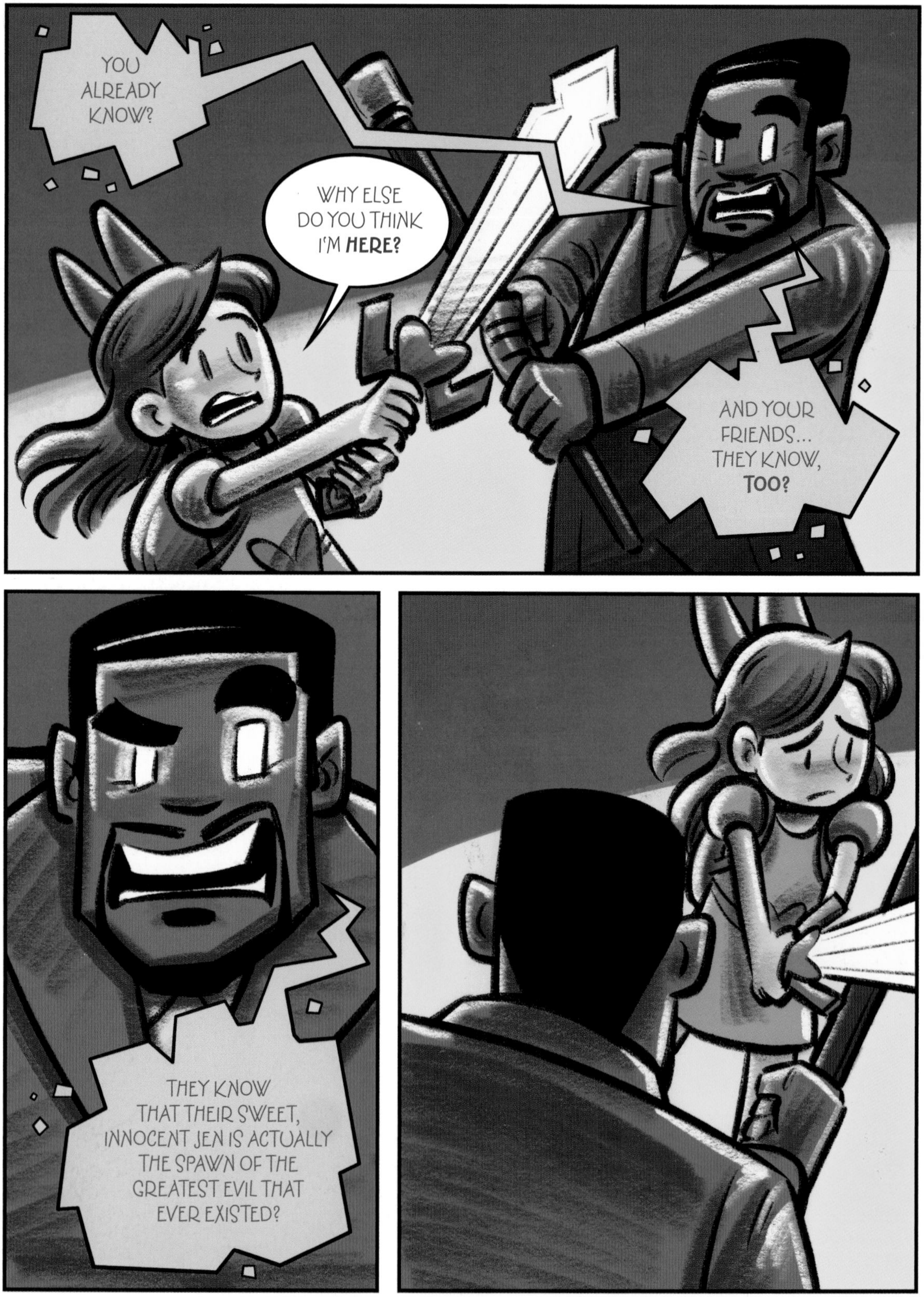
YOU ALREADY KNOW?
WHY ELSE DO YOU THINK I'M **HERE?**
AND YOUR FRIENDS... THEY KNOW, **TOO?**
THEY KNOW THAT THEIR SWEET, INNOCENT JEN IS ACTUALLY THE SPAWN OF THE GREATEST EVIL THAT EVER EXISTED?

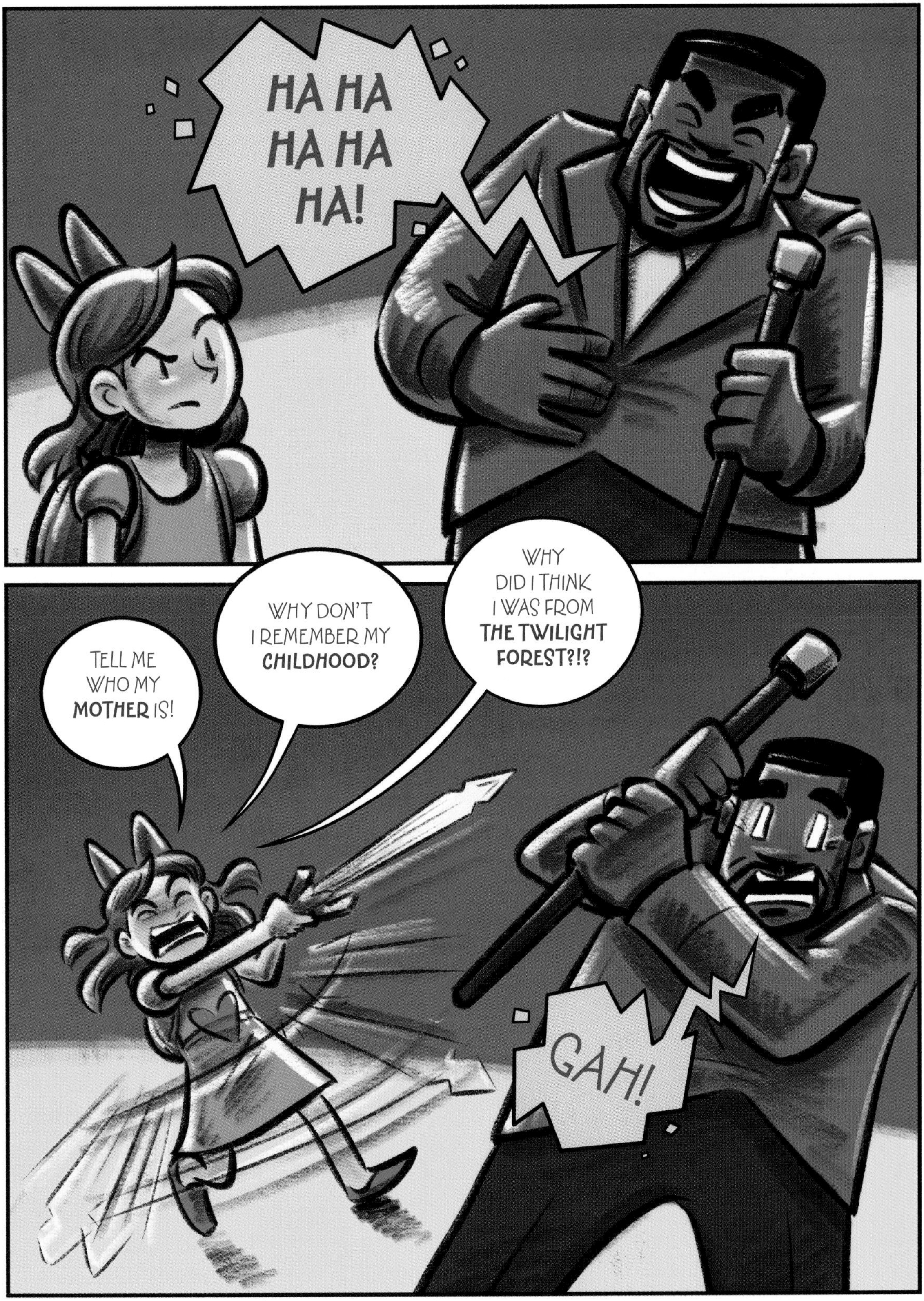
HA HA HA HA HA!
TELL ME WHO MY MOTHER IS!
WHY DON'T I REMEMBER MY CHILDHOOD?
WHY DID I THINK I WAS FROM THE TWILIGHT FOREST?!?
GAH!

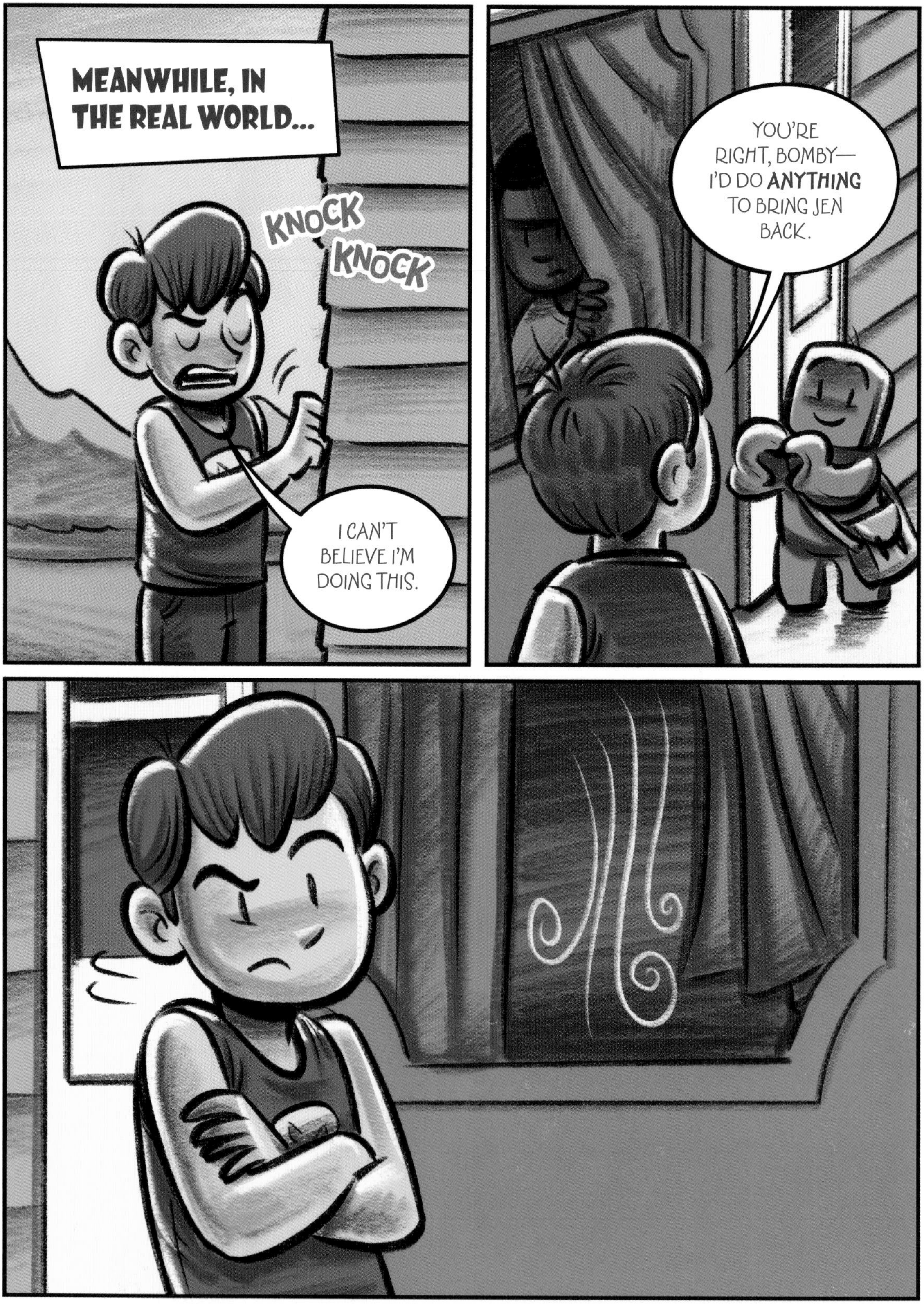
MEANWHILE, IN THE REAL WORLD...
KNOCK KNOCK
I CAN'T BELIEVE I'M DOING THIS.
YOU'RE RIGHT, BOMBY— I'D DO **ANYTHING** TO BRING JEN BACK.

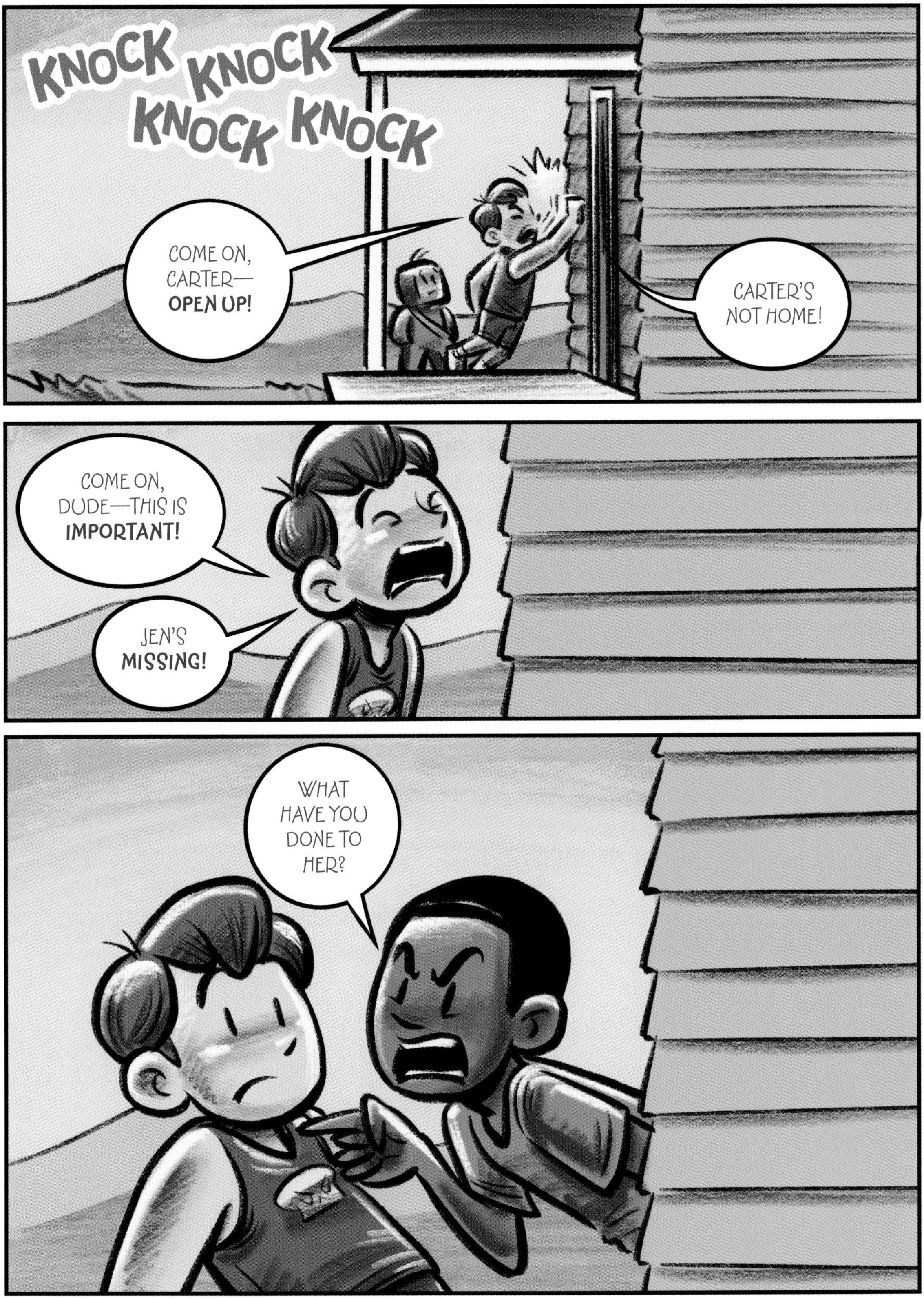
KNOCK KNOCK KNOCK KNOCK
COME ON, CARTER— **OPEN UP!**
CARTER'S NOT HOME!
COME ON, DUDE—THIS IS **IMPORTANT!**
JEN'S **MISSING!**
WHAT HAVE YOU DONE TO HER?

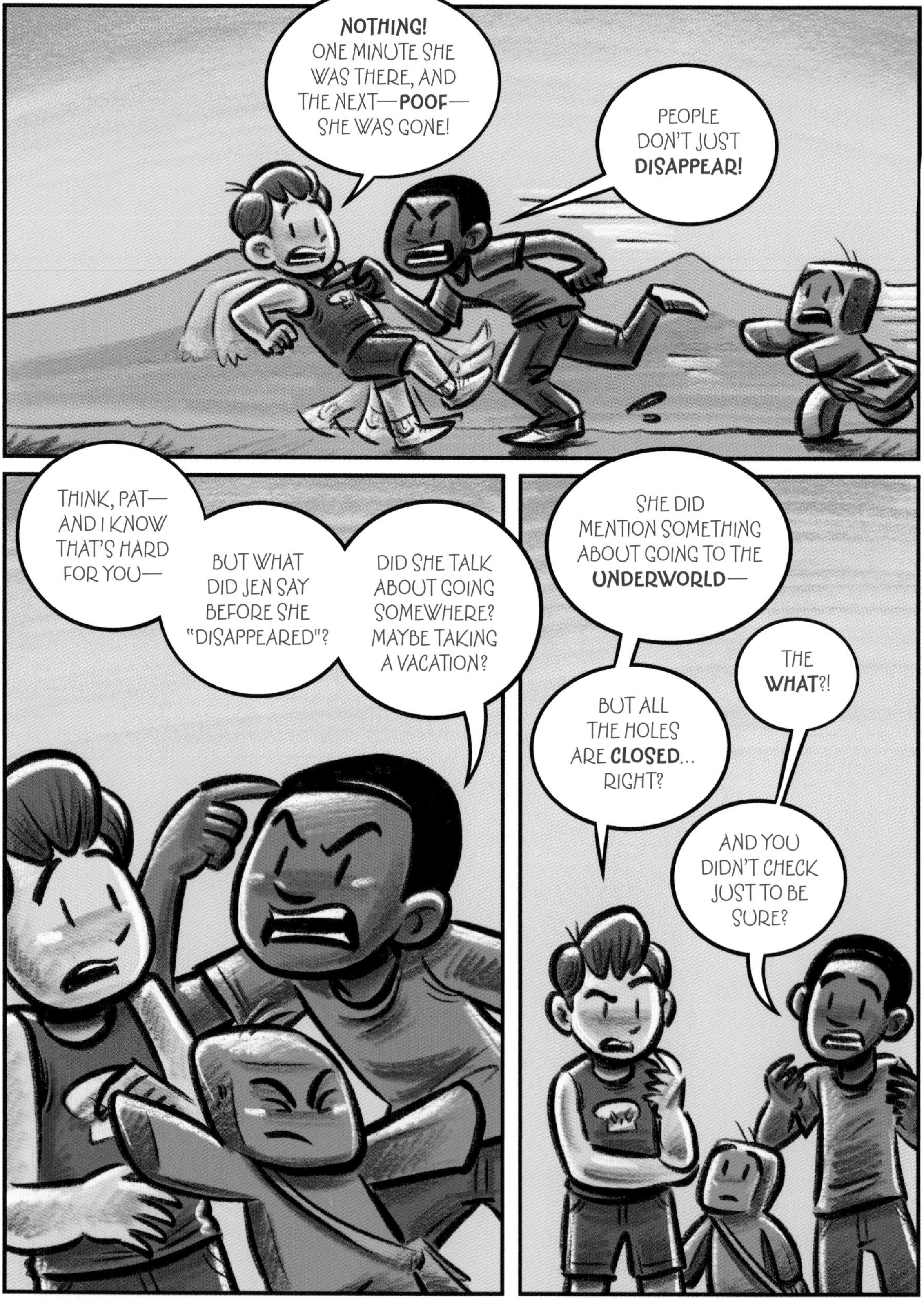
NOTHING! ONE MINUTE SHE WAS THERE, AND THE NEXT—POOF—SHE WAS GONE!
PEOPLE DON'T JUST DISAPPEAR!
THINK, PAT—AND I KNOW THAT'S HARD FOR YOU—
BUT WHAT DID JEN SAY BEFORE SHE "DISAPPEARED"?
DID SHE TALK ABOUT GOING SOMEWHERE? MAYBE TAKING A VACATION?
SHE DID MENTION SOMETHING ABOUT GOING TO THE UNDERWORLD—
THE WHAT?!
BUT ALL THE HOLES ARE CLOSED... RIGHT?
AND YOU DIDN'T CHECK JUST TO BE SURE?

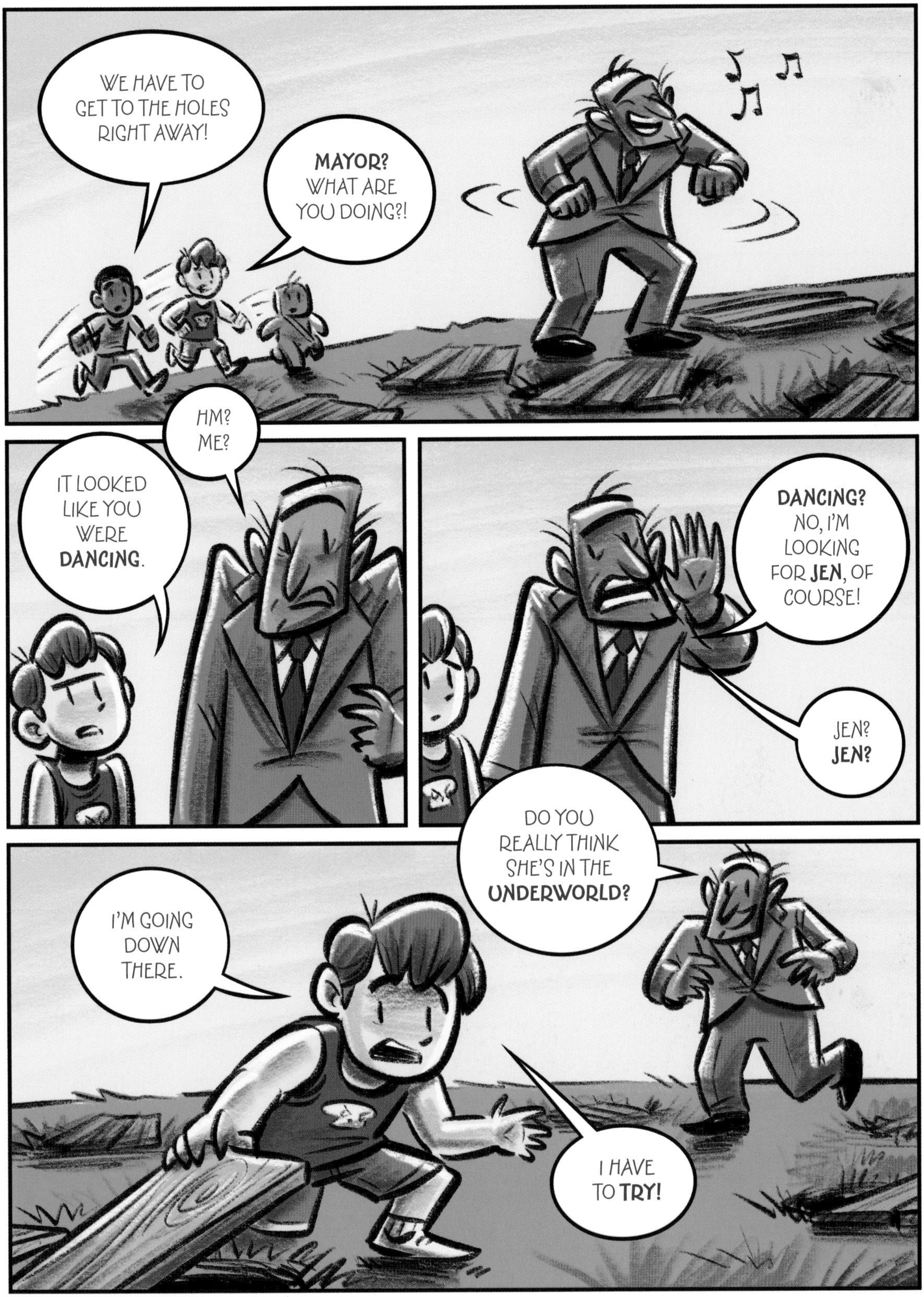
WE HAVE TO GET TO THE HOLES RIGHT AWAY!
MAYOR? WHAT ARE YOU DOING?!
HM? ME?
IT LOOKED LIKE YOU WERE **DANCING**.
DANCING? NO, I'M LOOKING FOR **JEN**, OF COURSE!
JEN? **JEN?**
DO YOU REALLY THINK SHE'S IN THE **UNDERWORLD?**
I'M GOING DOWN THERE.
I HAVE TO **TRY!**

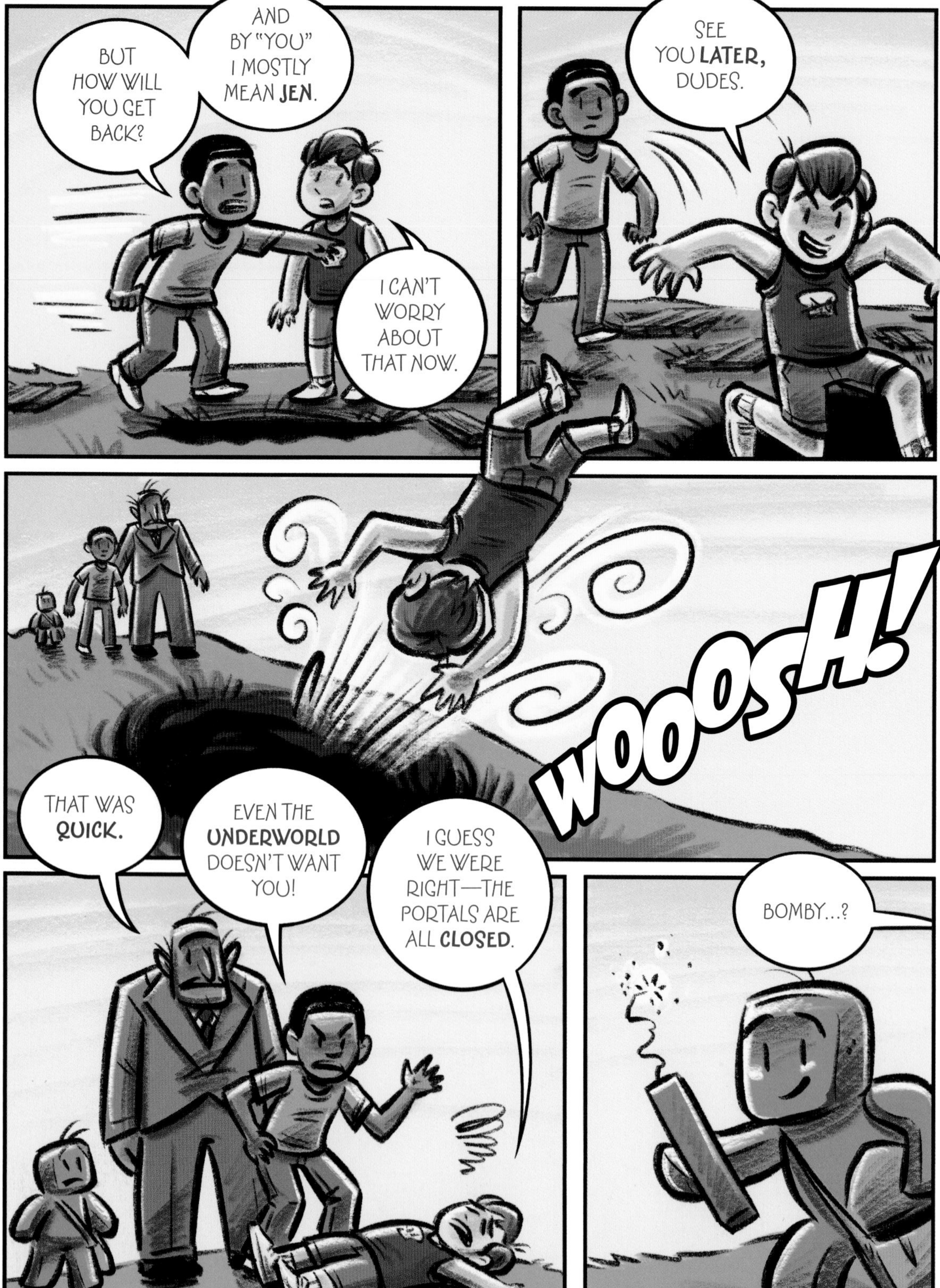

BUT HOW WILL YOU GET BACK?
AND BY "YOU" I MOSTLY MEAN **JEN**.
I CAN'T WORRY ABOUT THAT NOW.
SEE YOU **LATER,** DUDES.
WOOOSH!
THAT WAS **QUICK.**
EVEN THE **UNDERWORLD** DOESN'T WANT YOU!
I GUESS WE WERE RIGHT—THE PORTALS ARE ALL **CLOSED**.
BOMBY...?

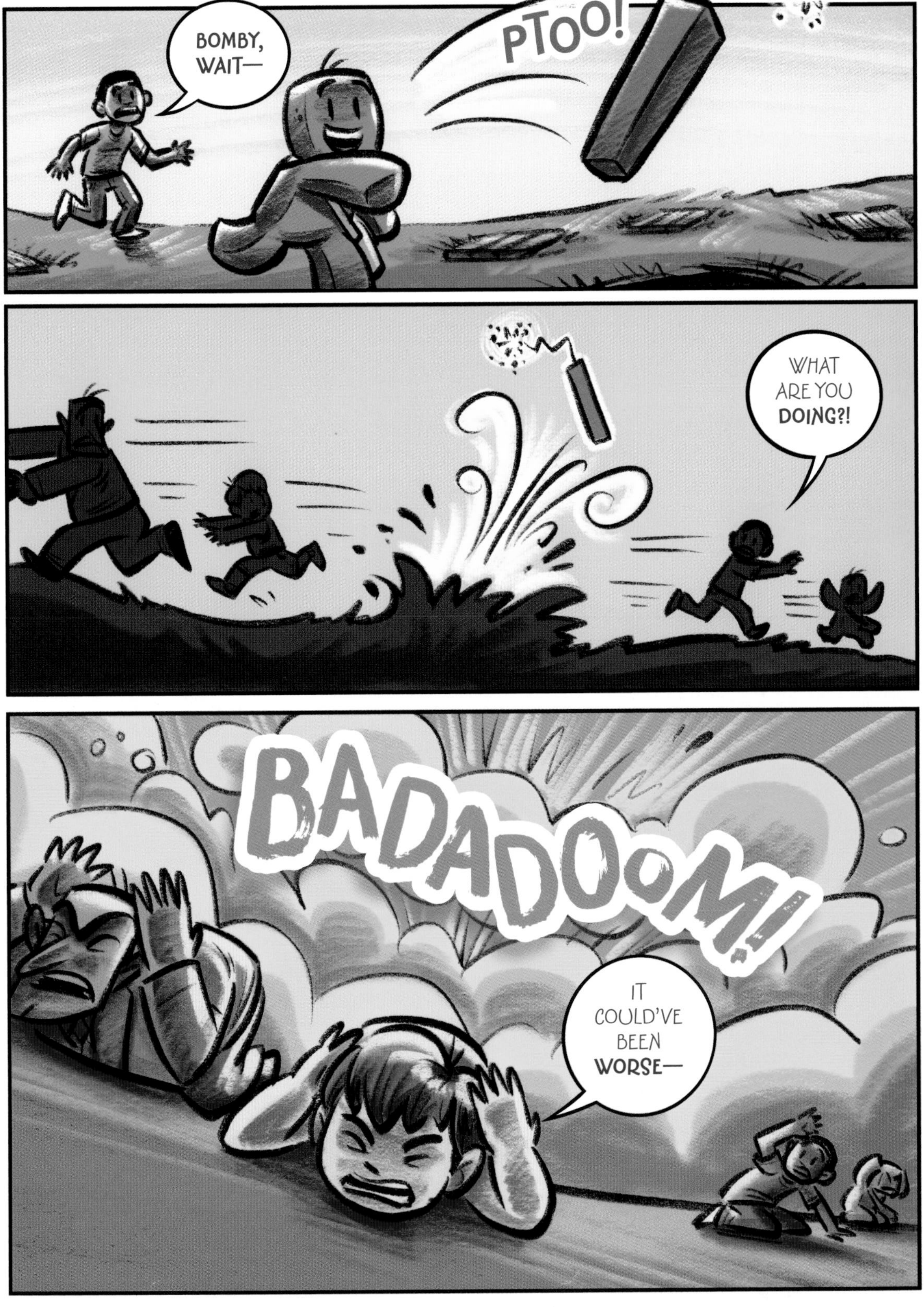
BOMBY, WAIT—
PTOO!
WHAT ARE YOU **DOING?!**
BADADOOM!
IT COULD'VE BEEN **WORSE**—

"—HE COULD'VE TRIED THE **BIG KAHUNA**!"

YOU—

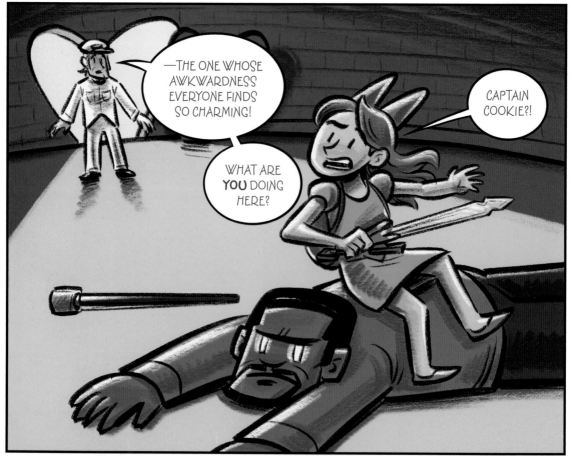

—THE ONE WHOSE AWKWARDNESS EVERYONE FINDS SO CHARMING!

WHAT ARE **YOU** DOING HERE?

CAPTAIN COOKIE?!

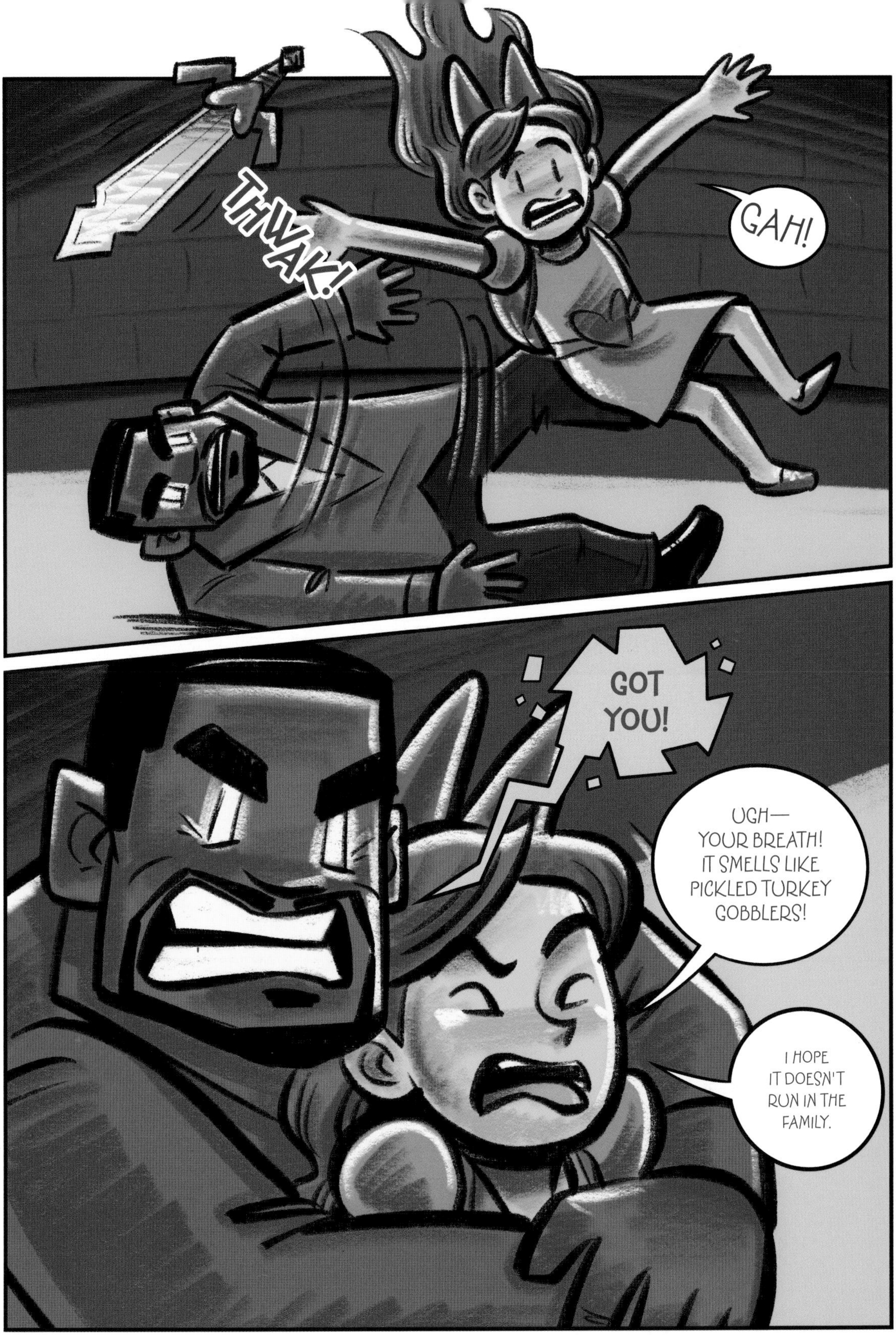
THWAK!
GAH!
GOT YOU!
UGH— YOUR BREATH! IT SMELLS LIKE PICKLED TURKEY GOBBLERS!
I HOPE IT DOESN'T RUN IN THE FAMILY.

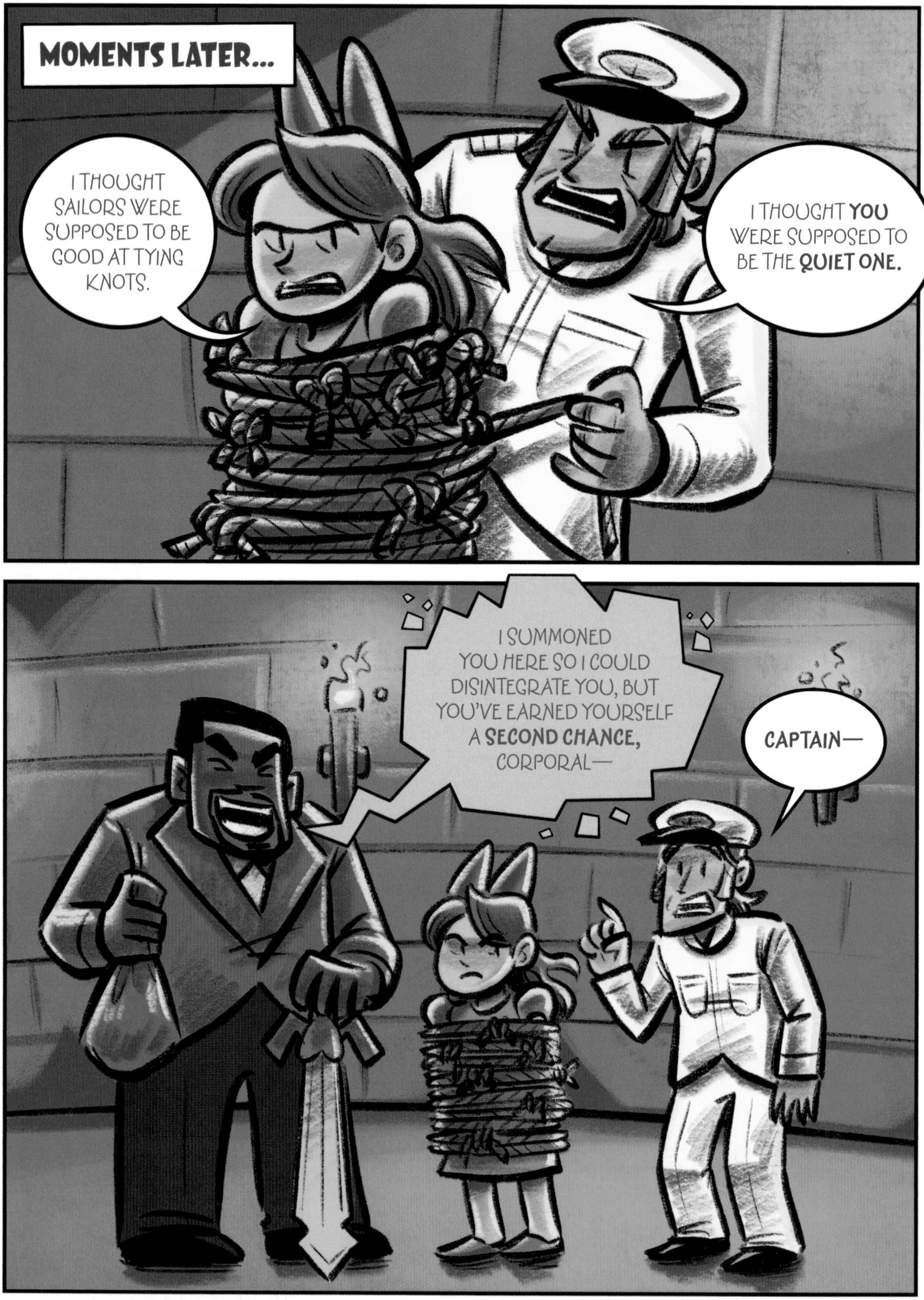
MOMENTS LATER...
I THOUGHT SAILORS WERE SUPPOSED TO BE GOOD AT TYING KNOTS.
I THOUGHT YOU WERE SUPPOSED TO BE THE QUIET ONE.
I SUMMONED YOU HERE SO I COULD DISINTEGRATE YOU, BUT YOU'VE EARNED YOURSELF A SECOND CHANCE, CORPORAL—
CAPTAIN—

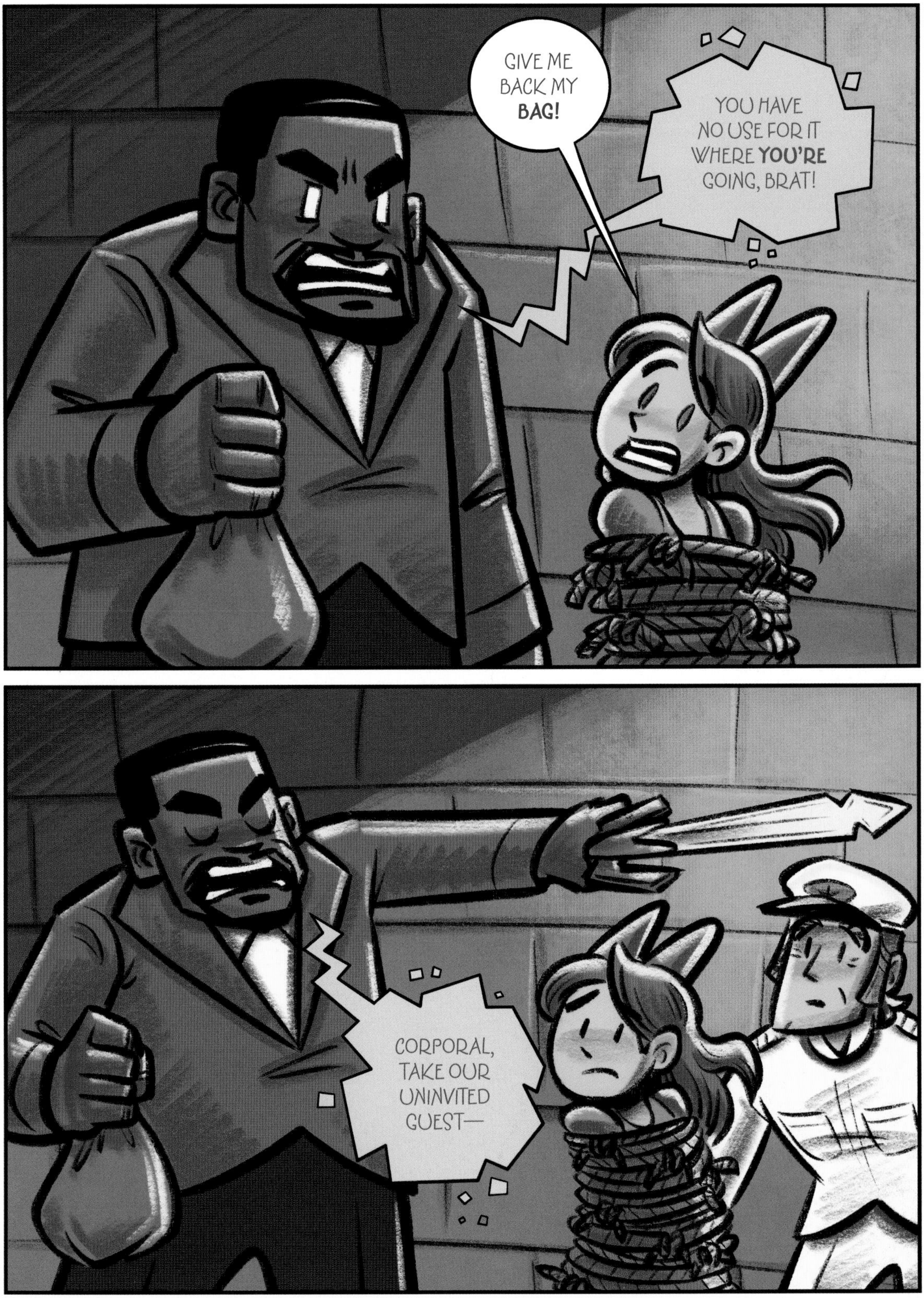
GIVE ME BACK MY **BAG!**
YOU HAVE NO USE FOR IT WHERE **YOU'RE** GOING, BRAT!
CORPORAL, TAKE OUR UNINVITED GUEST—

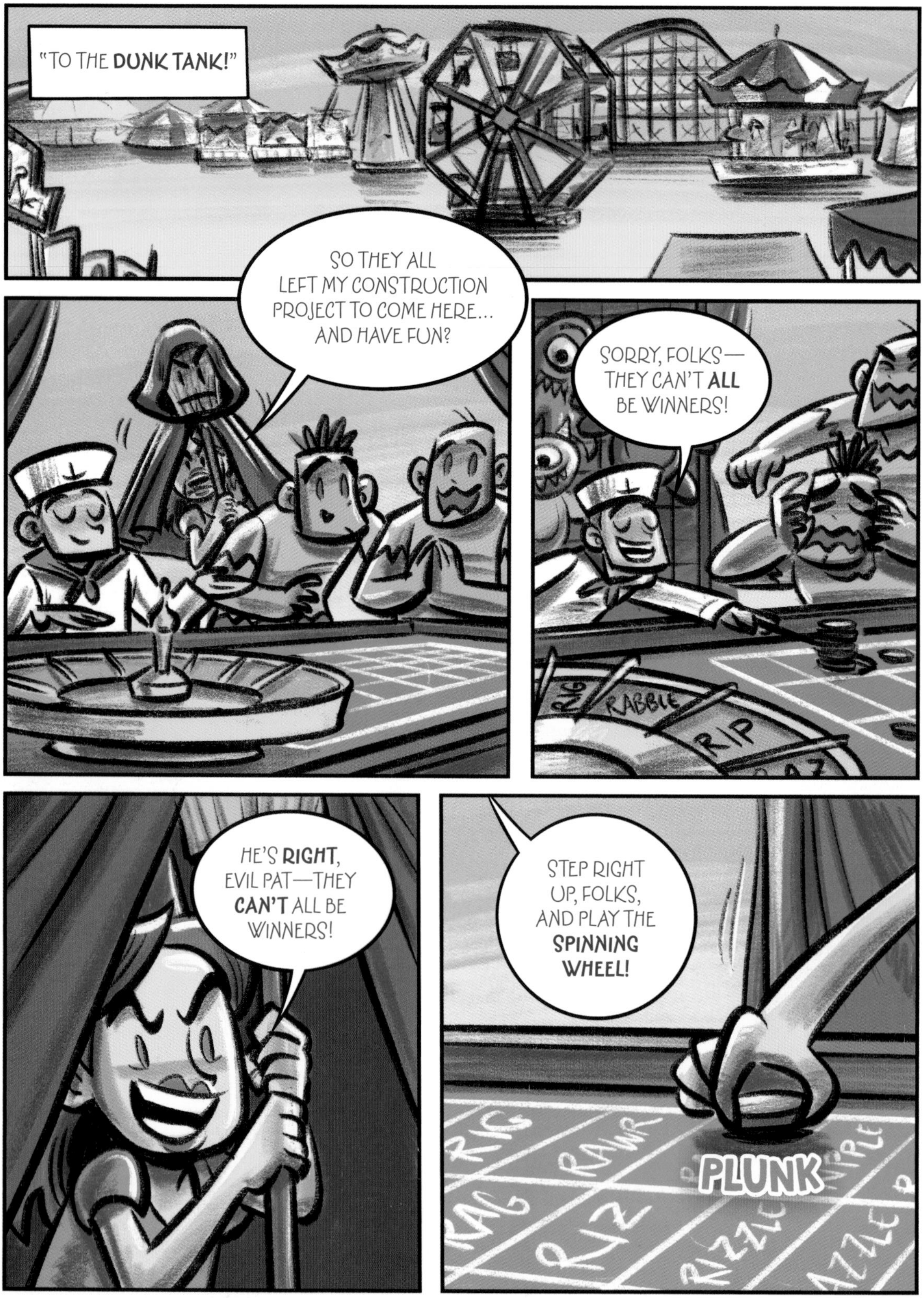
"TO THE **DUNK TANK!**"
SO THEY ALL LEFT MY CONSTRUCTION PROJECT TO COME HERE... AND HAVE FUN?
SORRY, FOLKS—THEY CAN'T **ALL** BE WINNERS!
RIG
RABBLE
RIP
HE'S **RIGHT**, EVIL PAT—THEY **CAN'T** ALL BE WINNERS!
STEP RIGHT UP, FOLKS, AND PLAY THE **SPINNING WHEEL!**
RIG
RAWR
RAG
RIZ
PLUNK

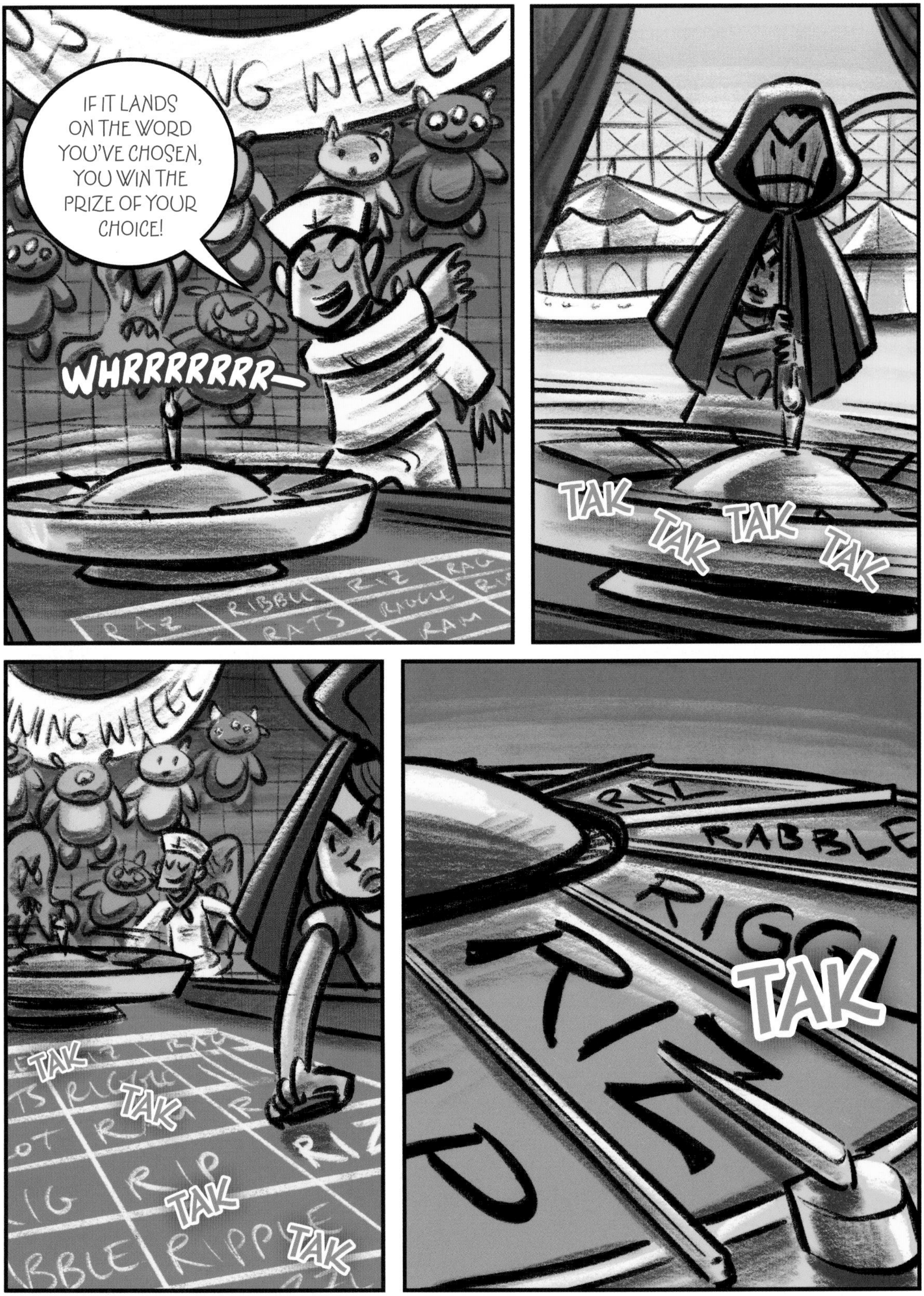
IF IT LANDS ON THE WORD YOU'VE CHOSEN, YOU WIN THE PRIZE OF YOUR CHOICE!
WHRRRRRRR—
TAK
TAK
TAK
TAK
TAK
TAK
TAK
TAK
RAZ
RABBLE
TAK

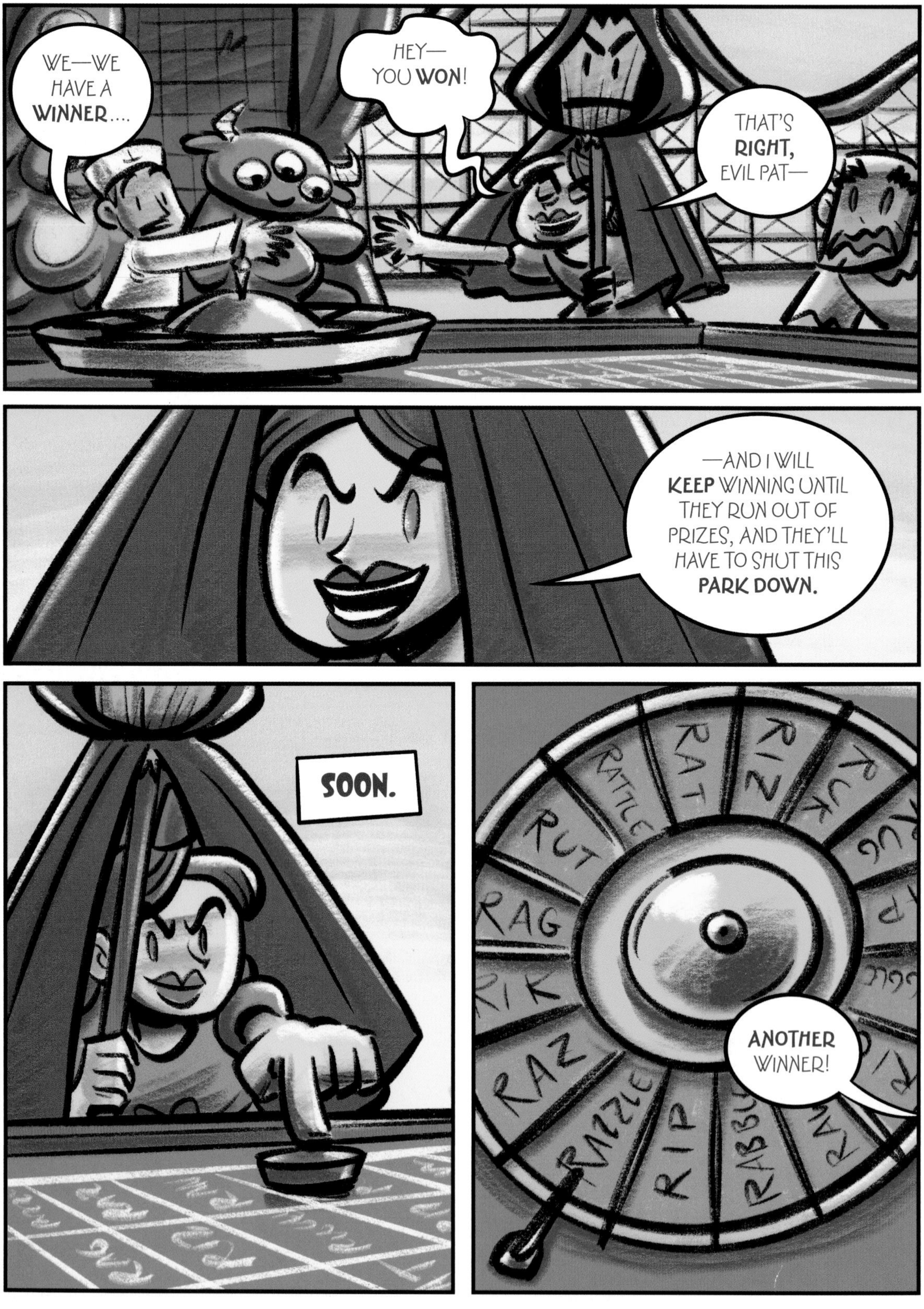

WE—WE HAVE A **WINNER**....
HEY— YOU **WON**!
THAT'S **RIGHT,** EVIL PAT—
—AND I WILL **KEEP** WINNING UNTIL THEY RUN OUT OF PRIZES, AND THEY'LL HAVE TO SHUT THIS **PARK DOWN.**
SOON.
RUT
RATTLE
RAT
RIZ
RUK
RAG
RIK
RAZ
RIP
ANOTHER WINNER!

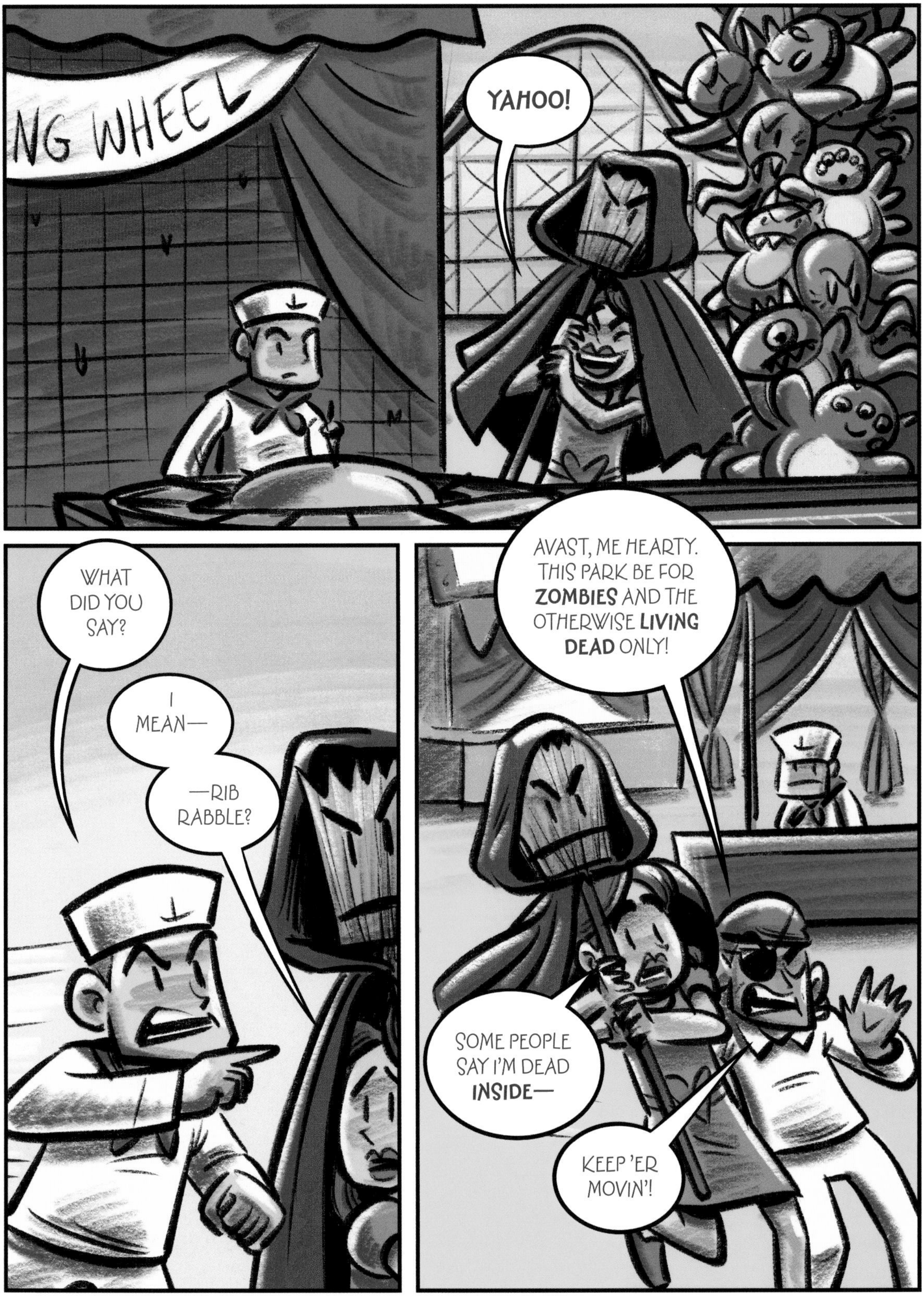
NG WHEEL
YAHOO!
WHAT DID YOU SAY?
I MEAN—
—RIB RABBLE?
AVAST, ME HEARTY. THIS PARK BE FOR ZOMBIES AND THE OTHERWISE LIVING DEAD ONLY!
SOME PEOPLE SAY I'M DEAD INSIDE—
KEEP 'ER MOVIN'!

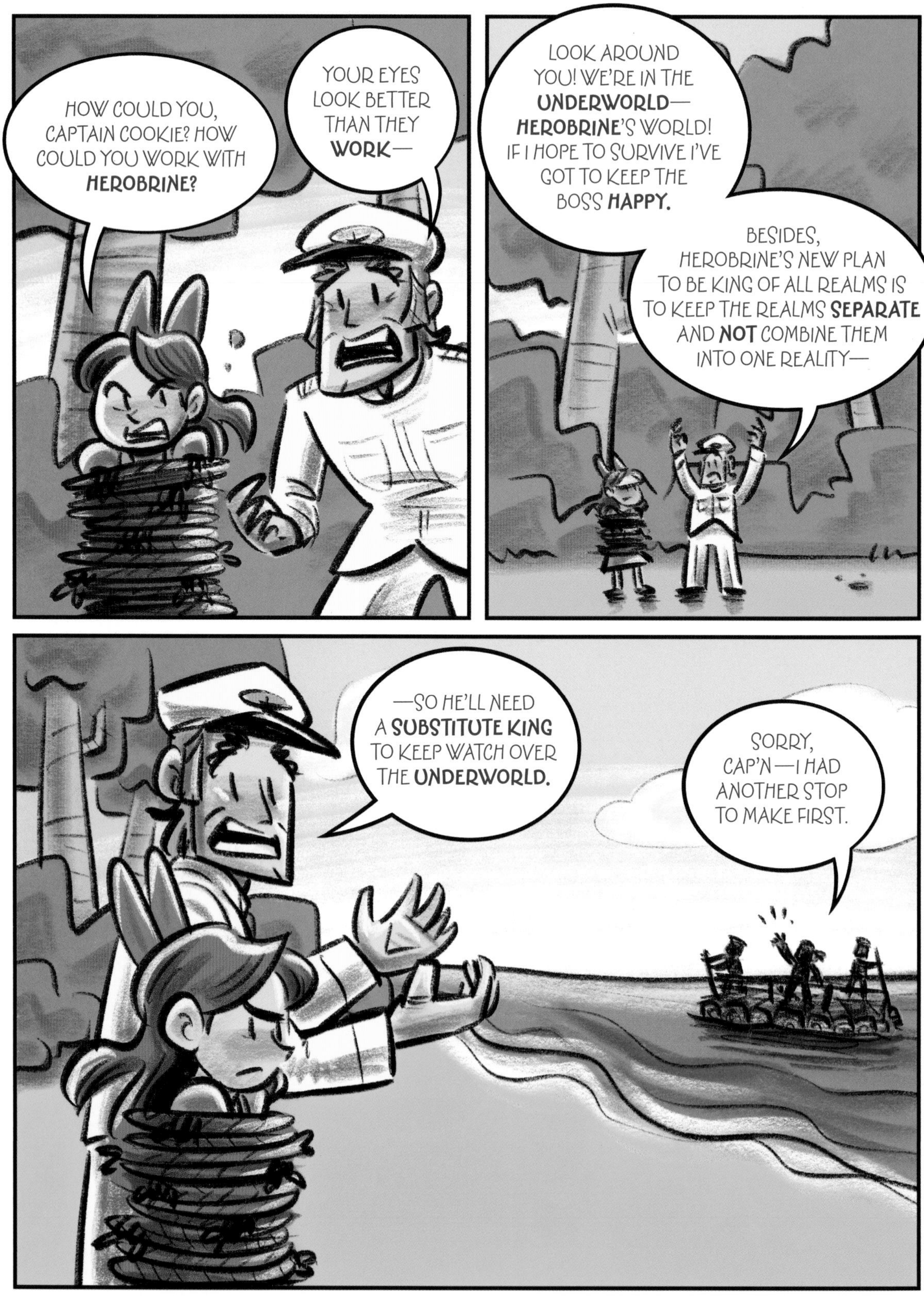

HOW COULD YOU, CAPTAIN COOKIE? HOW COULD YOU WORK WITH **HEROBRINE?**
YOUR EYES LOOK BETTER THAN THEY **WORK**—
LOOK AROUND YOU! WE'RE IN THE **UNDERWORLD**—**HEROBRINE**'S WORLD! IF I HOPE TO SURVIVE I'VE GOT TO KEEP THE BOSS **HAPPY.**
BESIDES, HEROBRINE'S NEW PLAN TO BE KING OF ALL REALMS IS TO KEEP THE REALMS **SEPARATE** AND **NOT** COMBINE THEM INTO ONE REALITY—
—SO HE'LL NEED A **SUBSTITUTE KING** TO KEEP WATCH OVER THE **UNDERWORLD.**
SORRY, CAP'N—I HAD ANOTHER STOP TO MAKE FIRST.

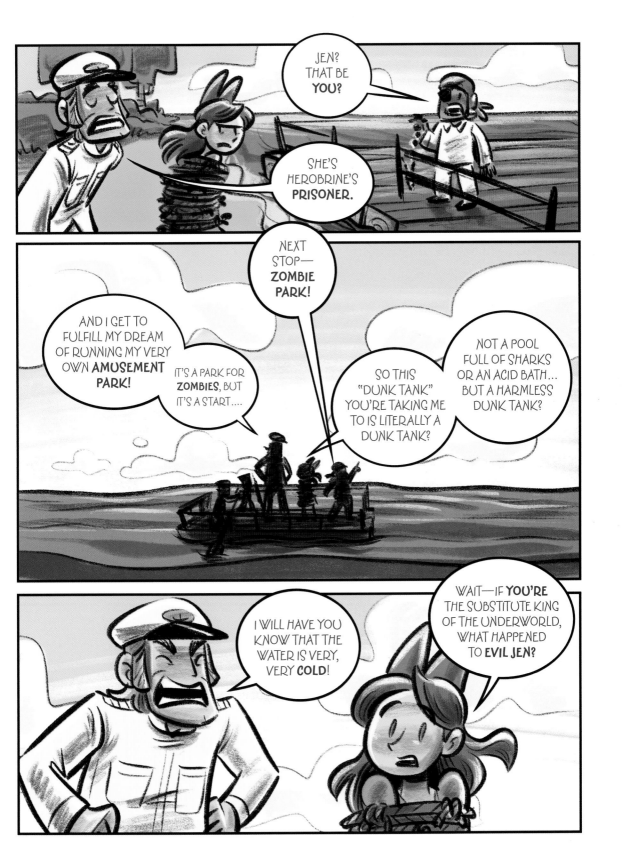

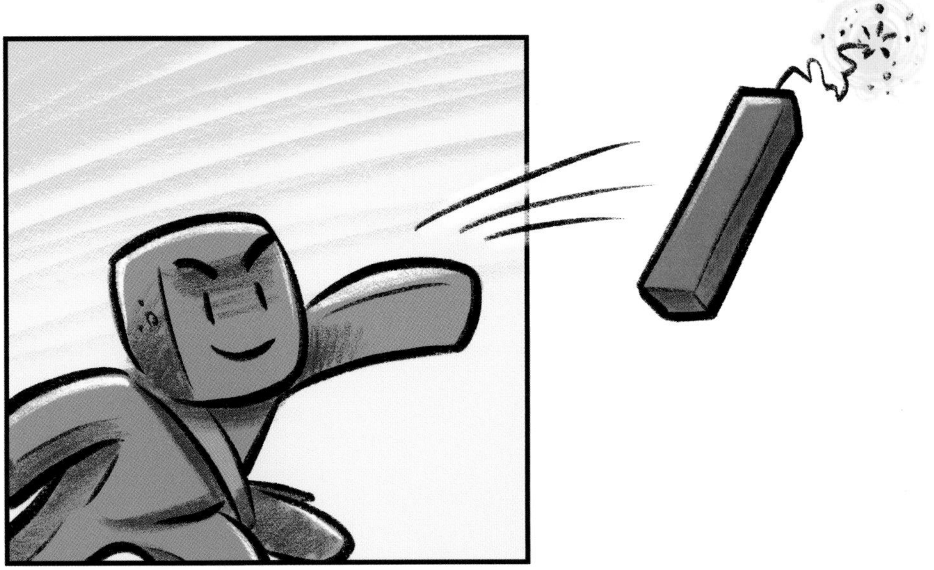

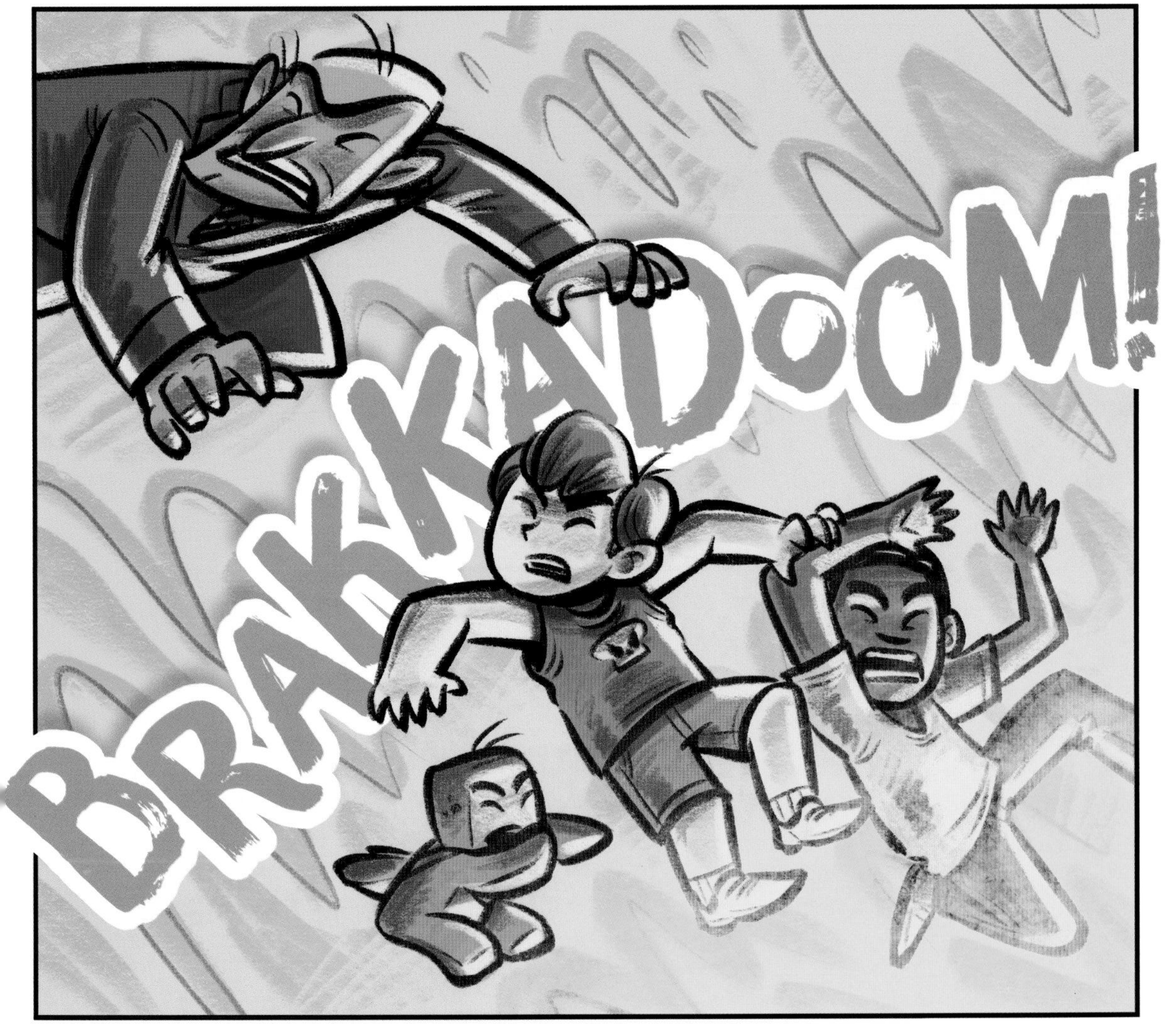
BRAKKADOOM!

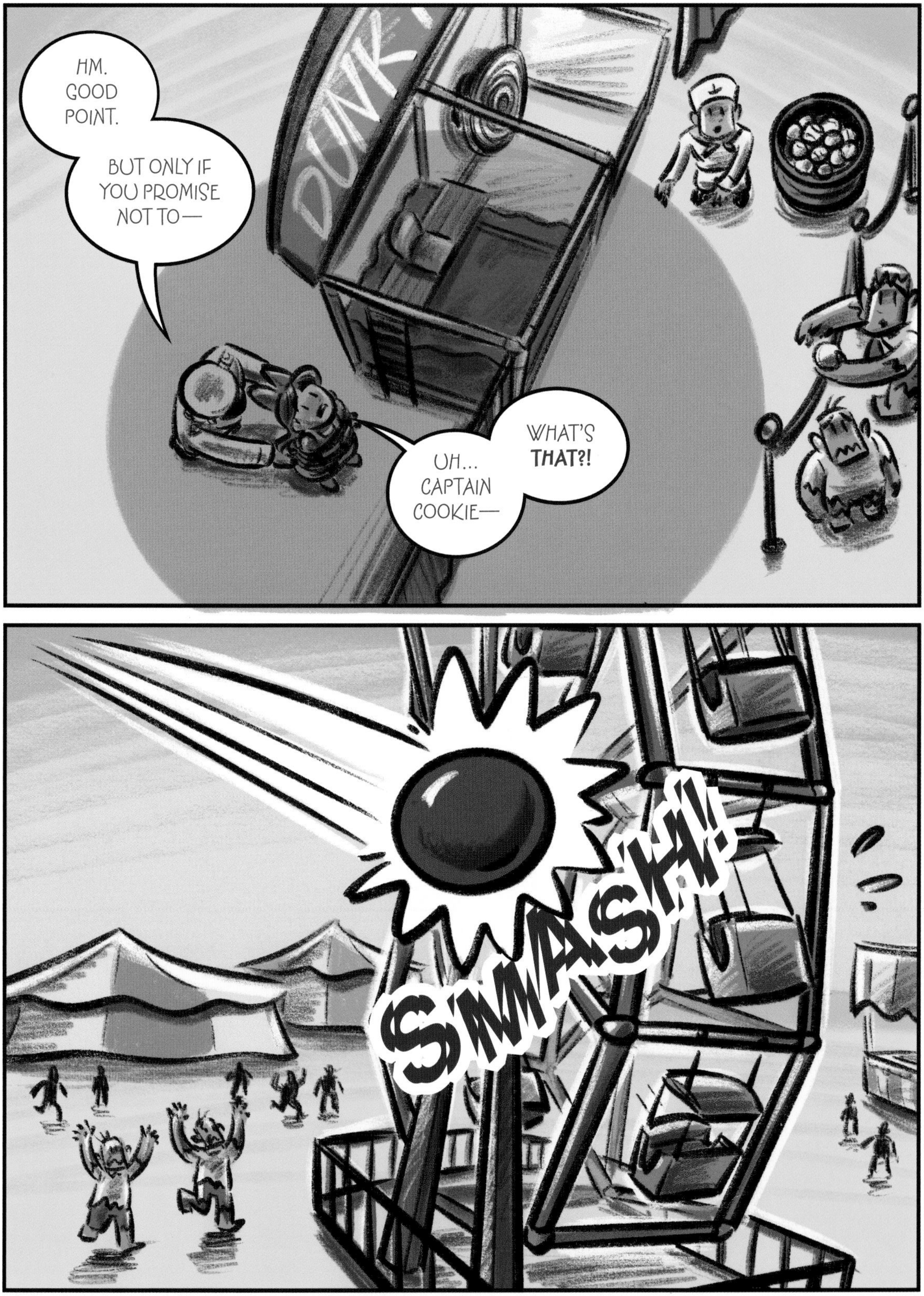
HM. GOOD POINT.
BUT ONLY IF YOU PROMISE NOT TO—
UH... CAPTAIN COOKIE—
WHAT'S THAT?!
SMASH!!

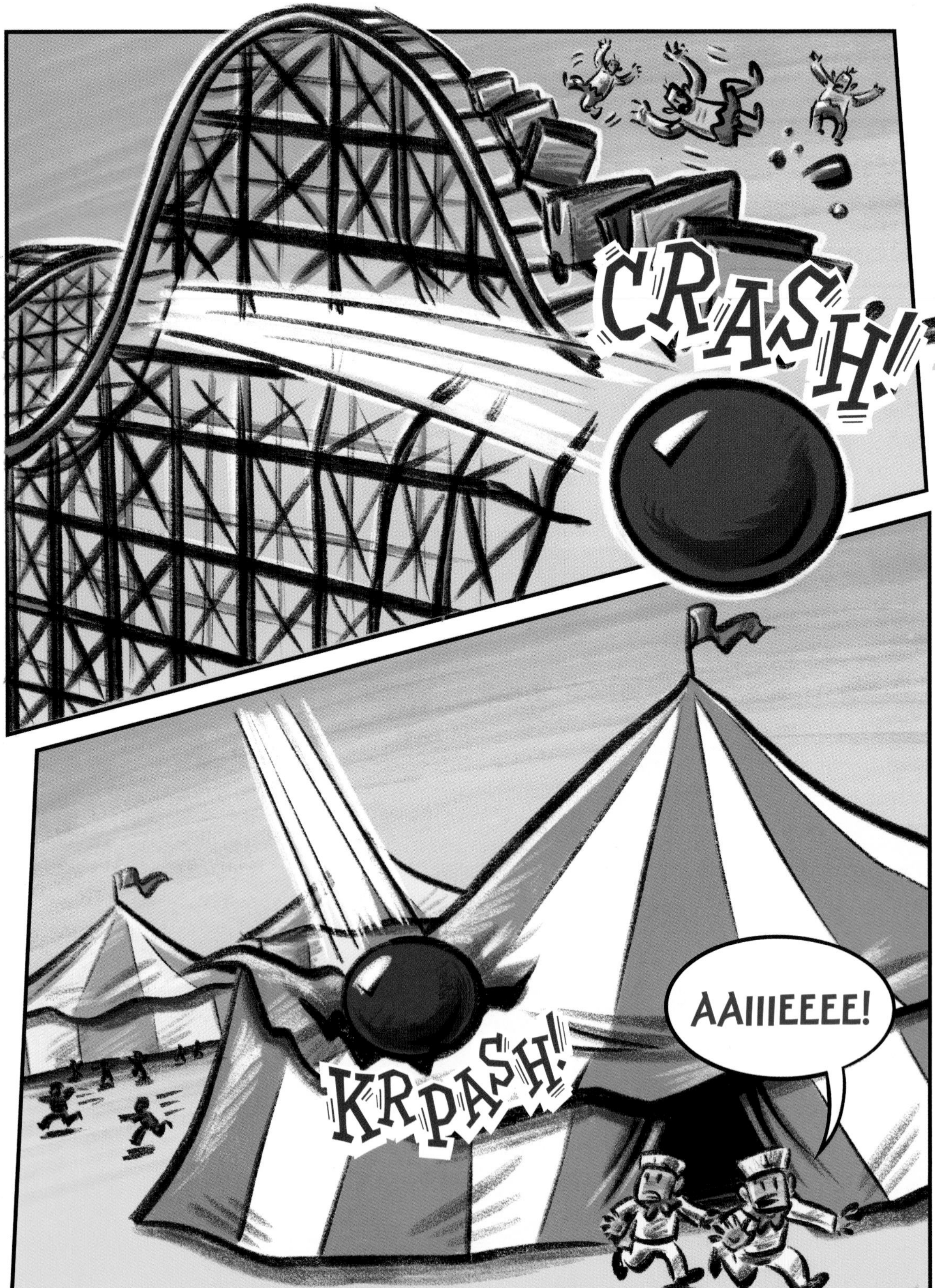
CRASH!
KRPASH!
AAIIIEEEE!

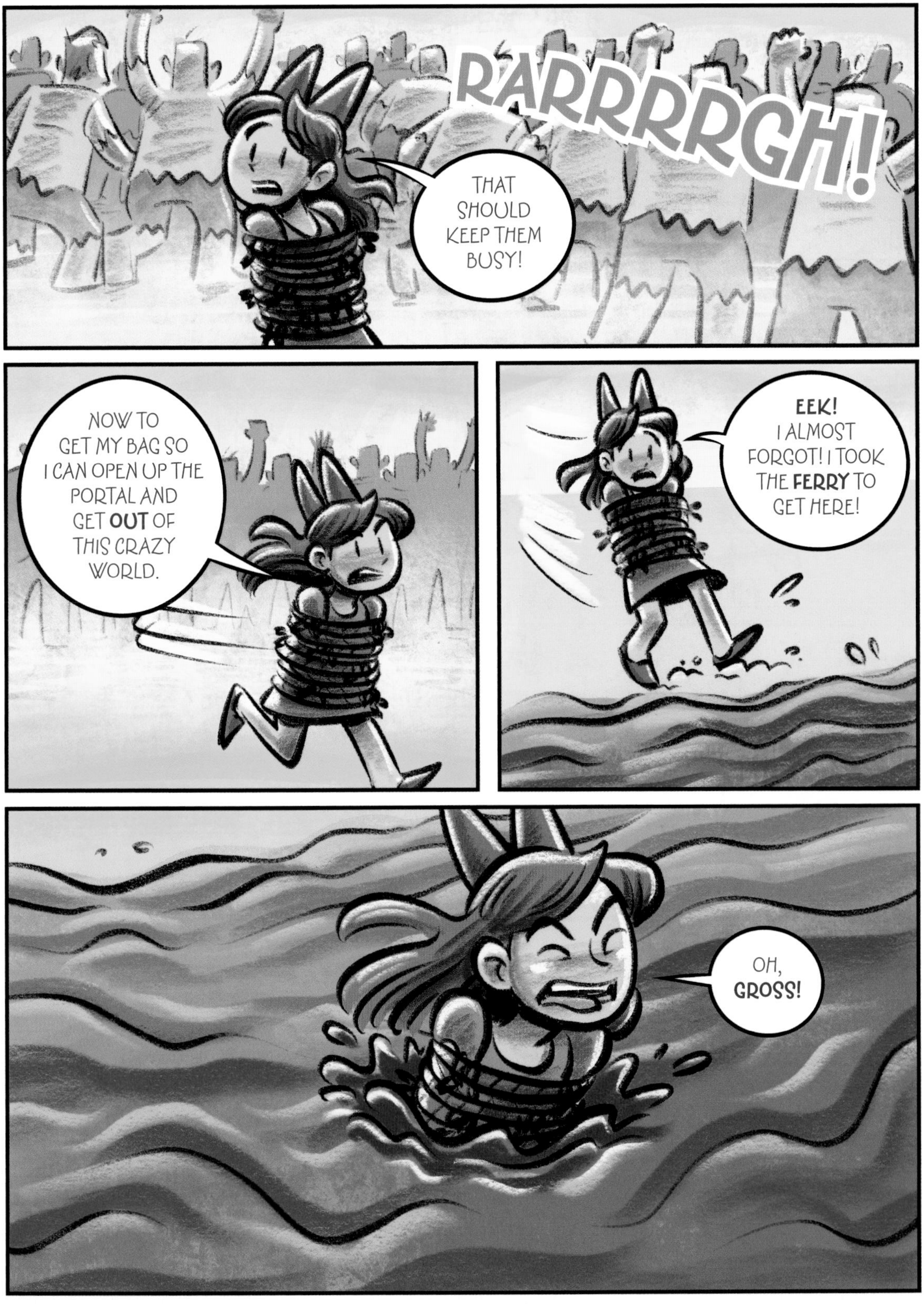
RARRRRGH!
THAT SHOULD KEEP THEM BUSY!
NOW TO GET MY BAG SO I CAN OPEN UP THE PORTAL AND GET OUT OF THIS CRAZY WORLD.
EEK! I ALMOST FORGOT! I TOOK THE FERRY TO GET HERE!
OH, GROSS!

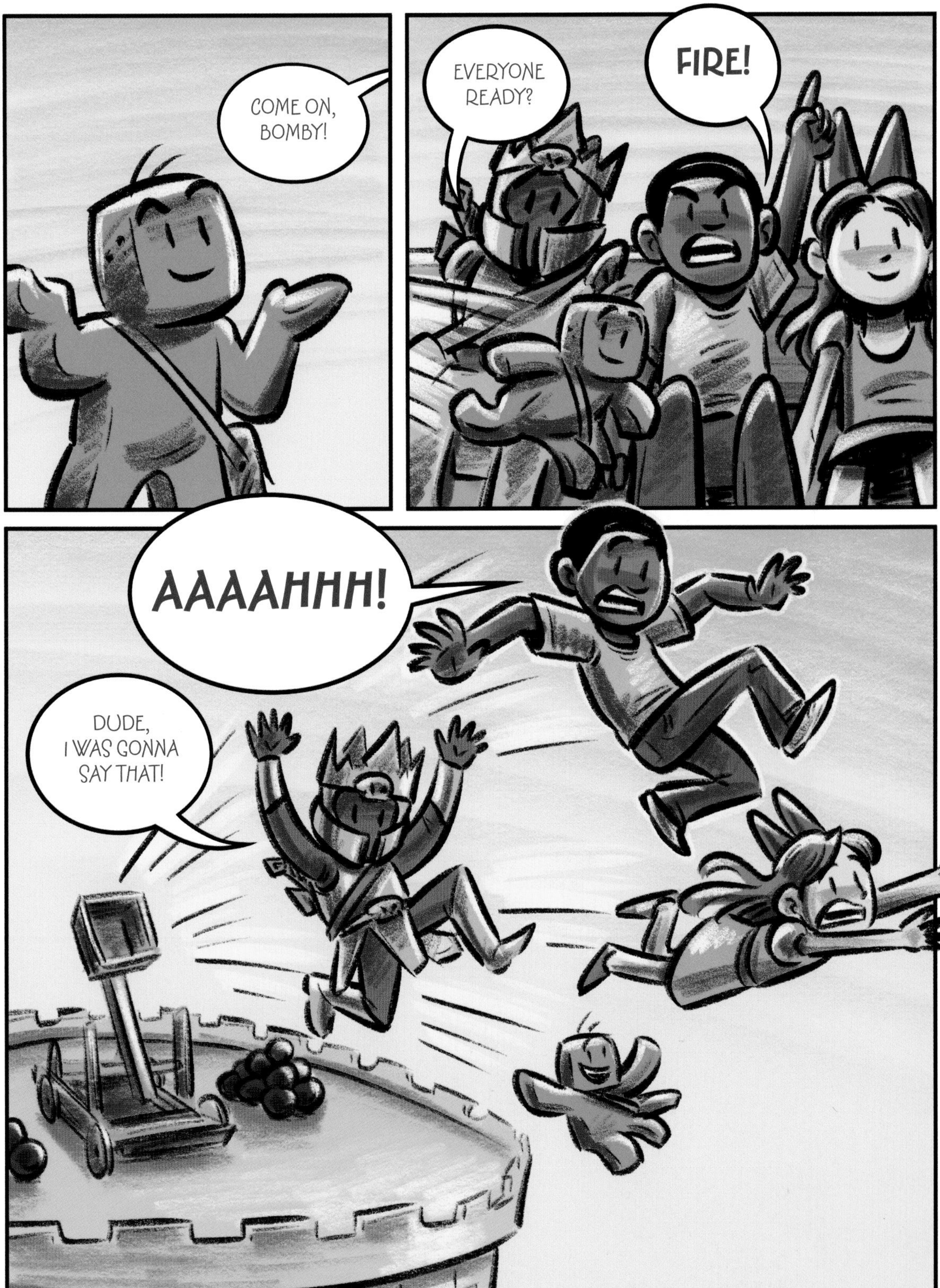
COME ON, BOMBY!
EVERYONE READY?
FIRE!
AAAAHHH!
DUDE, I WAS GONNA SAY THAT!

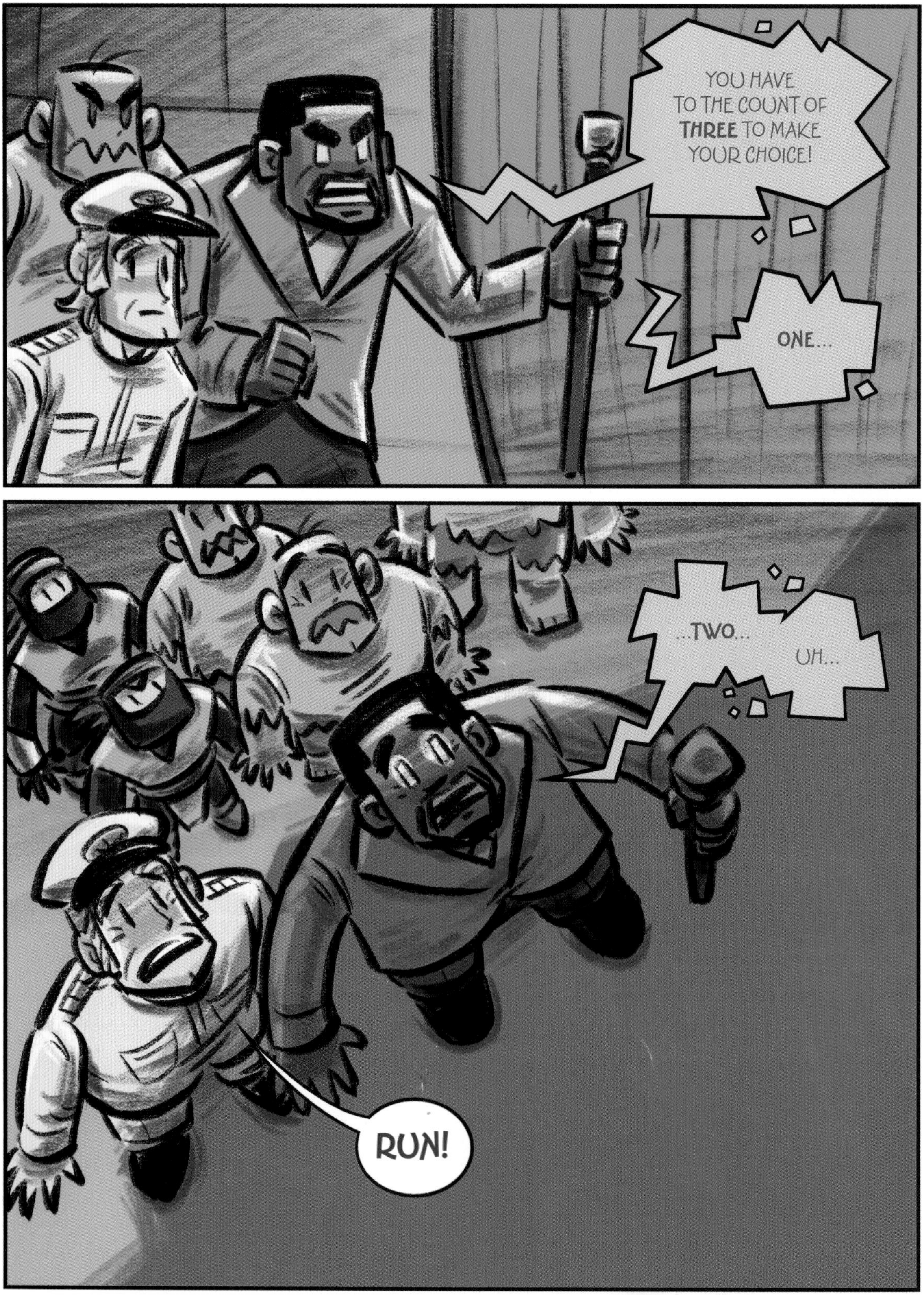
YOU HAVE TO THE COUNT OF **THREE** TO MAKE YOUR CHOICE!
ONE...
...TWO...
UH...
RUN!

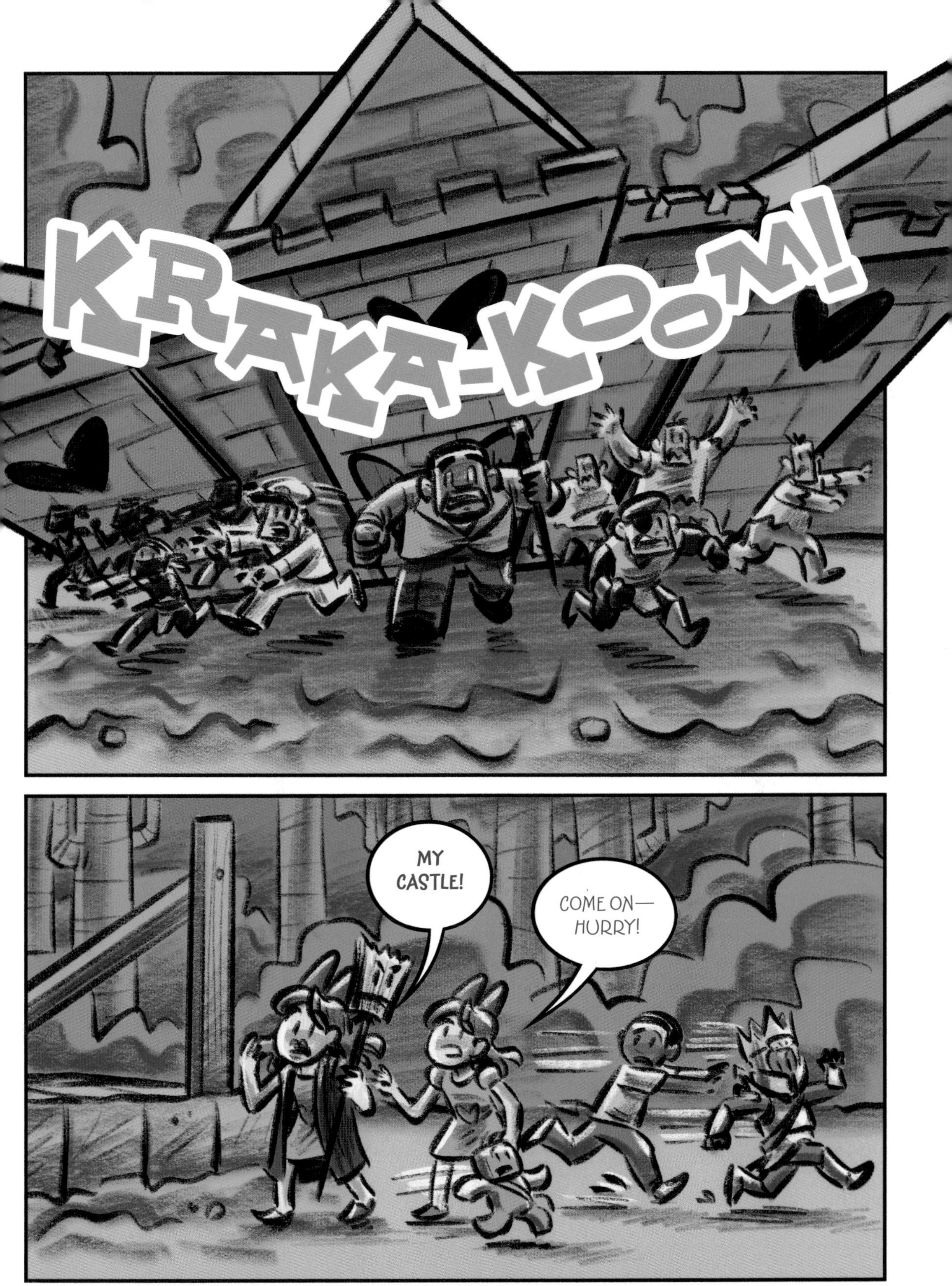
KRAKA-KOOM!
MY CASTLE!
COME ON—HURRY!

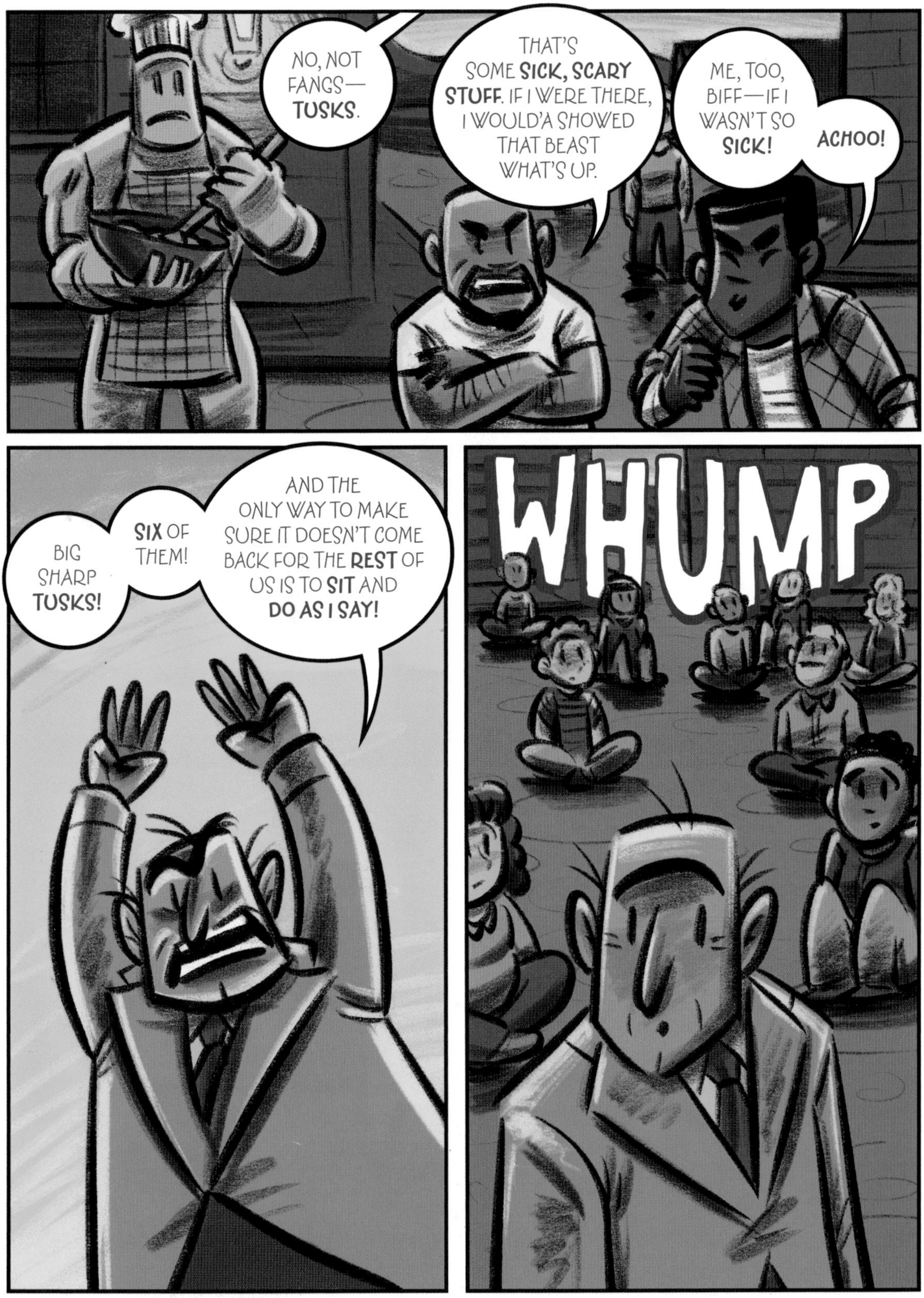
NO, NOT FANGS— TUSKS.
THAT'S SOME SICK, SCARY STUFF. IF I WERE THERE, I WOULD'A SHOWED THAT BEAST WHAT'S UP.
ME, TOO, BIFF—IF I WASN'T SO SICK!
ACHOO!
BIG SHARP TUSKS!
SIX OF THEM!
AND THE ONLY WAY TO MAKE SURE IT DOESN'T COME BACK FOR THE REST OF US IS TO SIT AND DO AS I SAY!
WHUMP

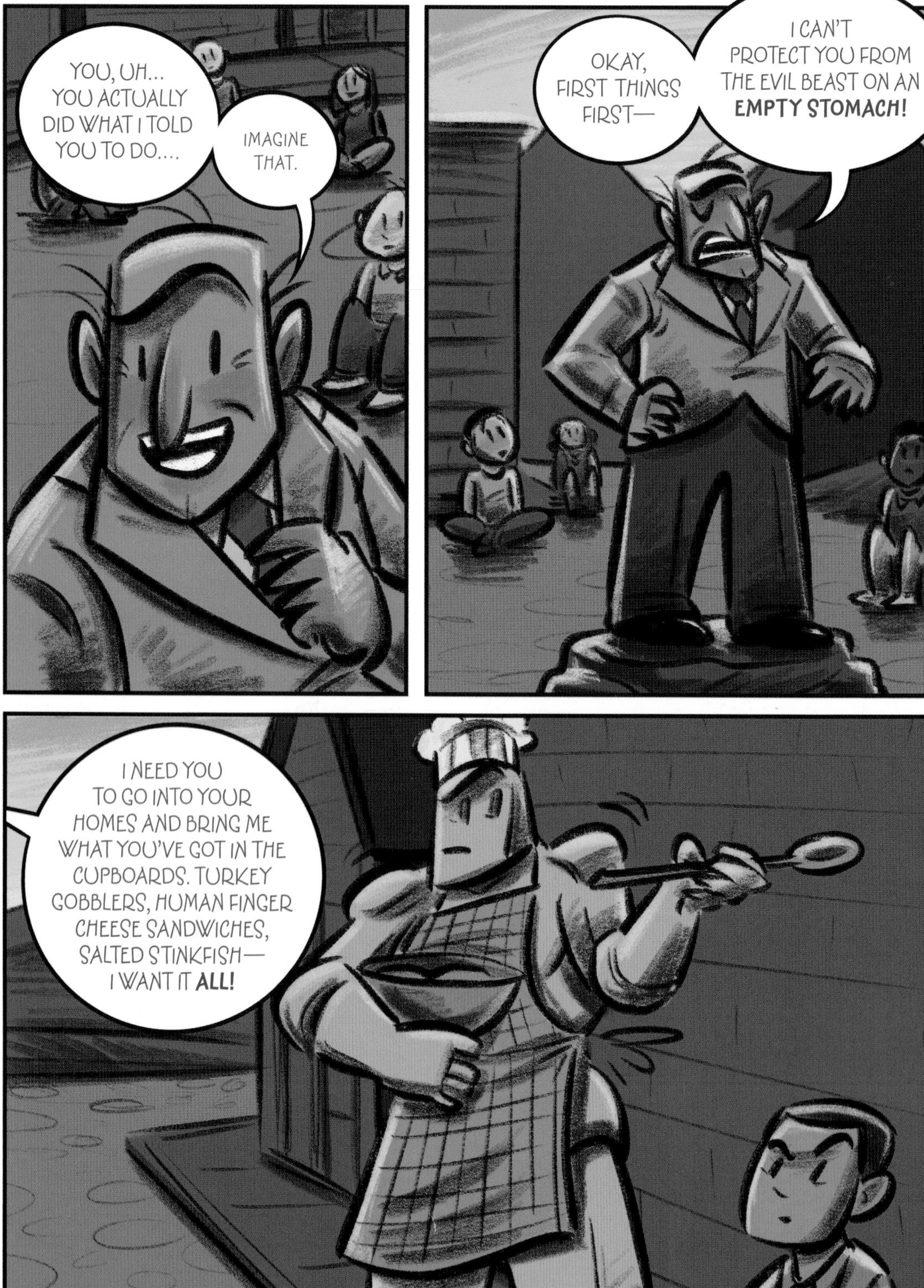
YOU, UH... YOU ACTUALLY DID WHAT I TOLD YOU TO DO....
IMAGINE THAT.
OKAY, FIRST THINGS FIRST—
I CAN'T PROTECT YOU FROM THE EVIL BEAST ON AN EMPTY STOMACH!
I NEED YOU TO GO INTO YOUR HOMES AND BRING ME WHAT YOU'VE GOT IN THE CUPBOARDS. TURKEY GOBBLERS, HUMAN FINGER CHEESE SANDWICHES, SALTED STINKFISH— I WANT IT ALL!

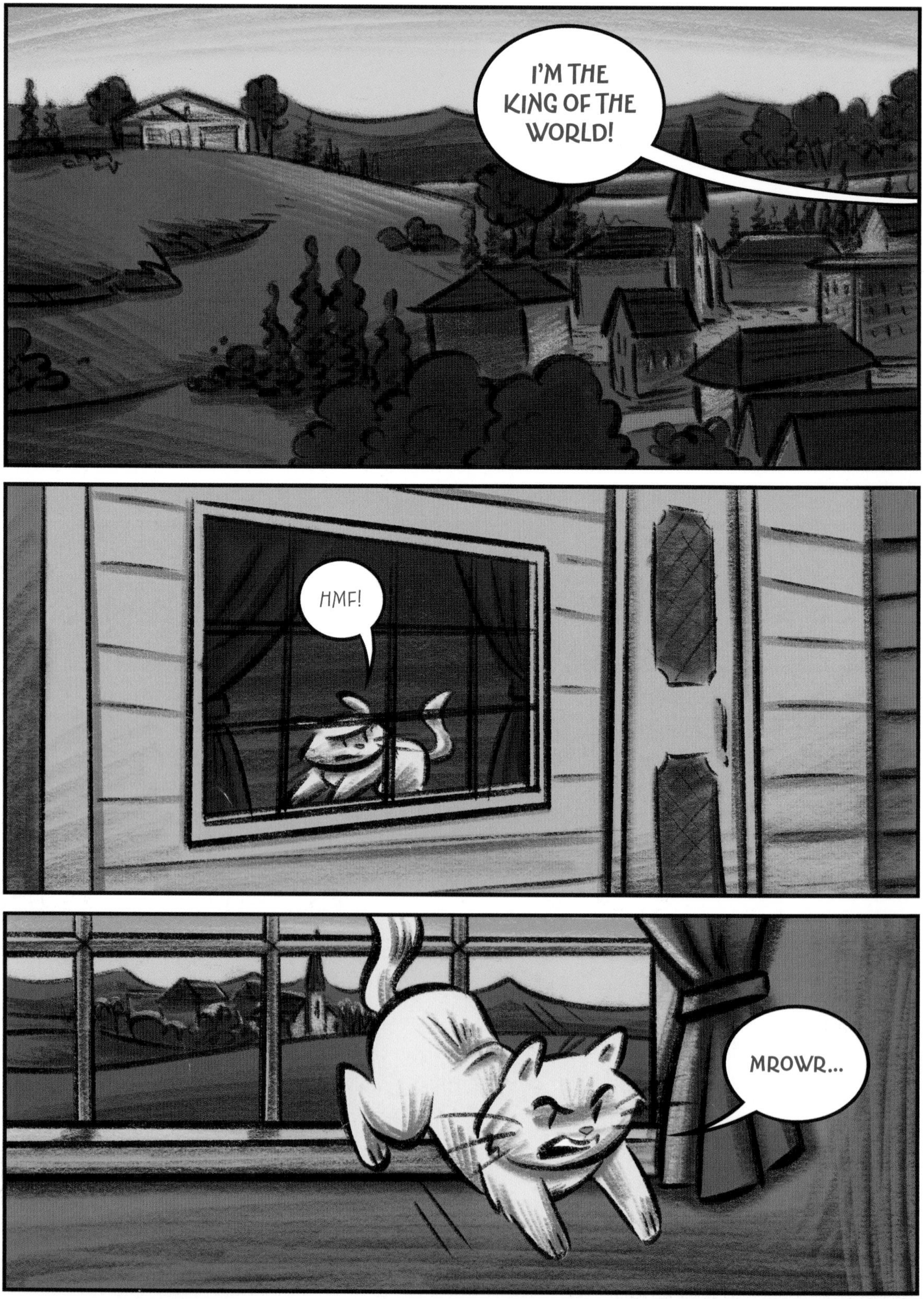
I'M THE KING OF THE WORLD!
HMF!
MROWR...

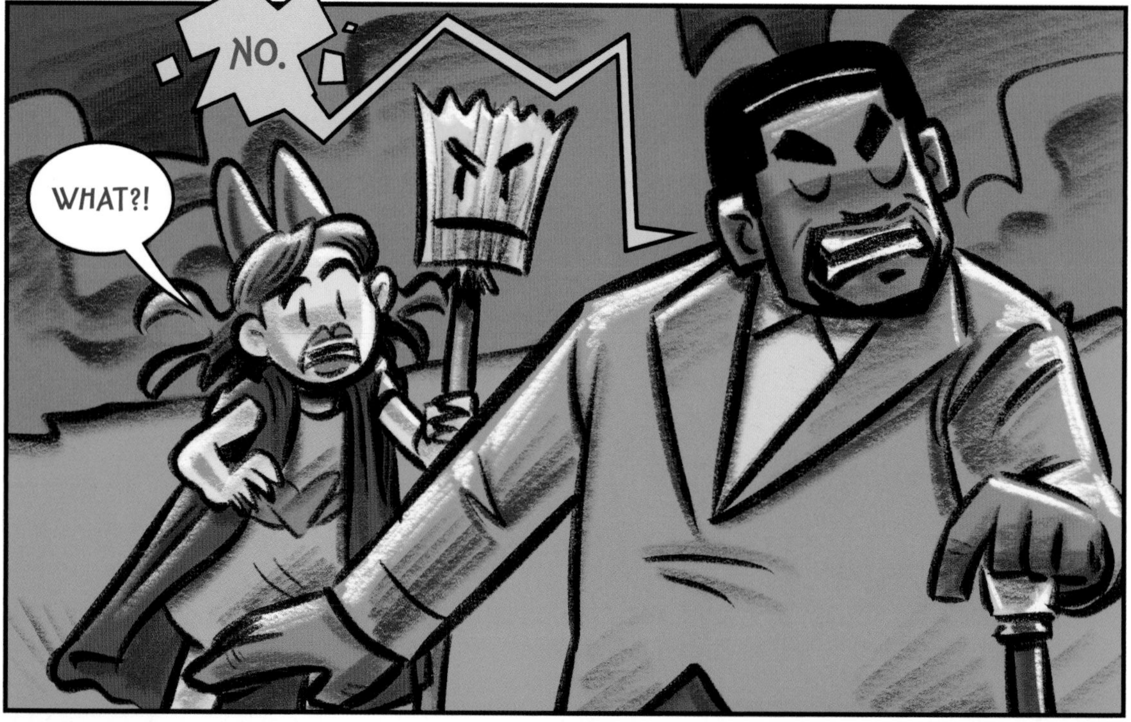
NO.
WHAT?!
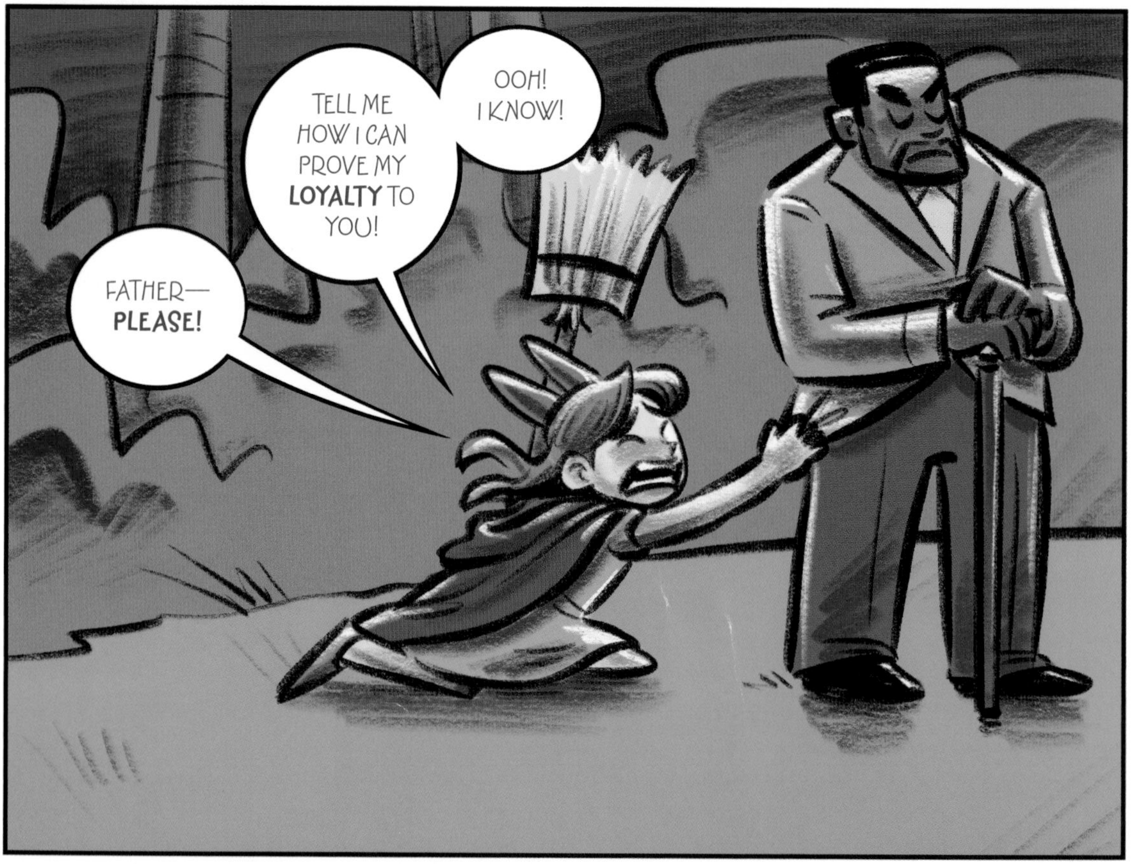
FATHER—
PLEASE!
TELL ME HOW I CAN PROVE MY LOYALTY TO YOU!
OOH! I KNOW!

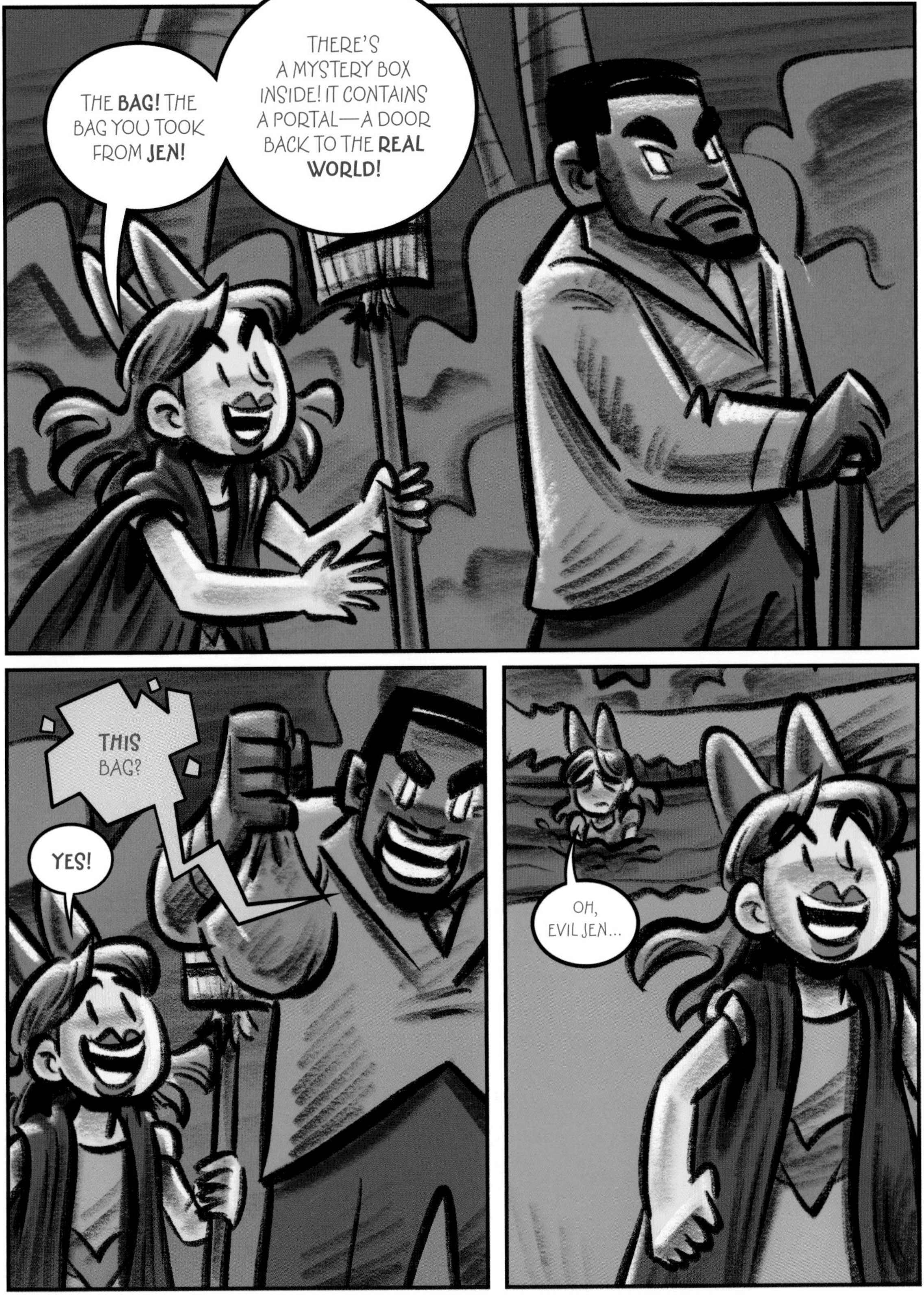
THE **BAG!** THE BAG YOU TOOK FROM **JEN!**
THERE'S A MYSTERY BOX INSIDE! IT CONTAINS A PORTAL—A DOOR BACK TO THE **REAL WORLD!**
THIS BAG?
YES!
OH, EVIL JEN...

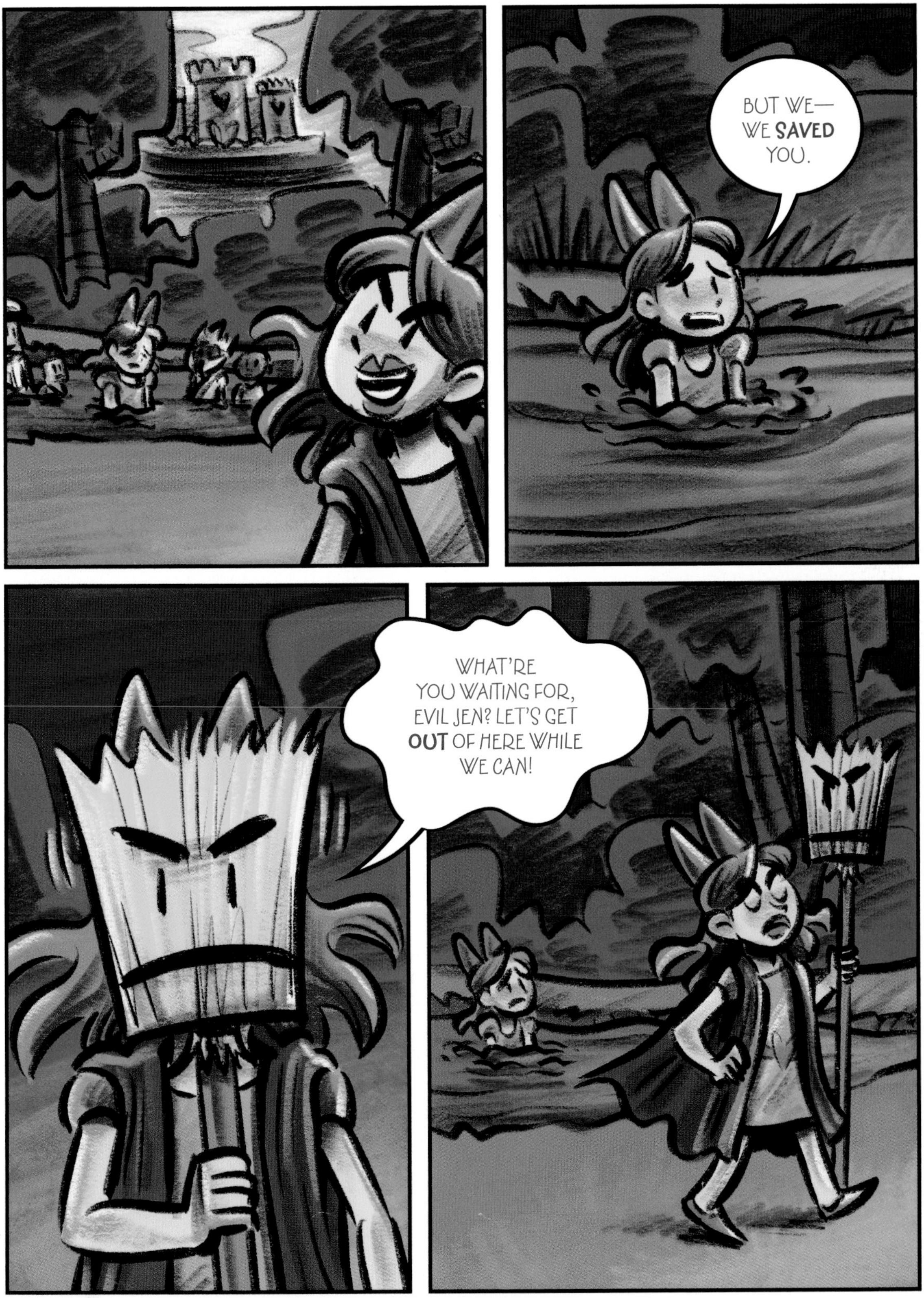
BUT WE—
WE **SAVED**
YOU.
WHAT'RE
YOU WAITING FOR,
EVIL JEN? LET'S GET
OUT OF HERE WHILE
WE CAN!

I CAME HERE TO SAVE EVIL JEN FROM OUR FATHER'S WORLD OF DARKNESS. FOR SO LONG I THOUGHT I HATED HER, BUT THE **TRUTH** IS I FELT **SORRY** FOR HER.

SHE'S NOT **EVIL**— SHE ONLY DOES EVIL **THINGS**...BECAUSE SHE'S **INSECURE**.

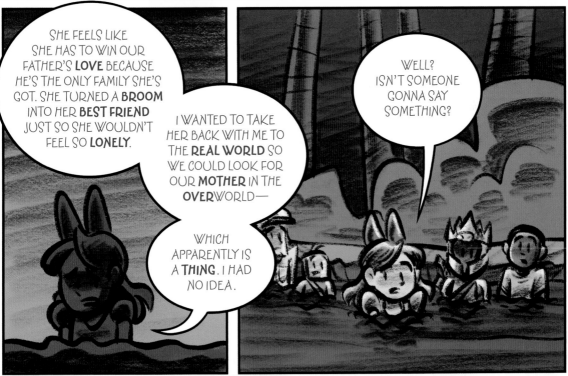

SHE FEELS LIKE SHE HAS TO WIN OUR FATHER'S **LOVE** BECAUSE HE'S THE ONLY FAMILY SHE'S GOT. SHE TURNED A **BROOM** INTO HER **BEST FRIEND** JUST SO SHE WOULDN'T FEEL SO **LONELY**.

I WANTED TO TAKE HER BACK WITH ME TO THE **REAL WORLD** SO WE COULD LOOK FOR OUR **MOTHER** IN THE **OVER**WORLD—

WHICH APPARENTLY IS A **THING**. I HAD NO IDEA.

WELL? ISN'T SOMEONE GONNA SAY SOMETHING?

NO WONDER YOU LOOK SO MUCH ALIKE....

WE—

DO **NOT** LOOK ALIKE!

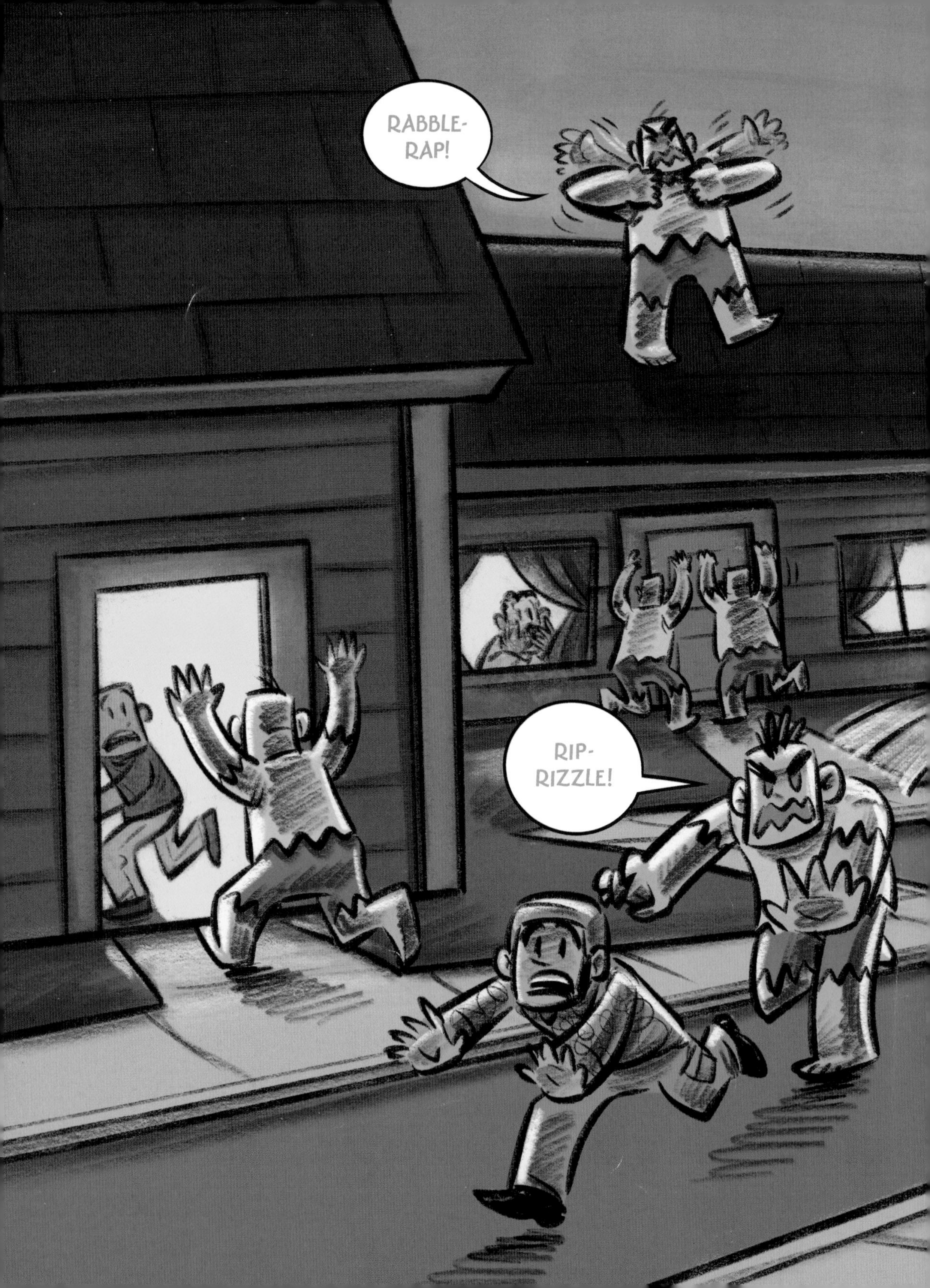
RABBLE-
RAP!
RIP-
RIZZLE!

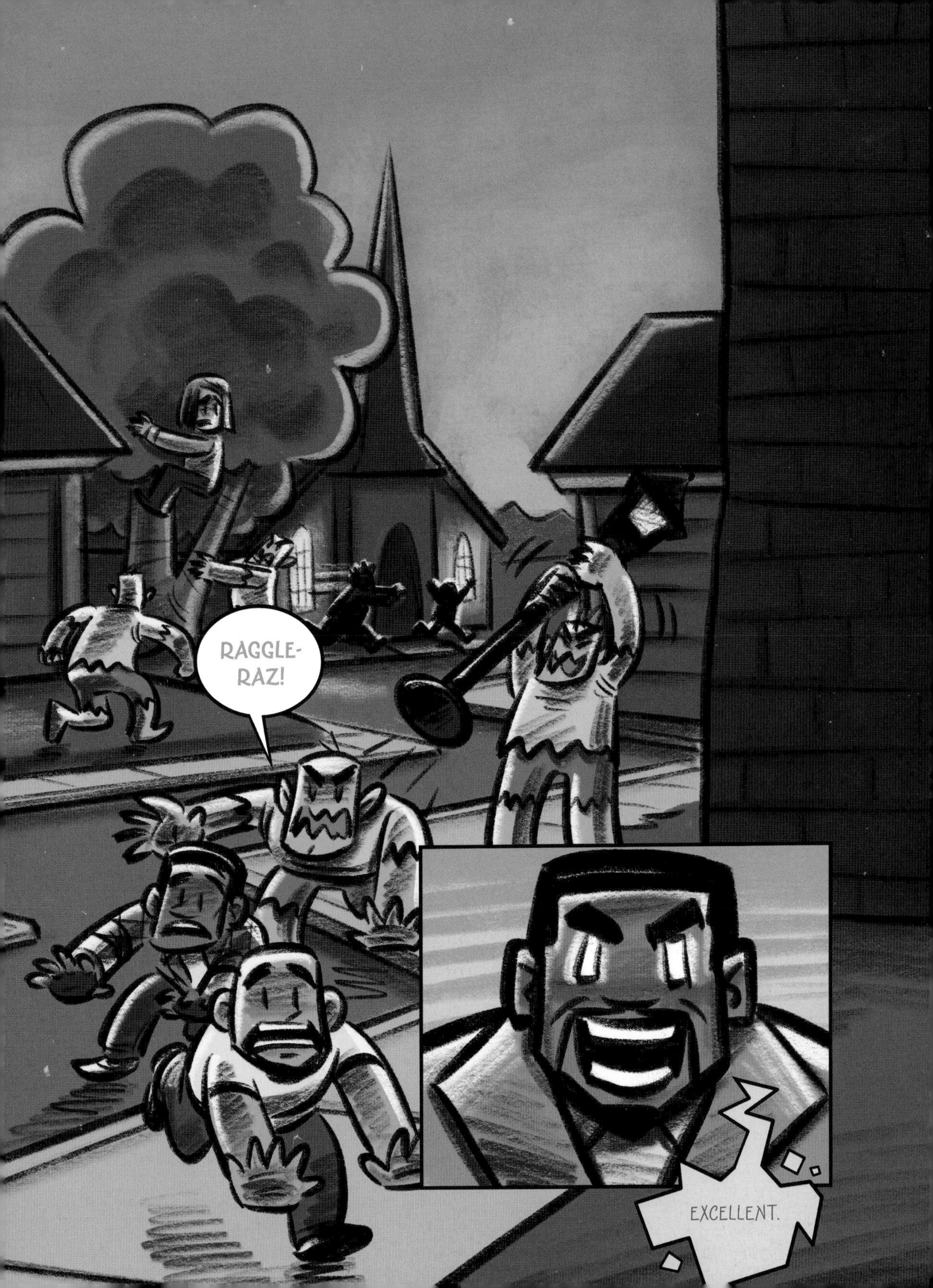
RAGGLE-RAZ!
EXCELLENT.

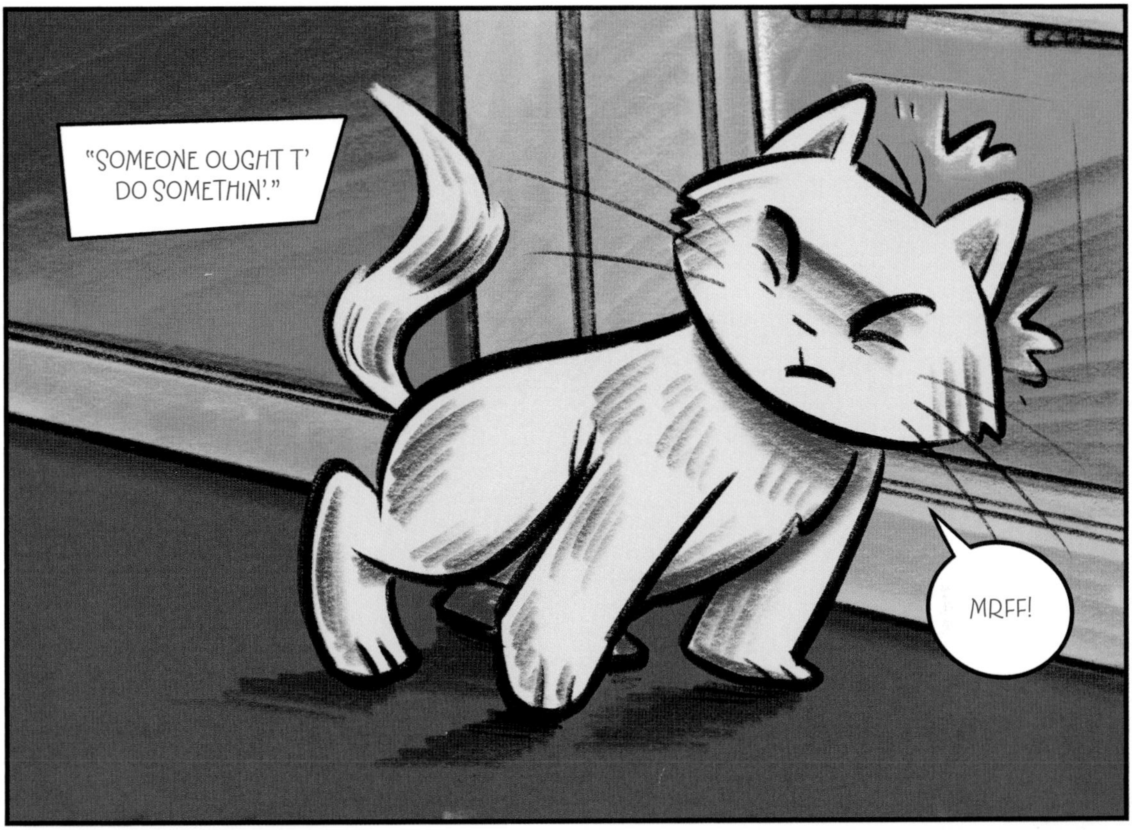
"SOMEONE OUGHT T' DO SOMETHIN'."
MRFF!

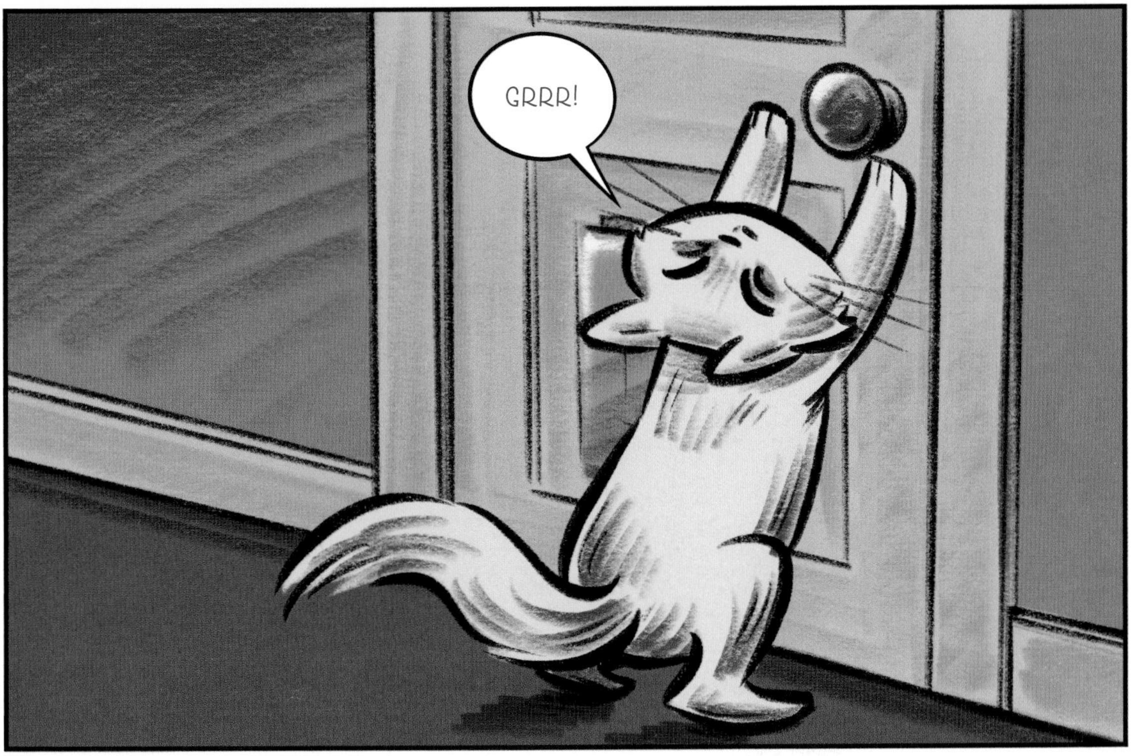
GRRR!

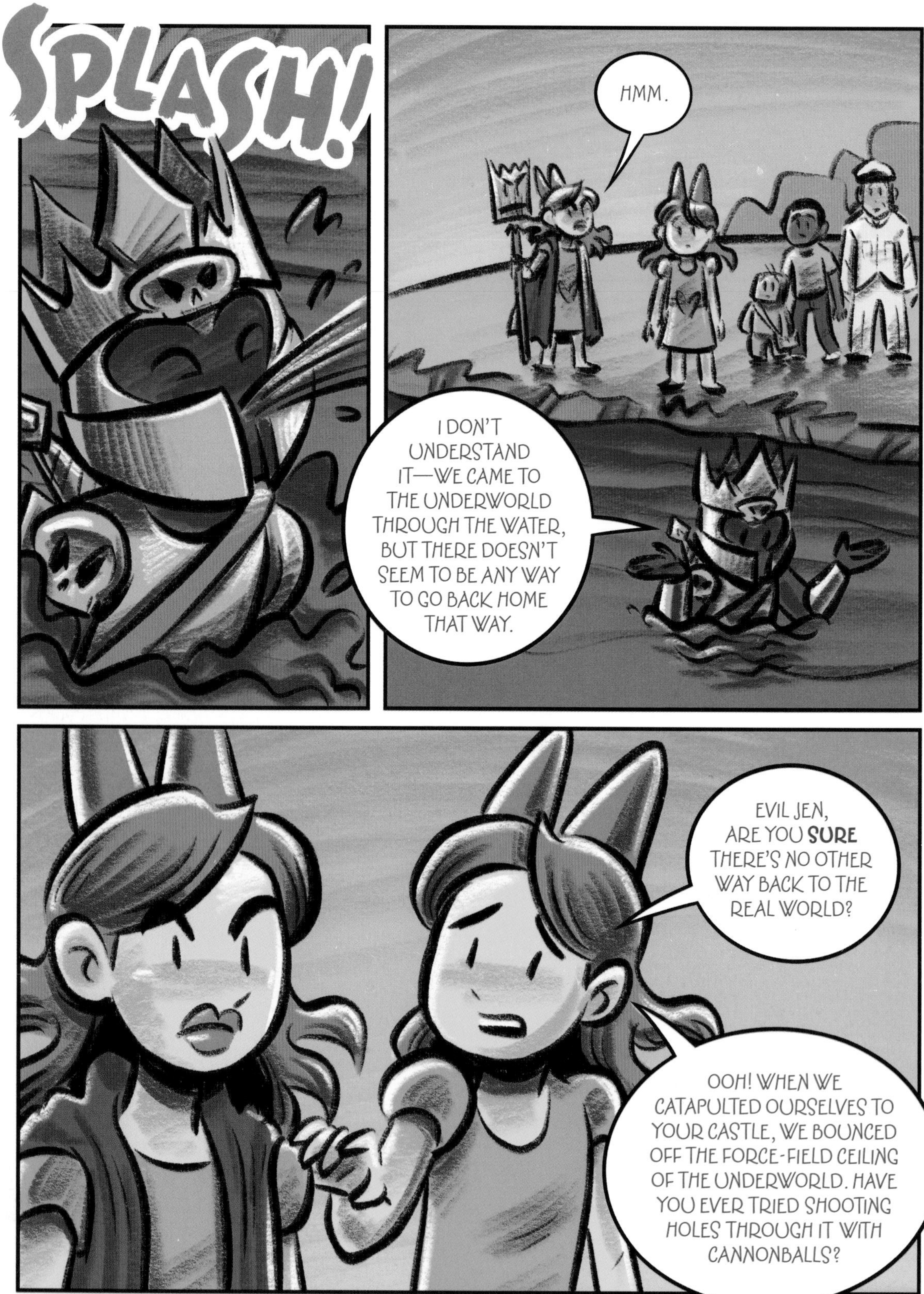
SPLASH!
HMM.
I DON'T UNDERSTAND IT—WE CAME TO THE UNDERWORLD THROUGH THE WATER, BUT THERE DOESN'T SEEM TO BE ANY WAY TO GO BACK HOME THAT WAY.
EVIL JEN, ARE YOU **SURE** THERE'S NO OTHER WAY BACK TO THE REAL WORLD?
OOH! WHEN WE CATAPULTED OURSELVES TO YOUR CASTLE, WE BOUNCED OFF THE FORCE-FIELD CEILING OF THE UNDERWORLD. HAVE YOU EVER TRIED SHOOTING HOLES THROUGH IT WITH CANNONBALLS?

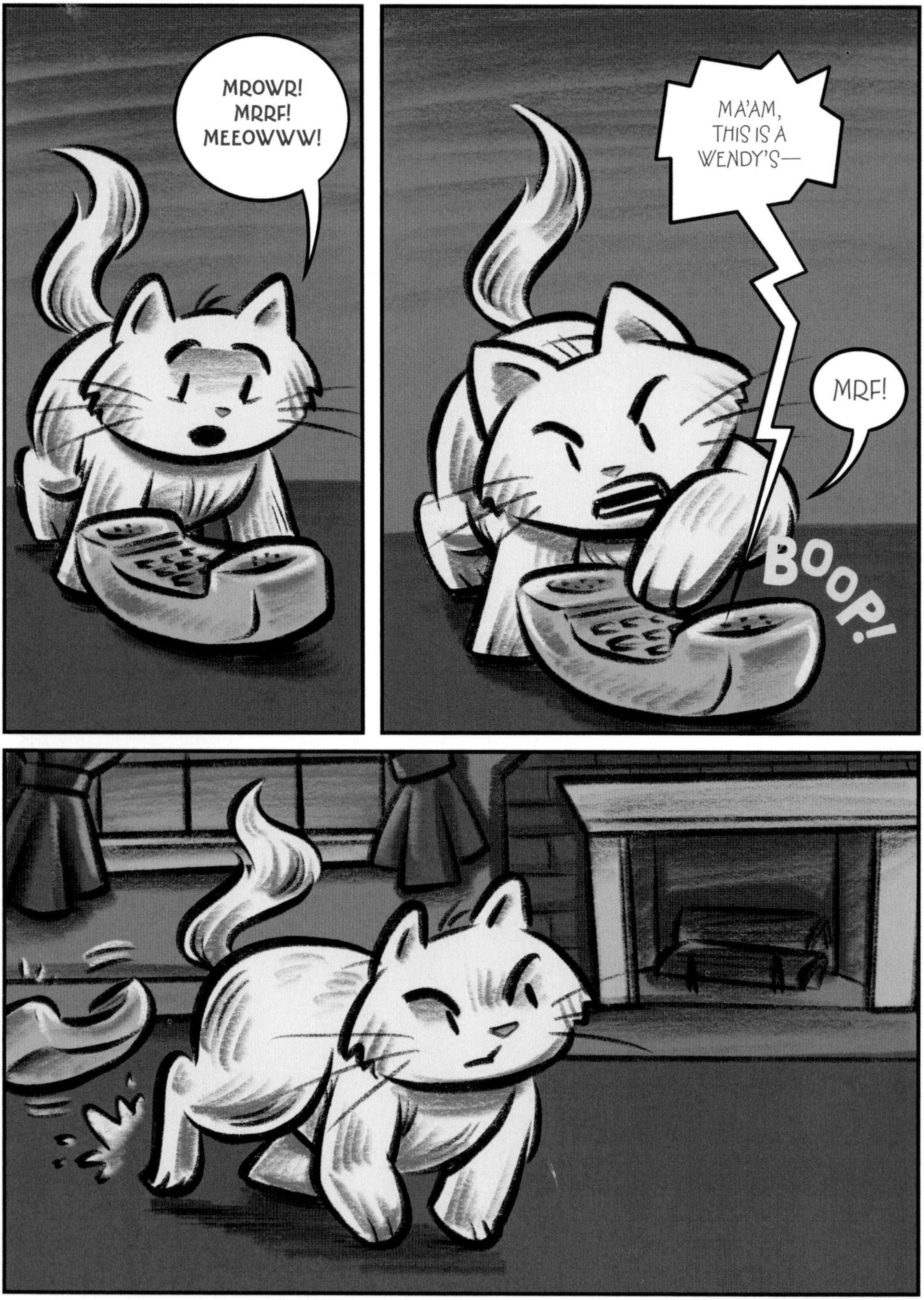
MROWR! MRRF! MEEOWWW!
MA'AM, THIS IS A WENDY'S—
MRF!
BOOP!

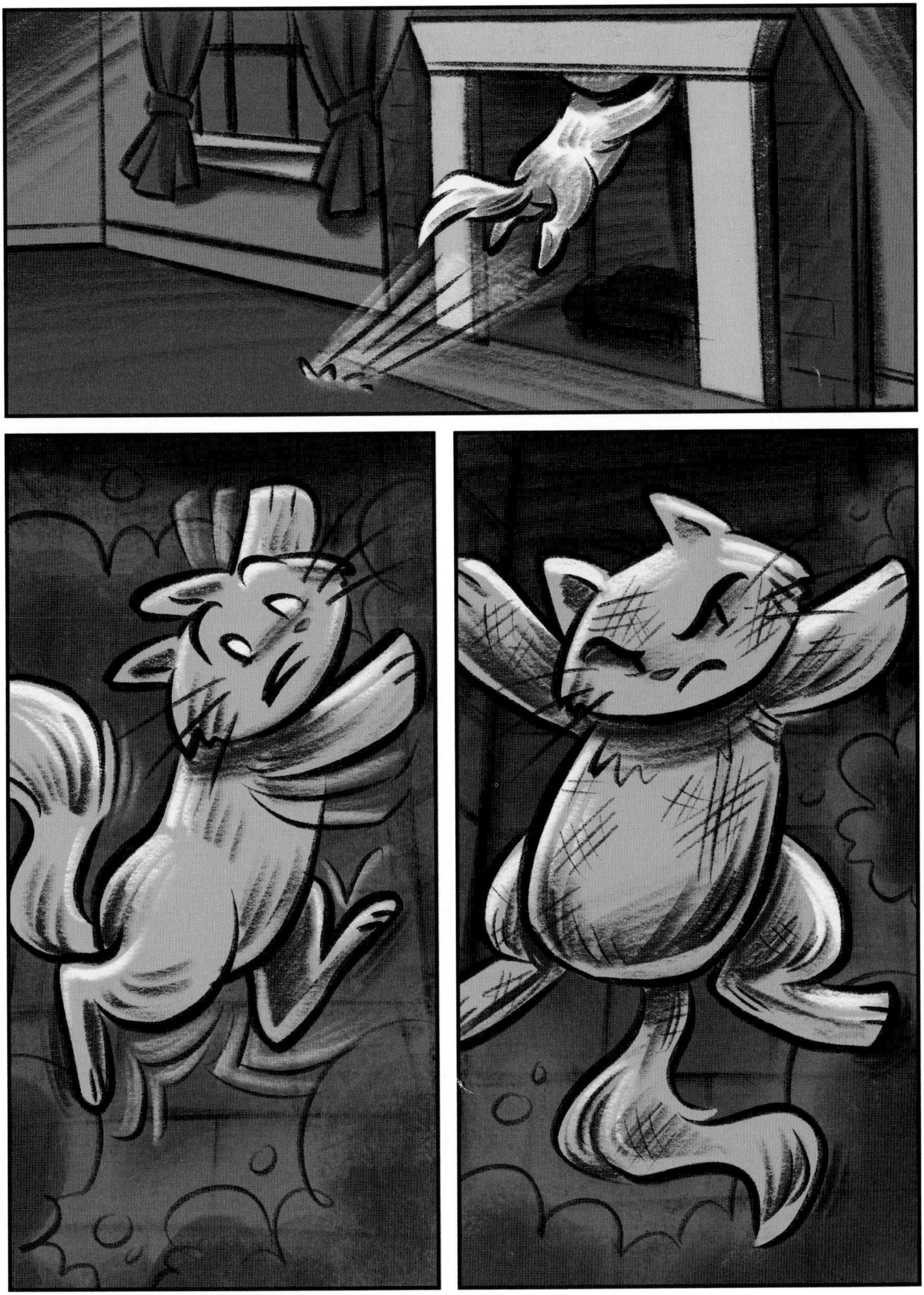

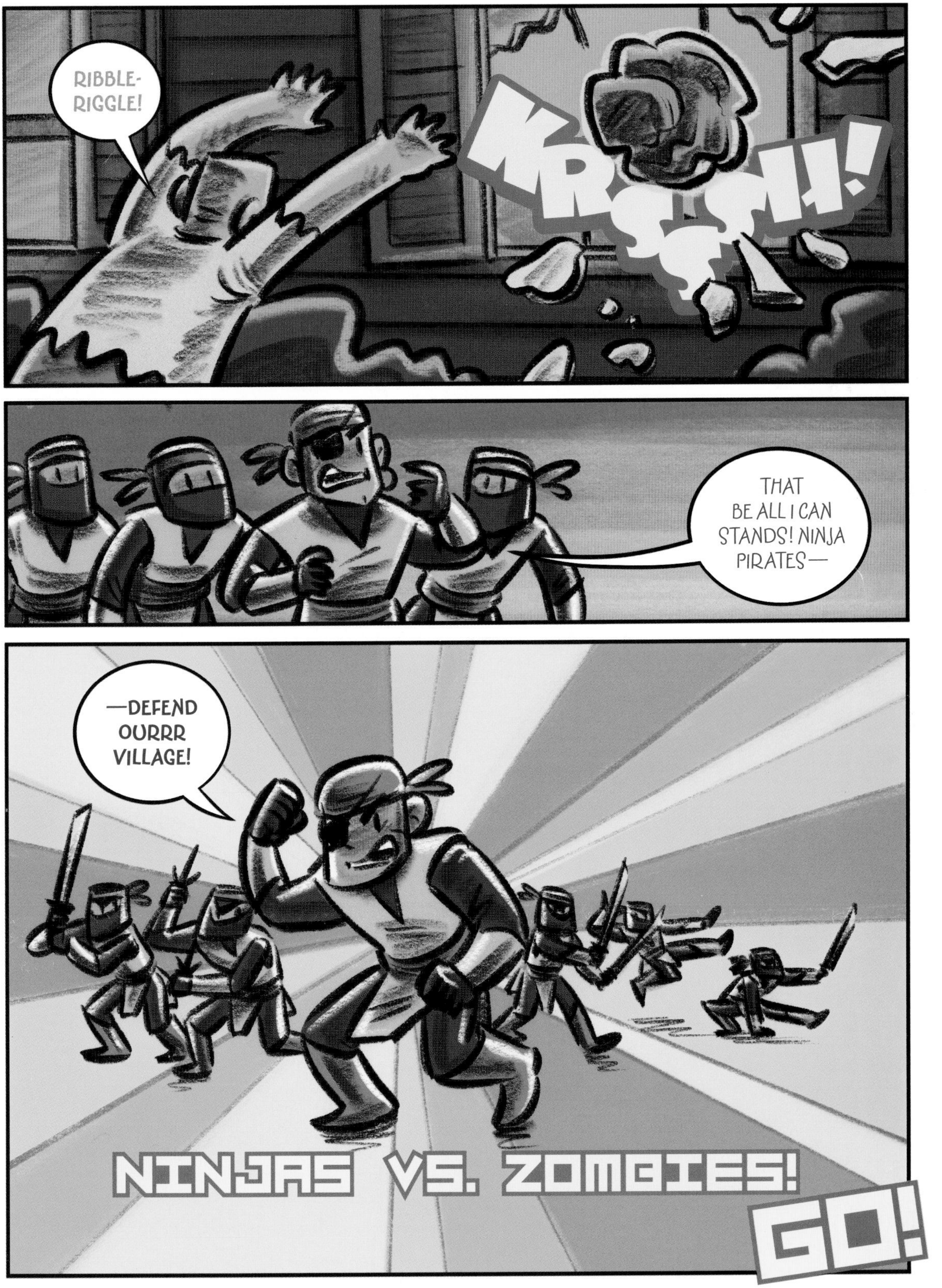
RIBBLE-RIGGLE!
THAT BE ALL I CAN STANDS! NINJA PIRATES—
—DEFEND OURRR VILLAGE!
NINJAS VS. ZOMBIES!
GO!

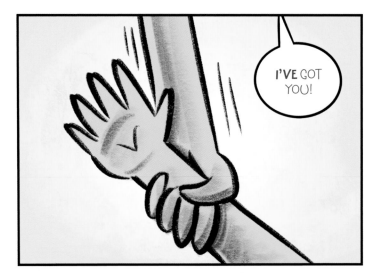

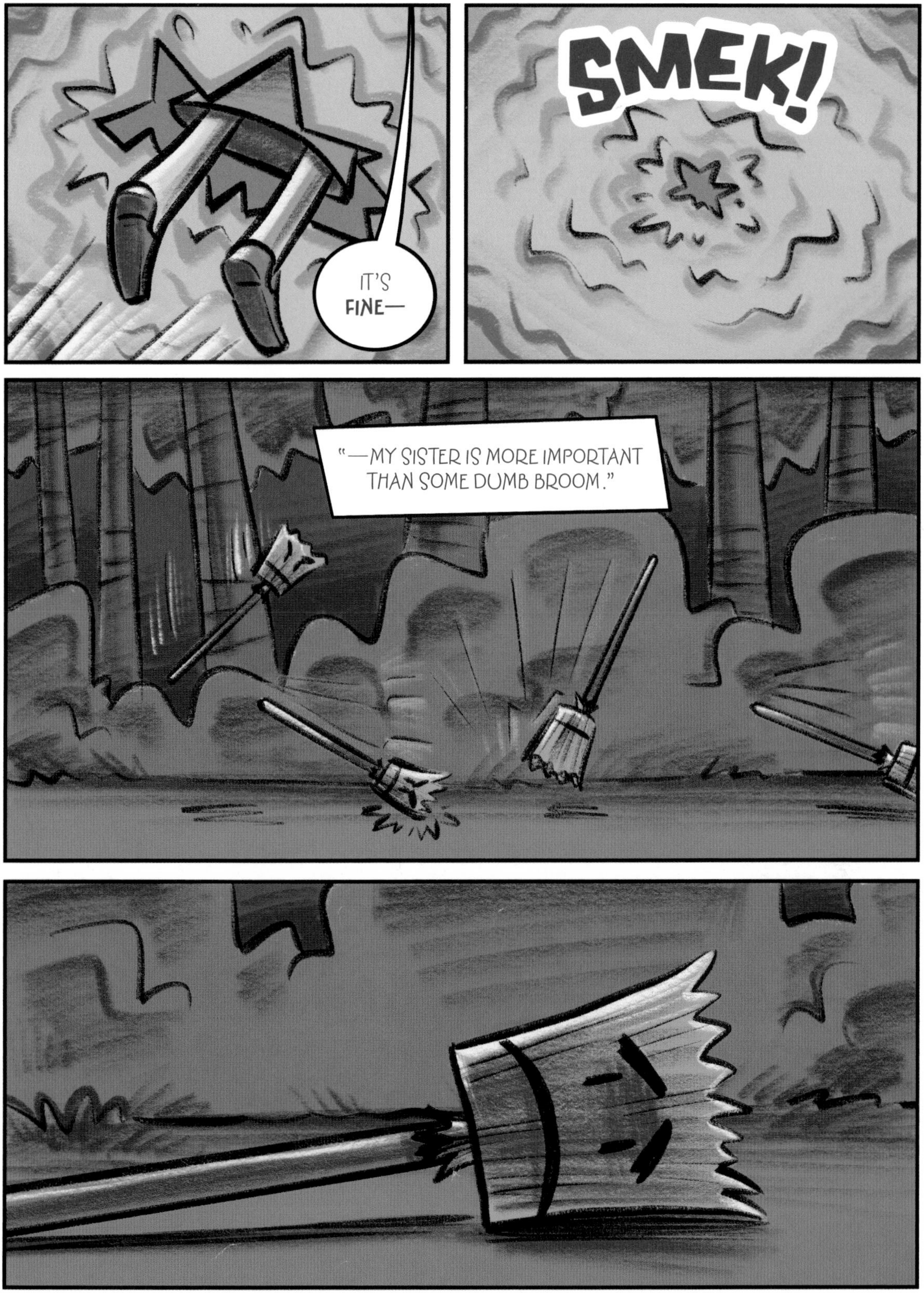
IT'S FINE—
SMEK!
"—MY SISTER IS MORE IMPORTANT THAN SOME DUMB BROOM."

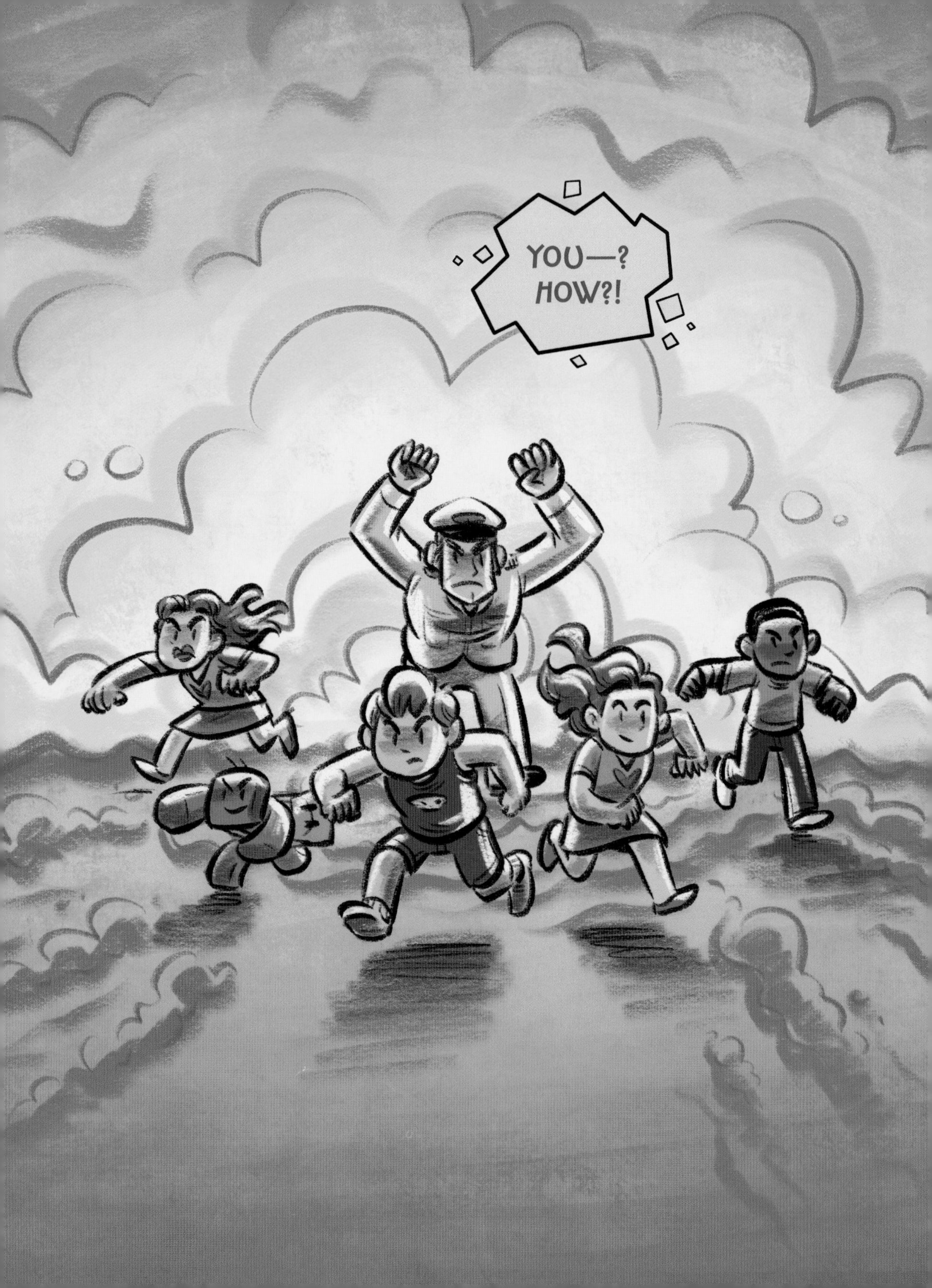
YOU—? HOW?!

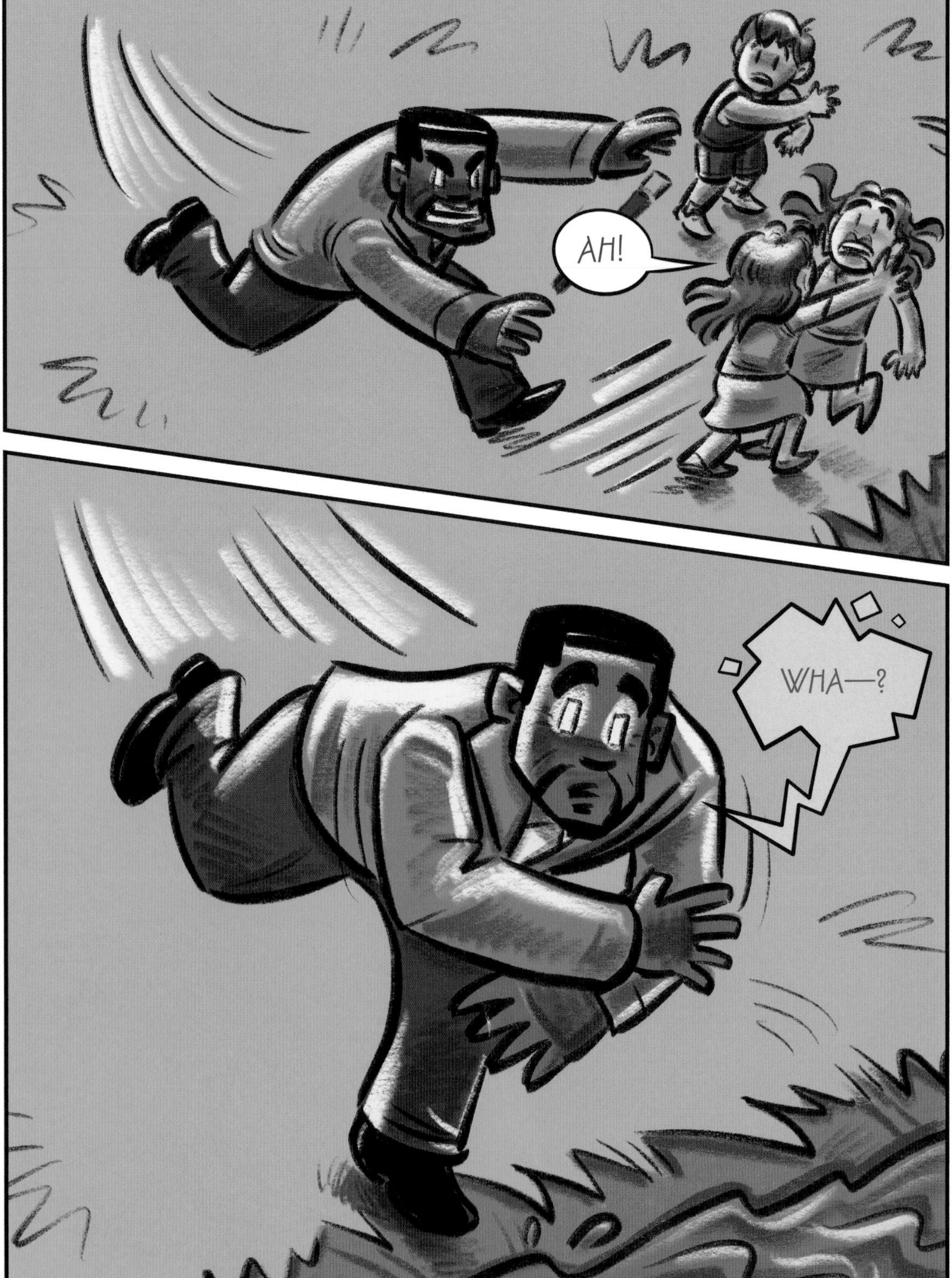
AH!
WHA—?

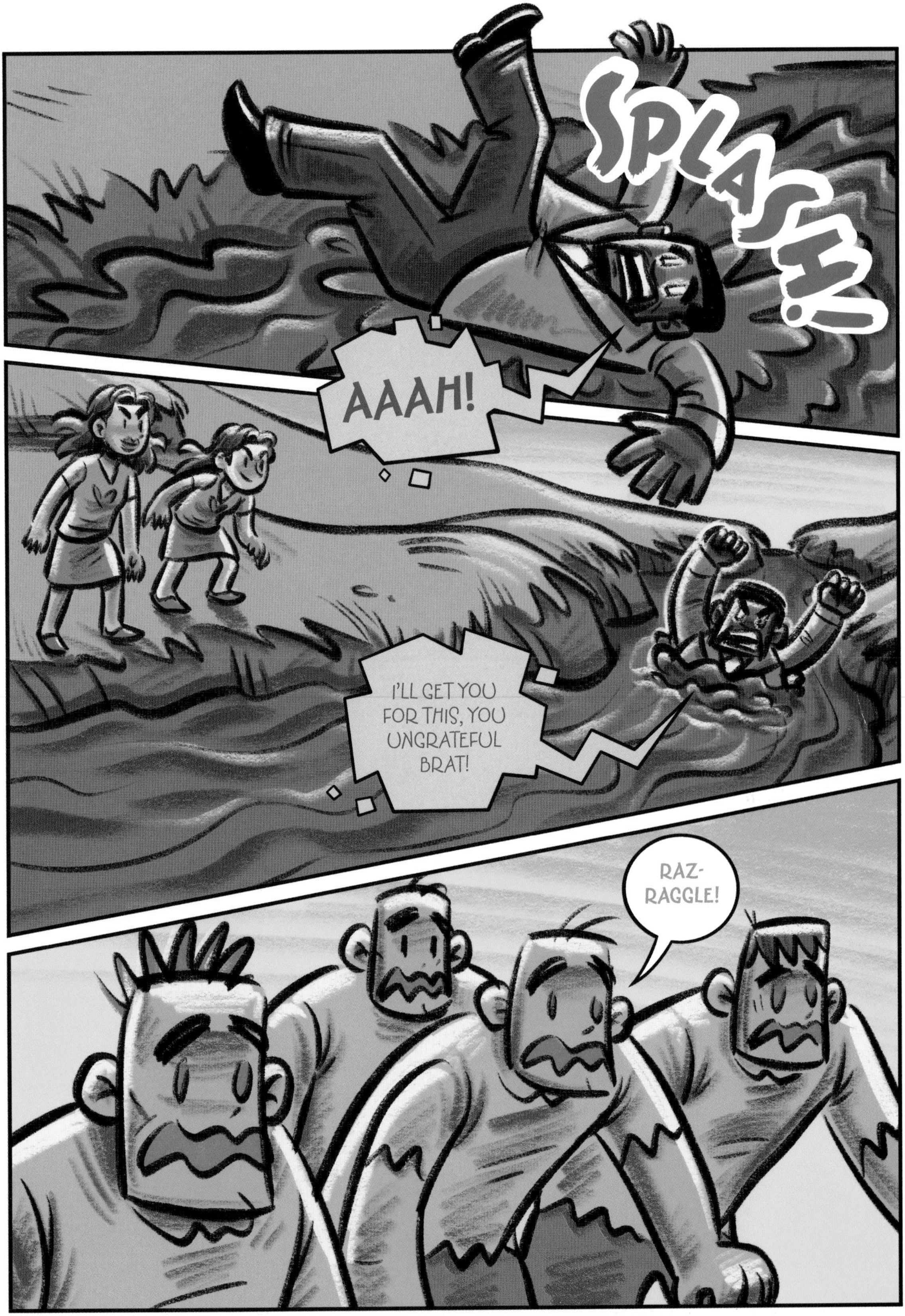
SPLASH!
AAAH!
I'LL GET YOU FOR THIS, YOU UNGRATEFUL BRAT!
RAZ-RAGGLE!

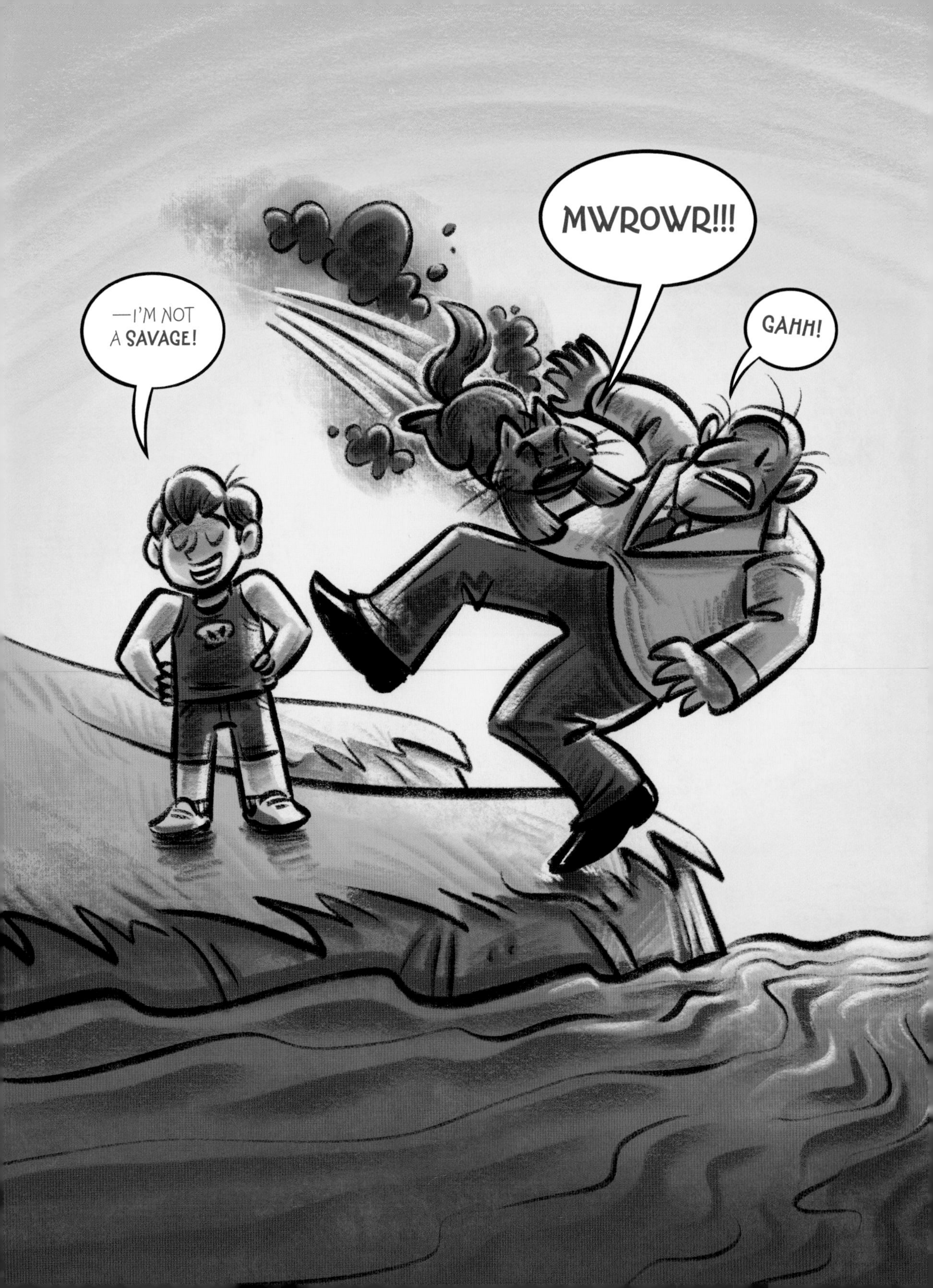
—I'M NOT A **SAVAGE!**
MWROWR!!!
GAHH!

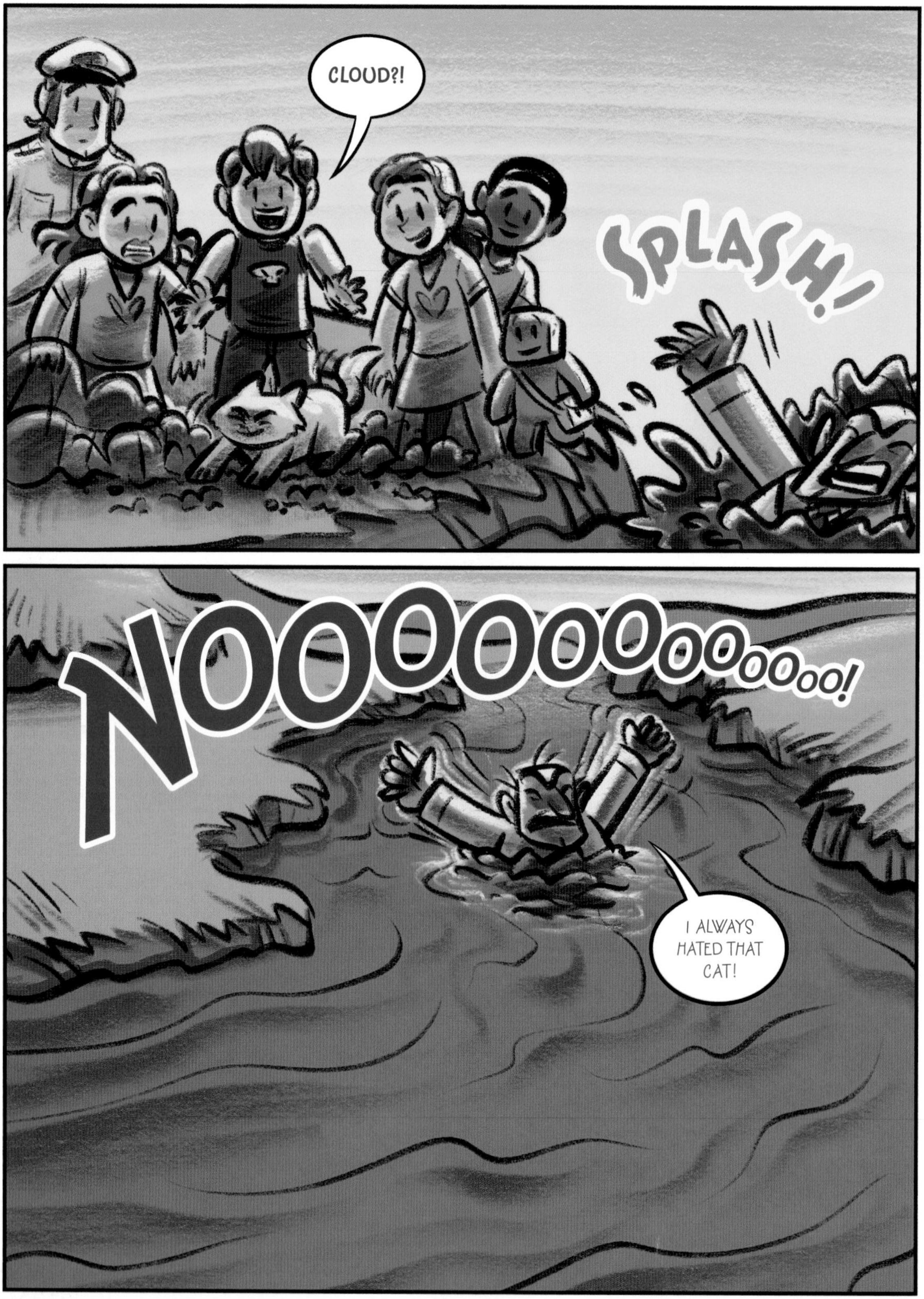
CLOUD?!
SPLASH!
NOOOOOOOoooo!
I ALWAYS HATED THAT CAT!

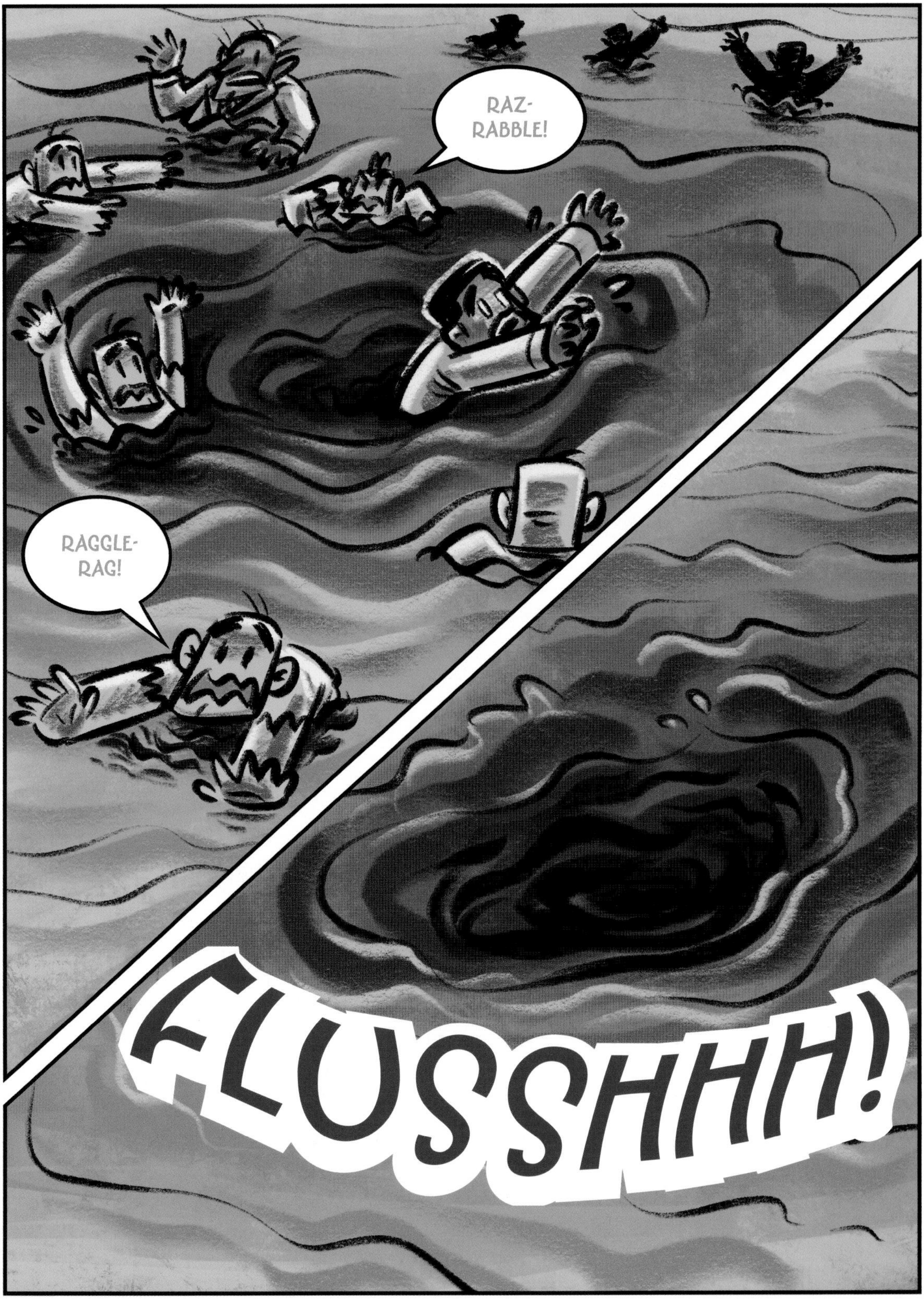
RAZ-
RABBLE!
RAGGLE-
RAG!
FLUSSHHH!

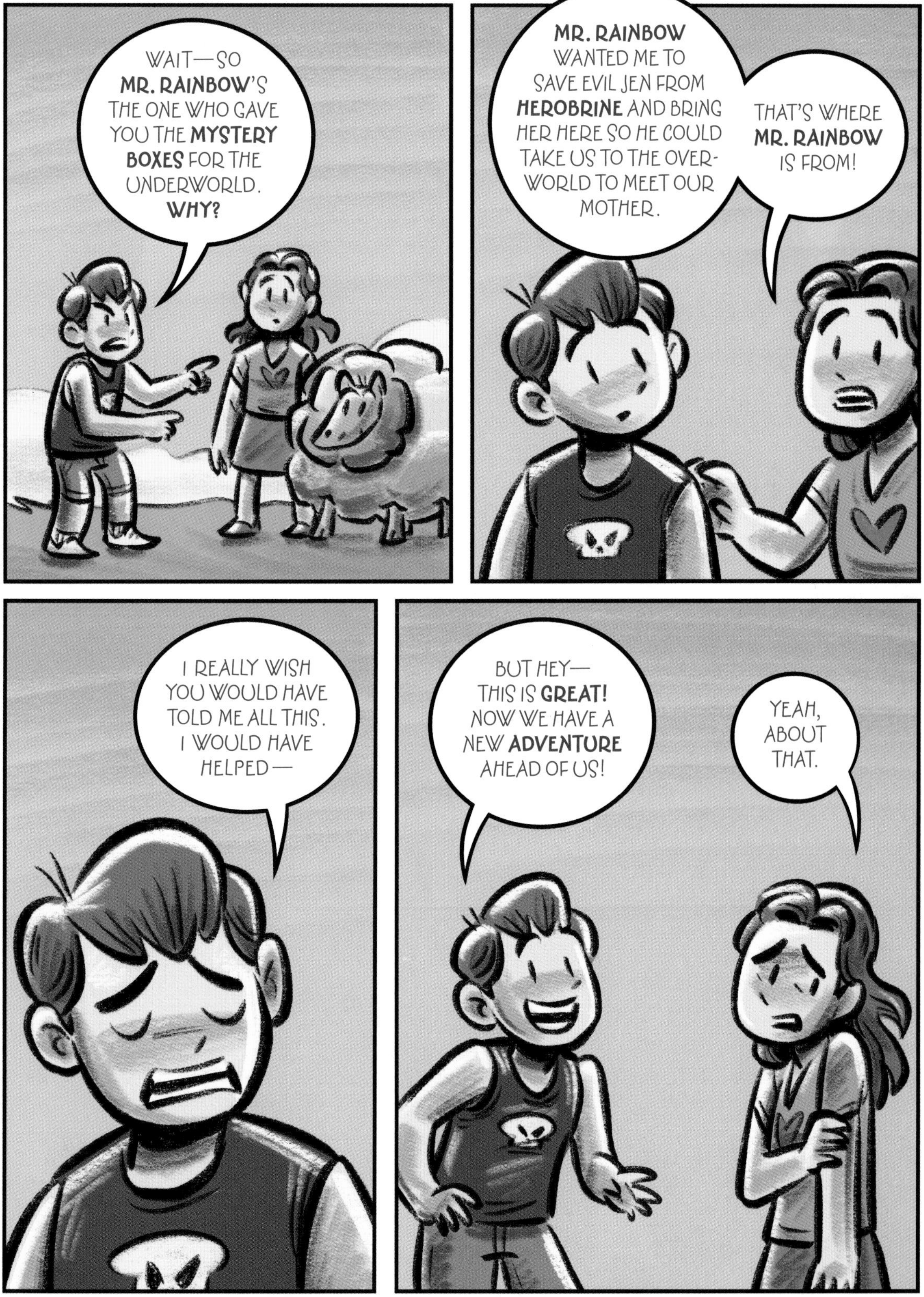
WAIT—SO MR. RAINBOW'S THE ONE WHO GAVE YOU THE MYSTERY BOXES FOR THE UNDERWORLD. WHY?
MR. RAINBOW WANTED ME TO SAVE EVIL JEN FROM HEROBRINE AND BRING HER HERE SO HE COULD TAKE US TO THE OVER-WORLD TO MEET OUR MOTHER.
THAT'S WHERE MR. RAINBOW IS FROM!
I REALLY WISH YOU WOULD HAVE TOLD ME ALL THIS. I WOULD HAVE HELPED—
BUT HEY— THIS IS GREAT! NOW WE HAVE A NEW ADVENTURE AHEAD OF US!
YEAH, ABOUT THAT.

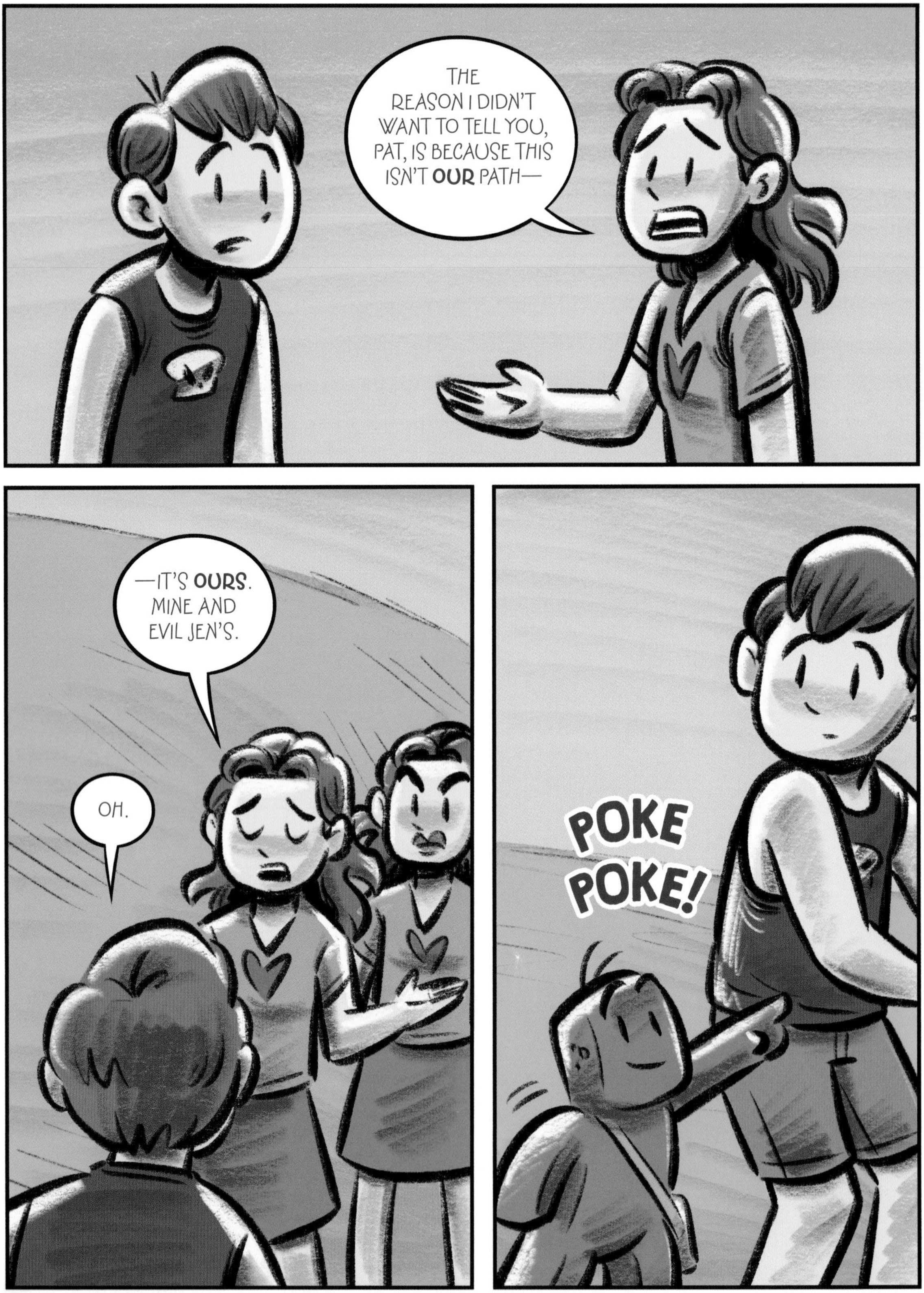
THE REASON I DIDN'T WANT TO TELL YOU, PAT, IS BECAUSE THIS ISN'T **OUR** PATH—
—IT'S **OURS**. MINE AND EVIL JEN'S.
OH.
POKE POKE!

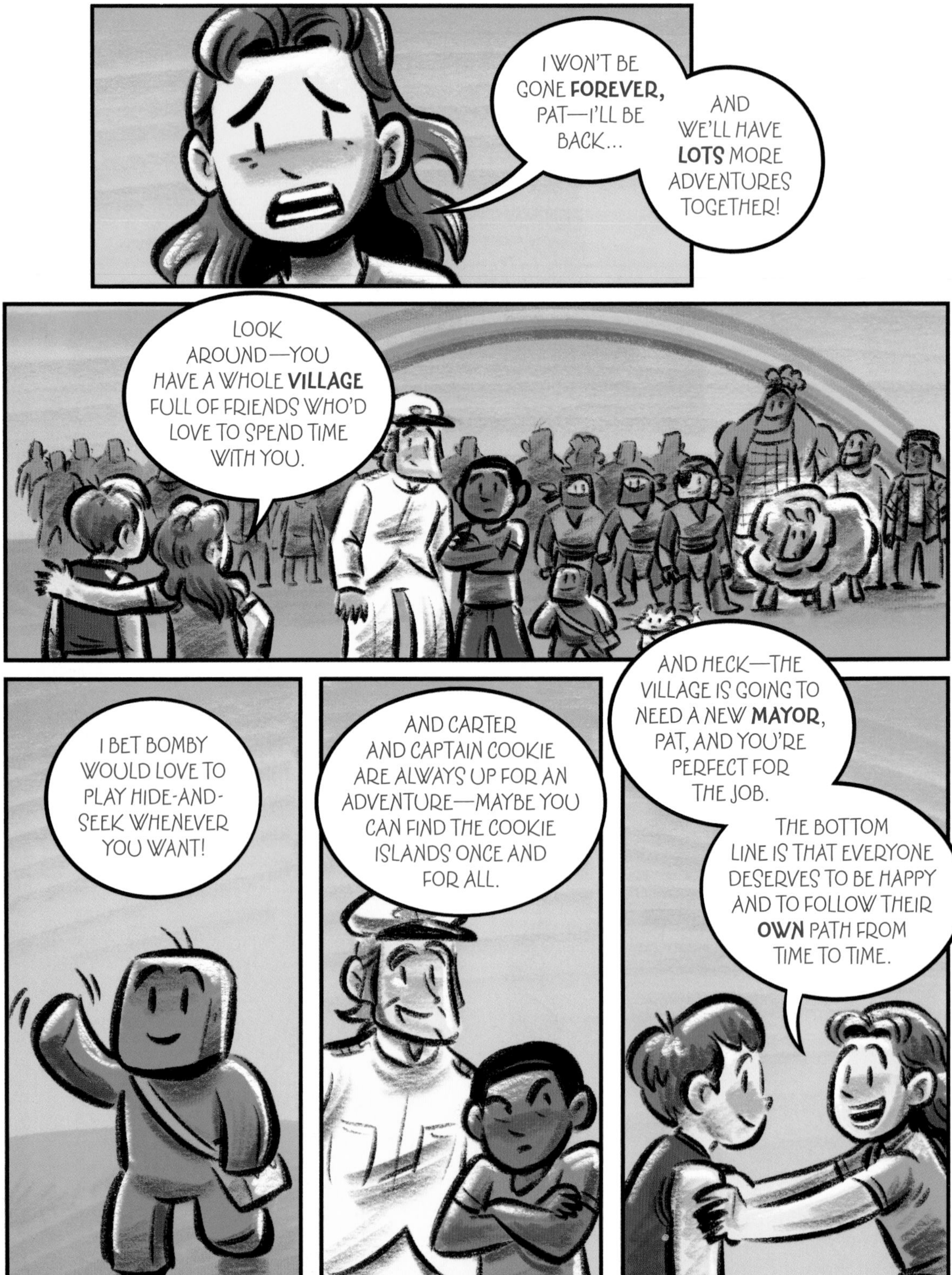
I WON'T BE GONE **FOREVER,** PAT—I'LL BE BACK...
AND WE'LL HAVE **LOTS** MORE ADVENTURES TOGETHER!
LOOK AROUND—YOU HAVE A WHOLE **VILLAGE** FULL OF FRIENDS WHO'D LOVE TO SPEND TIME WITH YOU.
I BET BOMBY WOULD LOVE TO PLAY HIDE-AND-SEEK WHENEVER YOU WANT!
AND CARTER AND CAPTAIN COOKIE ARE ALWAYS UP FOR AN ADVENTURE—MAYBE YOU CAN FIND THE COOKIE ISLANDS ONCE AND FOR ALL.
AND HECK—THE VILLAGE IS GOING TO NEED A NEW **MAYOR**, PAT, AND YOU'RE PERFECT FOR THE JOB.
THE BOTTOM LINE IS THAT EVERYONE DESERVES TO BE HAPPY AND TO FOLLOW THEIR **OWN** PATH FROM TIME TO TIME.

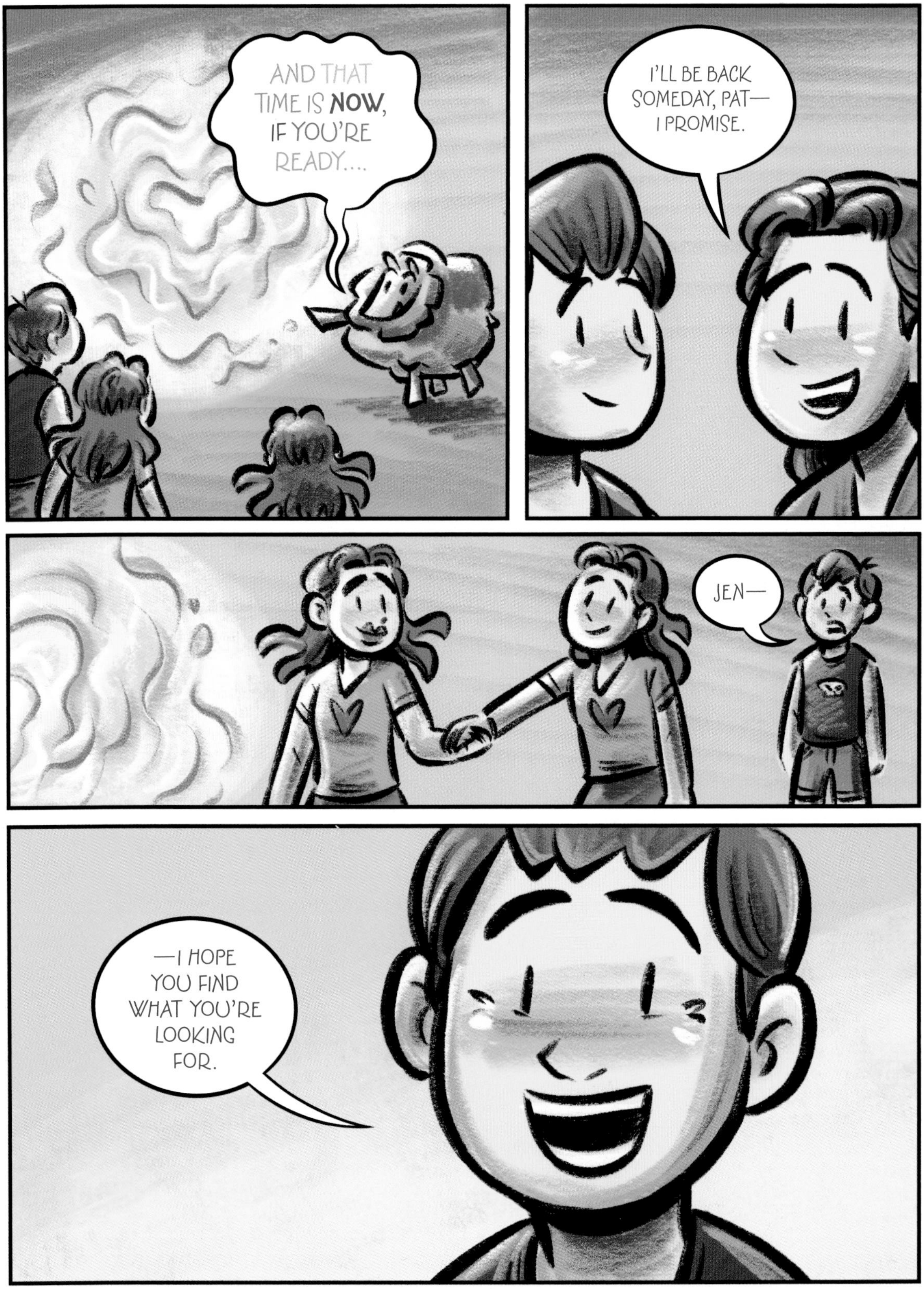
AND THAT TIME IS **NOW**, IF YOU'RE READY....
I'LL BE BACK SOMEDAY, PAT— I PROMISE.
JEN—
—I HOPE YOU FIND WHAT YOU'RE LOOKING FOR.